Allon

Book 1

Struggle for Allon

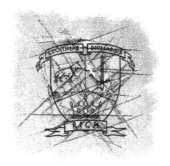

Shawn Lamb

Allon Books

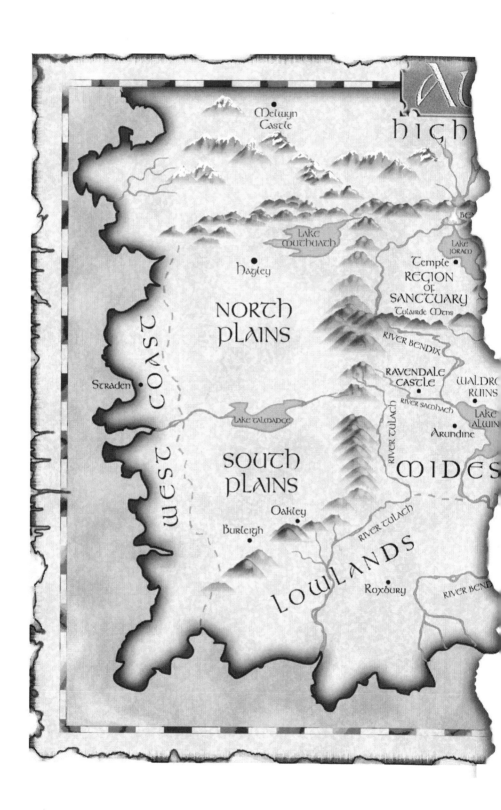

ALLON – BOOK 1– STRUGGLE FOR ALLON
SECOND EDITION
by Shawn Lamb

Published by Allon Books
209 Hickory Way Court
Antioch, Tennessee 37013
www.allonbooks.com

Cover illustration by Robert Lamb

Published by Creation House
Charisma Media (formerly Strang)
600 Rinehart Road
Lake Mary, Florida 32746

International Standard Book Number: 978-0-9964381-2-4

Books by Shawn Lamb

Young Adult Fantasy Fiction
ALLON ~ BOOK 1 ~ STRUGGLE FOR ALLON
ALLON ~ BOOK 2 ~ INSURRECTION
ALLON ~ BOOK 3 ~ HEIR APPARENT
ALLON ~ BOOK 4 ~ A QUESTION OF SOVEREIGNTY
ALLON ~ BOOK 5 ~ GAUNTLET
ALLON ~ BOOK 6 ~ DILEMMA
ALLON ~ BOOK 7 ~ DANGEROUS DECEPTION
ALLON ~ BOOK 8 ~ DIVIDED
ALLON ~ BOOK 9 ~ IN PLAIN SIGHT

THE GREAT BATTLE – GUARDIANS OF ALLON – BOOK ONE
REPRIEVE – GUARDIANS OF ALLON – BOOK TWO
OVERTHROW – GUARDIANS OF ALLON – BOOK THREE

PARENT STUDY GUIDE FOR ALLON ~ BOOKS 1-9
THE ACTIVITY BOOK OF ALLON

For Young Readers – ages 8-10
Allon ~ The King's Children series
NECIE AND THE APPLES
TRISTINE'S DORGIRITH ADVENTURE
NIGEL'S BROKEN PROMISE

Historical Fiction
GLENCOE
THE HUGUENOT SWORD

Preface

Struggle For Allon is the 2nd edition of the original *Allon Book 1*. Due to publisher constraints on word count and page length for *Allon Book 1*, scenes were deleted or shortened, and the character list excluded in favor of just the map.

Now, with rights reverted to the author, those omissions are restored in *Struggle for Allon*. The 2nd edition is 20% longer with 60 pages of replaced material and new scenes.

MORTALS

Prince Ellis
Sir Niles of Pollux
Shannan
Jasper
Edmund
Erin
Ned
Fagan
King Marcellus
Grand Master Latham
Hugh, Duke of Allon
Captain Tyree
Musetta
Iain, General of the Royal Army

Council of Twelve

Lord Darius	Southern Forest
Lord Allard	Meadowlands
Baron Erasmus	Delta
Vicar Archimedes	Region of Sanctuary
Baron Kemp	Northern Forest
Sir Gareth	South Plains
Lord Malcolm	North Plains
Lord Ranulf	Highlands
Lord Hollis	East Coast
Baron Mathias	West Coast
Sir Owain	Midessex
Lord Zebulon	Lowlands

IMMORTALS

Captain Kell, Commander of the Guardians of Jor'el
Lieutenant Armus
Lieutenant Avatar
Wren, huntress
Vidar, archer
Mahon, warrior
Zinna, archer
Jedrek, warrior
Mona, shape-shifter
Eldric, physician
Priscilla, Wind Guardian
Barnum, warrior
Valmar, warrior
Chase, Sea Guardian
Gulliver, Sea Guardian
Daren & Darcy, night twins

SHADOW WARRIORS

Dagar
Carvel, Shadow Archer Commander
Ashby, Shadow Archer
Commander Altari
Commander Witter
Griswold
Tor
Nari
Roane
Bern
Cletus

Chapter 1

BURIED DEEP IN THE SOUTHERN FOREST, THE JOR'ELLIAN Fortress at Garwood lay two miles from the province's main town. It was one of the more secluded conclaves of Allon's religious sect, those who worshipped Jor'el. Construction consisted of simple, weathered yellow stone framed by timbers. The main tower dominated the rear wall. The upper chamber of the tower served as the headmaster's private study. It contained an assortment of books, maps, scrolls and parchments.

Master Ebenezer looked his age of sixty with thinning hair and relaxed features. He wore the blue and silver robes of his order. He sat at the table with wrinkled brow of deep concentration, as the quill pen scratched across the paper. After signing his name, he placed the pen aside. He used the drying dust to sprinkle on what he wrote then gently blew it off to carefully fold the paper. On the seam, he placed his seal in wax. With a sigh of angst, he laid hands on the parchment to offer up a silent prayer.

The door to the chamber burst open. A man of thirty years appeared in the threshold. He wore a brown and gold uniform with a feathered cap on his head.

"Jasper?" asked a startled Ebenezer.

"Latham's men are heading this way. Sir Angus is preparing to flee with Ellis."

Seizing the document, Ebenezer hastily crossed the room. "We will make what defense we can to give you time to escape." He shoved the parchment into Jasper's hand. "Take this. Hide it in your boot or doublet, anywhere. Keep it safe until after you're away, then give it to Angus."

"What is it?" Jasper tucked it in his boot.

"Angus will know when he sees it."

Noise from outside drew their attention to the window. In the courtyard below, five soldiers in Latham's black and purple uniforms shoved and threatened the four priests trying to prevent entry into the main building.

"Quickly!" Ebenezer urged Jasper from the room.

Sir Angus of Garwood, lord of the Southern Forest, possessed strength and vigor equal to any man half his age of fifty-two. His gray leather doublet was gathered about the waist by a large leather belt. Black breeches were tucked into knee-high boots. An impressive dagger hung at his right hip. He held a two-edged sword in his hand.

In a rush, Angus ushered Ellis through the main hallway of the Fortress. A golden-haired, blue-eyed lad of sixteen, Ellis rushed to dress. His doublet was left open and the shirt partially laced. He held a sheathed sword and belt as they ran into the back room.

Angus pulled on a wall sconce. Instead of being ripped off the wall, it acted as a lever. A panel slid open to reveal a hidden dark passageway. Angus grabbed a nearby torch then motioned Ellis inside the opening. Ellis quickly buckled the sword about his waist before hurrying into the darkness. Voices from the corridor prompted Angus to close the passageway from the other side.

"It won't take them long to find the lever." Angus held the torch high to see their way through the damp, dark tunnel.

Worried, Ellis looked over his shoulder. "Do we have far to go?"

"A couple hundred yards then up steps to a hatch in the forest floor. There's a shed nearby where I had Jasper move the horses for escape, only I never expected it this soon." Angus nudged Ellis to keep moving.

The tunnel had several sharp turns, which made it difficult to keep one eye out for pursuit and the other on where they were headed. Ellis smacked into the wall when he tried to look back past Angus. Finally they reached the hatch.

Hearing the noise of pursuit, Angus struck the torch against the wall to extinguish the light. "Go!" he snapped.

Ellis scurried up the ladder. It took effort for him to push the hatch open then scramble out. Angus came close behind. He quickly closed the hatch. It slammed down on top of the lead soldier. Angus stood on the false forest floor to prevent the hatch from opening.

"Hurry! Find something heavy. I can't hold it if he's reinforced." Angus grunted at an effort that threatened to erupt beneath his feet.

Ellis struggled to roll a good size log from a few feet away. Being only sixteen, he was strong but not fully developed in muscle. When Ellis came close enough, Angus grabbed him to move him on top of the hatch so he could deal with the log. The veins in Angus' neck and shoulders strained when he lifted one end of the log over the hatch. It fell with a heavy thud just as an attempt was made from below to dislodge Ellis. Painful groans and cursing came from the tunnel.

"To the horses," Angus ordered.

Jasper did his job well. All three horses were saddled for quick flight.

Ellis mounted. "Shouldn't we wait for Jasper?" he asked with some anxiety.

Angus vaulted into the saddle. "He'll join us when he can. Ride hard and don't look back." While Ellis did as instructed, Angus glanced to the hatch. "Jor'el keep you safe, Jasper." He kicked his horse to leave.

They urged their mounts from the forest onto the open road. They headed northwest toward the River Conn, which lay five miles from the Fortress. Across the river lay the Region of Sanctuary and safety.

A shout came from behind. "Halt in the name of King Marcellus!" Three mounted soldiers rode in hot pursuit. "Bring them down!" the lead soldier ordered.

Two soldiers armed their crossbows. At that moment, a sharp whistle was followed by an ear-piercing screech from above. A massive eagle dove at the soldiers. The force from its talons sent one to the ground. The second ignored the eagle's attack and kept his course. He loosed the shaft when Ellis' horse reached the midway portion of the bend in the road.

The arrow struck the horse in the neck, killing the animal. The violence of the horse's collapse threw Ellis over its head. He landed hard on the ground where he lay winded.

Angus wheeled his horse about in time to witness a wolf leap from the outcropping to take down the soldier who shot the arrow. Two figures emerged from the trees. The largest newcomer wore a full-length cloak with hood up and armed with a sword. The smaller one was dressed in a forester jacket, cowl up, with a bow and quiver slung across the back. The cowl of the smaller figure became blown back by the wind to reveal a dark-haired girl. Even with this intervention, they would not reach Ellis in time to stop the last mounted soldier from trampling him.

Digging in spurs, Angus sent his horse on an intercept course. The terrific crash sent men and horses to the ground. A flying hoof of a startled horse staggered Angus. The soldier avoided the hooves to scramble to his feet with sword in hand. Still recovering from injury, Angus' only managed to partially draw his sword thus unable to parry the attack. The soldier landed a deep wound to Angus' chest. He collapsed to the ground.

An unexpected blow from behind sent the soldier pitching forward, critically wounded. The cloaked man knelt beside Angus. A low stunned murmur caught in his throat at the unconscious Angus. He took a moment to recover then assess the wound. He saw see the girl with Ellis.

"How is he?" the man asked.

"Alive, but wounded. No, stay down," she said when Ellis tried to rise.

12

Ellis fell back on his elbow with a grunt of pain. He stared at the girl, who watched him with compassionate green eyes. He reckoned her to be near his age with a tan complexion from living outdoors. Her dark brown hair was pulled back in a long thick braid.

The man joined them. He examined the large abrasion along with a few cuts on Ellis' forehead. "Not bad. How do you feel, my lord?"

"A bit dizzy. Who are you?" Ellis sat up to try and see the face under the hood.

"Someone who wants to help."

Over the man's shoulder, Ellis saw the wolf nudge Angus. "No!" He ignored the pain of his wounds to stumble over to Angus. The wolf backed away.

"Torin just tried to rouse him." She patted the wolf's head when it came to stand beside her.

"It's a wolf!" Ellis snapped. He became concerned for Angus. So much blood stained the doublet that Ellis could barely detect any breathing. "He can't die. I must get him some place he can be cared for."

The man knelt on the other side of Angus. "We shall, but it is up to Jor'el if he lives." He motioned the girl to Ellis. "Take him into the shelter of the trees while I see to his friend."

"No!" insisted Ellis, who jerked away from her attempt to help him.

The man said nothing to the objection, rather turned his attention to Angus. He used his dagger to cut away the bottom part of Angus' tunic to bind the wound. "Stay with him while we fetch the horses," he instructed Ellis.

Ellis tenderly brushed the hair from Angus' forehead. "You can't die. There are so many questions. What will I tell Darius?" He swallowed back a sob. He wiped his eyes when they returned with two horses.

"We'll lay him over the saddle. Where we're going it is best he is not on a litter," the man said.

When the girl moved to help with Angus, Ellis prevented her. He helped the man lift Angus to his feet then to lie across the saddle of one of the horses.

"Won't he bleed to death?" asked Ellis.

"His own body weight should be pressure enough to slow or stop the bleeding for a time. Now, mount, my lord." He indicated the second horse.

Once astride, Ellis anxiously glanced down the road. No sign of Jasper. The man mistook his concern.

"We must hurry before more soldiers come."

The girl headed into the forest. Ellis followed her with the man leading Angus' horse bringing up the rear.

"Where are you going? The Temple is that way." Ellis pointed across the River Plain.

"Nearly eighty miles. He won't last that long," replied the man.

Ellis shivered at the statement. "Then how far are we going?"

"Far enough to be safe from the King's men yet close enough for his safety."

They continued on a northeasterly course away from the road. It seemed like forever that they wound their way deeper into the forest. Ellis grew impatient. If the man's statement was true about Angus then they couldn't travel too far. Besides, the direction they headed led to a place he knew, or rather heard about since growing up in the Southern Forest. Thus he lashed out.

"Where are you taking us, the Kirsh Swamp?"

"The swamp isn't safe from the king's men. Where we're going is," she replied.

Ellis shoved a branch from his face when they broke into a clearing. He wrinkled his nose at the murky and stale smelling landscape. "We *are* going through the swamp."

She paused at the edge. "It's the fastest way to safety, so follow me closely."

Ellis kicked the horse forward. The animal warily picked its way through the mucky mire. He did his best to steer the horse, though both had difficulty navigating the boggy terrain. The horse protested to the increasing depth of the swamp. Angry, Ellis snapped the reins, which made the horse rear and pulled the reins from him. He seized the horse's neck to keep from falling. He grimaced when sharp pain shot through his head. Swift hands caught the reins. A voice spoke soothing, unknown words.

"*Nas ciuine, mo Raine,*" she said to the horse. The animal became quiet. At Ellis' befuddled gaze, she explained, "Her name is Raine. She wishes to be treated nicely." Then to the horse, "*Urrasair mi.*" She guided the animal unto solid ground.

On the other side, Ellis snatched her arm. "How did you do that? What did you say?"

His abrupt action startled her. "You're hurting me." Her fear drew a warning snarl from the wolf along with a cry from the eagle overhead.

Wary of the wolf, Ellis released her. He spoke in a more controlled tone. "What was that strange language?"

The man brought Angus' horse beside Ellis. "The Ancient language of the Guardians."

He waved the girl ahead.

"There are no more Guardians," refuted Ellis.

"Not at present, but who knows." He led the horse after the girl.

"How much further? He could die before we get to where we're going!" Ellis shouted then kicked the horse to follow.

"Not much further, my lord," the man spoke over his shoulder.

Ellis wondered about his two rescuers. They were more a mystery to him now than when they first arrived. In fact, everything seemed mysterious since leaving Uncle Phineas' home to return to Garwood. Angus ushered him from bed with a hasty explanation of betrayal. They fled to the Fortress for sanctuary until Angus could decide upon a course of action. Alas, the arrival of soldiers caused their desperate flight. All that, joined with the appearance of these two individuals, overwhelmed him.

Ellis looked to Angus. "I pray to Jor'el you live," he whispered. At a sharp pain in his head, he looked down in his attempt to rub away the throbbing. Hoof and footprints sank in the soft earth. "We're leaving tracks. We could be followed."

"If anyone makes it this far into the Greenwood *then* we shall be followed," he said.

"Jasper!" Ellis quickly looked back, which made the man alert.

"Who is Jasper?"

"A friend with us."

"If he's good at tracking, he may find us, only doubtful since the legend of Greenwood is most powerful. This makes it favorable for hiding a fugitive."

"The legend? Ah, the Guardians. What was her name? The one who protected the wilderness and spoke to beasts—" Ellis stopped to glance ahead to the girl.

"Wren is the name of the Guardian. Shannan is the girl's name," the man said to Ellis' sudden interest. "However, Wren is not the legend I mean. I speak of the Dark Master himself, Magelen."

Ellis paled with fright. "This is … Dorgirith?"

"So it was called in the tongue of the Ancients when the forest was alive with his black arts. The ruins of his wretched manor still remain. During the Age of Light its name changed to Greenwood."

Ellis noticed the towering trees permitted only occasional shafts of sunlight to reach the forest floor. "I would have thought Magelen's black magic left more destruction."

"This is only a portion of what the Greenwood once was. Vibrant with life and game, it began to die to the Dark Way. After Magelen's defeat, the magic faded and the Greenwood ceased dying. However, the animals Wren once commanded are fearful and aggressive toward mortals, hiding deeper and more cunning in their habits."

"So the legend of Dorgirith keeps men out."

"Ay. Which is good, because here we are," he said.

They stopped in front of a large mound, which made Ellis curious. "Where? I see no dwelling."

"If we lived in a man-made structure, we would be too easy to find."

Ellis slowly dismounted since movement made him feel dizzy. He waved off help from Shannan to enter the mound. To his surprise, it ended after ten feet. "What now?"

Neither Shannan nor the man answered. He tended to Angus, while she moved further into the dark. The scraping of stone came from her direction then soft light from behind an opening in the wall. To his wonder, Ellis stepped inside a well-furnished dwelling. Not at all what he imagined the inside of a cave to look like. He would pay more attention to such details later since Angus' groan demanded prompt treatment.

The man laid Angus on a well-stuffed cot before removing his cloak to tend the wound. It would be the first view Ellis had of him, and a surprising one. He was far older than expected by the way he moved along with his ability to carry Angus. His old, close-fitting, knee-length jacket with slide slits appeared to have been once blue now well worn with a faded crest upon the left breast. His white hair was well receded from his head and kept neatly trimmed, as were his thin beard and mustache. From the age-lined tanned face shone a pair of deep blue eyes, piercing and steadfast. Gazing into those eyes, Ellis could see the past, present and future.

"He's dying," Ellis said in a thick voice of dreadful realization. His knees grew weak, which forced him to clumsily sit on the ground. They helped him to a bench at the table.

"I can mix him a draught to make his passing painless, but that is all. You need tending," he spoke so gently that Ellis could only nod agreement. "Shannan, my bag."

The large satchel held knives, needles, salves and ointments. For being old, the hands were steady and sure in administration. He gently tied off the bandage about Ellis' head.

"How is that?" he asked.

"Better." Ellis heard a low groan and saw Angus move. "Father?" He knelt by the cot.

Angus' eyes slowly opened. By his furrowed brows it took great effort to come back to consciousness. "Ellis. You're wounded."

"Slightly. You—"

"Am dying."

"No!"

"Hush, lad. I must say what needs to be said. Jor'el will give me time." Angus gazed at Ellis with misty tears. "I have seen Allon's salvation and blessed to played a small part in it. No, Ellis, please," he insisted to stop a protest. "Somehow you must prepare yourself for what is come, for your destiny. I wish I could tell you how."

"Fret not for the lad, Angus. We have never met, but I knew your grandfather very well. You even look like Abner," he said.

Angus curiously regarded the ancient face. "How?"

"There's no time to explain. Just know I was there when the House of Tristan fell."

"Impossible! That was almost ninety years ago."

"I turned one hundred and fifty this past spring. Until today, I thought I lived too long, and would die without seeing Allon's salvation. In his graciousness, Jor'el answered my prayers." He laid a firm hand on Angus' arm. "Look at me closely."

Angus noticed the worn tunic with a faded crest. "A Jor'ellian Knight?"

With a nod, he said, "I am Sir Niles of Pollux, the King's Champion."

At the stunning pronouncement, Angus was unaware that he had raised himself to one elbow. "My grandfather said you were killed in the overthrow."

"No. And by your existence I know Abner survived. Now, rest in Jor'el's peace, Angus. Your charge will be well cared for." Niles eased Angus back on the cot.

Angus turned to Ellis. His gaze was now distant and dull. He was leaving the physical world for the heaven beyond. "Listen to him and grow in strength and might, my son, my prince," was all he could say before his eyes closed forever.

After conducting a proper burial, Niles withdrew a short distance from the grave to allow Ellis time to grieve. Shannan remained with Ellis. He accepted her offer of comfort. Although strangers until a few hours ago, they appeared so natural together. Of course, Niles expected that since prophecy linked their destinies. Still, reading something is far different than experiencing it in reality. Oh, he believed Jor'el's promise from long ago, yet time has a way of dampening hope.

In one fateful encounter, he saw the past and future in two individuals. While preparing the grave for Angus, he found it difficult not to dwell upon his old friend, Abner. The brief exchange with Angus told how he and Abner believed the other had died. It also told him Angus' character proved just as faithful as his grandsire.

Niles' gaze shifted to Ellis. If he thought Angus resembled Abner, Ellis' features more strongly reminded him of Akilles. In profile, Niles saw Akilles as a teenager. The full face is where he noticed some differences. Where Akilles had striking baby-blue eyes not easy to forget, Ellis' eyes were a deeper blue. His hair golden rather than pale blond, while the shape of his jaw angular compared to Akilles. Even so, there was no mistaking his bloodline.

The thought made Niles consider the medallion he wore: a multisided jewel with a gold embossed eagle clutching a crown with a sword through the crown. A nick marred the gold outline of the medallion.

"Jor'el, you have brought me full-circle," he whispered with reverence. Ellis and Shannan came toward him. He let the medallion fall back against his chest.

For a moment, Niles and Ellis regarded each other. In that youthful pair of blue eyes, Niles noticed grit and determination along with a stubborn gleam reminiscent of long ago. He flashed a wry smile. "If I didn't know better, I would take you for Akilles."

"But you do know better. And certainly more about my heritage than I." Ellis swallowed back emotions to look at the grave. "When trouble started two weeks ago, he said a few things about my true identity." His voice became choked. "Until then, I believed I was his youngest son ..."

The words trailed off, as he lowered his head to regain his composure. Shannan again offered comfort only this time Ellis became braced to continue his confronting of Niles. "Now you tell me I look like someone named Akilles."

"Your great-grandfather. A prince of royal blood from the House of Tristan, and my personal charge." Niles held up his medallion. "This is the crest of the King's Champion. My duties included instruction of the heir, and protection of the royal family."

Ellis reached under his doublet to withdraw a similar medallion from a hidden breast pocket. "Father ... Angus said this belongs to my family."

A poignant smile appeared when Niles took the medallion. "The royal eagle." He turned to the backside. His smile widened while his eyes soft with remembrance. "You see this faded etching of APR?"

Ellis tried to focus. "The letters are hard to read, but I suppose that's right."

"Trust me. These are A, P and R." Niles traced the letters with his fingers. "It stands for Akilles, Prince Royale. He had it when we escaped Waldron that fateful night. I kept it safe until he left to seek a wife so as to continue the royal line."

Perplexed, Ellis shook his head. "I don't understand. He lived here then left? Surely, they would kill him—like they tried to kill me and succeeded with ... Angus!" He face grew harsh with angry sorrow.

Niles gripped Ellis' shoulder. "There is much to tell. For now, return to the cave to rest. I'll be along shortly." He gave Ellis back the medallion.

"But—"

"You need rest to recover from your wounds," Niles insisted. "We will have plenty of time for discussion." He nodded to Shannan.

"Come, my lord. I'll fix you some food."

"I don't have much of an appetite."

When Shannan and Ellis disappeared from view, Niles heard the voice a moment before he appeared.

"Greetings, King's Champion."

"Kell?" Taken back, Niles stared into the tall being's golden eyes.

The captain of Jor'el's immortal Guardians kindly smiled. Standing seven and a half feet, Kell towered over Niles. "It hasn't been so long since we last spoke for you to forget me."

"No," Niles chuckled with slight embarrassment. He gazed in the direction the young people left. "She has been a blessing to me since her birth. My only regret is Colin didn't live to see his daughter grow up."

Kell laid comforting hand on Niles' shoulder. "He was proud her."

"All she remembers is his gentleness and laugh." Niles shook off his dreariness. "I can guess why you are here. Ellis."

Kell nodded. "The Daughter of Allon and Son of Tristan are now together under *your* charge."

Fretful, Niles again considered his medallion. "I am very old. Will I have the time to do what is necessary to prepare them?"

Kell's smile of encouragement returned. "Aye. That is why I am here—to reassure you; though the task and challenge will be greater than before." He motioned in the direction of the cave to say, "They need you. Allon needs you to once again fulfill your duty as the King's Champion."

"What about the Guardians? Will you help?"

"Our return is directly linked to the Daughter of Allon." Kell made Niles look at him. "We shall do what we can to make certain Jor'el's will and Prophecy are fulfilled. It will be clandestine until the time of our full restoration." He briefly directed his gaze toward the cave. "Now, go with confidence, King's Champion." He made the Jor'ellian salute.

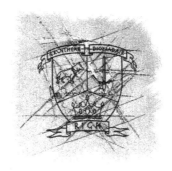

Chapter 2

ON TOP OF A RIDGE IN THE HEART OF THE MIDESSEX REGION, stood the ruins of the once proud Waldron Castle. It served as home to the House of Tristan for over two hundred years. Thirty miles way, lay another set of ruins, that of old Ravendale.

The original grounds covered twenty acres, taking thousands of men nearly twenty years to build. From every turret, gate, window, rampart and battlement, reminders of the past heralded the strength of Ravendale. Large stone griffins and wyverns guarded its massive front gate and four smaller side gates.

Although Tristan ordered the first Ravendale destroyed when he became king, it was rebuilt after Zared's successful coup. At Zared's direction, King Patrin chose the site right beside the ruins. Following the exact plans of the original, the new castle took twenty-three years to complete.

In the great hall, King Marcellus sat upon the throne, a large carved trunk of oak accented by gold filigree and covered with crimson cushions. At forty years old, Marcellus had strong features. Shining brown hair reached his shoulders. A neatly trimmed beard framed his face. Hazel eyes flashed like fire when angry. Being early morning, he wore a rich sable dressing gown embroidered with gold thread. To protect his feet from the cold marble floor he wore marching slippers.

Waiting on the King's pleasure was Grand Master Latham. Although near the same age as Marcellus, Latham was a thin wiry fellow with crystal clear blue eyes and black hair. Gaunt clean-shaven features were made more dramatic by deep blue robes over his long matching jacket highlighted with black and silver. A four-cornered dark blue skullcap covered his balding head. The marked contrast in eyes, skin coloring and regal dress, made a look from Latham unnerving by invoking both the physical and mental command he possessed. A large heavy silver chain hung from his shoulders across his chest. The chain held a black and silver raven-crested talisman.

"Any news of the pretender, Master Latham?" Marcellus spoke through a yawn.

"Not yet, my Liege, but soon. There are not many places in the kingdom they can hide to avoid your justice."

Marcellus skeptically eyed Latham. "Your revenge, you mean."

"My desire is to serve Your Majesty."

Marcellus snorted in refute. "Your desire is to see the old ways restored, same as Zared when he served my grandfather. Why else dissolve the Council of Twelve—again?"

"Those were the days when your family reigned supreme, my Liege. And will do so again once this pretender is dealt with."

The sounds of disturbance caught their attention a moment before a wounded soldier burst in upon them. Three guards raced to subdue him. He struggled against the restraint to shout: "Sire! I beg to report about the pretender!"

Marcellus surveyed the soldier, who had several deep scratches along with a large bruise on the right side of his forehead near the temple. "Leave him be," he ordered the guards. "Speak."

The soldier knelt before Marcellus. "We pursued them to the Southern Forest—"

"Angus!" Latham swore. "He went back home, perhaps to get Darius."

"You said he'd go to the Temple," Marcellus rebuffed.

"They were on their way to the Temple, Sire," the soldier continued. "We were on the Southern Forest side of the river plain about to bring him down when a giant eagle and great wolf attacked us!"

"You were stopped from capturing a boy by a wolf and eagle?"

The soldier grew apprehensive in self-defense. "The eagle had a wingspan greater than the width of my arms with talons three inches long." He motioned with his arms and hands in demonstration. "The wolf was a demon! With massive jaws it took Watters' horse down by the neck!"

"By the neck?" repeated Marcellus.

"Ay, Sire. The eagle unhorsed Ormand and gouged out his eyes. I barely escaped when the wolf knocked me unconscious from my horse."

Skeptical, Marcellus folded his arms. "Why didn't it kill you?"

The soldier balked in his answer. "Perhaps, it thought I was dead."

"Who controlled these beasts?" asked Latham.

"I don't know, my lord. When I came to, they were gone."

Marcellus eyed soldier. The bloody face, torn uniform and anxious demeanor lent credibility to the seemingly incredible report. At length, Marcellus said, "See to your wounds." He turned to pace in consideration signaling an end to the audience.

Unseen by either Marcellus or the soldier, Latham nodded to a nearby large man dressed in black. After he followed the soldier, Latham spoke. "Majesty, there is a Prophecy about a great eagle and wolf."

"I don't want Prophecies! I want them destroyed!" Marcellus stormed out of the Great Hall.

Latham left by another direction. He crossed one of the smaller courtyards to a building along the back wall. He ignored his servant's greeting to quickly mount the stairs.

By the look of the simple furniture one could not tell they were in the presence of so important a man as Grand Master Latham. When one passed from his bedchamber to his study, the simplicity ended. The circular room dominated the upper floor of the north tower. Large arched windows faced in the four directions of the compass, and gave a sweeping view of the countryside. The room contained numerous bookshelves full to overflowing, a laboratory, and an impressive oak desk covered with papers. Near the northern window stood an elaborately ornate tripod of wrought iron with a large black onyx basin. The basin held sod and water from the Region of Sanctuary.

Latham hurried to his desk. He produced a key from a concealed chain around his neck to unlock a large drawer. The only item inside was an old book. He pulled it out. The worn leather cover was embossed with the ancient symbol of the Temple of Jor'el. Deep gouges marred the symbol. He placed the book on the desk to open it. He murmured under his breath while his eyes scanned the pages in search of something. His face froze with concentration as he read aloud:

"'Yet take heed, O Man!
For in the midst of this shall come one
To whom Jor'el has appointed
The salvation of Allon'"

"I know that. What about these beasts?" he murmured with frustration. He flipped a few more pages before he stopped to read:

"'Those after his own heart shall he seek and find.
From the fowls of the air, to the beasts of prey
And the faithful shall he gather to himself
The hope of Allon.
Among them shall be one whose birth
Shall be linked to his own by a season.
Whose soul shall mirror his own.
The twain shall become one in desire and purpose.'"

Latham considered the words before venturing further in the book.

"'He shall give the Guardians charge over Allon—'"

With suddenness, he moved to a bookshelf. His hand ready to snatch the one he wanted. He turned the pages until he found what he was looking for. "Guardian of the Forest – Wren." For several moments, he held the book to consider what he read. Could this Guardian Wren have returned and aided the pretender? The beasts described seemed unusual in size. Not to mention an eagle and a wolf working together for one purpose. What do these beasts have to do with the *'birth linked to his own'*? Surely that phrase speaks of the Pretender, this promised Son of Tristan. He felt a chill deep at the thought of Prophecy being fulfilled.

He placed the book back on the shelf before he approached the basin. He closed his eyes and raised his arms. As he spoke the language of the Ancients, the talisman began to glow. "O mighty Dagar, hear me. I am in need of your eyes and ears, of your wisdom. Speak, O Dagar."

The water in the basin boiled to create steam. Dagar's image appeared in the cloud of steam. An impressive figure of noble and awesome perfection, tall and wearing a scarlet doublet and breeches trimmed in gold with a white shirt under the doublet. His boots and belt were of finely crafted black leather. A jewel encrusted dagger hung from the belt. In stark contrast to his dark clothes, sun yellow hair, matching small beard and mustache framed by a flawless complexion. Bright mahogany eyes shone forth with pure authority; authority of evil. By a look he intimidates, by a word he destroys. He wore an identical talisman to Latham.

"Why do you summon me?"

"My lord, I need your help interpreting Prophecy about what happened today. The usurper was aided by a wolf and eagle, only I can't tell if this is the person linked to his birth or the return of the Guardians."

Dagar snarled with intense displeasure. "Both! Through the guise of a weak mortal female, the Guardians will make their return. Find her and you may stop them." His eyes mercilessly stared at some unseen spot beyond Latham. His voice filled with malice. "Their return will signal meeting my old nemesis. This time, I shall have my revenge." He then ordered Latham, "Summon me again when you have found her."

Latham bowed to Dagar's disappearing form. He relaxed when the steam vanished. Dealing with Dagar was always difficult.

Latham left his apartment to head for the courtyard. There he found the man in black. He stood unusually tall at six and a half feet by standard measure. Even under the clothes his shoulders were broad and chest massive. He had large hands capable of crushing a man's throat. Cold, dispassionate hazel eyes missed nothing. A long scar ran from above his right eye, across the bridge of his nose to his left cheek. All this didn't intimidate Latham.

"Is he well taken care of, Tyree?"

"Ay, my lord. No one will ever find his remains."

"I know Marcellus wants the Pretender found and to deal with rebellious Council members, but I have another task for you. One more important than the Council. You're to look for a maid of about fifteen years old. She should be somewhere in the Southern Forest near the river plain. Take Shadow Warriors with you."

Tyree's shoulders squared with insult. "Shadow Warriors for a girl?"

"She's no ordinary girl. The two beasts you heard reported accompany her. I don't care how, just find her and bring her to me."

⁂

The nether dimension to which Jor'el banished Dagar was a cavernous domain. He managed to make it homey, as far as the decor he required. An identical basin to that in Latham's chambers stood in one part of the cavern. Beside the basin was a stone altar decorated with emblems of ravens and lizards. By way of these stations, he communicated with the outside world. The basin served as his direct link to Latham, and the Grand Masters before him. The talisman was a conduit of power. From the stone altar, Dagar received the worship of lay people who dabbled in the Dark Way. The influx from the outer world served to inspire and infuriate Dagar. Since being imprisoned centuries ago, he had time to think, to plan, to brood, and to hate. That hatred inspired him towards his goal. Now things were about to change.

"Tor! Tor!" Dagar shouted with impatience.

A red-haired Shadow Warrior arrived. "I'm here. Now what is so important that your bellowing can be heard in the reconditioning chamber?"

Dagar's lethal snarl made Tor recoil a step. "Mortal ineptness! The Pretender escaped—again!" In agitated steps, he paced. "Have there been any reports of unusual mortal activity involving animals?"

Tor thought for a moment before answering. "No. Witter and Altari haven't reported anything like that. Why?"

"Latham said a girl and two beasts helped the Pretender."

Curious, Tor asked, "You think she maybe the Daughter of Allon?"

The question brought Dagar to a stop. "Of course! What other mortal is prophesied to control beasts?" He glared at a large map of Allon that hung on a cavern wall. "If this Pretender really is the Son of Tristan, and she the Daughter of Allon, they must not be allowed to unite!"

"What about using *madah-dunes* to track her?"

Dagar didn't immediately answer, as he studied the map. "Not yet. So far we have been successful in keeping the mortals in check by simply manipulating animals and nature. However," his voice grew bitter and lethal, "if this is Prophecy being fulfilled, the enemy will soon show *his* face. Then, we will unleash the creatures of *infrinn*."

Tor understood Dagar's use of the pronoun *his* to speak about Kell, the Guardian Captain. No comment needed, so he asked, "How do you suggest we confirm their identities?"

"I instructed Latham to find her. No doubt he will employ Shadow Warriors." A cunning smile appeared. "Still, clandestine help is appropriate. Send Carvel to Witter. Two can play at controlling beasts, and perhaps draw her out."

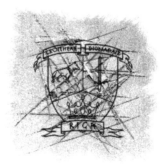

Chapꭲer 3

ARWOOD CASTLE SAT PERCHED ON THE HIGHEST PEAK IN THE
Southern Forest, overlooking the town for which it was named. It
stood like a stalwart sentinel protecting the town and the road
leading to Jor'el's Fortress. The ramparts offered a commanding view of
the countryside. Though rich in timber and the craftsmanship such
resource offers, the Southern Forest was the least wealthy of Allon's
twelve provinces.

With a worried expression Darius watched the sunrise from a top the
rampart. The warming rays met the rising mist to create a subtle sparkle
on the landscape. For his nineteen years, Darius' deep frown and
furrowed brow made him look older. The swirling breeze whipped nut-
brown hair while his face nipped pink by the morning chill. He paid no
heed to either wind or chill even though his russet doublet was open with
a thin shirt underneath.

He diligently fortified the castle after Angus and Ellis fled. Alas, he
needed to act wisely when Marcellus and Latham focused their attention
on the province in a relentless search for the *Pretender*. Any attempt to
interfere could bring disaster to the region and personal tragedy. He sent
word of the latest development to his Uncle Phineas, Lord of the

Northern Forest. Would Phineas alert the other members of the Council of Twelve? He wondered if Allon could withstand a rift between the King and Council.

"You should at least have your cloak," said Edmund. He mounted the final steps to the rampart with a russet cloak over his arm. He stood a half head shorter than Darius with graying auburn hair and hazel eyes set in a ruddy complexion. Neatly groomed facial hair framed a stout chin and thin lips. He wore the brown and gold livery that marked the house he served. A broach with the crest of a badger held his cloak in place.

"A cloak is the least of my worries. It's been a week since the attack on the Fortress and Ebenezer's death, and still no word of them!" complained Darius.

"There was nothing you could have done to prevent it without posing danger to Angus and Ellis." Edmund placed the cloak on Darius' shoulders then snapped the brooch closed.

Darius focused on the horizon. "Any word from Nando and Brody?"

"Not yet. Remember, Jasper is with Angus and Ellis. He won't let them come to harm."

The neighing of horses drew their attention. The watch called: "Riders approaching!"

They moved to get a clear view of the riders. "Erasmus. And he's not alone," Darius said to Edmund. He called down to the courtyard: "Open the gate!" They hurried down to the small courtyard. "Close it," he ordered when Erasmus and his cloaked companion arrived inside. The large hood created deep shadows that concealed a face.

Though the same age, Erasmus contrasted Darius' dark thoughtful countenance. Bright blue eyes sparkled from a rosy complexion. He kept his curly blonde hair short for manageability. Colorful clothes spoke of a lively nature. Rarely did Erasmus wear black or gray. Rarer was seeing him in a pensive or serious mood. Today proved an exception that Darius noticed.

"You have news?" he asked Erasmus.

"We must speak in private." Erasmus indicated his companion.

The hooded man appeared slightly bent in posture when on foot. His gait sure in step as they crossed the courtyard, entered the great hall and continued to the study. Once in the room, he threw back the hood to reveal an elderly gray-haired and bearded man with stern features. He tossed one side of the cloak over his left shoulder to show the steel blue and silver robes of a priest. The crest of the Temple of Providence was embroidered on the left breast. He wore a short sword, the type used for protection in traveling, not an offensive weapon.

"Vicar Archimedes!" Darius stammered in surprise that quickly turned to concern. "What brings you here? Have you news?"

"According to my scouts, Sir Angus and the Prince never crossed the river. They discovered signs of a scuffle on your side of the plain, but no trace of them."

All the color drained from Darius' face. "He shouldn't have gone to the Fortress! But would he listen to reason? No."

"Angus is not a man to be pressed into anything. He did what he thought best," said Erasmus.

"Don't you think I know that? Stubborn as an ox is my father."

"Jackass is a better comparison," snorted Edmund in ill-humor.

"You speak impertinently of your better," scolded Archimedes.

Edmund chafed. "A better only in the eyes of the world, not in character or affection."

Darius' quick hand on Edmund's arm stopped further words. Instead, he addressed Archimedes. "Vicar, you are apparently unaware that my father and Edmund are kin."

"A distant and poor relation," said Archimedes.

"Near or distant, rich or poor, they are kin. Edmund is my godfather."

Archimedes raised a brow yet refrained from further comment.

"Darius, the Vicar came personally to tell you," emphasized Erasmus.

Understanding the intervention, Darius assumed a more conciliatory attitude. "I appreciate the risk you have taken, Vicar. Be of good cheer, a search is under way by two of my best men. Secretly of course, I would not want to incur the King's wrath and make our situation worse."

Archimedes straightened to his full height. "You don't know what worse is."

Erasmus touched Darius' arm to get his attention from Archimedes. "Marcellus has dissolved the Council."

Darius flinched in surprise at the news. "What? Is he mad?"

Erasmus heaved an uncomfortable shrug. "The discovery of a possible challenger to his throne prompted him to take full control. Fergus and Malcolm were arrested. Ranulf badly wounded during his escape, and my father killed."

Darius groaned at hearing the report. "I'm sorry, Erasmus."

Erasmus simply nodded, though the painful loss evident on his face.

"Let's hope Nando and Brody find them quickly," said Edmund.

Archimedes tossed Edmund a displeased look before he spoke to Darius. "Were Sir Angus and the Prince alone when they left?"

"No, Jasper is with them," replied Darius.

"Jasper. Another servant," scoffed Archimedes.

To this Darius grew offended. "Garwood's master-at-arms, a most trusted and loyal friend."

Archimedes ignored the rebuff. "When the Prince has been found, bring him to me. The King would not dare to violate the Temple sanctuary."

"The King no, but Latham is another question."

Archimedes spoke boldly to the contrary. "Latham would risk too much by doing so. Now I must return. Jor'el be with you, with your father and the Prince."

Erasmus followed Archimedes in departure.

"Stick your nose back in your bloody books!" chided Edmund.

"Softly, Edmund," Darius warned the steward. "We don't need to make him angry. There is enough to worry about without you making matters worse."

"The man is an insufferable hermit who only comes out of his cloister when it suits him."

"Exactly why his coming here is so unusual!" Darius' rebuttal silenced Edmund. "Now, make arrangements for a new search."

On his way out, Edmund collided in the threshold with a young man in his mid-twenties. His ash blonde hair was unkempt while his face dirty and marred. "Brody."

Darius whirled about in anticipation to confront Brody. "Have you found them?"

"Not Sir Angus or Master Ellis. We found Jasper half-dead. His face is badly beaten along with numerous other wounds. Nando thinks he'll lose his left eye."

"Did Jasper say anything about them?"

"All he knew was that they left the Fortress."

"Is Jasper here?" asked Edmund.

Brody shook his head. "No, sir. We intended to fetch him back, only we stumbled upon Captain Tyree and Shadow Warriors—"

"Tyree!" Darius said with alarm to Edmund. "Archimedes and Erasmus."

"I saw him and a companion leave when I arrived," Brody said.

"Heaven help them," Darius muttered.

"Ay, but you must flee, my lord!" Brody urged. "We overheard Captain Tyree say he has orders to bring you in, *dead* or alive. Upon learning this, Nando and I split up. He to tend Jasper at the Dunlap ruins, while I came to warn you. They're only a couple of hours behind me."

"Indeed, you must flee immediately!" Edmund spoke emphatically, only to be rebuffed.

"Where? You heard what Erasmus said about the others. No. I must take up the search."

Edmund sharply disagreed. "Darius, be reasonable! You can't search with Shadow Warriors in the province. What about those here at Garwood? Would you leave them to face Tyree?"

"What do you suggest?"

"Order Garwood abandoned and retreat to Dunlap to form a new strategy."

Darius frowned with sigh of resignation. He noticed Brody watched him, thus he addressed the young man. "You did well. Return to your father with my thanks for your loyal service."

"Nowhere in Allon is safe. I would sooner perish fighting than huddled in fear. My father would understand. Besides, I told Nando I would return with provisions and medicine for Jasper."

Darius gave Brody an impulsive grin before he issued the disturbing order. "Edmund, tell everyone to flee for their lives. Brody, make haste to gather what provisions we need. We'll meet at the postern gate as quickly as possible."

***

Darius and the others were not the only ones avoiding Shadow Warriors. From the tree line of a bluff overlooking a small village on the outskirts of Dorgirith, Shannan watched a patrol leave the village. Torin lay beside her, also watchful. She saw significant damage with several homes burned. Numerous villagers lay either dead or seriously wounded.

A nearby thunderclap startled her from her vigil. It began to rain, hard and heavy. She shrank back into the forest, disturbed and frightened by what she witnessed. She rushed back to the cave. Torin entered a moment before her.

Niles stood in the library section thumbing through a book. Ellis sat at the table with parchments and books before him. She threw back the cowl of her jerkin to give an urgent report.

"Grandfather! Patrols are everywhere. Men unlike any I've ever seen. Large soldiers dressed in black from head to toe, riding massive black horses. From the bluff I saw villagers try to resist, but it was useless."

Niles grew grim with concern. "Shadow Warriors."

She fought back upset to nervously nod. "That's what I thought. They looked exactly like you described." Her voice grew mournful. "Those poor people."

Ellis grew curious at the exchange. "What are Shadow Warriors?"

"Nearly invincible soldiers that have been employed by the enemy since the Great Fall. If you had read further you would have learned about them." Niles indicated the book Ellis read.

"He might not have time to learn from books," began Shannan. "So far they have skirted Dorgirith, but it may only be a matter of time—"

"No!" Niles snapped. "Jor'el has brought us together for a great purpose. He will give us time to make ready. Return to your watch while Ellis continues his studies."

"Come, Torin." Shannan left the cave.

"Why do you send her to do a man's job?" Ellis argued.

Niles raised a scolding brow. "You have much to learn, my lord. Shannan was raised in the forest. She can come and go unseen. I would not purposely place my granddaughter in harm's way, only Jor'el has plans for her. It is for his plan that she, and *you*, must be prepared to fulfill." He again indicated the book.

Frustrated, Ellis shoved it aside. "What good are books when everything is falling apart?"

"You said Angus only had time to tell you the truth about your royal heritage, but not much history. These books and maps will tell you what he could not."

Subdued, Ellis lamented, "He was the only father I ever knew." He sniffled with sorrow. He wiped several tears from his face. "How will any of this help me fight Marcellus and Latham?"

"Knowledge is power. You can't fight what you don't understand. Weapons are just one way. Wisdom, knowledge and faith are other ways. Take for example your ancestor King Tristan. His faith in Jor'el helped him destroy Magelen, not warfare." He sat opposite Ellis to continue.

"When Jor'el created mortals, the Great Maker lived among us in a grand palace called *Jor'el-l`ahair*, which in the Ancient means *Jor'el With*

Us. The compound consisted of the Palace, the Temple of Providence and the Fortress, where those who were called to the priesthood learned from the Heavenly Ruler Himself."

"Where is the Palace? It must be magnificent."

"It no longer exists. Nor does the Fortress. Both destroyed during the Great Battle. Only the Temple remains."

"The Great Battle?"

"To aid the mortals, Jor'el called upon his Guardians, immortal beings possessing wisdom, power and strength beyond mortal capabilities. Mortals and Guardians co-existed in a unique balance of need and mutual admiration. Together they frequented Jor'el's holy compound. Only Captain Kell, the supreme Guardian, and a few divinely chosen mortals were allowed into the inner sanctum of the palace on a daily basis. For a thousand years, all lived in peace and prosperity until Dagar, the Guardian Trio Leader of the Region of Sanctuary grew discontent with his station. Mortals became the object of his unrest, and would play into his scheme by spreading dissatisfaction."

Ellis listened with furrowed brows of confusion. "What does that have to do with the Great Battle?"

"Patience. All will become clear if you stop interrupting and just listen. By means of other Guardians, Jor'el warned Dagar to curb his attitude. Alas, Dagar wouldn't listen. He vented his anger and maimed a fellow Guardian beyond recognition. Jor'el set him free from suffering."

Ellis became surprised. "Jor'el killed the Guardian? I thought they couldn't die?"

Niles shook his head at Ellis' obstinacy of interrupting. "Jor'el is all powerful. He can uncreate what he created. Have you so little faith that you question his abilities and power?"

Chided, Ellis colored. "Not really. I'm just trying to understand. If Jor'el is all powerful, why does he want to use me to topple Marcellus?"

A fair question, and one Niles often asked Jor'el during his mediation concerning Shannan and himself. The answer always came back to trust and faith. For whatever reason, the Almighty chose to use weak mortals to bring about his will for Allon. Now it was Ellis' turn to grapple with the question. Niles could only guide Ellis, not make up his mind.

At length, Niles replied, "That, my Prince, is for you to inquire of Jor'el. Be assured, He will answer you. For now hear the history to which you were born without further interruption."

Ellis nodded, though by his expression, Niles knew the young man didn't like the answer. Still, he proceeded. "Finally, Jor'el sent Kell to remove Dagar from his position. Alas, Dagar escaped. He met Haggar, a female mortal disowned by her family for her sinful life. Filled with bitterness, she willingly agreed to his plan. She gave birth to his twin sons, Ram and Razi. Dagar raised them to hate Jor'el."

"Razi was Dagar's son? I read something about him being Vicar Elias' father." Ellis grabbed a book, but Niles stopped him.

"Ay, Razi was Dagar's son. Only he came to believe in Jor'el, and denounced Dagar's plan. This infuriated Dagar. He and Ram led a rebellion that divided mortals and Guardians. This became known as the Great Battle." Niles grew thoughtful in shaking his head. "Somehow Dagar succeeded in defeating Kell, and crowned Ram King of Allon. As a result, Jor'el withdrew his presence, banished Dagar to a nether dimension and removed all Guardians from Allon."

Ellis sat up at hearing about the Great Battle. "Why did Jor'el allow Dagar to win?"

Niles took a deep breath to continue without answering Ellis' question. "Banishment did not curb Dagar's hate. Although confined, he found ways to employ Shadow Warriors over the centuries."

"The same Shadow Warriors Shannan reported seeing?"

"Hard to say. During one such mission, Dagar learned of a surviving female descendant of Ram. She was brought to him, and once more the powerful Guardian had son, Magelen. He became the conduit for unleashing a torrent of evil upon the mortals not seen since the Great Battle. Then came Tristan, who armed only with a dagger and faith in Jor'el, slew Magelen."

"Faith and not warfare," Ellis muttered under his breath.

Niles grinned at the understanding. "Tristan became Allon's most beloved king and ruled for one hundred years. He reestablished the worship of Jor'el and created the Council of Twelve. He was the first Jor'ellian Knight of the Temple, sworn to defend the honor of Jor'el and Allon. With the Fortress rebuilt, the order swelled into a great army. Their faith gave them unparalleled strength. Many believed a Jor'ellian could defeat a Guardian, against which no other mortal stood a chance."

"Have you ever defeated a Guardian?"

Again, Niles ignored the question to earnestly regard Ellis. He came to the heart of the matter. "Despite Dagar's victory, Jor'el didn't leave us without hope. He prompted Elias to rewrite the Book of Prophecy to include the promise that a Son of Tristan would return to restore the throne of his ancestor. Also mentioned is the Daughter of Allon, in whose fate lays the return of the Guardians. Joined in purpose, they can stem the tide of evil brought about by Dagar, and begin clearing the path for the Almighty's return." He saw Ellis understood. "Ay, my Prince. *You* are the Promised Son of Tristan, and Shannan is the Daughter of Allon."

"I can see my birth, but Shannan? Where are her parents?"

Niles fondly smiled. "Kell told us of her pending birth. Joyous news since my son, Colin, was one hundred and ten years old while his wife, one hundred. After forty years of marriage we thought her barren. Alas," he said as smile faded, "she died in childbirth. Colin three years later."

Ellis spoke with due consideration. "You said Kell told you. Have the Guardians returned?"

"Not completely. Their full time hasn't come yet."

Ellis looked confused. "Father—I mean Angus—said you were killed in the overthrow. Did Kell help you survive? How have you lived so long? The oldest person I met was ninety, and born just after the coup."

A look of deep melancholy overcame Niles. "Although the escape was planned, it didn't happen as we hoped. Abner and Gordon had their parts, while Colin and I took your great-grandfather, Akilles and his brothers from Waldron. After reaching the safety of Dorgirith, word came that Waldron burned to the ground. There were no survivors." Niles paused to gather his emotions from painful recollections.

"That's why you and Abner thought the other died," said Ellis.

Niles nodded. "*And* the reason I've lived so long, is to help you fulfill your destiny."

Ellis let the reply sink in for a moment. "I understand much of what you say, but your age and that of Colin, still puzzles me. I didn't think anyone could live that long."

Niles frowned with discouragement. "Part of the curse that mortals suffered for helping Dagar. Before then it was common to live up to two hundred and fifty years. Since then, our life span has grown shorter."

"So why wasn't I born here?"

Niles became annoyed. "You ask too many questions rather than consider what you've been told! We fled to insure the continuation of the royal line. Akilles and his brothers couldn't stay here and find wives! Not until Shannan was born did I even hope to live to see prophecy fulfilled. Now time grows short. *You* must be prepared for the journey ahead." He then groused, "I must calm myself from this discussion so I can consider how to structure your training." He rose from the table.

Niles paused in cave threshold. Ellis read; his brow deeply etched with intensity. Not only did Ellis bear a strong resemblance Akilles, he also possessed the inquisitive, impulsive and impatient nature of his great-grandsire. "Jor'el, give me wisdom and patience to guide him," Niles prayed and left.

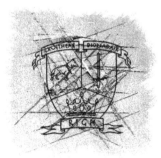

Chapter 4

UNDER DIRECTIONS FROM KING MARCELLUS AND GRAND MASTER Latham, Captain Tyree and the Shadow Warriors carried out a ferocious search. The brief spirit that bonded the people of the Southern Forest vanished under the onslaught. Small settlements were completely wiped out while all storehouses raided and burned. Sounds of devastation followed Tyree as his troops left the Southern Forest.

The next to feel their wrath was the Northern Forest under the lordship of Baron Phineas, younger brother of Angus. After receiving word from Darius, Phineas gathered his troops in support. On his way, he met Tyree's forces. Even with offering stiff resistance, his men could not defeat the Shadow Warriors. Almost to a man, the field lay littered with the fallen from his ranks. Phineas himself lay slain along with his son-in-law. His son Kemp barely managed to escape with his life. He fetched his family and fled into the wilderness.

News of Phineas' defeat preceded Tyree into the Highlands. However, Lord Ranulf chose to fight. Despite still suffering from earlier wounds, he used guerrilla tactics against the Shadow Warriors until the first snowfall. This forced the Shadow Warriors to face the rough Highland winter while Ranulf and his people disappeared into the mountains for safety.

Winter spared the Highlands the destruction that scarred the Southern and Northern Forest. However, when Tyree departed in early spring, he ordered hundreds of cattle slaughtered to deprive the people of their main source of trade and food.

With Lord Malcolm in prison, the North Plains fell easy prey. The people had no desire to fight without their overlord. Being spring, all seeds, plows and plow animals were destroyed. Fields already planted became trampled while those in bloom left untouched. Tyree coerced the farmers to agree to send sixty percent of their harvest to his army, with twenty percent going to the King at Ravendale. This left a mere twenty percent for the people to live on. Cheating meant death.

Sir Gareth of the South Plains faced a most difficult challenge; fight or yield to save his people. Knowing what became of Phineas and Ranulf, he chose to yield. Being summer, he offered the best of the South Plains bounty in tribute. He hoped the generous offer would prevent devastation. Alas it did not. Tyree ordered many fields burned, as they passed into the West Coast to confront Baron Mathias

Known for swaggering bravado, Mathias would not let his ne'er-do-well reputation or the feared invincibility of the Shadow Warriors stop him. He combined Phineas' frontal assault with Ranulf's guerrilla warfare. It proved the most resistance Tyree and the Warriors experienced. Unfortunately, the same fate awaited Mathias. It ended in a blood bath, with a seriously wounded Mathias borne from the field by a servant and taken into hiding. All ports came under Tyree's command. Foreign trade halted until word from the King came in respect to such dealings.

So much violent bloodshed stained Allon that the normally gruff and ill-tempered Lord Zebulon of the Lowlands gave second thought to offering resistance. His people were weavers and craftsman. They took wool from Midessex to create beautiful tapestries, rugs and cushioned furniture.

Another winter began to settle in, and not the season to wage battle. Whereas Zebulon kept a small force trained for war, he decided to follow the example of his younger brother Gareth. With a handful of men, he met Tyree at the border under a flag of truce to propose a bargain. He freely offered the region for the army's winter quarters in exchange for mercy upon his people.

Not normally known for mercy, Tyree considered the offer a good one. The previous winter spent fighting in the Highlands caused grumbling among the Warriors. During those months, they would not viciously pillage the Lowlands. However, they left their mark of revelry in every village, town and settlement. It became a heavy price in terms of property but did spare lives.

Sir Owain of Midessex may have held the title of knight, but in reality, a simple farmer. He thought best to serve his people by offering no resistance to Tyree. Similar to Zebulon, he considered the sacrifice of livestock and crops a small price to pay compared to the loss of lives. The Shadow Warriors were not as ruthless as in other regions, but Midessex did not completely avoid violence. According to Tyree, these random acts were object lessons to ensure Owain's continued cooperation.

The Meadowlands lay just south of Midessex. It provided ideal grazing grounds. Allon's three major rivers and small tributaries meandered through the rolling hills. Glass making and smithies of all kinds were prevalent on river settlements. The province's chief exports were horses and sheep. The best horses were raised and trained in the Meadowlands.

A highly intelligent and shrewd man, Lord Allard formulated an ingenious strategy for handling Tyree: commodities trading. By the time Tyree left the Meadowlands, Allard had the captain believing himself an astute businessman. Save for a few scorched fields, the province escaped unscathed. The people breathed a sigh of relief when the soldiers left.

For eighteen months, Baron Erasmus of the Delta received word of what happened to his countrymen. He waited with dreaded anticipation for his region's turn. The Delta bordered both the Meadowlands and the Lowlands. Rich in mineral deposits the mild climate proved well conducive for bathing and recuperating at the hot springs. Fancy spas lined the south coast. No coward, Erasmus found it difficult to justify resistance in the face of such examples as Phineas and Mathias.

With a wary eye, Erasmus watched Tyree make his path obvious in circumventing the country. His father died at Ravendale during the coup of the Council of Twelve. Erasmus could not dishonor his memory by simply giving in like others. When Tyree's army entered the Delta, they razed all the towns between the border and provincial castle of Deltoria. Such action forced Erasmus to back down to spare the rest of his region from violence. He hated himself for doing so.

Sir Fergus of the East Coast remained in prison while his teenage sons were too young to act in defense of the province. The wealthy merchants fell before Tyree to offer whatever they could to satisfy him and his Shadow Warriors. Such enormous booty convinced Tyree to be lenient. Minimal acts of violence made the people appreciate his benevolence.

At last, Tyree would make his way to Allon's most sacred shrine, the Temple of Providence in the Region of Sanctuary.

* * *

Atop a gently rising plateau surrounded by four majestic hills stood the Temple of Providence. The only building in Allon to rival the splendor of the Temple was the once magnificent Waldron Castle.

Each province contributed to the Temple. The pillars of marble came from a quarry in the far range of the Northern Forest where it bordered the foothills of the Highlands. Carved images of Verse and Allon's history decorated the pillars. These guarded massive wooden doors hewn and gilded by the craftsmen of the Southern Forest. Golden steeples topped twin bell spires of gleaming white marble. The bells came from the sister provinces of the North and South Plains. The entire facade of the Temple was white marble with gold accents. The arch shaped windows of colored glass were created and assembled in Midessex. At certain times of day, the Temple reflected the sun's rays in a brilliance of white with a kaleidoscope of gold and rainbow effects.

Inside, gold, white and crimson formed the colors of the décor. Metal workers of the Highlands forged the golden lamp stands. Tapestries from the Lowlands hung on the walls, while a crimson carpet from the weavers in the Meadowlands lead to the High Altar. Sun cascading through the windows made a bright mosaic of color on the white marble floor. Each window represented a province with six on each side of the Temple. The incense was supplied by the West Coast, exclusive importers of such finery. Not to be outdone, the exquisite Altar furnishings were donated by leading merchant families of the East Coast. Wood for the High Altar came from the oldest tree in Allon, which had been found in the Delta.

Vicar Archimedes and the priests participated in morning prayers. The front doors burst open, which created a thunderous echo in the cavernous room. Tyree's black uniform stood in stark contrast to the sparkling brilliance around him. At his back came half a dozen Shadow Warriors. They were three to four inches taller than Tyree's six and a half-feet, making them a more imposing sight than the dark captain.

Archimedes rushed to confront Tyree. "How dare you invade the Temple?"

Tyree ignored Archimedes. He signaled his men forward when Archimedes seized his arm. He snarled at the Vicar. "You can't stop me."

Archimedes spoke in a low voice full of deadly confidence. "Do not be so sure."

Tyree focused so intently on Archimedes that he didn't notice the one hundred priests take up position behind the Vicar. The priests shed their outer robes to expose white tunics emblazoned in gold and purple. All wore short swords, however the crest drew Tyree's attention. It was divided into three parts, each depicting an ancient symbol with an eagle, a wolf, and a crown surrounding a sword. A brief ripple of concern crossed Tyree's brow.

The lead Shadow Warrior grew stiff at sight of the crest. His cold grey eyes flashed with a surge of brightness. "Captain," he spoke with warning in Tyree's ear.

"Silence, Commander Altari. You don't take this charade seriously, do you?" Tyree tried to laugh off his concern, but a hollow, feeble attempt at best.

"This is no charade," said Archimedes.

"You would turn this holy place red with blood?" challenged Tyree.

"We would drive you outside before slaying you all." Archimedes spoke with such deadly earnest that Tyree gripped the hilt of his sword to cover his unnerved reaction.

Altari seized Tyree by the shoulder. "Captain!" he insisted.

The veins in Tyree's forehead twitched at Altari's intervention. He turned on his heels to march from the Temple. The Shadow Warriors followed him.

Archimedes stepped out onto the Temple steps to watch the Tyree and his troops ride through the main gate. Several priests joined him. "We have revealed ourselves. We must prepare."

⚜

Tyree never discussed what happened at the Temple, as he frantically drove the army back to Ravendale. His return could not have come at a worse time, for Marcellus entertained in grand style. Despite the disruption of his arrival, Tyree boldly entered the Great Hall. He did not even clean up his road-dusty appearance. Eyes of scorn, curiosity and confusion followed his approach of high table. Noise of celebration gave way to curious murmurs as Tyree fell humbly to one knee.

Marcellus snarled with displeasure. "This better be good, Captain."

Tyree cast a sheepish glance to the guests then back to Marcellus. In a clear, strong voice he said, "Sire, the Jor'ellian Knights of the Temple have returned."

After several initial gasps of stifled surprise from various parts of the hall, a deep hush fell. No one spoke or stirred until Marcellus leaned forward in his chair with eyes heavy upon Tyree.

"What did you just say?" Marcellus harshly demanded.

"The Jor'ellian Knights of the Temple have returned—"

Marcellus bolted to his feet. The force sent his chair tumbling backwards. Latham immediately came beside him. He seized Latham by the collar to draw him close, inches from his own face. "Did you not tell me yesterday that it was too soon for the Jor'ellians to return?"

"It is, Sire! Question him about them. Surely they were not armed for battle."

Marcellus demanded of Tyree, "How did you learn this, Captain?"

"At the Temple of Providence, Sire. We were attempting to obey your orders when Vicar Archimedes and one hundred Jor'ellians prevented our mission."

"Were they dressed for battle?" pressed Latham.

"There were armed with short swords though not fully dressed for battle."

"You let one hundred knights not in battle dress stop your army of Shadow Warriors?" challenged a middle age nobleman at the end of the high table.

"One hundred *Jor'ellian* Knights, my lord," Tyree corrected.

"*If* any still exist, they must be old men."

"Ay! We shall crush them and their legend," said another noble with bravado.

Tyree became rigid at the insults. "My army could have engaged them. Yet my only thought was to immediately inform His Majesty of this unusual occurrence."

"You have done so, Captain. And at great personal distress!" declared Marcellus.

"Forgive me, Sire," Tyree pleaded.

Marcellus' fiercely scowled. "Go! All of you!" he shouted at the crowded hall. He seized Latham to force him from the hall into an antechamber. "What does this mean? Could this be some trick by Archimedes to divert our efforts? To dress his priests as Jor'ellians to rally support for the Pretender?"

"Archimedes hails from a great lineage of Jor'ellian Knights. It is doubtful he would use such a trick."

"Then what? Raze the Temple itself?"

"Sire, to act prematurely will play into the Pretender's plan."

"What plan? For two years my men have scoured the countryside with no sign of the boy, Angus or Darius. Perhaps your precaution is for nothing and they all lie dead in some forsaken corner of the country."

Latham slowly shook his head. "If that were true, I would know."

"You didn't know he was alive until a few years ago!"

Latham's jowls tightened and his back stiffened.

Marcellus scoffed with ridicule. "You have nothing to say? For all your knowledge in the magic arts you are fallible."

"Sire, mock me all you want, but it does not change what Tyree said about the Jor'ellians."

Marcellus briskly opened the door to shout, "Captain Tyree!" Quickly, the captain appeared. He clapped his sword with a short bow to Marcellus. "Return to the Temple-"

"Sire," protested Latham.

"Silence!" commanded Marcellus. He continued to instruct Tyree. "Arrest the priests and Archimedes, only leave the Temple intact. We shall do to them my grandfather did."

Tyree again clapped his sword. "As you command, Sire."

Marcellus just closed the door upon Tyree's departure when Latham voiced his objection.

"Sire, we are dealing with Prophecy. The return of the Jor'ellians is clearly spoken of in connection with the Pretender. We must act prudently and not in a childish fit of temper."

Marcellus' eyes wrathfully narrowed, his voice strident in response. "Remember to whom you speak! Your Prophecy is tolerated only as far as it will aid me in gaining total control of Allon. I care not for your Dark Way. Now, go!"

Latham bowed with forced submission. His hand clenched the talisman as he departed.

When he returned, Tyree found the Temple and its compound deserted. The emotions that drove him the last few days were an unusual mixture of anger, insult, embarrassment, and a twinge of fear. The latter was an unfamiliar emotion.

Angry to the point of exploding, Tyree picked up a candlestick from the High Altar with the intent on hurling it through one of the windows. Altari snatched his arm to prevent the action.

"Let go!" Tyree sneered with a wince under Altari's crushing grip.

The Warrior's cold grey eyes filled with warning. Tyree loudly exhaled with frustration, but his expression showed recanting. Altari released him, which let Tyree to vent some emotion by slamming the candlestick back in its place.

Tyree spoke as they left the Temple. "The King won't like this, but hopefully, I can convince him that this is the end of it."

Altari stopped Tyree when they stepped outside. "We're not going to search for them?"

Tyree moved from Altari. He snatched the reins from the Warrior, who held his mount. He vaulted into the saddle. "Why? If they were priests in disguise, we have heard the last of them."

"They were not simple priests. We can't just give up. They are too dangerous to be allowed to roam free," Altari argued.

Tyree scowled with skepticism. "What do know you about them?"

The Warrior gave Altari a warning glare. This prompted Altari to reply with discretion. "I know that a Jor'ellian Knight—and priest—can slay a Guardian. The only mortals who can."

"You don't believe that legend, do you?" Tyree spoke with disdain.

Altari began to speak when the Warrior nudged him. Altari bit back his reply.

Tyree noticed the exchange. "So that is why you and the others are *afraid*. If they can kill Guardians, then Shadow Warriors should be no trouble."

Altari stiffened at the insult. His grey eyes flashed brighter than normal eye color. "We are not afraid! Merely cautious."

"Well, your caution costs us the opportunity to find out!"

"No, your withdrawal did that."

Fuming, Tyree lashed out. "I don't know how Latham tolerates your impertinence." He snapped the reins for the horse to gallop from the Temple compound.

"What were you doing?" the Warrior chided Altari. "Do you know what will happen if we are discovered? Reconditioning or worse."

"Trying to save us from being drawn into a confrontation with the Jor'ellians before it is time." Altari signaled the Warriors to follow Tyree.

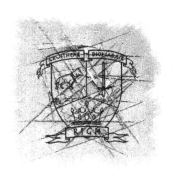

Chapter 5

SINCE THE DISCOVERY OF A POSSIBLE PRINCE TO THE HOUSE OF Tristan, every corner of Allon suffered during the ruthless two-year effort to be rid of the dangerous usurper. All corners except a hidden cave deep in the infamous forest of Dorgirith.

During this time, Ellis grew in knowledge and stature under Niles' instruction. It surprised him to discover the vast array of equipment the old Knight possessed and kept in good shape. However, before he could touch a real weapon, Niles had to be satisfied of his proficiency with mock weapons. He found Niles to be an amazing master in almost every art of warfare. Despite age, Niles proved a good wrestler. His acrobatic skills were a bit rusty in demonstrating climbing, jumping or landing techniques. In truth, Niles' skill and knowledge far exceeded Angus or Jasper. Nevertheless, if not for the foundation of their teaching, learning the advanced techniques from Niles would have been frustrating.

Raine, the captured horse Ellis rode that fateful day, became his mount for all equine training. Regardless of the weather, he completed a rigorous workout of physical strengthening and conditioning. This was followed by an hour ride on an obstacle course Niles laid out the day before. The entire regiment occupied the morning, with weapons instruction and formal education after the midday meal.

Ellis also found in Niles a devout worshipper of Jor'el. Inside the cave, Niles constructed a small altar for daily worship. The old Knight spoke of including Jor'el in all aspects of life. On Allon's holy days, they journeyed to a rugged outdoor altar Niles erected years earlier for special observances. By words and deeds, Niles showed that a Jor'ellian Knight's successes or failures often told of his relationship with Jor'el.

The twice-a-week exceptions to Ellis' daily regiment were the most frustrating part of his early days in Dorgirith. Training from Niles he could accept, but learning to hunt and move about the forest with stealth from a girl was embarrassing! His vigorous protests drew a harsh tongue-lashing from Niles.

"Shannan is blessed with hunting skills beyond even my abilities. Other than the Guardian Wren, you can have no better teacher."

However, not until Ellis' rebellious attitude nearly got him trampled and gouged by a wild female boar, did he learn the truth of Niles' words. If not for Shannan's expert shot, he could have been killed. From that day on, he never raised another complaint.

As time passed, Ellis realized how he fit into the Great Maker's divine plan for Allon. The sobering awareness made him keenly feel the need for spiritual strength. At night, he read Verse for hours. The more he meditated, the more his skill increased, even to the point of impressing Niles. Just as his skill grew, so did the difficulty of his training exercises. It was a great day when he defeated Niles in a wrestling match that left Niles sore for two days.

After a grueling morning workout, Ellis' clothes were soaked with perspiration, his face grimy. Now eighteen, he grew from a lanky sixteen-year-old into a handsome, muscular young man of six feet two inches. His features had bronzed by hardy outdoor living. Shoulder-length golden hair dripped with sweat while two days worth of whisker stubble framed his chin and lips.

Niles sat on a boulder by a small river that ran through Dorgirith to watch his protégé. Ellis' sword rested on his lap. He fought a smile. "Well done. I'll have to come up with something more difficult."

Ellis cocked a brow. He took a deep breath before asking, "More difficult?"

This time Niles widely smiled. "If you had been alive in my day, these trials would be child's play compared to what Vicar Wilbur put us through. Just ask Archimedes."

"I hardly picture the Vicar as a knight."

"Next to me, he was the most skilled. He bore the title First Jor'ellian Knight of the Realm. If I had not defeated him in the Contest, I would have been the next Vicar and Archimedes the King's Champion."

Ellis sat beside Niles. "The Contest?"

"The ultimate test of skill and cunning. It only happens when the King's Champion dies naturally or is killed in battle. The winner takes his place."

"Which you did."

Niles chuckled. "It wasn't easy. The Contest is a grueling three-day event in which all Jor'ellian Knights participated. The first two days consisted of various trials to test a Knight's cunning, strength, and skill. All came one right after the other with little to no sleep. Some didn't make it to the third day. Even those remaining were near exhaustion. The final day was combat between the contestants. Only after defeating all the others could one claim the rank of King's Champion."

"You had to kill other Knights?"

"No! We never fought to the death, only to defeat. Our oath forbids taking the blood of another Jor'ellian."

"So you've been testing me with events from the Contest?" Ellis wryly grinned.

Niles cocked a mischievous brow. "Not yet, though I have altered some events to sharpen your skills. When the time comes, I will recreate the Contest in its entirety. Then we shall see how good a warrior you truly are. For you will not be the King's Champion, *you* will be King."

Ellis' brows knitted at the pronouncement. It gave him great pause to consider his destiny, King of Allon.

Niles' hand clapped Ellis' shoulder. "Bathe in the river before we return."

Absentmindedly Ellis stripped before he plunged into the water. The coolness on his warm body startled him from his introspection. After the initial shock, the water felt refreshing. He immersed himself several times.

"Feels good. You should come in." He playfully splashed Niles.

"Grandfather—" Shannan emerged from the forest carrying several rabbits. Now seventeen, she wore her dark hair loose with the sides braided and drawn back. She stopped at seeing Ellis swiftly submerge.

Niles laughed. He tossed the clothes to Ellis once the young man's head tentatively came up for air. "These need to be washed, either on or off your body."

Shannan tried to hide a blushing smile. "Rabbit stew." She held up her catch to show her grandfather.

"Start supper. Ellis and I will be along after he washes the red from his face and dirt from his clothes."

Ellis gave Niles only a passing smirk. He tried to dress while keeping his lower half submerged, and an eye on Shannan's departure.

"Hail, King's Champion!" a voice came from the opposite direction of Shannan's departure. Two large beings appeared.

Niles smiled in greeting. "Kell. Armus."

Ellis hastened from the river to pull on his boots. He curiously eyed the new arrivals. At the name "*Kell*" he wondered if this was the Guardian Niles often spoken about. He had to be; while both stood taller than any mortal, past seven feet. Ellis fetched his sword, which Niles left against the boulder before he approached them.

"My lord," said Kell. He and Armus saluted Ellis with the right hand clenched in a fist over the left breast. They bowed at the waist.

"Ellis, this is Kell, Captain of Jor'el's Guardians, and his lieutenant, Armus," said Niles.

Up close, Ellis gaped at the Guardians. They towered over him by over a foot. Kell's black hair and bright golden eyes commanded attention. Armus equaled Kell in height with brown hair, light chestnut eyes and more rugged features. Both were powerfully built, only Armus stockier with broad shoulders, massive arms and chest. They wore tan colored close fitting jackets trimmed in gold. The jackets had side slits from the hem to the hip for ease of movement. From brown leather scabbards hung sheathed swords and daggers. The breeches were tan while the boots matched the belt.

"By the Heavenlies! Sirs." Ellis began to bow when Kell snatched his elbow to stop him.

"Do not bow to us, Son of Tristan. We are here on your behalf."

Niles told Ellis, "I've learned over the years, that Kell only makes an appearance when things are about to happen." He then inquired of Kell, "What is it?"

"A critical error has been made and must be remedied."

"Jor'el has erred?" asked Ellis confused.

Kell shook his head. "Not Jor'el. He is perfection. Alas, mortals are not. Archimedes exposed the presence of the Jor'ellians too soon. Tyree is hot on their heels. This has forced them to go into hiding."

"Leaving the Temple unguarded," added Armus, his brightened chestnut eyes direct on Niles.

The old Knight visibly shivered with surprised fear.

"Niles?" asked Ellis with concern.

Niles waved Ellis off to speak his concern to Kell. "He is not ready."

"That is why we are here. If he cannot defeat us, he will not defeat Dagar."

"How can I defeat a Guardian?"

"That is for you to discover, Son of Tristan. Be certain, we will test every aspect of your skill and character. We must, yet we do so with no malice, quite the contrary. The fate of Allon lies in your hands."

Ellis assumed a braced posture during Kell's reply. Niles' hand on his shoulder did not stop his scrutiny of the Guardian captain. At a rough shake, Ellis gave Niles his attention.

"Tell Shannan we have guests for dinner," said Niles.

Ellis hesitated, but Niles' firm nudge moved him on his way. He reached the cave a moment before the others.

"We have company for dinner. Guardians," he gruffly announced.

"Guardians?" Shannan echoed in surprise.

"Indeed." Niles entered with Kell and Armus.

Shannan froze upon sight of the two large, powerful beings. In awe, her gaze shifted between them.

"Shannan, this is Kell. I've told you about him," said Niles matter-of-factly.

"Kell," she repeated, and then started. "Captain of the Guardians!" Aside from being the most handsome being she'd ever seen there was compassion to his countenance. In his golden eyes she saw all the tales her grandfather told of his might; of his battle with Dagar, and his role in bringing Niles and the princes to safety.

Kell warmly smiled as he bowed. "Greetings, Daughter of Allon."

"This is Armus, Kell's lieutenant," continued Niles.

Shannan's gaze turned to Armus. Past a jovial gleam in his bright chestnut eyes she saw unflinching loyalty and trust; a good combination of qualities to have in one's lieutenant.

"My lady." Armus took her by the elbow to steer her towards the pot. "Rabbit stew?"

"Ay, but it won't be done for another hour."

"I'm certain we can find something to occupy ourselves until then."

"I didn't know Guardians ate. I mean mortal food," she said, halting his departure to join the others.

Armus' smile widened. "We eat. We also sleep, though ours is more a meditative state rather than a loss of consciousness." He tossed a wry glance to Kell as he continued. "The only thing we don't do is grow old ... or die."

This statement drew perplexed looks from Ellis and Shannan.

"Not in the mortal sense," said Kell, which added to their confusion. "Guardians are physical manifestations of the spirits from which we are formed. That is why we possess the attributes of both the physical and spiritual dimensions. When a Guardian *dies*, for lack of a better term, we simply return to our former spirit."

"How do Guardians die?" asked Shannan. She stirred the stew.

Kell's eyes darted to Ellis. "At present, it would be unwise of me to answer."

Ellis scowled in annoyance as he sat at the table. "He won't say anything that might help me."

"Information is knowledge." Kell sat opposite Ellis.

Not pleased by the answer, Shannan accosted Kell. "Knowledge of what? And why won't you help? Ellis *is* Jor'el's chosen, rightful heir to Allon's throne. Were Guardians not created to aid us? And where have you been all this time?"

She spoke so rapidly that an amused Kell couldn't answer.

"As fearless as her grandfather," Armus chuckled to Kell.

Kell grinned in reply to her question. "Most are at Melwynn, with a few of us remaining to protect the kingdom."

The answer stymied her. "Melwynn? I thought the Castle of the Guardians was a legend."

"No, it is real. Just like our Council Hall of Arundine. Only they have been hidden from mortals since the Great Battle."

"Is Melwynn were Jor'el went after withdrawing his presence from Allon?" asked Ellis.

"No. He is in the Heavenlies, until Allon is worthy of His return."

"When will that be?"

"Not until all of Prophecy has been fulfilled."

"When Ellis is king?" asked Shannan, a sharp eye on Kell.

"That is only part of the Prophecy, my lady." Kell began quoting,

"When the Great Enemy has gathered together his minions,
Uneasy shall lay his crown,

For when peace has come to his camp
They shall behold him who is to come.'"

Armus continued,

"'And with him shall be a shining multitude
Whose light shall gleam with heavenly radiance.'"

"'*Blood shall stain Allon,*'" Niles soberly concluded the quote.

Heavy silence followed the somber reciting. At length, Kell spoke: "The coming confrontation will be like nothing seen since the Great Battle. It is that for which you must be made ready, my lord."

Ellis chewed on his lip. He stared at an unknown spot on the table. "Will I win?"

"That is a question left for another time."

"Why?" Ellis demanded. Kell's calm expression infuriated him. "I know! Information is knowledge."

"If you know the outcome it could affect how you are prepared, spiritually, mentally and physically."

"Ellis, remember what I taught you," began Niles. "Jor'el is perfect power and knowledge, only he chooses to use imperfect, weak mortals to carry out his plan. Therein lies the stumbling block. Consider Archimedes."

Ellis' lips twitched with a frustrated sneer. His brows drew level.

"The question is, are you willing to face the Contest on faith and trust us and Jor'el? Or do you need complete answers?" Kell keenly watched for Ellis' response.

Ellis stormed out. Concerned, Shannan began to follow, but stopped when Kell spoke.

"He must come to terms with this himself. If not, he will do Allon more harm than good."

"I don't understand. Why bring him this far only to taunt him?"

Kell tried to temper his words. "Understanding isn't always the answer. Faith is what matters. Jor'el sent Armus and me to test him in every aspect. If he cannot tolerate what we do out of obedience then he will fall before Dagar."

She bit her lip. His words hard to hear, but he spoke truth.

After lunch Niles, Kell, and Armus planned the Contest, seemingly unconcerned that Ellis had not returned. Shannan was concerned, so while they were occupied, she grabbed her bow and quiver to quietly leave the cave.

Finding Ellis would not be difficult; after all she spent her whole life exploring the thousand acres of Dorgirith. She knew all the boundaries, the best hiding places and then some. Ellis had gone off before over the years. In her role as self-appointed watchman, she followed at a discreet distance but rarely disturbed his solitude.

Whenever troubled, he usually went to Angus' burial mound. For sixteen years Angus nurtured, trained, scolded, loved and sheltered him like his own son. That was the first place she went. No Ellis. She went to other places they frequented over the years, still no sign of him. Each failure made her anxiety grow. She knew she had to keep her wits thus forced her emotions to calm down when she grew careless in her search.

At the farthest western extent of Dorgirith, a massive outcropping overlooked the river plain toward the Region of Sanctuary. Now twilight, she discovered Ellis sitting on the largest portion of the outcropping staring off into the distance. With a sense of relief, she stopped within the shadow of the trees to take up her vigil.

She only saw a quarter of his profile, but she didn't need to see much to sense his conflict. Since a child, Niles taught her Verse and Prophecy along with her role based upon what Kell told him. She dutifully listened, only everything seemed abstract, without form or substance. She tried to imagine the Son of Tristan in how they would relate along with their adventures. Imagination is often far from reality.

The moment she met Ellis, she knew him, just like Niles said. The depth of awareness went far beyond anything she ever experienced. The keenness with which she felt his pain, joy and presence touched her very soul. Her every thought and action became focused on him, as if beyond her control.

On those occasions when conflicts arose between them, she tried to ignore, even fight the urges, to will them away. Ellis could be obstinate and condescending. Saving him from the boar was a turning point in their relationship. He became a more willing pupil, to a point. There were still times his ego took a bruising under her instruction or she bested him in hunting skill he thought he mastered. Eventually his strength and prowess grew to where he outdid her in everything. At those times, she found herself annoyed at Ellis becoming the master while she second best. Niles rarely interfered, expect on those occasions. He spoke wisely about not allowing her feelings to cause conflict with Ellis for their destinies lay together for the good of Allon.

Allon. Another abstract concept she wrestled with. The appearance of the Guardians made it a reality for both she and Ellis. The weight of reality now came crashing in upon their sanctuary.

"Oh, Ellis. Although you know in your mind what to do, you must open your heart to embrace it. When you do, I hope you find me there." With that, she left. He was safe and had much to consider.

Ellis heard a slight rustle. He caught a glimpse of Shannan leaving. He knew she was there. She was always there. He smiled in turning back to watch the sunset. It used to offend him that she followed to keep watch. He could take care of himself and didn't need a girl's help. How arrogant he acted. His behavior didn't stop her tenacious persistence in watching out for his welfare. Their moods and habits became second nature to each other. Often they sat in silence upon the very spot he now singularly occupied. Nothing needed to be said, or did it? She knew his thoughts and feelings as he did hers, or did he? Why did she leave so quickly?

He realized just how much he depended upon her steady presence. He drew strength from her silent support and peace in her confidence of his destiny. She taught him to hunt with patience, to track with the stealth of a fox.

"What have I given her in return?" he wondered to himself.

Hope for the future, a voice within him answered. Then in his mind he heard Niles' quoting Prophecy:

> *"'Among them shall be one whose birth*
> *Shall mirror his own.*
> *Unto her shall he pledge himself,*
> *For she, like Allon, shall be his desire*
> *And the twain shall become one.'"*

"'Unto her shall he pledge himself, for she, like Allon shall be his desire,'" Ellis repeated aloud. He glanced skyward. "Jor'el, show me what I must do to prepare for the Contest."

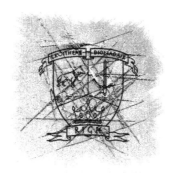

Chapter 6

NOT UNTIL THE FOLLOWING MORNING DID ELLIS RETURN TO the cave. Shannan sat against the outside entrance wrapped in a blanket asleep. Beside her were glowing embers of a dying fire. So soft did Ellis approach that she became startled when he touched her shoulder. He laughed.

"Did you not hear me, she who walks silently?"

She smirked in recovery from her momentary fright. "I suppose you enjoyed that."

He sat beside her. "Why are you out here? Not enough room inside with our guests?"

"I was waiting for you."

Ellis watched Shannan drew her legs up to place her chin on her knees. When he arrived, she was a fifteen-year-old slip of a girl. At age seventeen, she was well on her way to womanhood. Her profile showed a mature line to the jaw and curve of her cheek. The freckles had faded yet her complexion still robust from outdoor living. Her hair was disheveled from sleeping. She casually turned to him and rested her cheek on her knees. The long flowing locks fell to one side. Green eyes were soft in their focus. Her brow wrinkled.

"What are you looking at?" she asked.

He kissed her cheek. "Thank you for worrying." When he went to rise, she snatched his arm, which drew him back to one knee.

She gazed steadily at him. "You will succeed."

He flashed a confident smile before he went inside. Niles prepared breakfast. Kell examined several parchments on the table. Armus thumbed through a book. Shannan appeared beside Ellis. He glanced briefly at her before speaking.

"How long to prepare the Contest?"

Kell and Armus looked up from their respective places, then to each other with small, pleased smiles. "That's what we've been discussing," replied Kell.

Ellis reached for Shannan's bow and quiver to hand her. "We'll keep ourselves occupied while you three finish coming up with ways to test me." He fetched another set for hunting.

"Make it venison. You'll need the meat for strength," said Niles.

Shafts of light pierced the canopy of trees when they emerged from the cave. "I saw some tracks near the ancient ruins earlier," he said.

During their walk, Ellis cast several cursory glances to Shannan. He wanted to know the answer but did he dare ask? Finally, he spoke, "Why did you leave the overlook so quickly?"

"You knew I was there?"

He chuckled. "I can't recall a time I didn't know."

"I can recall times you didn't like it."

"I'm sorry for that," he admitted with true regret. "You haven't answered me."

She heaved an shrugged. "For the same reason you kissed me."

"Because you wanted to leave?" he asked with confusion.

"No. Because it felt right."

Ellis stopped their trek. With eyes direct on her, he said, "I wanted you to stay."

Shannan met his glance. "I wanted you to kiss me before now."

He did so, this time on her lips. In that kiss, all unspoken words and feelings were understood. For several moments, they remained in each other's arms.

"Did you stay at the outcropping last night?" she asked.

"No. After you left, I went to the altar where I spent the night in mediation. Now I know what I must do." He softly smiled at her, as he continued:

> "*Among them shall be one whose birth*
> *Shall mirror his own.*
> *Unto her shall he pledge himself,*
> *For she, like Allon, shall be his desire*
> *And the twain shall become one.*"

"My desire for Allon grows from our relationship. I only learned of my royal heritage shortly before we fled. I did not grow up nurtured in royal responsibility, though Angus spoke of Allon in ways of loyalty and sacrifice. Since being here, I have come to understand the meaning of my destiny. Yet where Allon is my duty, you are my heart. In order to love Allon, I must love you."

Her eyebrows titled in a challenging manner. "You love me out of duty?"

He laughed at her provoking ploy. "No. I love you with my heart. Armed with that love, along with Jor'el's strength, I will embrace my destiny." He went to kiss her again when nearby noises caught their attention, then a flash of movement. "Venison."

With stealth they moved toward the sound. Suddenly it bolted. They dashed into a small clearing between dense trees to follow. Nothing.

Ellis stooped to view tracks. "Two does and a buck."

"One doe and one buck," Shannan spoke to the contrary.

"There are three sets of tracks."

"Two deer tracks. This third, I've never seen such a hoof print. Look how it gouges deeper and longer. The cleft is not like the others."

He looked closer. "A large hoofed animal, though in the deer family."

Shannan swiftly followed the tracks with Ellis on her heels. They stopped after another half-mile. Here the hoof marks were numerous and overlapping. Several low hanging branches and bushes were trampled or broken.

Shannan studied the ground. "A confrontation between the buck and large one. Blood goes off that way."

They followed the trail until they came upon the buck, dead. Ellis examined it. "Killed by a single thrust to the chest. I see no signs of other grazes from antlers," he said a bit baffled.

Shannan made her own inspection of the buck. "If this came from an animal, I've not seen such a wound before. *And* I know all the creatures in this forest."

"Then we shall find out what it is." Ellis rose to follow the second set of tracks.

After a short time, he seized her arm to draw her behind the cover of rocks. He placed a silencing finger to his lips then pointed forward. Fifty yards away stood a doe easily grazing. He readied his bow. When he took aim at the doe, it appeared, stunning in beauty and noble form.

"A unicorn!" Ellis murmured in wonder.

Though deer-like with a cream color hide it had a single gold horn. Near the height of a horse, it took up position to shield the doe. With a steady turn of its majestic head, it looked straight at them.

In mesmerized awe, their eyes locked on the unicorn. The bow slipped from Ellis' hands. Shannan visibly shivered. She carefully gripped Ellis' arm to lean close to whisper.

"We must leave."

He shook his head in amazement. "It's magnificent."

She tore her gaze from the unicorn to look at him. His eyes transfixed on the unicorn with a small smile across his lips. "Ellis, I sense evil about the creature."

"How could such a beautiful creature be evil?"

"I don't know-" she barely spoke when the unicorn bolted. Ellis left in hot pursuit, and without his bow. "Ellis, no!" He did not heed her call so she ran after him.

Recklessly, Ellis raced after the unicorn. He didn't notice where he ran until he broke into a large meadow. The unicorn was nowhere in sight. He frantically looked about to find it. Shannan arrived.

"Did you see which way it went? It couldn't have vanished."

She stopped his further movement into the meadow. "We are outside of Dorgirith!"

Ellis visibly winced, as if waking from a dream. "What?"

"We are passed Dorgirith boundaries. We must go back."

A roar startled them. A large bear stood on its hind legs between them and Dorgirith. This was no ordinary bear with menacing fangs, reddish eyes and froth dripping from its mouth.

"Behind me!" Ellis assumed a defensive position in front of Shannan. Realizing he was without his bow, he drew his sword. "Ready your bow."

With a swipe of its massive paws, the bear came at them. The action made Shannan retreat a few steps to take proper aim. A frightening eerie ear-piercing sound came from behind Shannan. The attack happened so swift that she could not identify the creature. It knocked the bow away then came at her head. She turned to shield herself. Talons buried in the back of her shoulders. She cried out when the momentum forced her to her knees.

The creature had the shape of a reptile with small wings and scaly feathers. The powerful talons kept Shannan on her knees. A savage bite to the neck made her collapse to the ground. Her movement made the creature momentarily jump off her. It readied for another attack when a frantic screech made it look up. Kato snared the creature before it could bite Shannan a second time.

"Shannan!" Ellis tried to move towards her when the bear lunged at him. He stumbled sideways to avoid the attack. He again tried to move to her, and once again it prevented him. Angered, Ellis swung at the bear.

He landed a hard blow. The wound enraged the already rabid beast. It knocked Ellis to the ground. The bear let out a tremendous roar.

Torin launched at the bear. Ellis scrambled to his feet. He sent a deep savage slash to the bear's midsection. Another sword slashed across the bear's chest. It heavily fell to the ground. Torin lunged for its throat to insure the kill.

The winged creature and Kato were locked in combat. Suddenly, in a brilliant burst of light, the creature vanished. The blast sent Kato to the ground at Ellis' feet.

"Kato?"

The eagle squeaked and flapped its wings in response. With Kato unharmed, Ellis ran to Shannan. Torin nudged her face. No respond. Ellis examined the back of her ripped jerkin. He discovered flesh torn and a savage bite to her neck. Fearful, he felt for a pulse. Faint, but still alive. He swallowed back a lump in his throat. Torin whimpered.

"Run home and let Niles know we're coming."

Torin lowered his head to give Shannan another nudge.

"She's alive. Now, go." At Ellis' second command, Torin left. Kato landed beside him. "You will be our guard. Watch for any more of those creatures."

After an affirmed screech, Kato took to the air.

Ellis gathered Shannan in his arms. He did not know how far they traveled from the cave in search of the mysterious unicorn, but that didn't matter. He would carry her to the ends of Allon if needed to bring her to safety. His stupidity caused them to leave Dorgirith's security and straight into trouble. If it killed her, he would never forgive himself.

The distance passed in a blur of anger, fear and determination. Visions of the beautiful unicorn, rabid bear and leathery reptile bird flashed through his mind. What possessed him to go recklessly after the unicorn? Where had it gone? The bear appeared without a sound. Surely such a rabid beast would have made some noise upon approach? The way it looked in the eyes, face, fangs, and even the salivating seemed unnatural. What was that leathery creature? Where did it come from?

A cry made Ellis look up. Kato circled the cave. Being so deep in thought, he nearly passed it. "Niles!" he shouted as he entered

Niles knelt beside Torin to greet the wolf. He bolted up. "Great Maker! What happened?" He led Ellis to his room, where Ellis gently laid Shannan on a cot.

"We were attacked by a rabid bear and some hideous creature," replied Ellis between breaths.

Niles examined the serious wound on Shannan's neck. He found four punctures, two fairly deep and two superficial. "Kell," he said with an unsteady voice.

Kell's attentive glance passed from Shannan to an anxious Ellis. "Did you see the creature?"

At Ellis' description, Niles uttered a low fearful gasp. Harsh eyes turned to Kell. "How did it get into Dorgirith?"

"We weren't in Dorgirith. We pursued a unicorn—" Ellis said, then regretted his admission at Niles' fury.

"There are no more unicorns in Allon!"

"There was! A magnificent male with a golden horn. I chased it. Before I realized it, we were outside Dorgirith's boundaries."

Niles clenched his jaw. "That was foolish," he swore.

"I know," said Ellis with a woeful sigh. "Shannan warned me, but I didn't listen. I couldn't. I had to chase the unicorn. It's as if it drew me after itself." His eyes grew misty with painful regret. "I'm sorry!"

Niles abruptly turned aside. Kell and Armus watched in grim silence.

Ellis screwed his eyes shut to compose himself. "Will she live?"

The Guardians exchanged somber glances. "It only bit her once," Armus said to Kell in an attempt to sound hopeful. By Kell's expression, he wasn't so optimistic.

"What was it?" Ellis demanded at their exchange.

Kell spoke in a deliberate even tone. "A kelpie. A demonic creature Magelen once sent to prey upon mortals. Usually it bites more than once, and their bite is poisonous."

"But curable, right?" Ellis asked with near desperation.

Kell slowly shook his head. "It's only a matter of time."

"No!" Ellis cried. He fell to his knees beside the cot. He clenched Shannan's hand. "I won't let her die because of my stupidity. I'll pray for Jor'el to cure her."

Kell's tone shifted between sympathy and certainty. "Evil forces are at work. They will go to any lengths to stop you. Including summoning ancient demons."

Ellis boldly confronted them. "Am I not Jor'el's chosen, the Son of Tristan? Did you not call her the Daughter of Allon?" Silence was his answer. He turned back to Shannan and firmly spoke over his shoulder. "Leave us!"

"What?" Niles' brows furrowed at the dismissal.

"I said, leave, Knight!" Ellis roughly repeated.

Niles stood momentarily stunned. Ellis invoked his princely authority, something unexpected. Kell ushered Niles from the room.

Ellis held Shannan's hand against his heart. He placed his right hand upon her wounded neck. "Hear me, O Great Jor'el. Hear my prayer for my love." He bowed his head to begin a singular vigil. He offered prayer upon prayer for Shannan, for himself, for Allon.

Ellis had no idea how long he prayed, as he fell into a deep sleep. His head rested against Shannan's side. His hand draped over her still covered her neck wound. Upon waking, he raised himself to his knees. He flexed the numb fingers of his right hand. In doing so, he saw no blood on his fingers or palm. Further investigation showed no wound on her neck. He looked again from his right hand to her neck. Was he dreaming? He searched for her other wounds. Gone! He took her by the shoulders, confused yet hopeful.

"Shannan?"

There came a soft stirring followed by deeper breathing. Her eyelids flickered then slowly opened. "Ellis."

"I thought I lost you." He gratefully kissed her forehead. "Niles!"

Niles rushed in with Armus at his heels. His breath caught in his throat at seeing Shannan look up at him. Armus also appeared stupefied.

"I told you Jor'el would hear me," said Ellis with confidence.

"Forgive me for doubting you, my Prince." Niles sat on the footstool to embrace Shannan. He couldn't hold back tears.

"She needs food and wine," said Ellis to Armus.

"At once, my Prince." Armus made the Guardian salute.

Later, while Niles fed Shannan, Armus coaxed Ellis into the main room to sit at the table to eat. Ellis took a deep whiff of the food set before him.

"Not Niles or Shannan's cooking."

Armus cocked a smile. "Mine."

"You cook?" The food tasted excellent, so Ellis heartily ate.

Armus sat opposite Ellis. "In the old days, Guardians and mortals freely interacted. We taught each other much. The only thing we didn't do was marry."

"Why? Don't you feel love or loneliness?" asked Ellis with a mouthful.

"Our need for companionship is different than mortals. We take great pleasure in serving. Each of us has tasks that more than consumes our time and energies. Thoughts beyond such are rare."

"Dagar being the exception."

Armus lowly growled. "Ay. Dagar proved Guardians could reproduce with mortals, though hardly out of love or loneliness. His intention is to overthrow Jor'el. His strength, combined with that of his son, a half-Guardian, made him nearly unstoppable last time."

"Could that be why the Shadow Warriors are nearly unstoppable, because they're half-Guardian?"

Armus' eyes narrowed as he features grew fierce. "They are full Guardians; turncoats who joined Dagar at the Great Battle. I denounced them when I called them *shadow warriors* for following in his wake. I never thought the name would stick, but he chose otherwise."

Ellis carefully regarded Armus, the Guardian's lieutenant's wrath intimidating. "Then you can reproduce after you own kind also?"

Armus noticed Ellis' caution so he relaxed. "Not that I know of. At least, I've never tried. And I've been around a little over two thousand mortal years."

The answer astonished Ellis. "In all that time you've never felt love or loneliness?"

Armus' features soften in to a small smile. "No. Although, I've witnessed mortal love many times."

"With no curiosity?"

Armus shrugged. "A bit, but I've also seen its aftermath. Heartache, sorrow, despair. All are dangerous emotions."

Ellis warmly smiled. "The reverse is true also. There is no greater happiness then when love is discovered. The greatest emotion is the joy. Especially the first kiss."

"So I've been told before," Armus simply said, his features placid.

The unaffected expression puzzled Ellis. "Have you ever kissed a female?"

"No."

The answer further vexed Ellis. "If your need for companionship is different, and you don't feel love or loneliness like we do, then why have male and female Guardians?"

"Don't mistake the absence of mortal emotions for lack of any feelings. Kell explained we are manifestation of the spirit from which we are formed. Besides, it is the spirit of a mortal that feels emotion." Armus' tone grew a touch harsh.

"I meant no offense," Ellis recanted.

Armus sighed with some regret. "No, my lord. I forget my place." He leaned forward on the table, his voice sheepish. "In truth, I have often wondered what a kiss feels like."

Ellis thought a moment before he shook his head. "I can't think of a comparison you would understand."

"Just as well. If Kell knew what I admitted, I wouldn't hear the end of it." He chuckled.

"By the way, where is Kell?" asked Ellis.

"Here." Kell and another Guardian stood in the entrance threshold.

The new Guardian was a stunningly beautiful female with long auburn hair, bright green eyes and flawless complexion. She stood six inches shorter than Kell, making her seven feet tall. She wore a forester green jerkin with a brown cowl. The breeches were identical in color to the jerkin, and tucked into knee-high leather boots. A brown leather belt gathered the jerkin about her waist. A plain-sheathed dagger hung from the belt. Instead of a sword she carried a finely crafted bolt-action crossbow with quiver of arrows slung across her back. Any mortal man would feel his heart race and pulse pound at sight of such a beautiful woman.

Ellis swallowed back his reaction to change his focus from her to Kell. "Where have you been, Captain?"

"Laying out the plans for your Contest," replied Kell, though mindful of Ellis' efforts. "With what happened, we must move quickly."

"Shannan is alive."

"I know."

"You know?"

Armus smirked as he said to Ellis, "He has Jor'el's ear."

Ellis grew angry with Kell. "You cured her? But you said—"

"No, my Prince," began Kell in mild refute. "*Your* faith cured her. I just happened to be present when Jor'el answered you. He gave me instructions for your Contest. Time is short, so it will be combined with the task of assembling your Companions."

Niles emerged from the room while Kell spoke. "So soon?"

"Dagar is going to great lengths to thwart Jor'el."

"And Jor'el allows it?" asked a confused Ellis.

Kell patted Ellis' shoulder. "Fret not for things beyond your comprehension. Continue to exhibit the faith you did for Shannan, and all shall be revealed in the end."

Ellis' gaze passed from Kell to the beautiful Guardian. He brightly flushed when she smiled.

Kell grinned at Ellis' embarrassment. "This is Wren, a Guardian huntress. She's been the one protecting you all these years."

"That was until today," groused Wren. "The kelpie and bear I managed to keep from Dorgirith, but not the unicorn. To do so, would risk exposing my presence. I summoned Kato and Torin and sped them on their way to aid you, my lord."

"Why couldn't you deal with the unicorn?" asked Ellis.

Wren hesitated. A nod from Kell, gave her ease to reply. "It was no ordinary unicorn, rather an apparition controlled by Witter."

Armus and Niles stiffened upon hearing the name.

Ellis noted their reactions. "Who is Witter?"

"Witter was once the leader of the Southern Forest Trio," began Kell. At Ellis' befuddlement, he explained, "When Jor'el created Guardians to aid the mortals, he made three to act as one in watching over each province. The Trio. Their duties and special assignments would balance each other, yet with a leader to whom Jor'el personally spoke. Under each Trio member were thousands of other Guardians to serve in various capacities. The numbers varied depending upon the needs of the mortal population of the province."

"How many Guardians are there now?" asked Ellis.

Kell soberly sighed. "Many were vanquished at the Great Battle. I knew of only a hundred who survived with twelve remaining in Allon to keep watch. Now that Dagar appears to be aware of your presence, Dorgirith is no longer safe. You and Sir Niles must leave at dawn."

"What about Shannan?" Niles asked.

"I will remain with her until her time comes," said Wren, which drew a dubious look from Ellis. "I may not have been able to stop the unicorn from a distance, but now that I am here, and know what I'm up against, I will successfully defend the Daughter of Allon."

"Time is short, you both must prepare," said Kell to Niles and Ellis.

No need to tell Shannan, she overheard. Once the Guardians arrived, she knew it was just a matter of time before Ellis would begin his journey of becoming king. She did not expect it to be so soon or sudden. Feeling stronger, she slipped out of the cave to gather her emotions while the others made plans.

Alert to her departure, Torin followed. She sat on one of the boulders at the cave's entrance. A cool breeze told of an early autumn. She gathered her knees to her chest and rested her chin on her knees to stare off into the distance. Torin lay down next to her. A few moments later, Ellis emerged from the cave to sit beside her.

"You shouldn't be out here alone."

"Why? Because it's too dangerous?" she spoke more sarcastically than intended. She immediately apologized. "Sorry."

"Don't be. I know I'm ready to face the challenge. Are you?"

She grew shy, her voice sheepish. "I'm not sure. You are familiar with the outside world, I am not."

"Could you be happy if we remained in Dorgirith and allowed the dark times to return?"

"Of course not. It doesn't mean I have to like it. If we lose—"

"We can't lose with Jor'el on our side." He smiled with bravado.

She didn't take his attempted humor well. When she looked away, he took her hands to speak more seriously.

"That's not to say there won't be great sacrifice. Allon must be purged of the Dark Way. Such purging comes with a price. It has already cost me dearly." Pain crept into his voice. "Leaving you for a time is another part of the price. Please don't make me pay more with regret at our parting rather let me draw strength from your courage."

Kell, Armus, Wren and Niles' emergence from the cave preempted her reply. Niles wore a large, hooded brown cloak over his clothes. He handed a similar cloak to Ellis, who put it on.

"Begin your journey by going to the ruins of Dunlap," said Kell.

"I know where that is. Darius and I played there as children."

"From there, you will be instructed on your Contest and next destination."

"Will it be you who directs me?"

"I can't say." Kell clasped Ellis' shoulders, which made the mortal stare up at him. "Understand, Son of Tristan, you must be diligent and faithful in your task. If you succeed, I will be at your side to face the enemy." He turned to Niles. "Farewell, old friend."

Armus also bade them farewell then politely stepped back with Wren.

For a moment Ellis and Shannan regarded each other. She bit her lip in an effort to maintain her composure. He took her face in his hands.

"I will come for you. No matter what happens." He kissed her before he left without looking back.

"Courage, child." Niles kissed Shannan's cheek. "I have something for you." He withdrew a necklace from his tunic. An oddly shaped object hung on the chain. "I'm not certain of its connection to Prophecy. All I know is before Vicar Wilbur died, he charged me with its keeping. He said I would know to whom it was to be given and when." He fastened it about her neck then tucked it under her tunic. "Guard it well until the time you need to use it." He flashed a glance in the direction Ellis left. "I need to go. Jor'el protect you, my dearest child." He hugged her.

"And you, Grandfather." Shannan tightly clenched her hands as she watched him catch up to Ellis.

"Come inside. You still need to rest." With a gentle guiding arm, Wren escorted Shannan back to the cave.

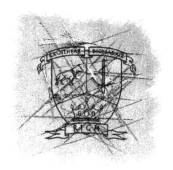

Chapter 7

IN HIS APARTMENTS AT RAVENDALE, LATHAM HARSHLY REGARDED the two beings before him. At seven and half feet tall, Witter had black hair and piercing green eyes. The distinctive glow of a Guardian's features was present, but weathered over the centuries to a grim aura of a Shadow Warrior. Six inches shorter than Witter, Carvel wore the black uniform of Shadow Archer complete with bow and quiver. Witter did most of the talking in giving their report.

"Is the girl dead?" Latham interrupted with impatience.

"She should be," replied Witter.

"You don't know for certain?"

Witter didn't like being questioned. "You wanted to know whereabouts of the Son of Tristan, and we found out. Be content with that." His sneer made his facial scar more pronounced and intimidating.

"Should I be content with that?" demanded Dagar. His image hovered over the basin.

Witter's bravado immediately faded. He made a hasty bow to Dagar. Carvel also assumed a submissive posture.

"Lord. We did what we could—" insisted Witter.

With a wave of his hand, Dagar sent a slap across Witter's face. The powerful Warrior staggered back a few step. A welt rose on his cheek.

At the abuse, Carvel quickly intervened. "My lord, Witter is correct. We only managed to penetrate Dorgirith's defenses with the unicorn. Still, we succeeded in drawing out the Son of Tristan …" His speech grew hesitant under Dagar's intense interest, until he stopped.

Dagar didn't accept the pause in speech. "And?" he pressed Carvel.

Girding up his courage, Carvel replied, "Guardian intervention saved him."

"Guardian!" bellowed Dagar. Furious, he demanded of Witter, "Who?"

"Wren."

"Since when could she singularly oppose *you*?"

"My lord, Jor'el's seal is on that place. It took all my strength to manipulate the unicorn apparition while Carvel moved the bear and kelpie into position—"

"Silence!" commanded Dagar. Witter and Carvel snapped to attention. After a moment of dreadful silence, Dagar spoke to Latham. "Despite failure in killing him, they did discover where he is hiding."

"And the girl with him?"

"Girl?" Dagar sent a snarl to Witter and Carvel.

"We couldn't clearly identify if she is the Daughter of Allon," said Witter.

"Although, more than likely she is dead since the kelpie bit her," added Carvel.

Dagar took a moment to consider the added intelligence. He wasn't pleased. "What if Wren's intervention saved her life?" When they didn't answer, he continued. "*If* Wren remained with her, that may serve as our confirmation of the girl's identity. A second attack will be impossible since we have lost the element of surprise." His eyes narrowed during his verbal contemplation. "The Son of Tristan is our primary target. With his death, she and the Guardians are of no consequence."

"As you say, my lord." Latham partially bowed in submission. A knock on the door followed by a voice addressing him made Latham launched toward the door. Dagar pulled back from clear view. Witter reached for his sword. Latham's stiff hand stopped Witter from drawing his blade. "What is it?" he spoke behind the door.

"The King has returned from his hunt and wishes to see you, my lord. He is in the Great Hall," came the reply.

"I shall be there presently." Latham listened for fading footsteps before speaking to Dagar. "I must go."

"Ay, we need to remain cautious until the time comes." Dagar sent a last reproving snarl to Witter and Carvel before he vanished.

Marcellus and his noble hunting party milled about the Great Hall exchanging hearty laughs and boasts. Pages offered them refreshment. Marcellus had yet to clean up as told by his road-dusty clothes.

"A successful hunt, Sire?" inquired Latham.

"Indeed. We shall be feasting on wild boar this night." Marcellus' reply drew gleeful comments from his companions. When the remarks ceased, he questioned Latham. "What have you been doing to keep yourself occupied while I've been away these past three days?"

"Tending to my duties, Sire."

Marcellus scoffed with disbelief. Using a heavy hand on Latham's shoulder, he drew the Grand Master aside. "Really? There is talk spreading throughout the countryside of another ruthless search for the priests."

"Jor'ellian Knights of the Temple."

"Priests!" Marcellus stoutly corrected. With harsh scrutiny, he stared at Latham. "They say you will proclaim yourself Vicar once you have Archimedes' head. The most interesting part is the description of large, powerful beings." His hand moved off Latham's shoulder to the back of Latham's neck where his grip grew tighter. "Some call them demons, others the Guardians returned. What I want to know is who they really are," he spoke in taunt voice.

Latham tried to maintain a calm façade despite the painful grimace across his lips. "Sire, with talk of Prophecy possibly being fulfilled, it is natural for some to mention Guardians."

Marcellus grew skeptical. "Your Shadow Warriors wouldn't be Guardians, would they? You would not be so bold as to circumvent my wishes in bringing about the Dark Way prematurely?"

The increased pressure on his neck made Latham grit his teeth in pain. "Sire, they are large men of Captain Tyree's ilk. Nothing more."

"I hope you are telling me the truth, Grand Master. If I learn otherwise, that day will be your last." His rough release made Latham shift a few steps to catch his balance.

Latham squared his shoulders, as his hand reached to clench the talisman. "Sire, may I ask a question simply for my understanding?"

Marcellus regarded Latham from over the brim of a tankard while taking a drink. Latham's voice was cool, posture haughty and clear blue eyes fixed in level regard of him. Many became unnerved by such a look, and Marcellus slightly flinched. The King averted his gaze when he made a curt nod of permission.

"Why are you reluctant to embrace the Dark Way like your forefathers did?"

Marcellus wiped his mouth on his sleeve. "By doing so, they compromised and shared their power. They were nothing more than puppets to your predecessors. I will not be a puppet king. I will have it all, and neither this pretended prince nor your Dark Way will rob me of that. Does that answer your question?"

"Fully. I am but a means to an end."

Marcellus chuckled in his tankard, yet shied from Latham's uncomfortable glare.

"How can I be certain that day won't be my last?"

Marcellus cast a skewed glance at Latham. "Do not interfere with my reign and you shall be free to do as you please. If you want Archimedes' position, it's yours. When this is over, replace the worship of Jor'el with your Dark Way, only leave me and my heirs to rule and all shall be well." Marcellus made his way to a side table to pick over some food.

Latham followed. "There are reported sightings of the Vicar and his followers that I am investigating. However, what you wished for has not happened."

"Meaning?" Marcellus tried to keep his attention on the food to avoid Latham's stare.

"I have it on good authority that the Pretender is hiding in Dorgirith."

Marcellus immediately flushed with rage. "Send out soldiers to fetch him! Dead or alive I don't care!"

"Sire, only the most stouthearted of men will enter Dorgirith."

"Foolish superstition brought about by your Dark Way." Marcellus strode to the center of the room to loudly speak. "The Pretender is alive and hiding in Dorgirith! Who among my brave nobles will drag him out?" He raised a brow of disbelief at the sluggish response. "Surely not every man here believes in ghosts and legends?"

"I will!" called a voice across the hall. The crowd parted to let the speaker through.

Latham stiffened upon sight of Witter. His reaction went unseen by Marcellus since the King watched Witter approach.

"One of your men? He looks like a Shadow Warrior," said Marcellus to Latham.

Witter preempted the Grand Master's reply. "Sire. I am Witter of Larkin. I fear no mortal man nor phantom legends."

Marcellus huffed a laugh. "I should say not." He noticed Latham remained stoic. He nodded to Witter. "Very well. Bring me his head and you shall be handsomely rewarded."

Witter bowed to Marcellus. He flashed gloating eyes at Latham before leaving.

Marcellus smiled in triumph. "You see, Grand Master, there is more than one way to deal with this problem."

Latham clenched the talisman to stem his anger at Marcellus' departing laughter. He left the Great Hall opposite the King. Somehow he needed to make Marcellus understand who was really in command, the same as his predecessor Zared did with Marcellus' grandfather. So far, Dagar seemed unaware of his trouble handling Marcellus. That could change if Witter continues to usurp him with the King.

Latham wondered why Dagar sent Witter. He had the situation under control. Perhaps Dagar gave a hint when he spoke of the prophecy connected to the girl. The Daughter of Allon, according to Witter. Naturally, Latham knew about Guardians since he dealt with Shadow Warriors. Having received his tutoring from the aged Zared, he understood the threat of an heir from the House of Tristan. The girl added a new detail he needed to deal with. This meant searching all his resources to understand more about her connection to the Guardians and Son of Tristan.

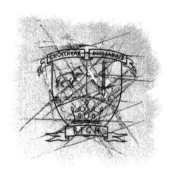

Chapter 8

UNLAP ONCE COVERED TWO ACRES, SMALL FOR CASTLES OF ITS DAY. Decay of over two hundred years had been its enemy, not war or siege. Wood of the roof, doors and floors were long eaten by insects or dry rot. With most support gone, the once proud stonewalls crumbled beneath the onslaught of weather. Nature laid bold claim to what remained. Overgrowth kept the ruins well hidden from the casual observer. This part of the Southern Forest was no longer well traveled since Garwood Castle replaced Dunlap. The forest also reclaimed the road when commerce took a different route through the region.

Kemp fled after his father Phineas died during the confrontation with Tyree's troops. He joined Darius, Edmund, Nando, Brody and Jasper in hiding. It grieved Darius to hear of his uncle's death. News of the devastating defeat curbed any plans to renew the search for Angus and Ellis. They lived as fugitives with carefully monitored activities.

Although ten years older, Kemp matched Darius in size. He wasn't athletic or agile compared to Darius. The family often referred to Darius as the warrior with Kemp the conversationalist. He also contrasted Darius in coloring, having inherited the blond hair and green eyes from his mother. With Kemp came his wife, Nancie, two young sons, Della, an nanny of sixty who cared for the boys, and Kemp's younger sister Erin. She was two years older than Darius, and a year wed when her husband died at Phineas' side. Erin's dark hair and eyes heightened her pale complexion. In stature, she only reached to their shoulders, but in tenacity she equaled her brother and cousin. Unfortunately, Nancie died the first winter of their seclusion. The trauma of flight joined with the harsh winter proved too much for her.

Rarely did any word from the outside world reach them, save those occasions Darius sent Nando and Brody to ferret out news. On those forays, they brought back supplies of grain and ale along with the occasional delicacy. They lived a Spartan existence compared to previous times. Even Erin and Della went about their day armed with daggers. The once rich, well-made clothes became severely faded and forayed. Learning some news about the suffering left from Tyree's rampage, they fared better than most living unmolested.

With little to occupy growing boys' idle time, Ned and Fagan found themselves schooled in the art of warfare and survival earlier than normal. By the time they were twelve and ten respectively, both showed great promise as warriors and hunters.

The late afternoon sun sank below the treetops. After a successful hunt, the boys accompanied Brody in returning to the ruins. Nearing the road from deep in the forest, Fagan spotted two cloaked men. Brody motioned the boys to quickly take cover to observe the men.

"Take our kill and warn Lord Darius of strangers," Brody whispered to Fagan.

After the boy quietly slipped away, Brody signaled Ned to go left. Brody aimed his bow at the road before the men. His arrow landed on the path in front of the men and made them halt. No sooner had the first arrow landed, when a second arrow from Ned landed behind them; a signal they were surrounded. The men carefully raised their hands.

"We mean no harm," called one in an older sage voice.

Brody stepped onto the path with his bow armed. "A sad day for you if you did."

"Brody?" asked the other man.

"Ay," Brody warily replied. "Easy!" he warned when the man's hands moved to remove the hood.

"Only to show my face," he said with a merriment that surprised Brody. Slowly, he pulled off the hood.

Astonished, Brody lowered his bow. "Master Ellis! We thought you dead! It's all right, Ned."

A rustling from behind was heard then Ned emerged.

"Do you remember your cousin Ellis?" Brody asked Ned.

"Ay," Ned answered, though tentative in regard of Ellis.

Ellis smiled at Ned. "It's been a few years. We've both grown up. You look like Kemp." This made the boy relax and smile.

"If you're on your way to Garwood—" began Brody.

"I know about Garwood," said Ellis glumly.

Niles lowered his hood. This made Brody flinch in defense.

"Easy! He's a friend," Ellis quickly assured Brody.

"What of Sir Angus?" Brody asked with anxiety.

Ellis swallowed back some discomposure when he made a somber shake of his head. "What of Darius? Is he alive? Jasper?"

Brody smiled. "Ay, Lord Darius is alive, and Jasper recovered."

"Only he wears an eye patch now." Ned held a hand over his left eye.

"What?" Ellis asked with disturbance.

"Compliments of Latham's men," chided Brody. "Nando and I found him barely alive, but you know stubborn soldiers, they won't die easily. Nor has it lessened his skill. He can still beat us all, even with one good eye."

The explanation didn't fully allay Ellis' concern.

"Come, sir. I know they will be overjoyed to see you." Brody put up his bow to escort Ellis.

Based upon Fagan's warning, Nando and Edmund took position on the rebuilt rampart. Darius, Fagan, Kemp and Jasper stood by the rickety gate, all armed. Fagan, Erin and Della hid behind a nearby wagon.

Nando saw them first. "Brody and Ned are with them."

"Ay," added Edmund in agreement. "I see—Great Maker! Jor'el be praised! It's Ellis!"

The news sent Darius racing from the ruins, yet he drew to a halt with some uncertainty. Hearing Ellis call his name dispelled all doubts. Overjoyed, he heartily embraced Ellis. Emotions choked Darius at seeing Ellis no longer a gangly teenager, but a young man taller than he. Catching sight of another man's approach, Darius made a hopeful movement then balked at sight of Niles.

"Darius," said Ellis with compassion. He took hold of Darius' arm.

"Your father was a brave man," said Niles.

Darius turned away from Niles to regain his composure.

Ellis' arm encircled Darius' shoulders. "I'm sorry. He died protecting me."

Darius' voice was thick in response. "No need to apologize. At least you're alive."

"Ay. Angus would have wanted that," said Edmund. With a sober smile, he motioned them to the ruins.

Ellis visibly winced at seeing Jasper standing by the gate. "Jasper—" was all Ellis could say, before embracing him.

Jasper warmly smiled with bravado. "Don't mind this. As long as I have one good eye to see you alive and well, I am content."

Kemp snickered at Ellis. "You've grown."

Erin wryly looked Ellis up and down. "Sad. You used to be shorter than me."

Ellis laughed, so did Darius and Kemp.

"To celebrate Master Ellis' return we can feast on what we killed," said Brody.

"We've already taken them to be prepared," said Della.

The women, Brody and Nando left to tend to the food. Darius grabbed a jug of wine. He led Ellis and Niles inside one of the repaired dwellings. It was more humble and sparse than the cave with straw beds covered in old blankets for sleeping. A rough-hewn table with benches used for eating. In the middle of the room was a stone-ringed fire pit to chase away the early autumn chill.

"Where have you been? How did father—?" Darius began with difficulty.

"First tell me all the news, then perhaps what I have to say will make sense," said Ellis.

For a little over an hour Darius, Kemp, Edmund and Jasper explained events of the past two years. Ned and Fagan quietly sat in on the conversation. With expressions ranging from anger, regret and sorrow, Ellis and Niles listened. The conversation became interrupted when Nando, Brody and the women brought food.

"Let us give thanks," began Darius. "Gracious Jor'el, once again you have provided for our needs. Today you have returned to us a most beloved brother, cousin and master. For that our hearts are overjoyed. May your blessings be upon him and us. *Tangie?*" He said to Ellis, "This is not a suitable feast to welcome you nor a home fit to hold it."

"No, Darius, it serves well."

Darius kindly spoke to Niles. "In all this time we have not been properly introduced. Forgive us our lack of manners, sir."

"Do not trouble yourself about the social niceties of the past, my lord. Preparing the feast shows genuine love," said Niles.

"You are most generous, sir. What is your name?"

"His name is part of my explanation. Only you haven't finished telling me what happened," said Ellis.

Annoyed, Darius cut off half a leg of the wild pig. "What more is there to tell? No one could stand against Shadow Warriors."

"What did Vicar Archimedes say when you spoke with him?" asked Niles.

"Nothing much past his concern for Ellis."

Edmund grunted in annoyance. "The Vicar is a man of few words. And those words are often laced with pious condescension."

"Softly, Edmund. We don't want to give our guest the wrong impression of the venerable Vicar," quipped Kemp.

"I take it, he is not well liked," Niles commented.

Darius shrugged. "He looks down upon Edmund for being a low born kinsman of my father. While Jasper has felt his horse whip for an inappropriate response. Or rather, what the Vicar thought was inappropriate. Father believed otherwise."

Ellis chuckled. "I remember."

"As for Kemp's reason—"

"I don't need a reason. It's generally thought I dislike everyone. Which isn't true, I just go along with the consensus for fun," said Kemp in good humor. He tossed a wink at his sons, both of whom chuckled.

Ellis ignored Kemp to ask Darius, "Archimedes didn't tell you what happened?"

"Only that there were signs of a scuffle on the Southern Forest side of the river plain. With Captain Tyree around, I couldn't save my own people much less look for you and father. Garwood may be no better now than these ruins!"

"Darius, the fault is mine—"

"No!" Darius seized Ellis' arm. "You are Allon's hope! My hope. The hope of us all."

In stunned silence most stopped eating, all eyes curiously on Darius. Only Edmund and Jasper sat unaffected by his declaration.

Kemp broke the silence. "Darius, what are you talking about?"

Darius regretfully looked to Ellis, who flashed a soft smile before speaking. "All of you know me as the second son of Sir Angus and Lady Agatha. In truth, I bear no blood relation. My family is very old and revered." He took it off the amulet hidden under the neck of his doublet to lay it on the table for them to view. "Angus found this wrapped with me in my blanket."

Della marveled upon sight of the amulet. "The Royal Seal!" She turned inquiring eyes upon Ellis. "You are the Son of Tristan?"

Kemp laughed, which made all turn toward him. "Him? Impossible!"

Forgetting himself, Edmund slapped Kemp's arm. "Mind yourself. He is! I saw him in the blanket with that amulet when Angus brought him to Garwood."

"I was with Sir Angus when he found Master Ellis," began Jasper. "It was an autumn day much like today when we left Midessex to return to Garwood because of King Unwin's orders to slay the infants. Shortly after we made camp for the night, there was a strange occurrence in the heavens. A shadow crossed the moon and it became almost pitch black. Suddenly a brilliant flash of light burst on the horizon. We thought we heard music but no words. Neither one of us said anything, for we sensed this was no ordinary night. We immediately broke camp, and headed in the direction of the light. At dawn we came upon a small settlement." Jasper's face grew grim in recollection. "Razed to the ground. The inhabitants lay in huddled masses of dead or dying. Then, among the dreadful silence, we heard a baby crying. We followed the cry to find her mortally wounded yet clinging to her infant. She said she was waiting for Angus to give him the babe."

"She mentioned Angus by name?" asked Kemp.

"No, rather she asked about his signet, if he was from the House of Dunham. When he confirmed it, she told us the babe's name along with instructions to seek out Master Ebenezer. Then she died. Angus unwrapped the blanket to see if the babe was injured. That's when we discovered the royal amulet."

A longer heavy silence followed until Erin spoke, tentative and low. "Did Master Ebenezer confirm everything?"

"Ay. Apparently she and her husband came to see him upon learning she was with child. Since the days of Sir Dunham, a second royal birth record has been secretly kept at the Fortress of Garwood. Ebenezer told them what every generation since the overthrow was told, that someday the slaughter would occur. At that time, a heritage of loyalty would fulfill a vow of fealty. Ebenezer charged Sir Angus with the child's keeping because of the vow made by his ancestor Dunham."

Darius solemnly nodded. "He told me of the vow before going to the Fortress."

Jasper again proceeded. "Master Ebenezer gave me a document for safe keeping until I could give it to Sir Angus. Alas, that never happened. I believe it has to do with you," he said to Ellis.

"Where is the document now?" asked Ellis.

"I still have it."

"I've seen it. Ebenezer's seal is unbroken," affirmed Darius.

"Continue to keep it until I need it," Ellis told Jasper.

Kemp's face showed an effort to keep his temper as he confronted Darius. "Why were we not told this before?"

"The fewer who knew the better, though father told Uncle Phineas," began Darius. "For the rest, he devised the story of how mother was with child when she went to care for her dying widowed sister in the Lowlands. She returned to Garwood months after her sister's death and Ellis's birth. That way the story could not be confirmed or denied."

The explanation did not set well with Kemp. Edmund's harsh glare kept him from speaking. Erin regarded Ellis with befuddlement.

Ellis kindly smiled. "I haven't changed that much."

"Oh no? A few moments ago you were my pesky younger cousin. Now you are heir to the Throne of Allon. I'd say that's quite a difference."

"I can assure you, he's still pesky," snickered Niles.

Kemp could only hold his temper so long. "This is incredible! Why tell us? Are you planning to overthrow Marcellus to proclaim yourself king? Are we your army?"

"He seeks his Companions," Della said before Ellis could reply.

"You are familiar with Prophecy?" asked Niles.

"My father served as the headmaster at the Fortress of Mulbury. He became blinded during the coup and left for dead."

Niles brows knitted in recollection. "Jen. I knew him."

Kemp laughed with high ridicule. "Few survived the overthrow. Next I suppose you'll say you trained Ellis in combat. The last time I saw him he could barely hold a sword or lance much less challenge Marcellus. No offense, Jasper," he added with a mock snicker to the wily master-at-arms.

Niles sternly replied, "I have done exactly that! I am Sir Niles of Pollux. The King's Champion." He took off his amulet to place it beside Ellis' amulet. "See for yourselves the truth of what we say."

Kemp cautiously stared at the amulets. Della examined them.

"This is the amulet of the King's Champion," Della confirmed. "My father described how the royal eagle clenched the crown and sword. These are only found on his amulet. To wear it was an honor that only a few Knights ever achieve."

Kemp snatched them from Della. Upon Ellis' amulet, he saw the royal eagle. On the second was the joining of the eagle, crowd and sword. He carefully placed them back on the table without uttering a word.

"How did you survive?" Edmund asked Niles.

"Queen Myla and I conceived a plan of escape. Unfortunately, things didn't go as planned. The Queen gave herself up to Zared to ensure our safety. Once away, we hid in a most unlikely place, Dorgirith. Akilles stayed until he felt the calling to find a wife and continue the royal line." He turned over the royal amulet. "These initials belong to Akilles, Prince Royale. Ellis is Prince Akilles' great-grandson."

In awe, Della regarded Ellis. "To think, I use to change your diapers when you visited Denley." This brought a subdued laughter from all.

Niles picked up the amulets for him and Ellis to replace about their necks. They also tucked the amulets underneath the neckline.

"What now?" Darius asked Ellis.

"I continue to gather my Companions from the Council of Twelve along with whatever tasks are necessary to prepare for my destiny."

"You've succeeded in convincing two." Darius indicated himself and Kemp. The latter slowly nodded.

"I'm afraid the food has gotten cold," Della said apologetically.

"Cold or hot, we gratefully eat in the presence of our Prince," said Darius. He raised his cup in salute of Ellis. The rest mimicked him.

After the others retired, Ellis found it difficult to sleep. He climbed one of the remaining ramparts to take up a solitary vigil. Accepting the truth that Angus' death was not his fault took many months. Reconciling his true heritage and destiny also required diligent reading of Prophecy along with deep soul-searching. Now, discovering Darius hiding like a fugitive brought back the same disheartening emotions of two years ago.

Just like Angus, Darius willingly embraced his role. Darius' words echoed in Ellis' mind; *"You are Allon's hope. My hope. The hope of us all."* Jasper recalling the night of his discovery as a babe gave Ellis a new appreciation for the loyal master-at-arms. Even Della voiced her support. He couldn't blame Kemp for speaking with angry skepticism. Being at Dunlap brought a fresh reality to what Ellis had to do. It gave him a glimpse of what awaited him—the various reactions of those he would meet on his journey.

Ellis became so absorbed with consideration that he paid no attention to the passage of time. Heavy dew of a frosty autumn morn blanketed the forest floor. A mist rose from the ground. Dew even dampened his hair and cloak. Being so deep within the forest, it would not be until mid morning that the sun's ray penetrated the canopy of trees. The dim gray light signaled dawn. He didn't rouse from his introspection until Darius joined him.

Curious, Darius followed Ellis' rapt attention. "I don't see anything."

Ellis cast a side-glance to Darius. "When did you learn the truth about me?"

Darius' focus shifted from the forest to Ellis. "When I was eleven, I stumbled upon father and mother discussing your future. Father abruptly tried to leave. In doing so something fell from the bundle he carried. I snatched it up before he could. From my history lessons, I recognized the royal amulet. There wasn't much he could do but tell me the truth and swear me to secrecy. It hurt to learn you were not really my brother." A tremor of pain crept into his voice.

Ellis heartily gripped Darius' shoulder. "Only in blood. In my heart you *are* my brother. Same as Angus will always be my father and Agatha my sweet mother."

"Ay. However, that does not change your true identity. You are my Prince, my liege lord. To convince the rest of the Council, we must journey to each province."

Ellis ruefully snorted at the word *we*. "It won't be easy."

Darius heaved a casual shrug as he turned his attention to the forest. "Since when has having you around been easy?"

Ellis smiled. He too gazed at the forest. Suddenly—"Did you see that?"

"What? Where are you going?" Darius demanded when Ellis scrambled down the rampart.

Niles arrived in a rush to intercept Darius. "No! He must go alone."

"Why?" Darius jerked away from Niles.

"His Contest is part of this journey."

"Contest? What are you talking about?"

"Come, I'll explain. He will be safe," Niles spoke with assurance when Darius hesitated.

Thirty

Ellis ignored Darius, as he raced to where he had seen the mysterious shape. Nothing! He stopped to listen. His eyes scanned the surroundings. Though the mist, the dark vague forms of trees loomed. It was eerily silent. No meadowlark sounded the arrival of morning nor did the slightest breeze stir the trees. Yet something or someone lurked nearby. He felt a presence, not discernible in shape rather in spirit. The sense drew him to this spot. Who, what, and why were the questions? His hand gripped the hilt of his sword ready to draw. Tension grew in the pit of his being.

The hairs on the back of his neck stood on end when a cold presence brushed past. He turned to see a trail in the mist and ran to follow. He found himself in a clearing void of dew yet ringed by the morning mist. A sense of compulsion gripped him, a sense reminiscent of—

Ellis whirled about to come face-to-face with the unicorn! It somehow seemed larger than he remembered since it looked at him eye to eye. His whole being became seized by the compulsion to reach out and touch it. The same compulsion as when he chased the unicorn from Dorgirith. He sneered at the remembrance of Shannan's wounding.

"Not this time, beast!" The compulsion disappeared when he spoke.

The eyes of the unicorn grew malicious. "So be it, Son of Tristan," it unnaturally spoke. It lowered its head to charge him.

Ellis barely avoided it. He drew his sword. The beast skidded to a furious halt. Ellis' blood ran cold at seeing its countenance alter before him. Beauty became replaced by evil in the menacing eyes, snarling mouth with flaring blood red nostrils. The golden horn changed to the silver of a sword. For a brief moment he stood mesmerized by the transformation. When the unicorn reared, the sensation passed. Another charge. He parried the blow meant to knock him off his feet. His swing of retaliation caught the unicorn in the rump. It screamed in anger.

Ellis braced in anticipation of another attack. The horn flashed crimson while the hide turned pale red with fury. The beast trembled and pawed at the ground. The horn flashed! Suddenly, Ellis realized what he saw that drew him from the ramparts. *The horn!*

The beast charged. Ellis raised his sword. He willed himself not to step aside until the absolute last possible second. In quick fluid action, he moved and sent a savage blow that severed the horn from the unicorn. An unearthly cry of pain came from the beast as it stumbled forward. It desperately tried to regain its balance but unable to. The unicorn fell headlong to the ground. With labored breath, the bloody hornless head turned toward Ellis. The unnerving hate-filled eyes made him retreat a few steps. With a bray of anger it raised its head to the sky. Blinding light forced Ellis to his knees. When the light faded, the unicorn was gone!

For several moments, Ellis remained on the ground trying to comprehend what just happened. Even during his battle with the bear and kelpie, he did not experience such an overwhelming sense of evil. This had to be part of the Contest.

"Kell, what did you do?" Ellis murmured with disconcertion.

"I didn't do anything."

Ellis scrambled to his feet. His sword poised at the tall being veiled by the mist.

Kell stepped out for Ellis to see him. "You can put up your sword."

"Not until you tell me what manner of Contest is this."

"This was not part of the Contest. When I sensed Witter, I came as soon as I could. It appears you didn't need help."

Perplexed, Ellis lowered his sword. "If this wasn't planned, then what did Witter want?"

"I don't know. A test of your strength, or perhaps a distraction."

"Some distraction." Ellis sheathed his sword. "Shannan?" he asked with concern.

"She is safe. As for the first test, this will serve. You have earned your reward." Kell motioned towards a tree. Against the trunk rested a large gold and white shield with the crest of the House of Tristan, an eagle with out stretched wings. "Upon each successful completion you shall receive part of your kingly armor."

While Ellis examined the stunning workmanship, Kell's brows deeply furrowed. He carefully cocked his head to one side as if listening.

"This will be cumbersome to carry." Ellis' voice drew Kell from his distraction.

"You will not take the armor with you. It shall be preserved until the day in which you take full possession." Kell took the shield.

"What about Witter? I could encounter him again."

"That's possible. No matter what happens you must stay your course. For now, go to the Highlands by way of the Northern Forest road. Once across the border, make your way to the Fortress at Ludlow." Kell smiled with encouragement, as he placed a hand on Ellis' shoulder. "You did well, Son of Tristan. Eat and rest a few hours before continuing your journey."

Ellis nodded. With weary steps, he left the forest. His battle with the unicorn took more out of him than he anticipated. If the remaining tests combined the physical and supernatural, he wondered if he could pass them all. Niles' knowledge may be of some help to understand what he faced, but in the end, this was *his* contest. He recalled what Niles once said; *we shall see how good of a warrior you truly are. For you will not be the King's Champion, you will be King.*

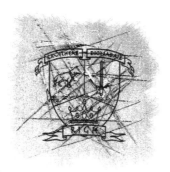

Chapter 9

SHANNAN AND WREN SWATTED AND STOMPED IN AN EFFORT TO avoid hundreds of small rodent-insect-like creatures devouring everything in cave. Shannan shrieked when one attached itself to her leg. It tried to bite her. She struck it aside with her bow.

"What are these things?"

"Drusi!" chided Wren. "An annoying cross between a rat and locust that Magelen sent to plague the Plains when they refused to send tribute." Wren snatched a lantern. She broken it and spilt the oil on the floor. Using a log from the stove, she set the oil on fire.

"No!" shriek Shannan in protest.

"Fire is the only way to destroy them. Outside!" Wren shoved Shannan to the exit. She waved the burning log at the drusi trying to flee the flames. In backing out, Wren knocked over a chair and set it on fire. She tossed the log into the cave. Outside, she fired her an arrow at the entrance. The impact started a cave-in. "That should finish them."

Shannan shivered at seeing her home destroyed. All she ever knew was gone in an instant. Torin quietly came along side to nudge her hand in support. She patted his head. Kato squawked when he landed on the boulder beside Shannan.

"I'm sorry, but Witter has penetrated Dorgirith. We must leave."

"I thought you said you could protect me here?"

Wren's jowls tightened with annoyed frustration. "If it were the old Witter, but it's not." She drew Shannan her from the cave. Torin and Kato followed. "Cover your head, we're outside."

Shannan put up her cowl. "What do you mean the *old Witter?*"

"Joined with Dagar, he can draw upon power I alone cannot repel at present."

"So you need help. What about Kell or Armus?"

"Kell went to help the Prince remember? Armus is occupied. Besides, summoning another Guardian isn't as simple as it used to be. It is not time for our full return. Until then we must perform our tasks singularly."

From out of the bushes, two wild boars rushed onto the path in front of them. Unusually large, they angrily snorted and chomped their teeth.

Shannan gaped in fear. "Those eyes. Like the rabid bear."

"They aren't rabid, rather unnatural," Wren cautiously said. Torin snarled at the boars. "*Fuirich, Torin,*" she spoke in the Ancient. Wren also addressed the boars in the Ancient. "Peace, my little ones. We mean no harm. Let us pass."

Instead of backing away, the boars lowered their heads. They pawed the ground to toss gravel aside as if preparing to charge.

"They're not listening," Shannan murmured with dread.

"Carefully ready your bow," Wren lowly instructed. "Torin, Kato, *Ionnsaigh!*"

Torin launched at one boar while Kato dove at the other. One boar head-butted Torin aside. Kato clung to the neck of the other boar. The second managed to shake Kato. A crossbow arrow slashed its throat, nearly decapitating it.

Wren became briefly distracted since the shot didn't come from her or Shannan. The first boar turned upon Torin. Wren let her shaft fly. The might of her shot passed through the boar from the chest out the flank, killing it.

Trembling at the display of such force against the boars, Shannan fought to hold her bow ready.

Wren took up a defensive position in front of Shannan. She aimed in the direction where the unknown crossbow shot came. "Be ready to run," she said over her shoulder.

"You never could have gotten them both in time," spoke a voice with nonchalance.

A tall man dressed in forester garb appeared from behind an oak tree. He held a loaded crossbow. He stood half a head taller than Wren, who was seven feet. His physique was trim and athletically built with auburn hair. Brilliant copper eyes caught attention.

Stunned, Wren's mouth open to speak yet barely said the name, "Vidar?"

"Time for reunion later. Witter is near. This way."

Wren drew herself from her surprise when Vidar guided Shannan into the wood. "Kato, fly. Torin, come."

After a short distance, Vidar raised a hand to stop their trek. He placed a finger to his lips to stifle Wren's forming question. He motioned for them to take cover behind a boulder. A few seconds later, Witter came into view. He reined the stallion a few yards away from them. His head turned as he scanned the surrounding area.

Seeing Witter for the first time, Shannan understood Wren's description. An aurora of evil surrounded him. Even the horse seemed different, unnaturally larger. Shannan dared a glance at the others. Wren held her bow ready while Vidar's eyes were fixed on Witter.

Witter let out a loud growl of exasperation. He spurred the stallion, which galloped off at a speed impossible for any normal horse. Not until Witter was gone did Vidar relax. He let out a low audible sigh of relief.

"What happened?" asked Shannan.

"I blocked our presence from being sensed," he replied.

Shannan's questioning glance shifted to Wren, who said; "Vidar was the leader of the Northern Forest Trio. His abilities are equal to Witter."

"Maybe. I'm just glad it worked," groused Vidar. His statement drew a concerned glance from Wren, which he ignored her to say; "I know a place to take her for safety." He took Shannan's hand to leave the safety of the boulder. "It's where I've been hiding if you're interested," he said to Wren's hesitation.

"Of course I am. How far?"

"A week's walk for a mortal. Unless we take the Guardian way."

Wren looked askew at Vidar. "You haven't changed. Still arrogant."

"You're wrong, Wren. Much has changed," he solemnly said. She still appeared reluctant. "It will be safer for her." He nodded to Shannan.

Wren took Shannan's right hand. Vidar still held her left hand.

"What about Torin and Kato?" asked Shannan.

"We will bring them later." Wren nodded to Vidar. "*Siuthad!*" the Guardians said together. In a brilliant flash of light they vanished.

A flash of bright white light appeared in the hollow cavern. When the light faded, Shannan swooned into Vidar's arms. Her cowl fell back. He balked at seeing her clearly for the first time.

"Something wrong?" asked Wren.

"Nothing." Vidar carried Shannan to a portion of the rock wall carved out for use as a bed. A folded blanket lay at the end of the bed.

"Do you have any wine?" Wren asked Vidar when Shannan began to wake.

Vidar went to a cupboard to fetch the wine. Wren grew curious at receiving an unopened bottle. She said nothing instead she turned her attention to Shannan. After uncorking the bottle, she offered Shannan a drink. She supported Shannan's head.

"Slowly," cautioned Wren. "You fainted. Mortals are not accustomed to dimension travel."

Shannan looked about. "Where are we?"

"In a cliff cave overlooking the East Coast. This is my hiding place. You'll be safe," said Vidar. He flashed an awkward smile at Shannan.

"You'll feel better after some rest," said Wren. When Shannan closed her eyes, Wren noticed Vidar's sober regard of her. "What is it?"

Despite obvious reluctance, he motioned her to a small table in a semi-circular part of the wall carved out as a bench. He sat opposite her. "I told you, much has changed."

"Indeed. Of all the mortal pleasures, wine was your favorite. No bottle remained unopened in your presence. Does this change include being modest about your abilities?"

The internal battle to choose his words was clearly visible on his face. "At the Great Battle, I witnessed mortals and Guardians fall before Dagar's forces."

"We all did," she gently reminded him. "I thought you vanquished. For over a century, I mourned your loss. Not until Mahon told Kell about your survival did I have a shred of hope to see you again."

Vidar shifted a bit uncomfortable. "Then you know the bomb of white light and deafening sound was a forced dimension travel." He continued after her sober nod of acknowledgement. "I awoke in the Cave behind stygian bars. I spent most of my imprisonment wondering if I would be another victim of Dagar's reconditioning." He snatched the bottle from her to take a long drink. "They also used spurean chains. Dagar thought of everything to torment and break a Guardian."

His tale so disturbed her that she could barely ask, "Were you tortured?"

He sluggishly shook his head. "Before my turn, I was forced to watch others experience horrendous abuse. Part of my breaking process; or so I was told. Some valiantly resisted, only to meet the ultimate fate for not renouncing Jor'el. Others broke and joined Dagar. They somehow became altered by the Dark Way."

"If you weren't tortured then—" Wren couldn't complete her thought.

"How am I here? Have I joined Dagar?" he finished for her, not hiding his sarcasm.

She flashed a discomposed glance at him.

"I escaped, along with a handful of others." Although she tried to appear sympathetic, he noticed uncertainty. With an angry grunt, Vidar stood and pointed to the cave opening. "There's the way out. You can take the Daughter of Allon and leave."

"Vidar—" Wren weakly began in protest.

He abruptly turned from her. In doing so, he noticed Shannan awake. She regarded him with green eyes so unpretentious he could not look away.

"Is something wrong? You are troubled," Shannan said with certainty.

Wren replied, "Vidar was captured by Dagar. He was telling me of his recent escape."

Vidar crossed the kitchen area, which consisted of a small hearth with a grated grill. A narrow table served for preparing food. A kettle and cast iron skillet sat on one end of the table. Six tubers lay beside the kettle. "I was going to make tuber soup. Will that do?"

"Ay." Shannan sent a compassionate glance to Wren before she went to help Vidar peel the tubers.

Kell departed the ruins the moment Ellis left. The Prince had enough to contend with than to worry about Shannan. Unfortunately, Kell used a good bit of strength hurrying from the cave in Dorgirith to the ruins of Dunlap then back again. Each time an overwhelming sense of Witter's presence urged his speed. Even for the mighty Guardian captain, the present use of dimension travel taxed his stamina. The greater the distance, the more energy required. Both locations lay at opposite ends in the vast Southern Forest.

To conserve energy in case of battle, Kell reappeared five miles short of the cave. He ran the rest of the way. Guardians easily out-distanced any mortal with little effort. He covered the five miles in a matter of minutes. It was not exhaustion that drew him to an unsteady halt, rather the sight of a cave in.

"Wren! Can you hear me?" Not receiving a reply, he took a deep breath, closed his eyes and reached out his senses into the cave. "Darkness. Fire. Evil!" His eyes opened.

Kell used his sword to knock a hole large enough to allow access. Smoke billowed forth with a rancid smell that struck his nostrils. It forced him to step back. When the smoke cleared, he cautiously entered the darkened cave. Something crushed beneath his feet. By the feel of his hand on the wall, he knew he reached the main room.

"*A'lasadh!*" He snapped his fingers. Immediately the cave filled with light by which to see. The inside had been gutted by fire while the room littered with dead—"Drusi. Jor'el has lifted his seal." After a quick search, he discovered Wren and Shannan were not inside. Satisfied, he sheathed his sword and left.

Kell took several deep breaths of fresh air to clear his head of the smell of smoke and burnt drusi. Kato landed on a boulder while Torin appeared from the trees.

"You two are safe. Do you know where Wren and Shannan are?"

Torin yipped before he ran from the cave. Kell followed Torin to the dead boars. He bent to examine them. Crossbow arrows lay near each animal.

"This one was killed by Wren, I recognize her shaft. This one, I don't recognize, though by the wound, it had to be a Guardian." Kell frowned when Torin yipped several times. "I can speak to you, but understanding is Wren's specialty."

"Perhaps I can tell you," came a voice from behind.

Instantly, Kell rose with his sword drawn. Annoyed, he lowered his blade. "Priscilla! Haven't I told you not to do that?"

"Old habits are hard to mend." Priscilla was fair with long pale yellow hair past her waist. Part of her hair was a braided coiled on her head like a crown. Sky blue eyes held a mischievous glint while the rich pink lips smiled. She wore a dress of light and dark green that reached her ankles. It gathered about the waist by a gold belt fastened with a shell buckle.

Kell slammed the sword into the scabbard. "One day your *old habits* will get you sliced in two."

"You can never tell where the wind will go."

His set jaw told he was not in a joking mood. "Well?"

She closed her eyes. The wind picked up around them. Her head turned in several directions until the wind died. "That way. To the East Coast."

Kell folded his arms across his chest. "Why didn't you just say they went to your province?"

"The wind is a fickle thing."

"Be serious!" he snapped, to which she looked hurt.

"They are safe. That is what I came to tell you. Vidar—"

"Vidar?" Kell echoed with surprise.

"Ay. He brought Wren and the Daughter of Allon safely to his hiding place when Witter tried to flush them out with drusi."

"I saw Witter's attempt. Is Shannan injured?"

"No. A bit shaken from dimension travel, yet that is to be expected."

"What about Vidar? How did he appear?"

"He recently escaped, though is vague with details. He did say Dagar used spurean chains and stygian bars."

"By the heavenlies! I would speak with him."

"On foot?" Priscilla questioned when Kell walked away.

He pulled to an abrupt halt. "I have dimension traveled multiple times, encountered trouble twice, battered down a cave-in and dealt with you. So, unless you can conjure up a wind to carry me there, I'm walking."

"It was just a question," she said defensively. She hastened after him. "I can keep you company. Better yet, I can help you get there faster."

Kell stopped at hearing sincerity, yet remained skeptical. "No fickle tricks or old habits?"

"I deserve that." She held out her hands. "Truce."

"Truce." He took her hands. "*Siuthad!*" they said together.

White light made Vidar bolt up from the table where they sat to eat. His crossbow ready to defend Shannan. Wren joined Vidar in wary anticipation. The light faded to reveal Kell and Priscilla.

"Kell," said Wren with relief. "Am I glad to see you. We had to leave Dorgirith."

"I know." Kell saw Shannan step out from behind Vidar. "Are you all right?"

"Ay. What of Ellis?"

"Well. He dealt with the situation before I arrived." Kell directed his attention to Vidar. With a warm smile, he heartily clapped Vidar's shoulder. "It's good to see you again. I hear you have a tale to tell."

Vidar timidly scratched the back of his neck. "Not really."

Kell pursed his lips in regard of Vidar. He appeared the same. Only upon closer inspection, the bright copper eyes lacked the confidence that once marked Vidar's character. Before the swaggering merry smile showed Vidar enjoyed his physical existence. Kell attributed the lack of spark to the imprisonment. He needed details to learn of Dagar and other Guardians. Thus he pressed his cause.

"How did you escape?"

Vidar shied from Kell. "With Rune's help."

"Rune?" repeated Kell with some discord. "How did he help you?"

"When he couldn't stand to see anymore suffering, he devised a plan. At a lull in the torture cycle, he helped me and a dozen others escape. We didn't get far when the cry went out so we scattered. I don't know what happened to Rune or the others."

"Who were they?"

Vidar heaved a hapless shrug. "I only knew five. Mahon, Elgin, a vassal from the Delta; Daren and Darcy, the night twins from the North Plains; and a warrior from the West Coast called Cyril."

"Mahon," said Kell with a small smile of relief. "Where did you emerge from the Cave? What province?"

Vidar uneasiness turned into annoyance. "I don't know."

"There had to be something familiar. Was it Midessex?"

"I said I don't know!" he snapped. This caused Kell's brows to rise at the rebuff. Vidar tried to bring himself under control by turning aside. He caught Shannan's encouraging glance. He began to relax.

Kell noticed Vidar's mood change. He took hold of Vidar's arm to get his attention. "I need to know what you can tell me. It could be vital in helping the Son of Tristan and Daughter of Allon."

Vidar spoke in a more controlled voice. "The white bomb forced a dimension travel to the Cave. Where that is, I don't know the province. Even if I did, I don't think I could remember. Time and place become distorted in the nether dimension. Priscilla said it's been five hundred years." He shrugged, as he continued. "Bridging the dimensional gap made me weak and disoriented, so I didn't really take the time to assess where I emerged. It was just a forest." Vidar grew pensive. "When I felt strong enough, I did a second travel, only to black-out. I woke to the sound of water."

"I found him and brought him here," said Priscilla.

"What made you come to our aid?" Wren asked Vidar.

"A sense of trouble compelled me to go."

Kell squeezed Vidar's arm though he spoke to Shannan. "Because of you, the Guardians are returning. Vidar is proof that even Dagar can't prevent it."

She noticed Vidar grow thoughtful. "That disturbs you?"

"No. I'm just beginning to realize how much imprisonment robbed me of perception. I don't know what I would have done if Rune had not helped me before my turn came."

"It doesn't matter, you're free. What you do from now on is what counts, not what might have happened."

"The Daughter of Allon speaks wisdom," began Wren. "You followed your spirit's calling and saved us from Witter."

"What now?" Priscilla asked Kell.

"Can you keep her safe until it is time?"

"Between myself, Vidar and Wren we can keep the Daughter of Allon safe, even from Witter."

"A simple *ay* would suffice," groused Kell.

"Even a gentle breeze ruffles feathers."

Kell scowled at Priscilla yet spoke to Wren. "If anything happens, take her to Melwynn."

"Where will you be?"

"My place is as the Prince's shadow."

"If you leave on foot, it's a long way down." Priscilla motioned to the cave opening.

Smoldering irritation filled Kell's glance. Shannan took his arm. "He can't leave until he has supped with us. I want to know all about Ellis and Grandfather."

"I'll bring some large sea bass," teased Priscilla before she vanished.

Kell huffed and sat at the table. "Why does she delight in taunting me?"

Wren chuckled. "Because you're too serious."

Kell shot her an arched glance.

"The Captain has much to be concerned about," said Shannan.

"Which shows the difference between them. Priscilla's carefree, flippant attitude irritates one as serious as Kell. The amusing part is he doesn't see it," said Wren.

"His great fatigue prevents it."

"How do you know that?" Kell asked Shannan.

"When I first met you, I sensed control of your emotions, words, and actions. You moved with ease and great energy. When you arrived with Priscilla, it was rather hand-in-hand. Your temper is short while your movement less fluid. I can only imagine the amount of energy you have expended the last twenty four hours to accomplish what you have."

Kell leaned back against the wall with a look of admiration at Shannan's assessment. "Ay, I need nourishment and rest. I'd never admit that in front of Priscilla."

"Then Guardian males have as much ego as mortal males."

Wren and Vidar's laughter made Kell flush in dispute.

"I've never been accused of having an ego. Have I?"

This only served to increase the mirth of his fellow Guardians.

"If it's as large as your appetite, I hope Priscilla brings enough to feed us all," said Wren.

Shannan gently touched Kell's hand. "Relax, Captain. Things will be easier to endure in the morning."

He shook his head. "I must be on my way before then. Even that delay pains me. Oh, for my full strength to return!"

"Full strength? Guardians are already more powerful than us."

"Since the Great Battle our strength is only half of what it once was. Jor'el rendered judgment upon all Guardians because of those who followed Dagar. As the time grows near, our strength and abilities will increase. That is why you are so important to us. Through you, Jor'el has ordained our full restoration."

"As we strengthen, so does Dagar," warned Vidar.

"Which is why we must tread carefully and keep her safe until time," said Kell with emphasis.

Shannan grew defensive. "Ellis goes about freely."

Kell tempered his response to soothe her. "You have different paths toward the same goal: he to unite the mortals, you the Guardians. Once that is done, we join forces to face Dagar." He softly smiled at her discouragement. "Fret not. Trust us, and have faith in Jor'el."

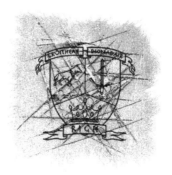

Chapter 10

EVERYTHING WAS READY FOR DEPARTURE FROM THE RUINS. Over the years they gathered items necessary to make life a little easier. They packed the essentials into one covered wagon pulled by a single horse.

Niles waited by the old gate to observe the preparations. Some ten yards away, Ellis spoke with Darius. For two years Niles tutored Ellis, taught him warfare, made him memorize Verse, joined him in hours of meditation, laughed and counseled him when the burden felt unbearable. Now came the time for proving his mettle. Was Ellis ready? True he defeated the unicorn to pass the first test only so much more lay ahead. Niles sighed with uncertainty.

"He has the heart and desire. Will he have the wisdom and strength of character to face all challenges?" He glanced skyward in anticipation of an answer.

"What is it?" Ellis asked.

Niles had not noticed Ellis' approach. He quickly covered his momentary surprise. Rather than give a direct answer, he changed the subject. "I don't think their coming is a good idea."

Ellis cocked a wry smile. "You tell Darius he can't go with me. The others are under his protection. If they are captured, word of me could spread."

"I thought you trusted them?"

"I do. This is for their own safety."

Niles flashed a grin of approval at the cautious bravado.

"We're ready," called Darius.

Ellis waved a reply. With Niles by his side, he headed the troupe west from the ruins. He used the wood to shield their movement in skirting the town of Garwood. The castle was strategically positioned near the intersection of two main roads. One road headed due north, the other northeast. Both roads led to the Northern Forest. The road north crossed the province to the Highlands. The other led to the Denley Castle, the provincial seat, located on the shores of the picturesque lake of the same name.

After six-miles, they crossed the border into the Northern Forest. Finding a cove off the side of the road, they paused for a meal.

Upon breaking camp, Erin called, "Sir Niles. Take my place on the wagon."

"I may be old, young lady, but I'm not infirmed."

"I never meant it as such. I could use a good stretch of the legs. Besides, someone needs to keep Jasper from falling asleep," she said with a twinkle in her eye. She motioned to where Jasper sat in the driver's seat. He yawned.

Before Niles could reply, Erin headed to join Ellis.

"Give you a hand up, Sir Niles?" offered Jasper.

Niles sprightly mounted the wagon by himself. "I'll drive, you rest."

"Don't mind if I do." Jasper handed Niles the reins. "Lady Erin kept me awake all morning. She insisted I drive even when Nando offered so I could catch up on sleep."

"Why wouldn't she let you sleep?"

Jasper shrugged. He settled into the back of the wagon. "I gave up trying to figure out women when my missus died."

"We should be leaving," called Ellis.

Niles snapped the reins for the horse to move. Up ahead, Erin walked beside Ellis. She focused on him, while he focused on the road. A seed of suspicion grew in Niles' brain. *More than the Contest may test you.*

Ellis kept his eyes on where they headed while Erin spoke.

"It seems so unreal. You being a prince and not my cousin."

He chuckled. "It took me awhile to accept reality. I couldn't imagine having any other father, mother, or brother." He tossed her a smiling side-glance. "Nor other cousins."

Her mirth was short-lived, as she grew melancholy. "Alas, it is true."

He took note of her somber tone. "Our blood relation may have changed, but we are still the same people. You're poised and pretty, while I'm pesky and princely," he teased.

"Do you really think I'm pretty? Lavi never thought so."

Her statement puzzled him. "I thought you loved each other?"

She shied at his question. "I loved *him*," she said with tone of bitter sarcasm. "He wooed me, as a woman desires to be wooed. When he had his prize, I learned he only married me because of father's station."

"I'm sorry."

She heaved an awkward shrug. "It did him little good since it cost his life. He may have been a scoundrel to me, but a brave fighter."

"I remember him on his charger. An awesome figure of a knight."

She laughed with mockery. "All boys dreaming of knightly glory make heroes of any man in a suit of armor."

"I'm not dreaming now," he said seriously. He changed the uncomfortable subject. "What happened to Nancie?"

"She died during our first winter in the ruins. It was the worst winter I can recall. Darius wondered if any of us would survive. Kemp took her death hard. He blamed himself for not stopping Tyree and being forced to flee. Oh, Ellis, there was nothing he could have done! It was horrible," she said with a visible shiver.

He placed a comforting arm about her shoulders. "The blame is mine. I am their quarry."

"No! It's all Marcellus and Latham's doing!" With a firm set chin, she looked directly at him.

He regarded her with mild wonder. "What did I ever do to deserve such loyalty from you and Darius?"

"It's nothing you've done rather who you are. After supper, Della fetched her old books. We read Prophecy concerning the Promised Prince. It confirmed everything."

"There is much to do before that happens, and much that can go wrong."

"I know, though while there is hope, I must have faith."

His arm dropped from her shoulder. "Not in me, surely."

Erin chuckled. "No, not in a pesky lad. Faith in Prophecy and Jor'el."

A smile of relief crossed Ellis' lips. "In that we agree." A cry from above drew his attention. "Kato?" he quickly called. He became disappointed at seeing a falcon.

"Who is Kato?" she asked at his letdown.

Fondness filled his face. "An eagle that belongs to someone I know."

His ardent expression made her tentatively ask, "You know this person well?"

Ellis smiled warm and tender. "As well as I know myself." He again looked up, unaware of her pained expression. His interest became diverted when Brody ran passed them. Darius arrived.

"It'll be dark in a couple of hours. I sent Brody to scout ahead for a campsite."

* * *

The Northern Forest was more hilly then the Southern Forest due to its proximity to the foothills of the Highlands. This meant the province was less populated, which served well for a group pretending to be pilgrims. It would take four long days of travel to reach the Highland border. Each day they began in the wee hours of the morning and continued until after twilight. The further north they traveled the colder the temperature. The snow-covered Highland peaks rose majestically in the distance. Soon the snow would lower in elevation, until the valleys were at least a foot deep.

In a vale of the foothill, stood the Fortress of Ludlow, three miles from the nearest town. It enclosed two acres. A central stone gatehouse greeted visitors while ten-foot high walls continued to the corner turrets. The wooden gate was large enough to permit wagons and horses, with a small inset door for foot traffic. Most wilderness Fortresses were built for defense as well as worship.

From a distance, everything at the Fortress appeared intact. However, they observed no smoke or signs of occupants. Darius sent Nando and Brody to scout ahead. Shortly, Brody returned to make report.

"The Fortress is abandoned. No livestock, except for a few loose chickens. Nando is making a complete search of the buildings."

Ellis curiously glanced to Darius. "I wonder why?" He told Brody, "Take the point. Jasper, Kemp, place the women and boys in the wagon. Edmund, Niles, guard the rear. Darius and I will take the lead."

Cautiously, they entered the Fortress. The courtyard showed no sign of damage or anything that would give a clue for the abandonment. An empty stable, chicken coop and livestock pens were located along the south wall. The living quarters and kitchen lined the north wall. A chapel dominated the back wall.

Once everyone entered, Darius said, "Brody, close the gate."

Nando appeared from the storehouse. "All is clear, my lord," he told Ellis. "I found supplies of salted beef, grain, cheese and beer. There's a fresh batch of butter along with milk in the cold storehouse. Also clean blankets, newly cut wood and oil in all the lamps. The armory is empty. Two dormitories are connected by a central hallway."

"That's very odd," muttered Darius to Ellis, who remained thoughtfully silent.

"Perhaps, but we'll eat well this night," said Kemp.

"And resupply our provisions," said Della.

"If only the stable had a few good horses," said Jasper, which made the horse neigh in protest. "To lighten your load, old girl."

Fagan climbed down from the wagon. "How long will we stay?"

"Until I feel Jor'el's leading." Ellis patted Fagan's shoulder when the boy frowned. "For awhile we shall have secure shelter and good food."

"We'll start supper," Erin said of her and Della

A figure jumped out from the shadow of the building to block the women's path. His appearance startled them. "Trespassers. Come to steal what is left?"

Ellis signaled the men to lower their weapons. He moved beside the women to make closer observation of the man. He appeared older than Della, with stooped shoulders under tattered clothes. The thick white hair was unkempt while icy blue eyes peered out from tanned skin. Despite the evidence of age, the texture of his skin appeared smooth and unwrinkled.

"We don't steal. We came to the Fortress in good faith only to find it abandoned. Where are the others?"

"There aren't any others, just me."

Kemp snickered in disbelief. "All these supplies just for you?"

His cold, hard glare turned upon Kemp. "What of it?"

Such insolence angered Kemp. "You look more the thieving kind."

Provoked, the man stepped forward. This made Kemp move to confront him.

"Peace!" Ellis intervened by raising his hands, one to stall Kemp and the other the old man. The man seized Ellis' arm. He twisted it to force Ellis to one knee.

"Release him!" ordered Jasper. He reached for his sword.

"No!" Niles intercepted Jasper. "Everyone stay back."

The man smirked. He exerted pressure on Ellis' arm. "Wisely done."

Ellis gritted his teeth against the pain yet managed a sly look to Niles, as he spoke to the man. "I may have underestimated you because of your age, but so did you about me." He made a move that freed him and ensnared the man about the chest. Ellis smiled at Niles. "Those wrestling lessons weren't wasted—" His boasting became interrupted when the man tossed him to the ground.

Surprised by the man's speed Ellis barely managed to roll away and spring to his feet. The man assumed an aggressive posture, which made Ellis say, "I don't want to hurt you."

"It'll be you who'll get hurt, laddie." He charged with lightning quickness. He snatched Ellis, and both fell hard to the ground with the man landing on top.

"Don't lie still!" scolded Niles.

"Easy for you to say," Ellis growled. He fought to get free.

Ellis gained enough leverage to push the man to one side. In the momentum, he rolled with the man and landed half on top. Ellis' dominant position only lasted a few seconds when the man pushed back. To keep from being bent in two, Ellis released his hold to fall backward. Due to the lack of resistance, the man followed Ellis down. This gave Ellis a brief advantage. He swung onto the man's back and attempted to pin him to the ground. The strength with which the man resisted shone in Ellis' face. With a loud grunt, the man heaved his shoulders and threw out his arms. The force knocked Ellis aside like a rag doll.

"Did you see that?" asked an astonished Kemp.

Niles didn't respond; his eyes fixed on the bout.

Ellis got to his knees just in time to dodge the man's lunge. He grabbed the man's arm. Ellis swung him around and landed a knee in the small of his back. With a hard thud, the man landed face first in the dirt with Ellis on top of him.

"We are not thieves! If you leave in peace, we may give you a portion of meat for your troubles," chided Ellis.

"I yield!" he said through clenched teeth.

Ellis released the man to stand. Ellis wobbled a bit unsteady since the battle required more effort than anticipated by the looks of the man. "Brody, Nando, see he gets what he needs and leaves."

"You would turn me out at night? There'll be ankle deep snow come morning."

"It's too early for valley snow, even in the Highlands," refuted Edmund.

He sneered in rebuff. "I've wandered these hills long enough to know when and how much it will snow. So unless you speak for your young lord, keep a civil tongue." He then demanded of Ellis, "Well?"

Their eyes continued the wrestling match their bodies completed. "Your word not to cause more trouble, and you may stay," said Ellis.

"Done!" he agreed with a stout nod. "I just finished dressing a feral pig when you arrived. The women can help me with supper."

"I suppose you wrung its neck for practice," Jasper dryly quipped.

"Too easy. I'd need a full size boar for a challenge."

Erin and Della were slow to follow him to the kitchen.

Ellis rubbed his shoulder, as he scolded Jasper. "Don't taunt him."

"He had me fooled," Jasper murmured in complaint.

"The master-at-arms fooled by an old man. I'll remember that," quipped Edmund.

Niles massaged Ellis' shoulders. "Highlanders are a hearty lot. I've seen eighty–year-old men in battle. Go rest in the hall while we unload," he said to Ellis.

Forty minutes later, Ellis had a good fire going in the hearth. He motioned to the sideboard when the others entered.

"He brought a cask of wine along with tankards. If anyone wants it mulled, I have the poker ready."

"Smells good," said Darius to the aroma from the kitchen.

They all had mulled wine when Erin and Della brought out side dishes for the meal.

"Done already?" asked Kemp.

"Ay. I've never seen a pig roast so fast," replied Della.

The man carried a carved roast pig on a large platter. "Eat your fill."

"Won't you join us? Here by me," said Ellis.

The man cocked a careful brow. "If you're always this trusting with the men you defeat you're not likely to live long."

"If you plan to kill me go back to the kitchen. If not, join us."

In stunned silence, the others watched the tense exchange between Elli and the old man. After a moment, the old man laughed with genuine good humor. He snatched a tankard.

"You have a noble heart, my lord. To your health and success."

During the meal they learned he was called Wanderer for his years of traveling the hills. It had been so long since he had a family and home that he couldn't remember his own name. Most fell into conversation with him, all except Darius, who remained warily quiet.

The meal just concluded when Darius left the hall. He made excuse of securing the perimeter. Upon completing his task of touring the Fortress, sounds of merriment still came from the hall. Unable to bring himself to return inside, Darius marched the rampart to a portion near the front gate. There he found Ellis.

"I've been waiting for you."

Darius folded his cloak about him. He leaned against the wall to gaze into the dark.

"I assume all is secure."

Darius still looked out in the darkness. "It' cold enough. He may be right about the snow."

"No, you mean he's right about not living long if I trust people like I trusted him."

Darius wrestle with a reply. "Ay," he droned at length.

"I did what I thought best. I knew I could trust him."

"How?"

Ellis shrugged. "I just knew. Perhaps Jor'el has granted me a sense of people. It's nothing I've experienced before this journey."

"Nor have I. It's unnerving."

"Think how I feel." Ellis clasped Darius' shoulder. "You may not approve of everything I say or do, but please, trust me and show support in public. If you wish to give me a tongue lashing in private, you may."

Darius gave a hollow chuckle. "I have your permission to scold you. Oh, Ellis," he gripped the arm on his shoulder. "In reality your are the

115

Prince, but in my heart, you will always be my little brother. I'm having difficulty reconciling the two in how to treat you."

"Then treat me as a man fully grown, not the youngster you remember. Perhaps in that, you can find a compromise. Now, the others are making ready for bed, join them."

"What about you?"

"I'll be along shortly. I wish to pray and meditate before retiring."

Darius no sooner left than Ellis heard someone approach. He became alert then relaxed when Wanderer stepped out from the shadows. Wanderer's appearance altered. He stood ramrod straight, taller than Ellis with white hair and bright violet eyes.

"Who are you?" asked Ellis.

"Valmar, Guardian of the Highlands. You fought well, Son of Tristan. The only other mortal to pin me was your mentor, Sir Niles."

"Did he recognize you?"

"Ay, as Wanderer. That is why he stopped any interference."

"Was this part of the Contest?"

"Ay, and you have gained your second reward."

"How? You could have thrown me off at any time."

Valmar kindly smiled. "My task was to test your heart and judgment. Jor'el has gifted you with wisdom. You dealt rightly with me." He motioned behind him to a gold breastplate, gauntlets and boots. "Rune forged these many years ago."

Ellis inspected the magnificent craftsmanship. Upon the breastplate was the eagle of Tristan. The shoulder guards crafted to resemble wings. "It's light."

"Yet can turn a Guardian's sword. Kell and Armus tested it when Rune finished." Valmar took the armor. "Come morning, after Wanderer has left, Lord Ranulf's wife, Lady Tilda, will arrive. Once you have met with her, proceed to the North Plains where you will meet Jora of Clive."

"Master Ellis?" Brody called as he climbed the ladder.

When Ellis turned to answer, Valmar quietly departed. "Ay."

"Lord Darius sent me to take the watch so you could turn in."

Ellis chuckled while he murmured to himself. "He must try harder."

As Wanderer predicted, four inches of snow fell overnight. Shortly after dawn, Darius and Ellis walked the ramparts. The smell of breakfast cooking lingered in the cool morning air.

"Riders approaching. Three men and a woman," said Darius.

"Lady Tilda," said Ellis.

Darius cocked a curious sideways glance. "How do you know that?"

"My journey is to gather my companions. With Ranulf in hiding, who else but his wife would come to see me? You told me their son Reid frequents Marcellus' court," Ellis spoke while they departed the rampart. "Open the gate!" he instructed Brody.

When the new arrivals drew rein, Ellis extended his hand to aid her dismount. "Welcome, Lady Tilda."

Tilda was shorter than Ellis by almost a foot. She wore her fifty years with an elegant grace. The large winter hat hid her hair. Deep brown eyes regarded Ellis with discernment tempered by wisdom.

"Your face shows your youth, but in your eyes I see knowledge, prudence and courage beyond your years. Indeed, Jor'el has blessed you, Son of Tristan."

Her use of his prophetic title surprised Ellis. "You know who I am?"

Tilda kindly smiled. "You are not the only one favored with a word from Jor'el on ocassion. Many years I have prayed to look upon your face. To see Allon's salvation. Ask what you will and it shall be done, my lord."

"My first request is that you join us for breakfast."

Inside the hall Della, Brody and Nando served the meal.

"Is it as we feared, that Angus is dead?" Tilda asked Darius.

"I'm afraid so. I take my father's place at Ellis' side."

"I wish I could say the same for my son." Heavy disappointment filled Tilda's voice.

"Do not distress yourself on his behalf," began Ellis. "Swords are only part of what is needed. The more support I can gather, the better. Merchants for supplies, farmers for food, metalsmiths for armor, and brave ladies willingly give of what they have. Now, tell me of Lord Ranulf. How is he?"

"His encounter with Captain Tyree worsened the wounds he suffered during his escape from Ravendale. He is confined to his hiding place. Rest assured, my lord, I speak as he would if he were here."

"If he trusts you, why should I do otherwise?"

Tilda tightly clasped Ellis' hand. The earnestness of her dark eyes fixed on him. "If anything should happen to us, all arrangements have been secretly made. As Ranulf's ancestor gave the family's signet to King Tristan in fealty, so we bequeath Clifton Castle and all our Highland holdings to you, our Prince." She kissed his hand in homage.

Her words stunned Ellis. "My lady, I'm overwhelmed. I accept with heartfelt thanks. Once we have finished breakfast and put things as we found them, we shall journey to Clifton Castle."

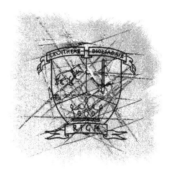

Chapter 11

D UE TO THE HARSH HIGHLAND WINTER, THE GROUP SPENT TWO months at Clifton Castle. Though unable to join them due to his slowly healing wounds, Ranulf sent messages from his hiding place. He confirmed everything Tilda said, pledging fealty of the Highlands in written oath to Ellis. Pleased by the Highland couple's generosity, Ellis did not want to impose any longer than necessary. Once the weather cleared, he insisted on leaving. He refused the horses Tilda offered since going mounted would alter their appearance of pilgrims.

The group became smaller since Tilda agreed to keep Kemp's sons and Della. The boys did not want to be left behind, but in the end, yielded to their father's persuasion. Della willingly remained. Despite Kemp's objections, Erin determined to continue. They convinced her to cut her hair to shoulder length and wear men's clothes for a disguise. Not skilled in arms, she wore a short dagger. Tilda also supplied them with new clothes for the journey, all except Niles. He refused to leave behind his old Jor'ellian uniform. The clothes would not detract from their ruse, though decidedly better than those previously worn for several years.

The clear weather turned wicked the fourth day into the journey. Icy snow and wind pelted them. Traveling the Highlands proved rough in the best of weather. An additional two inches of snow made it hazardous. Trudge on they did, through narrow passes, over steep climbs and slippery descents. By week's end they only managed to cover half the distance to the North Plains.

Years of outdoor living had strengthened her endurance. However, Erin began to weaken by the eighth day. She scrambled to catch up when the men slowed for a climb. A few times she caught Niles' reproving glance. Provoked by his looks, she picked up the pace. He never spoke a cross word to her. Since the day they left Dunlap, she sensed his disapproval. Why? She didn't know, but would find out.

After the ninth day of travel, they made camp in the shelter of a hollow. It nestled snugly between two of the lower peaks where the snow began to melt. A small brook ran through the hollow. The few trees were bare of leaves. Fallen branches would serve for firewood.

Erin gingerly sat on a boulder near where the men arranged camp. Brody and Nando built a fire, while Jasper and Edmund rummaged through their dwindling provision for the makings of a meal. Niles, Ellis and Darius had their heads together over the map. Erin gently pulled off her boots. Kemp arrived.

"Blisters worse? Perhaps you'll finally admit this was a bad idea." He squatted down to examine her feet. She shooed him away with a painful grunt. "Look, little sister, I told you not to come. You're too stubborn for your own good."

"Why didn't you want me to come? So you could leave Ellis to face trouble alone like you did Lavi and father?"

Kemp flushed with anger. Ellis' arrival stopped any reply.

"Is something wrong?" asked Ellis.

Kemp forced himself to relax "I was trying convince Erin to let me tend her blisters."

"Blisters?" Ellis noticed her bloody woolen socks. "Why didn't you tell anyone?" He tried to be careful in pulling off the socks to examine her feet. She still flinched. He discovered four large open blisters on her right foot, and three on her left. "It's a wonder you can walk. I'll have Niles tend you. He's excellent with medicine."

"I'll fetch him." Kemp hurried off.

"No need to bother Sir Niles," said Erin loudly. Kemp ignored her.

"It's no bother." Ellis again examined her feet.

Niles arrived alone. "You sent for me?"

"Ellis! I think I found an easier way," called Darius.

Ellis waved an acknowledgement to Darius then said to Niles, "Erin has been suffering cruelly from blisters. See what relief you can give her." He gave Erin an encouraging smile before leaving to join Darius.

When Niles went to examine her feet, Erin pulled her foot away. "Why do you hate me?" she said in a low voice full of bitter accusation.

Niles' head snapped up. "I don't hate you."

She balked at his penetrating gaze. "You don't like me."

"It's not a matter of like or dislike." He arranged the salve and bandages for treatment.

"Then why have you shunned me since we met?"

"You wouldn't understand."

The flippant answer infuriated her. "Try me."

Niles raised a brow. Despite her obvious pain and fatigue, she was determined to have an answer. "Very well. We can speak while I tend you." This time she offered no resistance. "What do you know of Prophecy?" he asked while gently applying the salve.

"Enough to believe in Ellis' destiny."

"Good." He wrapped her right foot. "Since you believe that, you would do nothing to interfere or distract him, correct?" He looked up at her, direct and probing.

His penetrating gaze unnerved her. "Of course not, only help."

"Even better. How's that?"

Erin marveled at her right foot. She momentarily forgot his administrations, since the conversation felt more uncomfortable than her feet. "I don't feel any pain."

Niles grinned. He reached for her left foot. "Since we are in agreement, let me ask you this: How long have you had feelings for Ellis? Since childhood?"

She gaped in amazement. "How—?"

"How did I know? It's obvious, if one knows what to look for. The more important question is have you told him?"

Again he stared at her with those probing eyes. Unmasked and vulnerable she muttered, "No," and lowered her eyes.

He lifted her chin to meet her gaze. "For his sake, keep your feelings hidden. His destiny does not include you."

She pulled her face away in an effort to fight back the painful anger at his words. Tears swelled despite her attempt.

"I don't say these things to hurt you. I merely seek to protect Ellis."

She shot him a caustic glance. "You think I would hurt him?"

"Not intentionally. Alas, all good intentions can go awry. If you truly care for him, leave him to his destiny, for his sake, and the sake of Allon. If not, we are all doomed."

At the pronouncement, Erin abruptly turned aside. Niles left. He might not hate her, but didn't he spare her feelings. She felt wet tears upon her cheeks. She shivered, this time from the cold. She wiped her eyes before she moved closer to feel the fire. She kept separate from the others not wanting any further conversations. She didn't remain alone for long. Nando placed a blanket around her shoulders. He kindly smiled before he returned to his duties of unpacking the night gear.

Jasper and Edmund made stew from wild onions and the two fish they caught in the brook. Niles occupied Ellis, which was fine. Until Erin could gather her thoughts and emotions she didn't want to deal with either of them. Darius placed a bowl of steaming stew under her nose. She took the bowl. He sat beside her to eat from his own bowl.

"How are your feet?" he asked.

"Better," she said through a mouth full of stew.

"Niles is a surprising old man."

Erin shoved the spoon in her mouth to stifle a reply.

Darius noticed her action. "Did he also scold you for coming?"

She huffed a grunt as she continued to eat.

For a moment, he regarded her with soft smile of admiration. "I'm proud of you."

She swallowed hard in surprise. "What?"

"I know I haven't said much. Perhaps appearing preoccupied. I *do* have eyes. At first, I agreed with Kemp that you shouldn't come. Not that you haven't the heart," he said with a chuckle to forestall her reply. "You've grown up from the spoiled girl who threw tantrums to get her way. I know Uncle Phineas would be pleased."

She stared at her soup. A new wave of tears swelled. "Thank you."

He placed an arm about her shoulders and kissed her cheek.

At daybreak, Erin felt a renewal of spirit. Darius' comments acted as a soothing counter to Niles' challenge. Unfortunately, a reinvigorated spirit did not translate into restored strength. She once again fell behind on the tough climb from the hollow. Kemp gave her a hand the final few feet to the plateau. For several miles the plateau stretched.

"What did Darius want last night?" Kemp asked.

"To say he was proud of me. That I'm no longer the spoiled girl who threw tantrums to get her way."

He chuckled. "Oh, you threw tantrums all right."

With a loud huff, she pulled ahead. Unfortunately, her feet were too painful to continue the quickened pace. He caught up to her.

"Was that all?"

She shot him a side-glance. "Isn't that enough? At least someone credits me for growing up."

Kemp frowned with wary consideration. He lowered his voice, though the tone irritated. "What you said last night isn't true. I didn't leave father and Lavi. I was somehow rendered unconscious. When I came to, they were dead."

"That's not what others say."

His anger kindled. "What others? Walsh and Thurman? I've been at odds with Walsh since winning Nancie. Thurman is a renowned liar."

"What about Grant and Hardwick? They too tell a different story. How you led them into an ambush."

"I don't know what they saw or think they saw, but it wasn't me!" He seized her arm, which drew her to a sudden, unsteady halt.

She winced in pain. "You're hurting me."

Nearby, Darius and Nando heard her. "What's wrong?" Darius demanded.

Erin jerked away from Kemp. "Kemp is being unreasonable."

"I'm concerned for her condition. Only she's being stubborn," argued Kemp.

"Leave her and join the others," said Darius.

Kemp's whole body went rigid. "You have no authority over me."

"I do," said Ellis firmly. He and the rest arrived.

With a throaty growl, Kemp marched ahead.

When Kemp passed him, Ellis visibly shivered. At least visible to Niles, who stood beside him. "What is it?" he whispered to Ellis.

"Something chilling passed with him or—" Ellis stopped to stare after Kemp.

"Are you all right?" Darius asked Erin, ignorant of the exchange between Ellis and Niles.

"Ay. Kemp was being Kemp," she complained.

"We know what that's like," groused Edmund. He received a jab from Jasper.

Niles said to Ellis, "We best go. We don't want Kemp to get lost."

"In his mood that might be a blessing," snorted Edmund.

Jasper rolled his good eye in defeat of his attempt to curb Edmund.

"Are your blisters better?" Ellis asked Erin.

After a brief uncomfortable hesitation, she answered, "Ay. Sir Niles did a good job." She flashed an awkward glance at Niles.

Niles tugged on Ellis' sleeve. "Kemp's out of sight. We best go."

"We'll slow the pace," said Ellis with an encouraging smile at Erin.

The group crossed into the North Plains late in the afternoon of the twelfth day. They stopped at a humble cottage inside the border to ask directions to Clive. The elderly couple greeted them, and insisted the group stay for a meal.

So advanced in age, their house was in ill repair and not well stocked. Ellis instructed Brody to snare some small game. Nando and Edmund fixed the table. Erin helped the wife, Tess, with bread and potatoes. Jasper fetched wood to begin a fire for cooking. Kemp and Darius repaired the roof since the sky threatened an afternoon rain.

Cedric, the husband, took Ellis and Niles down the small path from the cottage to the road. While giving directions, Cedric kept eyeing Ellis. In turn, Ellis studied the old farmer. Neither said anything directly to the other, it was all in their eyes.

Within two hours of their arrival, the sat to eat. After offering a simple prayer of thanks, Cedric began the conversation.

"For pilgrims, you have the look of nobility. Him especially," he said of Ellis.

"What makes you say that?" asked Kemp cautiously.

Cedric chuckled. "I've lived long enough to see all kinds. I'm one hundred."

"I've not met many who have your age," said Niles with impressed curiosity.

Cedric soberly nodded. "Sometimes I think I've lived too long. You, I think, are also of an age," he said of Niles.

"I am."

Cedric became wracked by a terrible coughing fit. Tess aided him.

"Let me make you a draught to ease the cough," said Niles.

Cedric waved Tess aside to speak. "My time is short. Nothing can help. My only concern is for Tess."

"I shall carry on well enough."

"The house is falling down because I cannot tend it."

"Hush now. We have guests." Tess then said to them, "Pay him no mind and finish eating."

They followed her instruction. When Cedric found his voice, he told stories of his life. At the age of ten he lived through the fall of the House of Tristan. He emphasized the evil of Zared and his kind, those who practice the Dark Way. Once settled with his family in the cottage he helped his father build, Cedric met Tess.

Ellis took to heart every word of sorrow and hardship to the point he felt they were his own sufferings. After supper, he slipped outside to gather his thoughts and feelings about his family's past. Other than Niles, he had not heard a firsthand account of what happened. Then again, Niles didn't go into great detail about the overthrow. Whether that was good or not, Ellis couldn't judge. He didn't know his family personally. Still, they were his heritage. Their actions dictated the course of his life.

Before leaving Dorgirith, Ellis settled in his mind the question of pursuing his destiny. Since then reality challenged him. Some folk they encountered were bitterly hateful toward all nobility. Others clung to the hope of Jor'el fulfilling his promise. Ellis was that promise. The burden weighed heavily upon him. Equally burdensome was how miserable all would be if he failed. Yet the most deeply touching encounter happened with Cedric.

Something drew them together, something happy and tragic at the same time. In their earlier visual exchange Ellis realized Cedric felt the same. He didn't know Ellis' identity, rather guessed at his nobility. A voice startled Ellis from his introspection. Cedric. The old man moved a bit unsteady when he joined Ellis.

"I'm sorry if my stories disturbed you, my lord. Perhaps I should listen to Tess, but my time is near. I feel compelled to speak what I know to whomever Jor'el brings across my path." He tried to stifle another coughing fit, but unsuccessful. Ellis gently steered Cedric to a nearby bench. When the coughing subsided, Cedric earnestly regarded Ellis. "You are so young, you could not possibly know what Allon was like before the evil came."

"I know more than you think. What did you father do at court?"

"He took his shame to the grave for not helping to prevent Zared's overthrow."

"Your father was close enough to King Berk to influence him?" Ellis asked, but Cedric fought a coughing fit, so he shook his head. Ellis knew in his heart there was a reason for their meeting. With time pressing, he gentled encouraged Cedric. "Please, tell me who your father was."

Cedric took a deep breath to clear his throat. "Alvin, the King's chamberlain. He witnessed many meetings between Berk and Zared. Fear for his family kept him from acting. By the time he resolved to do something, it was too late. We barely escaped, and kept running, until we arrived here. The shame of his cowardice plagued him the rest of his life." Cedric voice grew thick. He coughed worse than before. When the fit passed, he was deathly pale.

"Will you not accept Niles' remedy to ease your discomfort?"

"I kept thinking he looked familiar, only it couldn't be," Cedric said more to himself. He continued at Ellis' sympathetic regard. "I knew a Niles once. Sir Niles of Pollux, the King's Champion, a brave knight. When he discovered I stole a meat tart from a royal banquet, he smiled and shooed me way. Father would have tanned my hide. I grieved to hear he died protecting the royal children. So he cannot be the same man."

Ellis wondered if he should tell Cedric the truth about Niles. Before he could, Cedric continued.

"If only Jor'el would send his chosen to take back the throne those days can return. Alas, I shall not live to see it." He tried to stifle several deep coughs. This time a trickle of blood appeared at the corner of his mouth. He sheepishly wiped it away. "I need to be in bed."

Ellis helped Cedric to his feet. He hastily said, "You have lived to see it! You were right about my nobility. Jor'el's chosen stands beside you."

Cedric studied Ellis. The strong tanned features made his blue eyes even more striking. The golden hair hung like a thick mane to his shoulders. "I thought you looked like Prince Akilles."

"My great-grandfather." Ellis showed Cedric the royal amulet with the initials. "APR, Akilles, Prince Royale."

Cedric touched the initials. He cried and laughed at the same time. "My Prince," he whispered before he collapsed.

Ellis carried Cedric to the house when he laid Cedric on the bed. Cedric grabbed him. The voice barely a whisper, Ellis knelt close to listen. "I promise," he said. Cedric closed his eyes for the last time.

Tess wept. "We were married eighty-five years."

Niles, Darius and Erin entered. Ellis indicated for Erin to take Tess.

Ellis spoke to Darius. "Tell Brody and Jasper that tomorrow they are to take Tess to their youngest grandson in the Meadowlands. It was his last request and I promised it would be done."

With teary compassion, Niles gazed at Cedric. "Listening to his stories, I realized I knew him as a lad. His father was Alvin."

"Ay. He told me he grieved about your *death*."

Niles screwed his eyes shut to maintain his composure. "How many more of us from that time are left scattered about suffering?"

"I told my identity, and showed him the amulet. He died comforted."

Muted by grief, Niles simply nodded.

After giving Cedric a proper burial, the group split; Brody and Jasper to take Tess to her grandson while the rest would continue to Clive. Tess insisted they divide the remaining supplies to use on their journeys.

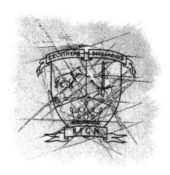

Chapter 12

THE VILLAGE OF CLIVE WAS A TWO-DAY TRAVEL FROM CEDRIC'S cottage. Just after sundown the second day, Ellis, Niles, Kemp, Darius, Edmund, Nando and Erin arrived at what was no more than a few buildings. The only source of light came from a small cottage. The top half of the split door stood opened.

Kemp knocked on the doorframe. "Anybody home?"

"Come in if you have a mind," replied a gruff female voice.

Kemp entered with Edmund and Nando. Candles and a fire in the hearth lit the cottage. A kettle hung over the fire. Stirring the contents of the kettle was an old woman, perhaps the same age as Tess.

"We're looking for Jora of Clive. Where can we find her?" asked Kemp.

The woman straightened. With an arrogant sneer, she accosted them. "Who wants to know?"

"It's a simple question, no harm meant."

"How can I be sure?"

"You have the word of a nobleman," said Kemp.

"I'd rather take the word of the King," she scoffed.

"You can take my word, Jora of Clive." Ellis stood in the threshold with the others at his back.

She cocked a sarcastic grin at Ellis. "It's about time."

"You knew it was she and still made me enter?" Kemp chided Ellis.

"Precaution. The village is deserted. If a single woman remains, it would more than likely be Jora. I had Niles and Darius search the outside," Ellis said to Kemp's chagrin.

"Smells good," said Erin.

"Help yourself. I don't stand on ceremony." Jora gave Erin the spoon. "Bowls are in the cupboard. Now, my lord, what kept you?" She crossed to a rocking chair, sat, and picked up some knitting.

"We supped with an old farmer named Cedric. He died," said Ellis.

"What about Tess?" Jora asked with concern.

"Two of my men are escorting her to her grandson in the Meadowlands."

Jora regarded Ellis with dark scrutinizing eyes. "You made me wait while you helped a dying farmer?" She scowled when he didn't reply, rather kept staring at her. "We'll see how far your mercy extends. If it's just to the poor or those more powerful."

"Ellis." Erin fixed him a bowl and drink. She placed it on the table.

"Will you join us?" Ellis spoke to Jora in a tone more suggesting a command than question.

"Of course. It's my food."

Once they sat to eat, Niles asked; "How goes it in the North Plains?"

"Our men were cowards," scoffed Jora. "We suffered greatly under Captain Tyree. Payment for the smarting Ranulf and his Highlanders gave him."

"We heard they imprisoned Lord Malcolm. Without their overlord, the people may have been acting wisely," said Darius.

Jora learned forward, malice in her eyes. "He's not imprisoned, rather in his sick bed being nursed back to health. They use him as a warning to the people about non-compliance."

Darius grew offended by her attitude. "You dislike your lord?"

"No. It is weakness and cowardice I dislike."

"Are you calling Malcolm a coward?" asked Kemp.

"Ay! He and anyone else who kowtows to Marcellus and Latham."

Kemp grew red-faced. Ellis stopped a reply with a grip upon Kemp's arm. "Everyone is entitled to his or her opinion," said Ellis.

Jora challenged Ellis. "What if I spoke villainy against you, my lord?"

Darius and Kemp stiffened in their seats. Nando and Edmund exchanged glances of concern. Erin bit her lip. Niles watched Ellis. For being continually insulted, Ellis kept his temper.

"If I tolerate you speaking treason against the present king, why should I take exception to myself?" Ellis slyly grinned. "Besides, to do so would oppose the reason you're here, to help me."

"*If* I choose to help you, it is a decision based upon your character, not any title you claim to hold, *my lord*."

"Then I shall not take offense to either your coarse words or base behavior."

Jora flushed at Ellis' retort, which made the others laugh. She then smiled with approval. "You give as good as you get, my lord."

"I should hope better."

"So do I," she said in all seriousness. "Tomorrow I will take you to Lord Malcolm. Now, eat. Then get what sleep you can."

By late afternoon the following day, Jora brought them to Hagley, a walled town of about ten thousand people. They entered by way of a small abandoned gate in a rundown part of town. In the largest house on the hill overlooking the city, lived Lord Malcolm with his mother, Lady Matrill. They met Matrill in the main drawing room.

A spry woman of forty-two with chestnut hair and matching eyes, Matrill's smile brightened up a room. She approached Ellis before introductions were made. "My lord."

"How does everyone else know you but we were ignorant?" chided Kemp.

"Jora is a prophetess. She told us of his lordship's coming. You may find others are not so enlightened." Matrill spoke so sweetly that Kemp bowed with apology.

"By your reception, I take it support is forthcoming," said Ellis.

Fretful, Matrill tugged on her fingers. "The matter is complicated, my lord. Malcolm desperately wishes to speak with you, if you will grant him an audience."

Ellis took hold of her hands in a gesture of support. "Madam, I have no power to grant or forbid anyone. If Lord Malcolm wishes to speak to me, it is I who am obliged."

"Then, come. There isn't much time."

"There will be time enough," said Jora confidently.

Matrill took Ellis' arm to escort him. "Please, only his lordship, Sir Niles, and Jora. The rest of you wait here." She led them upstairs.

"Is Malcolm so ill that you fear for him?" asked Ellis.

"It is not the illness I fear, but other forces," she said with heavy discretion.

"What forces?"

She paused at a bedroom door. "You will know soon enough."

Upon the cushions of a four-poster bed, lay Malcolm. For all his twenty-two years, he looked much older, the illness taking its toll. His mother made certain he was presentable with his auburn hair pampered and mustache trimmed. The gray-blue eyes told of weariness, while his complexion pale. He tried to raise himself on the cushions.

"My lord!"

Ellis approached the bed. "Easy. Do not trouble yourself."

With urgency, Malcolm snatched Ellis' hand. "I owe you an apology. I failed to hold the North Plains for you. They allow my mother and I to live here, but that is all. My authority is as weak as my body. You must not stay too long or they will find out and hunt you!"

"Easy, my son," Matrill cautioned. Her gaze flashed to Ellis. "You see, my lord, he is in great fear for your safety. We wished for Jora to speak with you in secret rather than bring you here, but she insisted meeting in person was for the best."

Ellis tossed a reproving look to Jora before he spoke to Malcolm. "Now that I am here, tell me what it is you wanted Jora to relay."

"I am not the coward others have branded me only because of how you see me now!" Malcolm rose on the cushions. He spoke with as much fierce determination as he condition allowed. "I fought at Ravendale when word came of a Prince from the House of Tristan. For my stance, Marcellus threw me in prison." His arms grew weak and he fell back. "Alas, my body failed my spirit! In my weakness, I lost the only thing I could offer you, the fealty of my province."

Touched by devotion of the ailing young man, Ellis said, "You lost a possession, not your heart and courage. I have no home, no castle or throne. I wander Allon in search of a prize I'm still not certain I can obtain. What you offer me is all I can offer you, my courage and pledge to do what is needed to free Allon from Marcellus and Latham. More importantly, to end the Dark Way."

"My lord!" said Malcolm, nearly in tears.

"Rest. You did all you could. I can neither ask nor expect any more."

"Listen to him, my son, and be at ease."

"I will. Now, my lord, you must leave. Remaining any longer may place your life in jeopardy. Jor'el be with you."

"May he grant you a complete recovery." Ellis left with Matrill, Jora, and Niles.

"Who are *they* you refer to in fearing for Ellis?" Niles asked Matrill.

"Lord Harkin, cousin of Marcellus. He brought Malcolm back to be used as a pawn! To parade his weakened body before the people." Matrill's voice cracked with anger. "He claimed a royal edict gave him command of the province. Since then he rules with an iron fist!"

In passing the drawing room, Matrill summoned the others to lead them to the front door. She took Ellis' hand in both of hers. "Please, be careful, my lord. Soldiers are everywhere."

"We shall."

They just rounded the corner from the house when—

"There! After them!" A dozen soldiers appeared a few blocks away

"Run!" shouted Jora.

At breakneck speed, Jora lead them through the streets to same abandoned gate where they entered.

"You run fast for an old woman," said Edmund.

"You run well for a young man. Now, open the gate!"

Hearing pursuit, Niles, Darius, Kemp and Ellis drew their swords to make defense.

"Hurry!" Erin urged Edmund and Nando at the gate.

The arrival of soldiers forced Edmund and Nando to abandon the opened gate to join the foray. The odds were not good. For having battle experience, Kemp found himself overpowered and captured.

"Kemp!" Darius shouted. Soldiers prevented him from going to Kemp's aid.

Niles, Ellis and Edmund skillfully handled the soldiers the fought. Although not a trained knight or squire, Nando did well against another two. He employed any means he could. At one point he lost track of one of the soldiers. Hearing Erin's outcry, he quickly wounded his opponent with a savage slash of his sword. The soldier manhandling Erin never knew what hit him since Nando came from behind.

"Look out!" warned Erin.

Nando turned in time to deflect a lunge at his body. The blade nicked his upper left arm. He landed a swift kick in the soldier's midsection. He then struck him with the hilt of the sword in the back of the head. The solider fell unconscious. Nando ushered the women through the gate where they waited for the others. One by one, each made their way outside. Niles came last. Edmund helped Nando bar the gate closed.

"What of Master Kemp?" asked Nando.

"Captured," Darius growled through set teeth.

"No!" cried Erin.

"There is nothing I can do," he argued to her upset.

Arrows whizzed over their heads. They raced to the woods. Jora reached the trees first.

"Aren't you winded yet?" asked Edmund.

"A bit," she admitted. "Return to Clive. I'll follow."

"You're not going to do anything foolish?"

Jora flashed a wry smile. "I'm an old woman. I have a right to act foolish."

"Not alone," insisted Edmund.

"Your bravery is commendable, though unnecessary. See to Ellis."

Edmund left Jora when Ellis called to him.

By the time they reached Jora's cottage, all were exhausted. Being the last to enter, Nando locked the door.

"No signs of pursuit," he said.

Niles peered out the window. "She bought us time."

"At the expense of her life?" rebuffed Edmund.

Ellis accepted a drink from Darius. "We don't know that."

Distraught, Erin sat at the table. "We know Kemp was captured!"

"I tried to help him." Darius offered her a drink, which she refused.

"You did what you could. We all did. Including Jora," Ellis said to Darius then Edmund.

"Do you think we'll be safe here?" Nando asked Ellis.

"At least until nightfall, then we leave."

Fearful, Erin sat upright. "We're leaving without Kemp?"

Her pleading eyes made Ellis mute. At his discomposure, Niles replied in firm yet even tone. "We have to. It could be a trap for Ellis. I don't think you want that."

"No." She lowered her head with a sob.

Ellis sat to hold her as she wept. "I'm sorry that we have no choice."

Niles watched Ellis speak soothing words. He knew Erin's heart toward Ellis, but what of Ellis for Erin? Niles argued with himself that such sympathy was natural and platonic since they once believed to be kin. What if it wasn't? What of Shannan? Such a breach in affection could place her, and Allon, in jeopardy. Surely Ellis wouldn't do that? *Alas, he's young, naïve and inexperienced.* Niles pushed the vexing thoughts from his mind as he determined to speak with Ellis at the first opportunity.

~~~

After dark, they left Clive heading south-by-southwest. Barely an hour into their trek, a figure bounded out of the trees. The men readied their weapons. Ellis shielded Erin. Darius stood at his shoulder.

"It's me!" The figure skidded to a halt with raised hands in surrender.

"Kemp." Erin ran to meet him. She flung her arms about his neck.

"Are you all right?" asked Darius.

"Ay. No thanks to any of you!" Kemp sneered at Ellis.

"What did you expect us to do? Storm Hagley? It could have been a trap for Ellis," rebuffed Niles.

Kemp got in Niles' face. "You'll risk everything for Ellis, but I'm expendable?"

"We are all expendable! Did you not understand that when you agreed to come?"

Ellis fought exhausted exasperation. "I must gather my Companions! If I could spare any and all of you I would, but I can't! I need you to be willing to make the same sacrifice I must."

"What sacrifice?" demanded Kemp.

Ellis stared at Kemp in an attempt to see beyond the anger. He only met stubbornness in the fix jowls and stiff back. Such obstinacy made Ellis lash out. "I have denied myself every comfort even the poorest people enjoy. Forfeited all safety to my person, and been forced to abandon the one I hold dearest to my heart, all for Allon!"

Kemp's brows slightly rippled at the passionate response. "That's your choice. You do not have the right to ask it of others."

Darius jerked Kemp about to face him. "Ellis is heir to the throne! He doesn't have to ask! It is our duty to support him. We have nothing to lose, but all to gain if this succeeds. I'm disappointed in you."

Kemp's obstinate glare shifted between Darius and Ellis. "Stay, if you want," he said to Darius then looked at Ellis to add, "Erin and I are returning home."

Thunderstruck, she gasped, "What?"

"You want to risk your life when he admits being in love with someone else?" Kemp spoke with such acidity that her hurt became immediately seen.

Ellis curiously regarded brother and sister.

Seeing his interest, Erin scolded Kemp. "It's not about feelings. Darius is right about duty!"

Sounds from nearby alerted Edmund. "Hush!" he commanded. He placed himself on guard. Nando and Niles took up position on the flank.

"Great! You led them to us," Darius accused Kemp.

"I—"

Darius clamped his hand over Kemp's mouth.

Jora appeared. She accosted Kemp. "I see you found them."

Kemp shoved Darius' hand away. "I was about to tell them it was you," he chided to Jora.

"You told them a few other things also. If I could hear you down the road, so can soldiers. We must keep moving. This way."

Without further words, most followed Jora. Kemp delayed Erin. "We leave at the first opportunity."

"I'm not leaving."

"You will do as I say. I am your brother, and the one you answer to, not him."

The rebuke stymied her. Raw emotions made her lower lip quiver.

He softened his tone. "Dear sister, this is for your protection. I don't want to see you hurt again." He gently wiped away a single tear from her cheek and kissed her forehead. "Let's go before they get too far ahead. We'll reach safety before leaving."

Prior to dawn, Jora lead them to a cove hidden on the South Plains border. She instructed them to eat and rest for several hours. Thick tension hung over the group, as Kemp and Erin kept to themselves.

Ellis wanted to encourage Erin but he didn't want to deal with Kemp. He noticed something different about Kemp when he and Niles arrived at Dunlap. He recalled the chilling sensation when Kemp past him after leaving Clifton castle. Despite all they suffered, Kemp still acted surprisingly selfish. Or maybe self-preservation? Whatever the reason, it drove a wedge between him and the others. His attitude drew Erin along with him. Alas, nothing would be resolved that night, thus Ellis settled down for sleep.

Sometime later, Ellis felt a hand wake him. Jora, only she didn't appear old. The first gray light of dawn rose behind her. Placing a finger to her lips, she motioned Ellis to follow her. They paused in a small clearing that overlooked a road.

"That road will take you to Burleigh, home of Sir Gareth. Beg for shelter as pilgrims."

"I knew you were a Guardian."

She smiled. "I am Mona. Jora the Prophetess is my identity when dealing with mortals. I try not to be obvious in my disguise. With you, it became necessary."

"So what part of the Contest are you to test me with?"

"That has already been done. A good king must not only be strong in arms, and act wisely with his enemies; he also needs to show mercy to those less fortunate, and those to whom fate has not been kind. Cedric was the less fortunate, while Malcolm the latter regarding fate."

Ellis brows arched with surprise. "This was staged for my benefit?"

"Oh, no! You heard for yourself how greatly Malcolm suffered on your behalf."

He accepted the explanation. "I told Cedric who I was before he died."

Mona's expression grew sympathetic. "Cedric was a good, faithful man. As reward, you have gained your helmet." It materialized in her hands. The helmet matched the gold armor, being crafted to resemble the head of an eagle topped with golden and purple plumes.

Ellis examined it. "It's as light as the armor."

"And just as strong." Mona took it back. "Give them two more hours of sleep then be on your way until nightfall. It's a long journey to Burleigh." Her expression grew thoughtful in regards of Kemp. "As for the man Kemp, do not seek to restrain him or attempt further reasoning. There is something amiss. I sensed it when I freed him from Lord Harkin's soldiers."

"Kemp has always been ill-tempered and contrary."

"No, there is more, something deep in his spirit. Unfortunately, my abilities are not so attuned to mortal emotions." Mona returned her attention to Ellis. "Jor'el is with you, Son of Tristan." She disappeared into the forest.

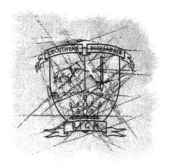

Chapter 13

ALTHOUGH DAGAR COULDN'T LEAVE THE NETHER CAVE FOR the outside world, those he chose to know his location freely came and went. No restrictions were placed upon their movements. However, it required great energy to bridge the dimensional gap. Witter appeared slightly drained upon arrival to give his report.

As Dagar sat listening about Ellis' battle with the unicorn, visions of past triumphs and defeats played across his mind. At the Great Battle, he wounded Kell, though not before Kell unknowingly wounded him. Dagar remained on his feet long enough to install his son Ram as king. He almost ceased to exist during the coronation. Tor brought him to the Nether Cave just in time. For numerous reasons, Kell became a focal point of his hate. The memories invoked by the report infuriated Dagar.

"Enough!" Dagar snapped. He pushed himself out of the chair. "He must have had Guardian help. A mortal could not defeat your unicorn."

"I sensed no such presence. Also, this *mortal* is Jor'el's chosen."

"Once my time has come, he will be no match for my full strength."

"Kell will—" Witter gargled in painful surprise when the words stuck in his throat.

Dagar's eyes narrowed as his lips snarled. "Haven't I warned you about mentioning that name in my presence?"

"Ay—!" gasped Witter with difficulty.

Dagar relaxed, which released his hold on Witter. "What about the rest of the plan?"

"It has been implemented," Witter replied in a strained voice of recovery.

The pitiful howl of a female could be heard in the tunnel leading to the reconditioning chamber.

"Come, I want to see how Griswold is doing," said Dagar.

Witter cautiously followed Dagar through a narrow passage. One hundred feet in diameter, the reconditioning chamber contained various implements of *instruction*. Cages surrounded a central floor. Stone stairways with narrow walkways circumscribed the chamber on various levels. Guardians of different stations and genders occupied the cages and cells. Many showed signs of suffering.

In the torture portion of the chamber, stood a formidable Guardian. He had a couple of inches on Dagar's height of seven and a half feet. He wore only a leather loincloth and boots, exposing massive arms and chest. He was darker in feature than most of his kind with yellow eyes. When he snarled, the scar on his left cheek became more pronounced. At his feet lay a heap of chains.

Dagar's attention went to the chains. "Griswold?"

"She gave me no alternative, my lord. She refused to yield."

Without looking up or giving warning, Dagar made his displeasure clear by a wave of his hand. Griswold gasped in surprise. He fell to his knees in distress. A gash appeared on his right cheek.

"You disappoint me, Griswold. I wanted her alive. Let that be your last lesson in disappointing me. Unless you want to end up like Rune!" Dagar motioned to a nearby cage.

Inside, sat a wretched male Guardian. One leg was gone below the knee, and his left hand missing. His entire body battered with a bloody bandage over his left eye.

Witter winced upon sight of Rune. He covered his discomfort to ask; "Why not kill him?"

Dagar heaved a disinterested shrug. "Too easy. For as long as I desire, he shall live to witness with his one remaining eye the wonders his instruments cause."

Rune tried to speak but only managed a pitiful wheeze through his nose.

Dagar saw Witter's confusion at the attempt to communicate. "I ripped out his vocal chords. Punishment for arranging that escape attempt." He sent a look of warning to Griswold before he left the area.

"He'll kill us all if he gets the chance. You included, Witter!" called a male from another nearby cage.

Piqued, Witter sneered at a stout Guardian with silver hair, beard, dirty ruddy features and bright sea-green eyes. His clothes were soiled, though he showed no signs of abuse. "Gulliver. How have you escaped unscathed?"

Gulliver's shrug made his spurean chains rattle. He ignored the pain such movement caused. "He hasn't gotten around to me yet." He leaned forward; his eyes narrow and voice a harsh whisper. "I've seen enough to know what's in store. Your giving in only saved you temporarily. He keeps poor Rune alive just for *you*."

"Witter!" bellowed Dagar from the other chamber.

"Your master calls, whelp."

"I hope I'm around to see you reconditioned!" Witter marched from the chamber to rejoin Dagar.

The Dark Lord stood before the basin. He impatiently called, "Latham. Latham! Why is he never around when I need him?" He complained to Witter.

Latham's image finally appeared in the mist. "I'm here, my lord."

"What is the status regarding the Pretender?"

"Marcellus summoned Tyree to make a report. I'll know more then."

Dagar scratched at his beard. "Witter will include his findings." He waved both hands. The steam disappeared to sever the communications.

Latham entered the King's private study to find Marcellus at the desk. Behind the King waited his brother Hugh, the Duke of Allon. Though five years younger than Marcellus, Hugh had a similar build. His hair and mustache were light brown with a fair complexion and hazel eyes. In his rich blue suit, he cut a dashing figure.

Also present was General Iain, Commander of the Army. He was Marcellus' age with dark red hair and whiskers. A strong athletic figure dressed in a suit of crimson, black and gold. In height, he stood a few inches taller than Hugh and Marcellus.

Tyree and Witter stood in front of the desk at attention. Latham cast a cursory glance at them before he addressed Marcellus. "You wish to see me, Majesty?"

Marcellus waved at the men. "Tyree and Witter have returned."

Side-by-side, Tyree and Witter were an impressive sight. Witter stood head and shoulders taller than Tyree, which was quite intimidating since Tyree was six and a half feet tall. Both wore black; both were dark, rugged and swarthy in appearance. Yet, Witter's commanding countenance demanded attention.

"If I didn't know better, I'd wager they were related," said Marcellus.

Tyree's glance at Witter made no attempt to hide his disdain. Witter met the glare with equal scorn.

Marcellus hid a smile of pleasure at the rivalry. "What news, Witter? Have you brought me his head?"

"No, Sire. I did encounter him on the border of the Southern and Northern Forest."

"You could not apprehend him?"

For a brief moment Witter locked eyes with Marcellus. Witter fought a smile when the King flinched. "He was not alone. There were too many for me to handle. Seven is my limit."

"Only seven?" said Tyree with a grunt of scorn.

"Ay." Witter's narrow gaze made Tyree wince.

Marcellus observed the palpable tension. "Why stop your pursuit?"

"Grand Master Latham summoned me to make report." Witter's answer made Latham sneer.

"First the Southern Forest then the Northern Forest. Why?" Iain asked.

"According to Prophecy he must gather his Companions from the Council of Twelve," said Latham.

Marcellus sarcastically chuckled. "He won't get far. Phineas is dead, Fergus rots in my dungeon, Malcolm is dying of weak lungs, and three others are in hiding. Which brings me to Captain Tyree's assignment."

"Sire, I'm pleased to report, all Fortresses are abandoned. Some razed, others emptied as they fled before us."

"What about the priests and Archimedes?" asked Hugh. A tone of concern crept into his voice.

"We have imprisoned three hundred priests, while cutting down another hundred when they offered resistance. Unfortunately, there has been no sign of Archimedes."

Marcellus pursed his lips. After a moment's thought, he spoke to Witter. "Return to where you last saw the Pretender. Send word if he moves, but *do not* return until you have his head!" he said with dreaded emphasis.

"I hear and obey, Majesty." Witter bowed and departed.

"I do not trust his boast, Sire," said Tyree.

"Neither do I. That is why you will take a platoon of my best men and follow him. At first opportunity, capture the Pretender and rid me of this Witter."

Tyree's lips twisted into a warped smile. He saluted the King.

"That is unwise, Majesty," said Latham after Tyree's departure.

Marcellus' stern features showed he was in no mood for objections. "I shall decide what is wise or not. He may have size and strength, but is short on brains. Returning empty-handed shows his flaw. Spare me your lectures! I have other duties," he snapped when Latham begin to object.

"More important than securing your throne?" brazened Latham. His hand encircled the talisman.

"You are too impertinent to question the King!" Hugh rebuffed.

Marcellus rose to seize Latham. This made Latham loose his grip on the talisman. "You come at him by way of Prophecy, with some of your Dark Way thrown in for good measure. I come at the problem like a warrior. There are numerous ways to thwart one's enemy. Remember that on your way out!" He shoved Latham backwards.

Latham regained his balance to leave without bowing. Upon entering his chamber, he noticed steam over the basin. A sigh of fatigue escaped when Dagar appeared. The Dark Lord noticed his weary vexation.

"You look tired, Latham."

"Marcellus' resistance is considerable. After Witter gave his report and left, Marcellus ordered Tyree to follow him. Since me intervention to stop it did not work, I will send word to Witter." He shook his head with another weary sigh. "However, I fear if I press Marcellus further, others will grow suspicious. His brother questioned me."

Dagar flashed a distracted smile. "Perhaps, the duke needs another reminder of whom he is dealing with. He has obviously forgotten about his sister."

Latham displayed some hesitation in speaking. "My lord, I do not question you, however, if something were to happen to Hugh, Marcellus' resistance could double. He cares very much for his brother."

"I didn't mean Hugh. Someone as close to Marcellus' heart as he."

Latham tried to hide a sinister smile at the suggestion. "Lida."

"Ay. She would have been queen, if I allowed. Now she must suffer. Don't have her join Vera. I want the point driven home."

"I understand, my lord."

"Now drink your strengthening tonic." Dagar snapped his fingers. A chalice appeared to hover in the air beside Latham. "Rest to allow the tonic to work before confronting Marcellus again."

For the remainder of the day, Hugh and Iain remained with Marcellus to tend to business. An array of papers lay scattered upon the desk. Tankards along with plates of half-eaten food covered the side table. The room's lamps grew brighter as twilight had fallen.

Two road-dusty noblemen entered the King's study. The younger man a ruddy complexion, auburn hair and brown eyes similar to his mother Tilda. The second nobleman was middle age, darker, and stout.

"Reid. Firth," greeted Marcellus. "What news?"

"I'm afraid you are correct, Sire. Grand Master Latham is in communication with Witter. He is ill disposed about your instructions to Captain Tyree," said Reid.

Marcellus snarled at the news. "Does he interfere with Tyree?"

"Not as far as we can tell, Sire," said Firth.

Marcellus swore. He tossed a quill pen onto the desk where he sat. "One day he will go too far!"

"Sire, why do you tolerate Latham?" asked Reid.

"His Majesty tolerates me because he knows I desire the best for him and Allon," said Latham. He moved silently into the room. A new aura of confidence and vitality seemed to radiate from his features. Everything about him seemed brighter. The color of his suit, even the talisman shone as if newly polished. He purposefully directed a steady, penetrating glance at Marcellus. "Is that not so, Sire?"

Marcellus replied in a weaker tone than he had spoke to Reid a moment earlier. "Ay, though I sometimes disagree with your methods."

The others noticed the subtle mood change without comment.

"Our methods may differ, Sire, but the desire is the same."

Hugh regarded the situation with a careful eye. "Really?"

"Ay, Your Grace." Latham directed his attention to Hugh.

The duke tried to withstand the commanding and condemning stare. He sheepishly looked away.

"Any more questions, gentlemen?" Latham gaze passed to each man.

At Hugh's thwarting, none of the others dared to speak.

Latham smiled with wicked triumph. "You gentlemen can leave now. His Majesty and I have matters to discuss." He gave Hugh a not to subtle prompting nod.

Hugh marched out. The others followed.

Once in the hall, Iain chided; "What manner of man is he?"

"He is evil. I could not tolerate his eyes," said Hugh in voice of hushed distress.

"Does he pose a threat to the King?" asked Reid.

Hugh shook his head with uncertainty. "I don't know. My brother speaks in two minds. One moment he is against Latham, the next defending him. Just like he did now."

"The longer Latham is here, the more his influence grows, as you just witnessed" chided Iain to Reid and Firth.

"Perhaps his association should be ended," said Reid.

"No!" Hugh seized Reid to draw him across the hall from the study. "When our sister tried, she suddenly took ill. Latham suggested she retire to the Delta to take the waters for her health. Marcellus agreed. She has been there these past twelve years, and is no better than the day she arrived. Since then, I've been more subtle in my approach so not to incite Latham."

"What gives him such sway that the King will not listen to his brother?" asked Firth.

"The Dark Way," Hugh replied in harsh whisper.

Reid appeared puzzled while Firth grim.

"Make no mistake, Latham will return the Dark Way to Allon once the *Pretender* is dealt with," Iain warned Reid.

"That will be a sorry day for Allon," said Reid.

Hugh deeply frowned. "If it wasn't treason, I'd agree. However, I'm still uncertain who poses the worse danger - Latham, or the Prince of Tristan."

"Should we return to our task, Your Grace?" asked Firth.

"No, it's too dangerous now that Latham knows. Remain here until Iain and I can find a weakness in Latham's plans."

"As you command, Your Grace." Reid and Firth bowed and left.

"What weakness? He stared you down," complained Iain.

"Ay, which confirms my belief that his influence ebbs and flows according to his own energy. The other day he acted like a whipped puppy when Marcellus gave him a tongue-lashing. Today he appeared renew, so that when he exerts himself Marcellus gives in and I yield. Don't you see? His limited powers must be renewed."

"Most certainly by the Dark Way."

"Of course. If we can learn *how* perhaps we can gain the advantage to break the cycle."

Iain snickered. "And you warned Reid of dangerous talk."

"Reid is a boy. This is my brother and the future of my family! Of our family," he reminded Iain in low urgent voice. "We must do it for Lida, for Vera and the children."

Iain grabbed the hilt of his sword. "You can depend on my help to protect my sister and the children." A small friendly smile appeared. "Speaking of, Lida is probably worried. Retire."

"What of you?"

Iain wryly smiled. "After a bit more ferreting out, something might be discovered. Now, go. We'll speak more in the morning."

⁓⸂⸂⸃⸃⁓

In the darkest part of the night, a great cry of anguish arose from the part of the castle where Hugh lived with his family. An alarm roused everyone.

In a dressing gown, Marcellus rushed to Hugh's apartments. A hastily dressed and armed Iain accompanied Marcellus. The crowd outside the duke's apartment, parted to let them enter. Hugh sat on the end of the bed sobbing.

"Hugh? What is it?" asked Marcellus with great concern.

"See for yourself!" Hugh motioned to the bed.

Marcellus' breath caught in his throat. Lida lay ashen and shriveled in age. Large sores covered her face. Vacant eyes stared up at the ceiling. All signs of death.

Iain reacted with vocal horror. The sight made the sword slip from his hand. "Lida."

Marcellus drew back with unsteady steps. "How?"

Hugh bolted up. "What? Can't you see what you've done?"

Marcellus' eyes grew wide in horrible surprise. "You're saying I'm responsible for this? I would never harm Lida. I wanted her as my wife."

Hugh drew close to hiss; "You brought him to us! First Vera and now Lida. When will it end, Marcellus? Will we all die like this?"

"No! It will end tonight." Marcellus raced from the room. He burst into Latham's chamber. Furious, he demanded, "What have you done?"

Latham casually sat in a chair beside the hearth, a glowing talisman in his hand. His cold expression matched his tone. "I have done nothing. Your resistance is to blame."

"Me? How dare you!" Enraged, Marcellus approached Latham.

Latham sharply raised his hand. Marcellus stopped in mid-stride, as if frozen against his will. A whirlwind of emotions played across Marcellus face. Latham rose. An aura surrounded him while the talisman glowed brighter. His eyes flashed like fire at Marcellus.

"Unlike your grandfather and father, you have no appreciation of the Dark Way. Until you learn to submit, those about you will suffer. Tonight it was Lida, tomorrow your brother, or one of your nephews or nieces. The choice is yours."

Marcellus stared at Latham in fearful comprehension. "Vera was right. You are evil."

Latham suppressed a taunting smile. "Too late now. You can't help either her or Lida. *But* you can help the rest of your family and Allon." He held up the talisman in front of Marcellus' face. His eyes filled with commanding malice. "What is your choice, *Sire?*"

Marcellus' mental anguish of emotional battle was clearly visible. His warring gaze shifted between the glowing talisman and Latham's unrelenting glare. Finally, with a great wail of sorrow, he collapsed to his knees. "I yield! Please, don't hurt anyone else! Not Hugh. Not the children." He sobbed.

"You have acted wisely, *Your Majesty.*" Latham then spoke with disdain. "Pull yourself together, man!" He jerked Marcellus to his feet. "Go. There is much to do to rid Allon of this Pretender."

Marcellus staggered as he left the apartment.

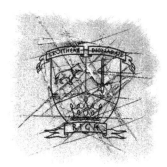

Chapter 14

AT THE CLIFF CAVE, SHANNAN BOLTED UP IN BED. HER BREATHING labored while her body trembled. In her mind she screamed. Vidar and Wren's swift appearance told her she had cried out loud. To their expressions of concern she said, "Ellis is hurt!"

"Are you sure?" asked Vidar.

"I saw it."

"It could be a future event. Kell is nearby. He wouldn't let anything happen," he tried to reassure her.

Shannan took several breaths to calm down. "It wasn't life threatening." Her angst returned. "He wasn't alone." Wren stopped her from rising off the bed. "I need to do something," she insisted so Wren released her.

Shannan moved to the front of the cave. "Kato!" No response. She asked Wren, "Have you not brought Kato and Torin here yet?"

"Try calling again."

Vidar noticed Wren mouth the name *Kato* when Shannan called for the great bird a second time. Wren also mouthed *Torin*. The eagle and wolf appeared at the threshold. This brought a wry smile to Vidar, who leaned closer to Wren.

"You forgot to bring them," he whispered to her chagrin.

Ignorant of the exchange, Shannan greeted the animals. She took the small pouch from her belt to tie around Kato's neck. "Take this to Ellis." Kato acknowledged.

"Why are you doing that?" asked Wren.

Shannan watched Kato fly off. "To remind him of his pledge."

"Something in your dream made you fearful he would forget," said Vidar. Her eyes told him the answer. He held her shoulder. "You are linked together in prophecy. Trust in that."

"As you need to let go of the past and trust in yourself again," Shannan spoke so only Vidar could hear.

Her statement amazed him while her steady gaze struck him mute.

Wren tried to be circumspect in her observation. She found it hard to ignore Vidar's bewildered expression. She chose to change the subject. "I think breakfast is in order. Any tubers left?"

"I believe so," he slightly stuttered; slow to shift his focus. "Though I believe seagull eggs would be better. I'll fetch some." He flashed a self-conscience smile at Shannan as he left the cave.

Wren questioned Shannan, "What did you say to him?"

"Nothing but the truth of how he needs to let go of the past."

Pricked, Wren looked to the cave entrance. "I hope he listens to you." Her voiced concern barely rose above a whisper.

"Is he more than a friend? A brother, perhaps?"

"Oh, no," said Wren with a soft smile. "Vidar became my mentor shortly after I was created over eighteen hundred year ago. We served together for centuries. We became very close friends. That's normally the case with mentors and protégés."

"Then he was captured."

"Ay, during the Great Battle." Wren again stared out the cave. "I mourned his loss for more than a century before I learned he survived. Imprisoned like so many others." Her brows furrowed with angry dismay. "He's different now. I scorn Dagar for that!"

Shannan touched Wren's arm. With a reassuring smile, she said, "Together, we will help him recover."

Wren's green eyes brightened in her regard of Shannan. "Your confident faith shows wisdom well beyond your years. In all my centuries of existence, I've not met a mortal, who with a word or single glance can dumbfound a Guardian like you did to Vidar."

Shannan shied, uncomfortable. "In truth, I have not met anyone outside of Dorgirith. Mortal or Guardian." She wrapped her arms like wanting to rub away a chill. "It's a bit frightening actually."

Wren wryly smiled. "I didn't think we frightened you."

"No. I meant leaving Dorgirith. With you, Kell, Vidar and other Guardians I feel almost invincible."

"You are very important to us. We will do anything to protect you."

Shannan's eyes grew misty in regard of Wren. "I don't want anyone harmed because of me."

"In our struggle with the Dark Way, that can hardly be helped."

Vidar returned and announced, "Four eggs. And green onions. Not a great haul, but will serve for breakfast. I'll scramble the eggs so we can each have some." He didn't notice any upset.

Shannan gathered her emotions. "With fried tubers on the side."

He nodded in agreement. "I noticed Kato did a few overhead circles before he headed inland, due west."

"Probably awaiting direction before leaving," said Wren. "Jor'el does lead animals also." She winked at Shannan.

"Which way is the Southern Forest?" asked Shannan, as she thinly sliced the tubers for frying.

"Northwest." Vidar chopped the green onions.

Wren noticed Shannan's puzzlement. "Due west means Ellis is on the move. Remember, he is to gather his companions. With Jor'el's guidance, Kato will find him."

Silence fell. Shannan concentrated on preparing the tubers. She had much to consider thus gave one word answers to Vidar's questions. He wanted to know how she liked her eggs, soft or hard scrambled. If the tubers were crisp enough. Even while eating, she barely conversed. Neither Guardian remarked on her change in attitude.

"I'm going to check the perimeter," said Wren.

"When you get back, I need to scrounge up something for dinner," Vidar told Wren.

"Better yet, I'll trap it."

"Vidar can go too." Shannan took the stone plates from the table to the kitchen area.

"You shouldn't be left alone," countered Wren.

"How long will it take you to check the perimeter?" asked Shannan.

"Fifteen minutes, at most."

"And to trap game for dinner?" Shannan inquired of Vidar.

"The same time frame."

"If you leave together, it's only fifteen minutes instead of thirty when going separately. In that short a time, I'll be fine. Torin is with me."

The wolf lifted its head from where it laid to yip an affirmation.

"Stay inside the cave," urged Vidar.

"I'll clean the dishes." Shannan scrapped the leftovers onto the cavern floor for Torin to eat. She proceeded to wash the dishes.

Despite their reassurance, and dispatch of Kato, a sense of uneasiness about Ellis gnawed at Shannan. She didn't recognize the woman in her dream. Then again, she didn't know anyone beside her father, grandfather and Ellis. All of them had been raised in the outside world. They experienced aspects of life she hadn't. Perhaps that fact alone caused her uncertainty. Ellis made a pledge, and gave her no reason to doubt his word. She argued with herself how dreams were not necessarily reality. Perhaps the woman was someone from Ellis' past, or what Vidar said about a future event. No amount of logic eased her angst.

She could almost hear Kell's voice telling her to trust Jor'el and not worry. He spoke with certainty, no glibness or hesitation. Just like with Ellis, the strong attachment she felt for the Guardians surprised her. Another aspect of her prophetic title became real. With them she felt confident, determined thus self-assertive. Kell was strong and sure-minded, Armus loyal and unwavering in support. Wren exhibited tenacity that bordered on brashness. Priscilla's flightiness could be amusing, though she did perform her duty. Vidar ... he was the most perplexing of the Guardians.

Wren mentioned how his character had changed since capture. Yet, Shannan sensed something more. A hidden secret that deeply scarred him. Whatever his secret, she felt that bolstering his confidence could act as counter. She truly meant what she said about him finding a way to trust in himself again.

Close sounding birdcalls startled her. She listened. "Kato?"

She moved from the kitchen area. The moment she reached the entrance, Torin's hackles raised. He growled a bark of alarm. Four ravens flew into the cave. Shannan ducked to keep from being attacked.

In the small confines of the hollow cave, the ravens dove at them. She seized her bow to swing at the birds. Torin snapped his jaws. He caught one raven by the leg. The others came to its rescue.

The attacking birds drove Torin yelping from the hollow. Shannan too became driven outside. She tripped and tumbled down a small incline to the beach. She lost her bow in the fall. The ravens followed them.

Torin leapt to snatch a raven before it attacked Shannan. Held in his powerful jaws, Torin shook his head to render the raven immobile. He threw the bird against the rocks. Being severely injured it couldn't escape when Torin picked it up a second time. Again, he shook his head before throwing it against the rocks. This time, the raven didn't move. Torin pawed it to make certain it was dead.

Shannan dodged the ravens coming at her head. A passing talon cut her right cheek. She fell to her knees to avoid them. She reached for a piece of driftwood. Hearing a caw, she swung the driftwood. She hit the raven square in the head, killing it.

Twang! Twang! Two shots took down the other ravens. Vidar and Wren arrived in a rush.

"What happened? Are you all right?" Wren asked Shannan.

"They flew into the cave, attacked us and drove us out," she said in winded reply.

"Your cheek." Vidar examined Shannan's face.

Priscilla arrived. Wren immediately accosted her. "I thought you kept the winds contrary so no one could find her!"

"I have. I didn't sense the ravens until a moment ago."

"Are there any more nearby?"

Priscilla shook her head. "Not that I have seen or sensed."

"Let's get you back inside and tend to your wound." Vidar escorted Shannan into the hollow cave.

"Return to your station and keep a sharp weather eye. I'm going to dispose of them," Wren instructed Priscilla.

Priscilla grabbed Wren's arm. "I really didn't sense them until it was almost too late," she insisted with heartfelt urgency. "I do not want any harm to come to her. She is our hope."

Wren's temper subsided. "We rushed back when we sensed trouble. We'll all keep a better eye on her."

Priscilla flashed a timid smile before she left to resume her post atop the bluff.

Wren dealt with raven carcasses. She used the same piece of driftwood Shannan did to cover each raven with sand. In doing so, she spoke the Ancient. *"Sand of earth consume the remains, let nothing be found not a spot or a stain."*

The small mound that covered each raven diminished into stillness until the area appeared undisturbed.

Wren closed her eyes and spoke the Ancient, *"Falcons and hawks, eagles and osprey, keep watch above. Let nothing of wing come this way."* She took a breath of recovery from invoking her power.

Inside, Wren found Vidar wiping the blood from Shannan's cheek. "I have salve that will help in the healing so it won't leave a scar." She pulled a jar from her pouch.

"I don't recall reading or hearing about ravens attacking people," said Shannan, disturbed.

"Normal ravens, no." Wren carefully applied the salve to Shannan's face. She paused to ask, "You know Marcellus' castle is called *Ravendale*?"

"Ay."

"That the crest on Dagar's talisman is a raven?"

Shannan heaved a heavy sigh. "I guess I didn't consider the connection would become reality with the birds. Merely a symbol."

"No, not a symbol. The same as Kato is real, though an eagle is the royal symbol of the House of Tristan."

With understanding, Shannan regarded Wren. "And the wolf because of its connection to Jor'el's Ancient crest."

Wren grinned at the understanding. "Ay."

Shannan grew deeply thoughtful.

"That troubles you?" Vidar sat beside Shannan.

She heaved a slight shrug. "Not really *trouble*. Just adjusting to the reality of what my Grandfather told me, and I read in books. Until I met Ellis, and Guardians, everything was in the abstract."

"For one so young, you are doing very well."

She gazed into his copper eyes. "As are you for being imprisoned. We both need to let go of the past and move forward."

"We'll start by me not leaving you again," he said with wry smile.

She looked down to her hands in an attempt to stop a sniffle.

"No need to be upset," he tried to soothe her.

"I hope Kato finds Ellis soon so we can bring this to a quick end."

"Kato *will* succeed," said Wren with confidence. "Now lie down to rest for a bit." She escorted Shannan to the carved bed. Once certain Shannan was settled, Wren stepped away. She carefully motioned for Vidar to join her on the opposite side of the hollow cave. She spoke the Ancient in a near whisper. "We narrowly avoided discovery."

"You think Dagar used the ravens to find her?" he replied in the Ancient.

"Of course. He has used them in the past."

"So? Command them to withdraw."

Wren vehemently shook her head. "Since the Great Battle, ravens are the only natural birds that won't listen to any commands. It may be part of the punishment, I don't know. But nothing has worked to control them."

Vidar grew thoughtful. "I didn't know that."

"Which is why I'm telling you," she tried to sound encouraging. "Priscilla didn't see or sense others, meaning it was just those four. I buried them so they won't be found. I also called the birds of prey to keep other winged creatures from the cove. From now on, you remain with her. Let me tend to security and supplying food."

Vidar stared at Shannan with deep consideration. He simply nodded agreement.

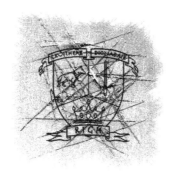

Chapter 15

Leaving the North Plains, Ellis found it difficult to follow Mona's suggestion about Kemp. He fought against the urge to reason with Kemp. However, their flight prevented any time for lengthy discussions. When pausing to rest or eat, Kemp continued to stay apart from the rest. He also made certain Erin was with him at all times.

On the third night since leaving the North Plains, Ellis and Niles sat together to eat. Kemp and Erin remained aloof. Niles noticed Ellis' interest in watching the brother and sister.

"There's nothing you can do or say to change his mind," said Niles.

"Perhaps. Only he forces Erin to stay with him."

"He is her brother. Being a widow, her welfare depends upon him." At Ellis' scowl of frustration, Niles asked, "Are you as smitten with her as she is with you?"

The question surprised Ellis. "What makes you think Erin is smitten with me?"

"I'm old enough to know when a woman is focused on a man." At Ellis' annoyance, Niles pressed him. "You haven't answered my question. Are you as smitten with her?"

Ellis looked sharply at Niles. "What kind of question is that? She's my cousin. Or rather *was* my cousin."

"It's a fair question, under the circumstances. What about Shannan? She is the Daughter of Allon. Your future queen if Jor'el blesses our venture. I would hope your wife, if he does not."

Ellis' blue eyes flashed with irritation. He managed to keep his terse voice to a private volume. "You question me wrongly. My heart *is* for Shannan." He sent a quick glance toward the brother and sister. "Despite the lack of blood relation, I still consider Erin my kinswoman. My feelings are honorable."

For a moment, Niles studied Ellis' resolute features. "Then I will say no more."

Ellis shook his head. "No, you're jealous, thinking I favor Erin."

Niles tried to sound casual even when he used the soup to motion toward Erin. "From several conversations with have had, I learned her heart *is* set on *you*. I needed to know your heart concerning her."

"I think you're confused. She loved her husband not me."

"Confused is something I am not!"

Niles' adamant statement combined with shoving food in his mouth, convinced Ellis he was right. "You refuse to admit it. Why? Because you delude yourself into thinking that at your age you are past such emotion as jealousy?"

Niles continued to eat rather than response.

Incredulous, Ellis huffed. "You *are* jealous, *and* protective of Shannan. Against me, of all people!"

Niles didn't speak. Instead, a heavy silence fell between them for the rest of the night. Even the next morning, they avoided the subject to focus on the journey.

After they crossed a small brook, Ellis stopped with a visible shiver of alarm. "Witter!" he warned.

"Who is Witter?" asked Darius. He walked just behind Ellis and Niles.

"I am." Witter appeared from the bushes. He reined in the spirit stallion. "I am here to deal with the Son of Tristan. If any of you try to stop me, you will perish."

Niles stepped forward to draw his sword. "I don't think so."

The look of recognition on Witter's face became quickly masked.

"Run when I strike," Niles spoke over his shoulder to Ellis.

Witter charged. Niles parried the blow.

"Run!" Ellis' shouted to the others.

Royal soldiers burst upon them with Tyree shouting; "A thousand talents to the man who captures or kills the Pretender!"

The intervention distracted Witter, which gave Niles a brief advantage. He thrust his sword deep into the stallion's chest. It reared to be free of the blade. Witter fell to the ground. The dying stallion landed hard on him and pinned his legs. Witter struggled to move from under the stallion's weight. With Witter down, Niles rushed to aid his companions.

From behind, the hilt of a sword struck Ellis' head. Stunned, he dropped to the ground. Through hazy, double vision, he noticed Darius kneel beside him. The sight didn't last long when a blurry blow sent Darius aside.

"Darius!" Ellis tried to reach for Darius, only his reaction delayed by the head wound. Erin's scream came from nearby. Rising to his knees made the dizziness worse. He collapsed down to all fours. He swallowed back a violent wave of nausea. He had to stay awake!

Erin managed to use her dagger to ward off a soldier. A second soldier arrived. Together, they overpowered her. She felt a blade cut along her ribs.

Nando rushed to help her. He slashed at the soldiers with his sword. "Run—" A fatal blow from behind made Nando pitch forward. His momentum carried Erin to the ground with him.

"Nando?" She fought back tears at seeing his ashen features and shrouded eyes.

Two soldiers surrounded Erin. Suddenly they cried out; "My eyes! I can't see!"

The soldiers dropped their weapons and staggered blindly. Hands grabbed Erin. She screamed in surprise.

"Be easy. We're here to help," said the large man holding her. He had black hair with cat-like yellow eyes. He wore a gray tunic and breeches. He spoke to another individual, identical in appearance. "Now, Daren."

Daren brought his hands together in a loud clap. At the deafening sound, all the soldiers became blind. Daren raced to Ellis and dead lifted him to his feet.

Niles called for the others. They hobbled away as best they could.

Witter ceased struggling at hearing the clap. He understood what just happened. "Guardians!" he angrily shouted.

From the shadows of the trees, Kell watched the Guardian night twins take Ellis' group away. He also heard Witter. One of Kell's hands was clenched. Effort showed on his face at energy needed to keep the stallion pinned. To follow the night twins meant releasing his hold. Daren's use of night blindness would only be effective for a few more moments. He had to keep Witter pinned until then.

"Be quick, night twins."

***

By nightfall, the wounds of the mortals needed tending. Erin could barely stand. Darius leaned heavily upon Edmund. Though battered, Kemp refused help. Niles appeared older than his years. Ellis' head had cleared and the nausea passed. Dried blood matted his hair where the hilt impacted his skull.

Daren and Darcy led them to a partially burned Fortress with no signs of occupants. They entered the remaining building, a dormitory. A long hall served for gatherings, as told by a table in the center of the room along with a hearth at the far end. Doors lined either side of the hall leading to individual rooms.

Edmund eased Darius unto a seat at the dusty table. Kemp was less gentle. He fell into a rickety chair. He rested his head on the table. Erin collapsed. Ellis carried her to a bedchamber on the north side of the hall. Niles checked his bag for medical supplies.

"What do you need?" Darcy asked Niles.

"Water, a basin and a fire in the hearth."

Daren went to fetch the items, while Darcy tended to the fire. He threw a few logs into the hearth then said, "*Na teintean.*" He snapped his fingers. A roaring fire appeared.

Edmund and Darius marveled as much as their battered bodies and fatigued minds could manage.

"They're Guardians," said Niles matter-of-factly.

"Guardians?" echoed Edmund in surprise.

Darius snickered with irony. "Why should we be surprised? With Ellis anything can happen."

Kemp's head rose only to the point where his could see Darcy. "Guardians. A lot of good they did. Just look at us."

"We saved your lives," said Darcy.

Kemp snorted and hid his eyes. It was all the emotion he could manage.

In the chamber, Ellis gently lowered Erin onto the bed.

She seized him in a panic. "Don't leave," she cried, her eyes pleading.

"Hush. You're injured and tired. You need rest."

"No, I need you!" She embraced him.

"Erin—" he began in mild protest, but she wouldn't be put off.

"Didn't you feel it? When you carried me in here? You have feelings for me," she ardently insisted

He grew awkward under her barrage of emotions. "Naturally. We grew up together."

"No, it's deeper," her voice passionate, as she caressed his face.

Ellis tried to remove her hand. His effort became cut short when she kissed him. He froze with confusion. When she grew bolder, he pulled away to hold her at arm's length. His befuddled features flush.

"You're trembling. You felt the same." She tried to kiss him again.

Ellis locked his arms to hold her off. "This is wrong, and you know it," he chided.

"I know no such thing."

"You do! You know my heart is for another." He abruptly released her to stand. He heard a muffled grunt of pain. "Your wound—"

Angry, she waved him away. "Take your sympathy elsewhere!"

For a brief moment, he lingered with regret. She retreated further from him. "I'm sorry," he murmured.

Ellis just emerged from the bedchamber when the night twins approached him. "Will the Daughter of Allon recover?" Darcy asked.

Startled by the questions, Ellis stared with perplexity at the twins. "Shannan is hurt?"

"My lord, you just brought her into the room," said Daren.

"Oh, no. She is not the Daughter of Allon," he said with relief.

"We assumed since she was with you. Forgive us," apologized Darcy.

"An honest mistake. Who are you?"

"Darcy and Daren, night twins of the North Plains," they replied.

Ellis flashed a cautious glance to the table. Edmund nursed his own wounds. Kemp slept. Niles finished tying off Darius' bandage yet noticed Ellis' concern.

"They know," said Niles in regards to those at the table.

"Nothing surprises me anymore," said Darius.

"He's grown as cynical as his father," snickered Edmund.

"Let me tend you now," Niles said to Ellis.

"No. See to Erin. My head is clear and the bleeding stopped." Ellis left the hall.

He walked to the battlement. His head may have cleared from the dizziness of battle, but it now filled with a new wave of conflicting emotions. He likened his relationship to Erin more as brother and sister than cousins. He tossed a thoughtful glance back to the dormitory. Her kiss confirmed what Niles said about Erin's heart toward him. Were his feelings still as platonic as he believed? He pursed his lips at recalling her kiss. He heard Niles question echo in his mind, *What about Shannan?* Frustrated, Ellis slapped an open palm against the wall.

"It's not right!"

"Ellis," said a female voice.

He came face-to-face with—"Erin. What are you doing here?"

"I wanted to speak with you. Your hand." She tenderly examined the wound on his hand.

At her touch, Ells felt a strange sensation. "I must have scraped against something on the wall." He tried to determine the sensation, as he looked into her deep dark eyes. He felt himself drawn into her eyes, and to her inviting lips.

"Don't fight your feelings." She passionately kissed him.

Ellis did not have the will or desire to stay her. Again he experienced her ardor. He felt his own passion rise, though accompanied by an annoying sense that something was different. It didn't even feel like earlier. He tried to will away the gnawing. He caressed her back, her sides—Nothing! His ripped himself from her arms her to view her side.

"Impossible! You have no wound."

Her face immediately changed to hatred, and she lunged for his throat. Ellis began to suffocate beneath the unusually strong hold. There was a wild, hateful glare in her eyes. It took all of his strength to rip the chokehold from his throat and shove her aside. He gasped for air. He braced one hand against the wall for support to stay on his feet.

"Ellis?" called Niles.

Due to pain in his throat from the near choking, Ellis couldn't reply. He turned back to the fallen Erin. Gone! How could that be? He didn't see her anyway on the rampart or in the compound. Niles arrived in a rush. Ellis forced the words from his throat. "Did you see her? Did you see Erin?"

"Of course. I just came from dressing her wound. What happened you?" Niles tried to examine Ellis' neck.

"What?" Overcome with confusion, Ellis seized Niles arm. He sank against the wall to sit on the battlement wall.

"Ellis?" Niles knelt beside him.

He waved Niles off, as he tried to gather his thoughts between gulps of air. "The sensation. No wound. Not Erin. Witter!" Irate, Ellis screwed his eyes shut. "Fool!" he swore. "I should have seen it and not been daydreaming."

The night twins came running. "My lord, are you hurt?" asked Darcy.

"No. Simply cursing myself for not recognizing Witter sooner. Return and make sure Erin is safe," Ellis told the twins.

"You think Witter means her harm?" asked Niles.

"I'm not certain. He used an apparition of her to try to weaken me."

Niles made a fatherly frown. "It is a weakness you gave him to use."

Pricked, Ellis clenched his fists to keep from lashing out. A screech brought him to his feet in time to see Kato land on the wall. "Kato." Concerned, he quickly removed the pouch to look inside. "Empty?"

"Shannan knows. She sent Kato to remind you of your pledge to her," said Niles with certainty.

"How could she know? Nothing happened," insisted a disconcerted Ellis. He fretfully regarded the pouch. In doing so, he admitted, "A single kiss. That she initiated. Nothing else, I swear!" When Niles didn't answer, Ellis continued with perplex urgency. "I knew it was wrong, which is why I left Erin in the room! You can't deny that Witter used the Dark Way to lure me." He again looked at the pouch with painful regret. "I didn't mean to hurt her. You believe that, don't you?"

Niles sighed with dismay. "You are young, and the young are prone to folly. Until now, I wondered when you would make a mistake. Oh, I don't doubt your desire or sincerity, but experience, and the wisdom it brings, is another matter."

Ellis waved the pouch in Niles' face. "You believe this shows my lack of experience?"

"I didn't mean to insult you. Don't insult me with sarcasm."

Ellis took a deep breath to regain his temper. "Niles, you have been my teacher, instructor and counselor. For that I owe you a debt I can never repay. However, you had your Contest. This is mine, to learn *my* strengths and weaknesses. You think me incapable of seeing them? I have only to look at the wounds people endured for me." He held up the pouch. "The is another bold example of my weakness." He abruptly turned aside when his voice cracked and eyes grew misty.

Niles took hold of Ellis' shoulder. "Injury and fatigue are getting the better of both of us. I expressed myself badly. As you are young, I am old, very, very old. Sometimes youth clouds your judgment and increases your zeal, while age makes me cynical and wary."

Ellis cocked a grin. "Perhaps, between the two of us we can find a balance." A screech reminded them of Kato's presence. Ellis stroked the bird's head. "Faithful, Kato." He attached Shannan's pouch to his belt. From his pouch he withdrew the brooch that held his cloak. "I don't have any string."

Niles pulled out a piece of bandage from his bag.

Ellis attached the brooch to the strip then tied it about Kato's neck. "Return to Shannan with my love." With an acknowledgment, Kato took to flight. "I'm truly sorry we had words."

"So am I. You still have many tests and trials to face."

Ellis snickered. "I wonder if this was one of Kell's tests?"

"No, it was Witter." Kell arrived. "He knows mortal weaknesses well. To play with the heart is a dangerous gamble. If he had succeeded in dividing you and Shannan, the hope for the kingdom would be halved."

"Where were you when all this was going on?" Ellis pointedly asked.

"Here, ready to intervene. Sensing the twins is why Witter canceled his apparition. The real Erin is safe and unharmed, save for her earlier wound."

"You know about that?"

Niles laughed. "Why do you think Witter couldn't get up after falling off his horse? Certainly not due to my feeble blow against a spirit stallion."

Darcy returned. "Captain. It is good to see you again."

"And you both," greeted Kell. "The South Plains is not safe. Escort the Son of Tristan to Armus in the Meadowlands. Take the shortest route through Midessex." He said to Ellis, "Time is pressing, my lord. Guard your heart and mind."

"How is Shannan?"

"She is well."

"My lord, we have supper ready," said Darcy.

Niles reached for Kell when Ellis left with Darcy. "Has Shannan begun her part?"

"No, but soon. With each returning Guardian, her understanding deepens. You taught her well." Kell noticed Niles' pensive expression. "Why so glum?"

Niles cast several discerned looks at Kell. "After each encounter, I wonder if it will be my last. Tell her—" He couldn't finish, instead he gripped Kell's arm.

Disturbed by Niles' statement, Kell glanced skyward. "Will you not let him see it? He who has fought so long and hard?" For a moment he waited for an answer but none came. "Let it not be as he fears."

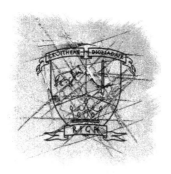

Chapter 16

WEARY, YET FULLY AWARE OF THE DANGER, ELLIS' GROUP left the Fortress six hours after Kell's warning. In their battered condition, they made slow progress. Traveling just inside the border of Midessex helped to use the forest as a scene between themselves and the open fields. Where the south part of Midessex bordered the Lowlands, the forest consisted of spindly beech, thin low level evergreens and scrawny brush. These were not woods to hide in or get lost. Here they needed to change course to travel due east to the Meadowlands.

For several days they traveled without sign of pursuit. This caused both concern and relief. Concern, because Witter and Tyree could be anywhere; relief because they didn't have to take frantic flight in their injured condition.

The journey prevented Darius from healing quickly. He sustained the most serious wounds with a slash to the chest and gash to his lower right leg. When Edmund wasn't assisting him, Darius used a crutch made by Niles. Darcy offered to carry Darius but he refused. He was not the only one who slowed their progress due to injury. It was best to keep a pace everyone could maintain. Unfortunately, they barely travelled twelve miles a day.

Late afternoon of the fifth day, they sat to eat. Ellis noticed the twins off to one side speaking with an unfamiliar female Guardian. She wore clothes similarly to Wren, only armed with a longbow. Ellis joined them.

"My lord, this is Zinna, Guardian of Midessex," said Daren.

"My lord." Zinna bowed to Ellis. "I was telling the night twins that Captain Tyree sent men to Sir Owain requesting assistance in your capture. Sir Owain is a few moments from arriving here."

Ellis regarded those in his company. "We can't move quickly. Darius is in great pain while Erin sleeps."

"Together we may be able to give you enough time to reach safety," said Daren.

Darcy shook his head. "Too risky to leave them unguarded. Not to mention disobeying Kell's order to take them to Armus."

Ellis pursued his lips. "I have a better idea." He carefully called: "Niles. Edmund." When they arrived, he continued; "Owain is coming to capture me."

"We can't fight," said Niles.

"I intend to preempt him."

"You're not going to surrender—" Edmund's loud protest became stopped when Ellis clamped a hand over his mouth.

"Sometimes, Edmund, you try all patience." No one stirred, so Ellis released Edmund. "I have no intention of giving up. Perhaps I can reason with him. If not, we shall capture Owain. His surety will bring us safely through Midessex."

Edmund slyly smiled. "For not having an ounce of Angus' blood, you're as foolhardy as he was."

Ellis grinned. "Thank you. Take the night twins to keep watch over the others. Niles and Zinna will accompany me to intercept Owain."

Sir Owain was a simple man in his middle thirties. A tanned complexion, trim body and rough hands showed his love for the farming life. He rode a placid mare in front of four others, also plainly mounted.

"How now, my lord?" hailed a voice from just off the road. "Are you looking for me?"

Owain drew his men to a halt. He nervously looked to find the speaker. "Show yourself. Or are you a coward?"

"Coward!" shouted the voice filled with ridicule. "That's funny, since you come to take me to Captain Tyree, who in turn would hand me over to his devilish master."

Owain fidgeted in the saddle. "I don't know what you're talking about, my lord. I came to speak to you." He signaled his men to the sides of the road. An arrow landed in front of Owain's horse, which made the docile mare shy.

"Don't move!"

"What do you want?" Owain's voice quaked.

"What did Tyree offer for my capture?"

Owain chewed on his lip in consideration. An arrow landed closer, which prompted him to burst out, "Nothing!"

"That's very insulting."

"You have caused enough trouble for my people already. I don't need more," Owain spoke with haste.

"I shall remember that when my time comes. And mark your cowardice."

For a long silent moment, Owain and his men anxiously waited.

"Dismount and throw down your weapons," ordered Ellis.

"Why?"

"Do it! Or the next arrow won't miss."

They did as told.

"Have your men place themselves face first around that large pine."

Once the four men followed instructions, a root sprang from the ground. It bound them to the tree. Owain paled with fright at the phenomenon.

171

"Take your kerchief and cover your eyes tightly."

Owain fumbled in obeying, his nerves frazzled. "Done!"

Ellis, Niles and Zinna emerged from the trees. They wore their hoods up to conceal their identities.

Owain made a small outcry when Niles laid hold of him. "Please, don't hurt me!"

"You are our surety to make it out of the province alive," said Ellis. "You men, carry word back, that if we see any soldiers, Sir Owain dies."

After murmurs of affirmation from the unnerved men, Ellis, Niles and Zinna left with Owain in tow.

Upon return, the others still slept with Edmund and the twins on guard.

"Did he give you any trouble?" asked Edmund.

"More a verbal nuisance than serious threat," replied Ellis.

"You boast now, but when you face the King's men, we'll see how far your boasting goes," said Owain with bravado, despite his blindfold.

Niles sneered in Owain's face. "Have you faced the King's men sword-to-sword? Or did you roll over like a scared dog?"

"I did what I had to do to save my people," Owain said, his bravado ebbing.

The shouting woke the others. Darius painfully stood. "What's this? Owain?"

Owain cocked his head to listen. "I know that voice. Angus?"

Ellis seized Owain, his tone angry. "Angus is dead! Fighting the King's men." He shoved Owain away, who stumbled to the ground due to blindness. "He was coming to capture me with the intent of turning me over to Tyree. All because he considers me an inconvenience. We foiled his plot, and will keep him for safe passage through the province."

Darius sneered at Owain though he spoke to Ellis. "Father always considered him the weakest on the Council."

"It will be nightfall soon, my lord. My abilities will only last till then," Zinna warned Ellis.

"You heard me give instruction concerning Owain. We'll rest a few hours and be on our way before dawn. It will take them until then to organize and come after us."

Kemp became angry. "You expect pursuit? What good is capturing him, if it will only increase our danger?"

"We have a trump card."

"Owain yielded the province. Why should Tyree cares what happens to him?" Kemp continued with his ill-tempered argument.

"His family does. They hold the province for Marcellus. He would have to expend precious time and energy from chasing me to calm them. It's a risk, but one we must take," said Ellis.

"You said you'd kill me if you see signs of pursuit. Was that a bluff?" challenged Owain.

Ellis knelt. He whipped out his dagger to press cold steel against Owain's throat. "Does this feel like a bluff?" Owain carefully shook his head. "Don't try my patience. You are a base coward. I have no stomach for cowards. If forced, you shall die a coward's death by my hand." He skillfully drew the dagger across Owain's throat, but drew no blood. He abruptly released Owain to stand. "Secure him until we leave," he ordered Edmund.

Erin muffled a gasp of horror at Ellis' action. His cold features very disconcerting. She found voice enough to ask, "You would kill him in cold blood?"

Ellis turned a sharp eye to her, his voice resolute. "I will do what is necessary to save Allon."

At Erin's discomposure, Darius gently took hold of her arm. "Men must make difficult, sometimes harsh choices. A future king, harder ones for the sake of his kingdom." He led Erin back to where she had slept.

Kemp barely kept the contempt from his face when following them.

"Shannan would understand," said Niles.

Ellis leveled an annoyed brow. "That doesn't make it any easier."

"Regrets?"

Ellis shot Niles a hot glance before leaving to find a spot to sleep.

During the wee hours of the morning, they pressed themselves harder than the previous day. Having Owain for a hostage called for haste in leaving Midessex. At dawn, Edmund spotted a small patrol on the horizon. He called them to Ellis's attention.

"Owain's men."

Ellis scanned the horizon. "Darcy, how much further to the border?"

"A mile. However, crossing the border won't ensure safety from attack."

"Owain will."

"No. They will." Daren pointed to another troop. "Lord Allard's men. A more fierce fighting force than Sir Owain's."

"How did they—?" Ellis began, then snorted; "Never mind. Once we are safe with Allard, let Owain loose," he instructed Edmund.

"My lord." Darcy indicated a rider from Owain's men coming towards them holding a white flag.

"Stay where you are, we can speak from here!" called Ellis.

"I have been sent by her ladyship to offer a trade for her husband."

"You have nothing I want, save to leave Midessex safely."

"Oh, we do, my lord. Two men, one called Jasper, the other Brody." He pointed back to where two bound men were brought to stand before the patrol.

Ellis scowled at the indication. "How can I be sure? I can't see them clearly from here."

"I have proof." The man produced Jasper's eye patch along with Brody's hunting knife. He gave them to Darcy, who in turned handed the items to Ellis.

Ellis heavily sighed with resignation upon receiving the items. "It's them all right," he told the others. "Are they harmed?" he asked the man.

"No, my lord. What of Sir Owain?"

"See for yourself." Ellis waved Edmund to bring Owain. His hands remained bound, though he no longer wore the blindfold.

"My lord, what shall I tell her ladyship?"

Ellis thoughtfully regarded the items before replying. "Tell her that once we have reached Lord Allard's men safely we shall send a man forward with Sir Owain. You shall send one with Jasper and Brody. When the exchange is made, we depart in peace."

"Ay, my lord." He turned his horse to gallop back to the patrol.

Ellis kept one eye on the patrol as they moved closer to Allard's men. The man with the flag dismount to take up position with Jasper and Brody.

"My lord." Allard came on foot to greet Ellis. He was a few years old than Ellis and five inches shorter. He dressed for battle with a helmet covering his head. He glared maliciously at Owain. "You always lacked backbone, but I never thought you would go this far."

"Ellis, they're on the move," said Darius of Owain's man.

"Go," said Ellis to Edmund.

"My lord, I have archers at the ready should there be treachery," Allard informed Ellis, who merely nodded. His attention focused on the exchange.

The man's jowls clenched when the groups met. "My lord," he greeted Owain with a titling nod at Jasper and Brody. "Her ladyship hopes you have not been ill used."

Owain's eyes flashed to Jasper and Brody then back to his man, as he acknowledged with a curt nod. "Ill enough," he chided.

"Ill? That is hardly a word to use when being graciously allowed to return home unscathed," rebuffed Edmund.

"Gracious would be not tying my bounds so tight. You'll have to cut me loose," groused Owain. He raised his hands in Edmund's face.

Edmund snatched them to hold in a manner for cutting. "Loose them," he said to the man concerning Jasper and Brody.

Edmund no sooner cut the rope then Owain seized the knife. A brief struggle began. Edmund proved no match for the farmer lord's large powerful hands. He fell with a deep dagger slice to his side. Owain made ready for another attack.

Jasper was free, but Brody still bound when the attack occurred. Jasper intervened to protect Edmund. He wrestled Owain for control of the dagger. Alas, this left Brody vulnerable to Owain's man. He died from a knife between the shoulder blades.

Shafts whizzed. An arrow seriously wounded the man who killed Brody. Another arrow deeply grazed Owain's left arm. He released Jasper. When a shaft hit the ground beside him, Owain bolted towards his men. An arrow struck his left leg, bringing him to his knees. Allard and his men charged.

"My lord!" shouted a mounted man. He reached down for Owain.

Owain dragged himself to his feet. He ignored the pain in his leg to seized the man's hand. In the time it took Owain to mount, two more of his men were struck down by Allard's archers.

"Retreat!" Owain ordered.

Jasper tended to Edmund when Ellis and a hobbling Darius knelt beside them.

"Edmund?" Darius anxiously said.

"I'll live," he groaned.

"Brody's dead. Knifed in the back." Jasper sneered with repugnance.

Ellis' eyes narrowed with rage at the fleeing Owain. A group of Allard's men galloped past them in pursuit of Owain. Allard swiftly dismounted beside Ellis.

"I'm sorry, my lord. I had hoped my show of force would deter Owain from any duplicity," said Allard with regret.

"No, you did rightly. I underestimated him."

"Horses for his lordship and the wounded!" commanded Allard, which received prompt compliance.

Ellis gave Jasper back his eye patch before he accepted a horse. Once astride, he said, "Give me Brody."

Two of Allard's men placed Brody's body over the saddlebow and Ellis' lap. The knife remained in Brody's back so Ellis removed it. With sneer of painful anger, he tossed the knife away.

Darius could sit a horse by himself. Edmund needed aid so he rode double with Jasper. Kemp and Erin also rode together.

"Fool!" thundered Tyree. He and Witter met Owain at his home.

Owain sat on the sofa. Bandages were wrapped around his left leg and torso. His countenance was pale. He sipped an herbal tea for pain. "I tried to do what you asked, only he is very cunning. Not to mention my wounds or the fact I lost three men," he said in defense.

Witter snarled at Owain's rebuff.

Tyree became thoughtful in regard of Owain. "I've had favorable dealings with Lord Allard in the past. That may be useful, even advantageous."

"To whose advantage? Yours or the King's?" chided Witter.

Tyree stiffened at the accusation. "Your presence is only mildly tolerated. Don't presume upon that tolerance."

"Your interference allowed him to escape me."

"If you had lived up to your original boasts, he should have been captured by now. Instead you complicate my task by your bombastic blustering."

Enraged, Witter drew his sword. Incited, Tyree did the same.

"Not in here!" Owain exclaimed.

"Leave off, coward," Tyree commanded.

Owain slightly recoiled on the sofa yet chided in response. "I may be a coward, but what bravery makes you two fight when the real threat is alive and free?"

Witter growled at Owain, which made the mortal lord shrink back. Tyree seized Witter to prevent any action against Owain.

"I hate to admit this," began Tyree tightly, "but he's right. The Pretender is our main quarry. I suggest a truce until he is caught. Then we can settle our personal differences."

Witter lowered his sword, so Tyree sheathed his blade.

"Now," Tyree continued, "if you allow me to approach Allard calmly rather than storm in, we may achieve our goal more quietly."

Witter stiffened. "You immediately break your truce with insults?"

"Merely an observation. Ingenuity may work where brute strength has failed both of us."

"Very well. But I want to know everything."

"Agreed."

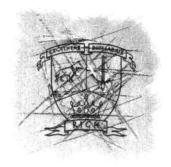

Chapter 17

ILTON WAS A GRAND SPRAWLING MANOR THAT SAT UPON A PLAIN in the heart of the Meadowlands. Defense could be made, but the manor reflected the wealth of the vast open province. Widespread destruction was not visible in the surrounding countryside. Horses and sheep lazily grazed on early spring grass. Workers busily repaired fences or fields damaged by the winter weather. All this Ellis keenly noted on their journey to the Milton.

Upon arrival, Lord Allard's personal physician aided Niles in treatment of the injured. Ellis tended to the dispensation of Brody's body, cared for the others then saw to his own needs. Allard generously provided every manner of noble toilette and clothing. He spared no expense to meet the needs of his royal guest and company. He even ordered a private banquet. Darius and Edmund declined, both too exhausted from injury to participate.

At high table, Ellis sat to Allard's right. This was the first opportunity to take stock of Allard since their meeting. He reckoned Allard to around age thirty, with a fresh clean-shaven face, bright green eyes and strawberry blonde hair. He carried himself with command accented by a look of slyness to his expression. Ellis recalled Darius telling him that

Allard possessed a quick, sharp mind, which he employed to strike a bargain with Tyree to save his province. Wed five years, he had a four-year-old son, eighteen-month-old daughter and expecting another child.

Ellis became distracted when Erin arrived with Lady Natalie, Allard's wife. One could not guess Natalie was seven months along with child. Erin's appearance commanded attention. Ellis had not seen her so beautifully dressed in years. The bodice of the rich velvet primrose gown fit snugly in the right places. The diamond and garnet accents match the sparkle in her dark eyes. Her short hair was well pampered to accommodate the small matching headdress. Diamonds in the headpiece shimmered when she tossed her head about. Ellis' eyes followed Erin when she and Natalie sat.

Niles occupied one chair over from Natalie. The chair between them reserved for Lady Erin. Ellis caught Niles' scrutinizing gaze. Ellis turned from Niles, as his mind instantly flashed back to their argument about Erin and Shannan.

"My dear Erin, you look marvelous," said Allard. "That gown becomes her," he said to Natalie.

"Indeed. Do you not agree, my lord?" Natalie asked Ellis.

"Ay," he replied. He avoided looking directly at Erin.

Erin smiled at Ellis, coquettishly obvious.

"It is a shame my sister has been denied such finery for years." Kemp made only a mild attempt to keep scorn from his voice.

"We were sorry to hear of your misfortune. You are welcome to the clothes you wear along with anything else I can provide," said Allard graciously.

"That is generous. However, I intend to return to Denley as soon as possible."

"Your sentiments do you credit. A lord's place is with his people."

In angry silence, Ellis tore at the chicken leg very aware of Kemp's meaning even if Allard wasn't.

Natalie noticed Ellis' action. "Is the food unsatisfactory, my lord?"

Ellis forced a smile in response to the question. "No. The food is wonderful. The best I've eaten in a long time. I'm greatly saddened by all the trouble that has plagued the kingdom. Perhaps I was wrong to accept your gracious hospitality. My presence will bring danger to your door, as it has for Kemp and Darius."

Allard gripped Ellis' arm. "Take no blame, my lord. I knew the risk when I rode out to meet you. It is my duty to give you shelter, arms, or whatever else you require."

Ellis looked Allard squarely in the eye. "You bargained with Captain Tyree to prevent your province from suffering. How can I be certain this is not a clever ploy to play both ends against the middle?"

Thunderstruck by the bluntness, Allard sat back in his chair. Natalie nervously bit her lip. She gave her husband a supportive squeeze of his hand. Allard recovered from his momentary surprise to reply.

"It is true that I used my wits to spare my people. Contrary to popular rumor, there *was* suffering. Thievery, drunkenness, riots. Tyree held a slack rein. When they left, I did what I could to soothe those injured or misused. Yet, not one person in my province was killed. If you fault me for saving lives, I am guilty."

"And earlier today? What did you tell Tyree?" Ellis continued his bold inquiry.

Allard bravely returned Ellis' regard. "Nothing, my lord. I swear," he affirmed. "I sent him away with a few trinkets, as per our earlier agreement. My servants are under strict orders to remain silent or suffer the harshest of penalties. Whereas I may use diplomacy, I loathe duplicity! That should be obvious when we dealt with Owain."

During the entire discourse, Ellis held a fixed eye on Allard. He watched for any sign of shrewdness or dishonesty. Allard's response appeared honest and blunt. "True, you came to my aid, and for that I am grateful. Your character beyond that is what I must determine. You see me for what I am, complete utterly without means. Being here," he motioned to the hall, "I cannot see you in the same light. Thus I ask hard questions to learn your heart and mind."

For a long moment, Allard stared at Ellis. "What do you want, my lord?"

"I ask of others what I can give, no secrets, no hidden agendas, only complete trust and loyalty. Nothing short of that can save Allon."

"You ask much, my lord. Of yourself and others."

"It should not be too much to ask of one who claims to loathe duplicity," Ellis countered.

Allard sat back, tugging at his lower lip in studious regard of Ellis.

"If you believe in Prophecy, you should understand," said Niles.

Allard met the piercing blue gaze of the old Knight. He returned his attention to Ellis when Ellis spoke.

"I am Jor'el's chosen. Latham is of the Dark Way. It is between those two you must choose. Anything less than a clear choice is as difficult as maintaining your balance on a fence. You may survive for a while, but at some point you will fall to one side or the other. It would be best by choice rather than by accident."

Allard's brows showed his consideration. "I went to help a future king in the worldly sense of fealty, for that is how your coming was told me since childhood. The hope of Allon wrapped in legend, not connected with Jor'el's Prophecy. What you say is of a spiritual nature that I must consider carefully."

"Of course. Yet understand, I do not have time to waste."

Natalie's hand on Allard's arm delayed his answer. Instead, she sweetly smiled to ask Ellis, "Can we at least enjoy the remainder of the evening, my lord?"

Ellis willingly nodded with a gracious smile. "Ay. The food truly is very good."

Allard's face brightened with relief. "I have musicians for dancing."

Ellis flushed with mild embarrassment. "I don't dance very well."

"That is true." Erin's eyes sparkled when she tossed a teasing smile to Ellis. "He always stepped on my toes at family celebrations."

Allard laughed. "Then music simply for enjoyment with our meal."

By late evening, most had retired. Allard yawned and stretched. In doing so, he caught Ellis' glance.

"It is the duty of a host to remain until all guests are satisfied."

"Do not stand on ceremony for me. Natalie retired two hours ago."

"As did Erin," said Allard with a faint smile.

Annoyed by the inference, Ellis took a long drink.

The action prompted Allard to ask, "Does she not please you? Your fair cousin?"

Ellis left the hall without answering. Agitated, he wandered the courtyard. Erin's coquettish behavior along with Natalie's hints, were all too obvious in trying to gain his attention. Visually Erin was stunning. What annoyed Ellis were the feelings of attraction. This time his stirring emotions were not due to Witter's interference.

As he wandered deep in thought, his hand absentmindedly hooked on his belt. He felt the pouch. He may have changed clothes, but he still wore Shannan's pouch on his belt. He removed it to trace the pattern.

"You are my heart, so why do I feel these things for another?" he wondered aloud. "If only you were here." The thought struck him. "That's it. It's not a desire for Erin, rather my loneliness for you. To see you jeweled and gowned, even to dance with you. To kiss you." He smiled at the pouch. "Forgive me, Shannan."

A bird's cry made Ellis look up. In bounding steps, he climbed up to the rampart. He heard the bird again, hopeful. Alas, it disappeared into the darkness.

"Aren't you going to bed?" Erin arrived unnoticed. She wore a shawl wrapped about her dressing gown.

Ellis tried to gauge any unusual sensation. "Erin? Is it really you?"

"Of course. Why do you ask?"

He grabbed her by the waist, which made her squeal with surprise and flinch in pain. "You still have your wound," he said with a smile of relief. "I had to be certain."

"Certain of what?" She took hold of his hand when he removed it from her waist.

"That is was you and not some dream." He tried to remove his hand, only she held fast.

"Do I feel like a dream?" She moved closer to place her arms around his waist.

He forcefully put distance between them. "Neither is this." He held up the pouch. "I made it for Shannan's last birthday."

Pricked, Erin folded the shawl about her. "If she gave your present back, she must not think much of it, or you."

Her scorn made him defensive. "You're wrong. This was just the reminder I needed."

"Some love if you forget."

"Some love if you must employ others to help seduce me. Whose idea was the gown, yours or Natalie's?" he shot back.

Erin flushed with embarrassment. She bit her lower lip.

Her reaction provided the answer. "Yours," he huffed with annoyance. "So was coming out here in the chill night wearing nothing but a shawl over your dressing gown."

Erin fought back tears. "You are crueler than I remember. Not only to me, but others."

"You mean Owain?" Ellis' face grew harsh. "Tell that to Brody."

She wept, as she fought with frustration. "I don't understand you. You've become some other person."

"Ay. As a boy, I was simply one of many playing in the field at Garwood or Denley. When I got older, I learned I was born to be king. Although," he said, growing reflective in tone and demeanor, "I always knew I was meant to do something. An inner compulsion that will not let me rest until I accomplish it."

At her befuddlement, Ellis seized Erin by the shoulders to ask with urgency, "Don't you understand? I have a destiny chosen by Jor'el. I must do all within my power to fulfill it. Even if it means my life."

She shook her head, unnerved. "I don't understand such self-destructive passion."

"It's not self-destructive! Allon stands on the brink of eternal darkness. Can't you see that?" He searched her face to find some spark of understanding. Met with continued bewilderment, he released her with a sigh of lament. "You can't."

She snatched his hand, urgent and pleading. "I will if you want me. I'll do anything, if you want me."

Ellis grew sympathetic in reply. "It's not your fault you can't see it. You weren't meant to. As for wanting you," he gently brushed the hair from her face, "I did once. And I almost yielded. A moment's gratification would only cause a lifetime of regrets for both of us. I wish better for you than that."

Hurt, she stepped away from him. "I don't need your sympathy! I know when I am being cast aside."

"No, Erin. You will always be like a sister to me."

"I have a brother. It is a man I wanted. I thought you wanted a woman, but all you want is a pouch!" She sharply turned to leave when he snatched her arm.

"Vent your anger on me, only leave Shannan out of this! I have done her as much disservice as you."

Kemp hurried up the rampart. "Let her go!"

Ellis complied.

Erin locked arms with Kemp. "I want to go home."

"We will, as soon as I can make arrangements for escort." Kemp sneered at Ellis before he ushered Erin from the rampart.

Ellis sagged against the wall. He eventually sat. Woeful, he looked at the pouch. "Oh, Shannan, what a fool I've been. Even apart, you remind me of the union of our souls, if not yet of body. A union ordained by Jor'el, and one I would be remiss to ignore or undo. I won't fail again. I promise." He kissed the pouch.

"That's all I wanted to hear. Though it took you longer to realize it than I hoped."

Ellis snickered when Armus sat beside him. "How long have you been here?"

"The entire time. What do you think drew Erin from her bed?"

Ellis became angry. "You used her like Witter?"

Armus shook his head. "She was no apparition. You felt her wound. As for using her, it could be taken that way. Yet, I just drew her from her room to here. I did not influence her speech. She spoke from her heart."

"All the same, you made me hurt her."

"Oh, no! You did that yourself. A funny thing is mortal love, confusing too."

Ellis snorted with annoyance. "Wonderful! A Guardian who never kissed a female is scolding me about love. What gave you the right to do such a thing?"

"Jor'el. This is part of your Contest," Armus calmly replied. "Since the time of Prophecy, the Daughter of Allon and Son of Tristan have been linked. Without the other, the one is only half of what they should be. Shannan knows that. The question was when would you realize it?"

Ellis' annoyance became replaced by sober understanding. "So Erin's whole purpose in all this was to test my commitment to Shannan."

"*More* than your commitment to Shannan is at stake. You are the hope of the mortals, while she is the hope of the Guardians. I can't tell you what a difficult task this was, especially after Kell told me of Witter's attempt with Erin's apparition."

Ellis stared at the pouch. He wasn't regarding it, rather seeing all the ramifications. "I'm sorry."

"Apology isn't necessary. You chose wisely. Shannan will soon begin her part in this enterprise. It is best she does so with complete assurance of your love."

"I sent her my brooch."

Armus lifted his arm level with his head. Kato landed on his arm. The brooch remained around the eagle's neck. "You mean this?"

"How? Why?"

"Kell intercepted Kato and brought him to me. It could not be sent in the spirit in which you did, incomplete and not wholehearted."

"I meant what I said!" Ellis insisted. Armus regarded him with skepticism. Guardians possessed eyes that could be both commanding and penetrating. Armus' gaze reminded Ellis of Niles probing of regrets. "No," he finally admitted. "I harbored regrets. There can be no regrets, no doubts. That is no longer the case."

The Guardian grinned. "That is all he needed to hear." He pointed to Kato. The bird squawked before it flew away. "Now he bears it with your complete love."

"How is it, that with no experience in love, you prove my best teacher?"

Armus smiled. "He who is untainted can see what those in the midst of heartache cannot."

Ellis wryly chuckled. "I'm going to bed." He stood.

"Don't you want your reward?" Armus rose. He unhooked a plain scabbard from his belt. "Your sword, my Prince."

Upon announcement, the scabbard transformed into polished gold with intricate engraving. The pommel resembled the body of an eagle with the head. Garnets served as eyes. The guard was carved like golden wings. The sword hummed when Ellis unsheathed it. The blade shimmered. He noticed writing etched in the blade.

"Guardian writing? What does it say?"

"'*With Jor'el's strength subdue and with this blade conquer.*'"

"Until now, I never felt a king, only a *should be*. This is a king's sword forged in the heavenlies." With anxiety, Ellis looked up at Armus. "Am I worthy?"

"My opinion does not matter. What matters, is what your heart tells you."

Ellis sheathed the blade. "You're wrong. You're opinion does matters. So does Kell's."

Visibly touched, Armus took the sword back. "Ay, you are worthy. As for Kell -"

"I can speak for myself, thank you."

187

Ellis huffed a laugh at seeing Kell. "I know; you've been here the whole time."

"Then you also know your next destination."

"Humor, Captain?" quipped Armus.

Kell ignored Armus. "At the end of the week you are to proceed to Arundine."

"Arundine? You said it was hidden from mortals. How will I find it?"

"The twins know the way. Now rest. You've done well, Son of Tristan."

Dagar paced his nether dimension chamber as he listened to Witter conclude his report. "Are you certain Tyree doesn't suspect you of being a Guardian?"

"I have made every effort to avoid detection. Dimension travel is becoming easier."

"Of course it is. Everything will become easier as the time approaches." Dagar chided with frustration, "Until then, we must employ more forces to counter theirs." He noticed Witter trying to suppress a smile. "You find something amusing?"

"Just recalling the look on Tyree's face when his diplomatic attempt to persuade Lord Allard into betraying the Son of Tristan failed."

Dagar's face took on an expression of offended curiosity. "Diplomatic? I don't employ diplomats."

"A tactic Tyree conceived when Owain's trap failed. He claimed the Son of Tristan would be on his guard so subtlety might work instead of brute force. I told him I didn't agree, but he insisted."

Dagar narrowly eyed Witter, which made the latter balk. "If only you had succeeded in capturing the Daughter of Allon. Since you failed, I shall boldly play upon mortal fears, no subtlety or diplomacy. What Tyree and the Shadow Warriors did, is nothing compared to what devastation I will unleash through Latham." He cocked a sly smile. "We shall begin with the crops. Gradually building to a crescendo of utter calamity that will divert attention. In short, we shall exhaust our foe of his resources and deplete his strength."

"What do you want me to do?"

"Continue in your pursuit. The Son of Tristan is still our main objective. As for the girl, you may have failed initially, but the backup plan may yet work. Return to duty. I shall see to the rest."

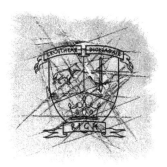

Chapter 18

PLAGUES AND MALADIES OF ALL SORTS DESCENDED UPON EVERY corner of the kingdom. The poorest to the most wealthy and noble suffered. Crops withered. Livestock died. The weather changed drastically from day to day with torrential rains, deadly thunderstorms, high tides and unseasonal blizzards in the Highlands, North Plains and Northern Forest. Calamity was not restricted to nature, as some mortals fell mysterious ill. Others encountered kelpies and gullet worms, legendary creatures of evil. Talk of hope in the return of a Prince to the House of Tristan dimmed under the onslaught of plagues.

Efforts by Council members to calm their people met with little success. Owain accompanied Lord Harkin to lead a procession of one hundred officials to Ravendale. Bewildered magistrates and frazzled mayors cried out in loud voices that echoed in the Great Hall. Neither Marcellus nor Hugh could soothe those assembled.

Reid and Firth arrived. Both appeared worse than when they returned from shadowing Witter. Each showed signs of minor injury from conflict. They pushed their way through the crowd to place themselves squarely before Marcellus.

"Reid?" said Marcellus. He finally lost his temper at the clamor of those assembled. He snatched the herald's staff to pound on the floor to get attention. "Enough!" When the room grew quiet, Marcellus spoke to Reid and Firth. "Trouble?"

"Sire, the kingdom is full of trouble. We have just returned from the Lowlands where neighbor turns violently against neighbor."

"The people are vexed by all matter of calamity," said Firth.

"So I've been hearing." Marcellus motioned to the crowd.

Reid drew closer to speak with low urgency. "Sire, there is more. For your ears only."

Marcellus motioned Reid and Firth to follow him from the great hall into an antechamber. "Well?"

Reid began the report. "When word of disasters in every province reached Ravendale, General Iain dispatched us to learn the cause. Upon hearing our report, he sent us to Your Majesty." Reid paused a moment, as he came to heart of the matter. "Sire, everything is a direct result of the re-emergence of the Dark Way."

Marcellus didn't react, which prompted Firth to insist.

"It's true, Sire! The unexplained plights upon the land. Creatures not seen since the Days of Calamity. People struck down for no reason. Witness our condition, Sire. The result of an encounter with a man in the last throngs of madness from a kelpie bite."

Reid grew bold in speech. "Sire, Grand Master Latham—"

Marcellus' expression turned harsh, which made Reid fall silent.

"Did I hear my name?" Latham moved from the threshold. His aura of command appeared to have grown in intensity.

"In reference to how the Dark Way, as the cause for all the calamities," said Marcellus.

"Really, Sire? From whom does the charge come?"

Marcellus waved at Reid and Firth. "General Iain dispatched them as *spies* to gather information against you."

The men balked in surprise. "No, Sire! We were sent to learn -" protested Reid.

"Silence!" snapped Latham. "Do not dispute your King."

"Dispute, no. Respectfully defend ourselves, ay."

"Only the guilty need defense."

"We are guilty of nothing!"

"Innocent spies?" challenged Latham.

Reid was nearly beside himself with outrage. "Military scouts."

Latham accosted Reid. His cold blue eyes stared down his nose at the young man. "Scouts against whom? The Pretender? No! Me, the King's Prime Minister. That is treason."

Reid's outrage turned to disbelief. "Treason? No, Sire!"

Marcellus said nothing. With fixed features, he regarded them.

"His Majesty knows treason when he sees it. Why do you think he brought you in here to speak in private?" continued Latham.

The men were dumbstruck. Reid stood on the verge of horror, while the older Firth fought to contain his dignity.

"Sire, please!" implored Reid.

Marcellus' voice was devoid of emotion. "Grand Master Latham told me of your assignment the moment he learned of it. By your own words you confirm him, and condemn yourselves."

"Guards!" Latham called. Six soldiers quickly responded. "Take Lord Reid and Sir Firth to the dungeon to await execution for treason."

Self-control vanished into desperation, as Reid rushed Latham. The soldiers intercepted him. "It's not true!" he shouted while being dragged from the room.

His features hard-set, Firth spoke to Marcellus. "You are making a mistake that will cost your kingdom. May Jor'el have mercy on you."

The pronouncement made Marcellus flinch. He pensively watched Firth leave willingly.

"What of General Iain? He is responsible for their actions," asked Latham.

Marcellus sighed with regret. "Since Lida's death, he hasn't been in his right mind."

Latham focused on Marcellus. He casually reached for the talisman. "Relieve him of command, and banish him from Ravendale."

Marcellus jowls tightened at the suggestion. He gave a curt nod.

Word of Reid and Firth's fate spread quickly through Ravendale. When Hugh arrived at Iain's chamber to warn him, Iain had already packed his saddlebags.

"Where will you go? Surely not to the Delta? Not to Vera," asked Hugh with concern.

"No, course not. I won't involve her." Iain hesitated, almost uncertain of continuing. "I didn't tell you this for fear of upsetting you. However, last time I went to visit her, she didn't recognize me. I tried to indentify myself, only she couldn't understand. First he robs me of my wife, and now my sister." Iain sneered back upset.

Hugh lowered his voice to a whisper. "Take heart, Latham doesn't know Vera is your wife. If he did, she would be dead. Maybe when this is over, by some miracle, her health and mind can be restored."

"The only *over* is if the *pretender* wins. Are you prepared for that?"

Hugh's eyes narrowed with deep consideration. "Maybe. Marcellus is falling deeper under Latham's influence. Every time I try to reason with him, Latham thwarts me by hurting those dearest to me." Hugh grew desperate. "I must protect my children!"

Iain drew Hugh into a shadowy corner. "Then let us level the field so you can freely act."

"What do you mean?"

"I shall come to the north gate at midnight. Have the children ready to flee with me to safety. It's the only way to protect them, and give you freedom to reason with Marcellus without fear."

"Where will you take them?"

"It is best you don't know. Trust me, for their sake and yours."

Hugh paused for a moment of thought before he nodded. "Ay. Until then, Jor'el keep you safe."

After a hearty embrace of Hugh, Iain quickly left Ravendale.

At the stroke of midnight, Hugh carefully ushered his four children along the castle wall to the north gate. The two boys were ages twelve and ten; the twin girls age seven. All wore plain clothes with hooded cloaks to conceal their identities.

Hugh brought them to a halt to allow the night watch to pass. Once the soldiers disappeared from sight, he whispered to his eldest son Wess.

"Wait against the wall."

Hugh opened the gate. He carefully looked for Iain. Nothing. He glanced back inside. No patrol. He focused back outside to search for any signs of Iain. Still nothing. He quietly closed the gate. Returning to where he left the children, he discovered them gone! At a touch his shoulder, he whirled about with dagger ready.

"Hugh!" A hooded figure held Hugh's dagger inches from his face.

"Iain?"

"Ay. The children are safe in the ditch. Return to your chamber before the watch comes. I'll take care of them."

"Are you certain they will be safe?"

"Of course. Now, hurry."

Hugh managed to venture ten feet from the gate when three soldiers appeared. By their talk, he reckoned them off duty, and drunk. Even to drunken soldiers he did not want to explain his presence so late at night. He hid in the shadows. Once they were gone, he began to leave the vicinity when a low familiar voice called.

"Hugh!"

The voice came from beyond the wall. He carefully approached the gate when the voice again called his name then asked, "Are the children ready?"

Terror gripped Hugh at recognizing the voice. "Iain?"

"Ay. The children. Are they ready?" Iain barely finished speaking when Hugh threw open the gate to pull him inside.

Hugh pinned him against the wall to demand, "What trickery is this? I just left them with you."

"Not with me. I just arrived. I was forced to wait for a mounted patrol to pass."

Hugh seized Iain by the collar and ripped off the hood. "What deception is this? You were just here."

"No deception." Iain rolled up a sleeve to show Hugh a bracelet. "You gave this to me during the Parathnos War in pledge to return and fetch me from the enemy. Now I give it to you as proof of my identity."

Hugh's paled with realization. "Oh, Iain! I thought it was you. I recognized your voice, but under the hood."

Iain's jowls clenched with angry realization. "Latham! He must not have thought I would elude the patrol. He did this to keep you in check. Only we are the wiser. Go back to your quarters, and pretend nothing has happened."

"What?" Hugh asked, slow to comprehend.

"You must play along."

"But he has my children!" Hugh protested with great distress.

Iain gripped Hugh by the shoulder. "I will find them. Trust the *real* me." Again, he showed Hugh the bracelet.

Hugh was slow to nod. "He mentioned a ditch."

"I know it. Now, go." Iain set Hugh on his way with a nudge. He waited a moment to make certain Hugh entered the main building.

Iain knew he had to act quickly. Fortunately, being the general of the King's army, he knew every inch of Ravendale. The *ditch* had to mean the old passageway used during the Frontier War. Marcellus' father, King Unwin sealed the passageway. What Unwin did, Latham could undo. All appeared normal when he arrived at the ditch's exterior hidden door. Upon close examination, he found it unlocked.

"Expecting me? Well, I won't disappoint you."

With no handle on the inside, he didn't want anyone to lock the door from outside. He used a rock to prop the door open in such as way as to appear closed. He felt along the ground until he found a twig the size of the exterior lock. He shoved the twig and other debris into the lock so that if rock dislodged it wouldn't work.

He slid inside the ditch. The slightly opened door also allowed some moonlight into the passageway. Ten yards down, he came to a hard turn right. Around the corner, shafts of lamplight came from under the interior door, and through the grated peephole. He knew this older portion of Ravendale's dungeon once served as a cruel torture chamber. They fashioned the interior door in such a way as to tempt the prisoner with notions of escape only to be locked in a dead end tunnel to starve to death.

Upon approach of the door, Iain heard weeping. Wess spoke words of encouragement to his sisters. Iain glanced back down the tunnel. With the possibility of a trap, he looked up and whispered a prayer.

"Jor'el, if you really are there, show this soldier mercy. Aid me this night. For the children's sake. Do not allow them to be sacrificed to evil."

Iain placed a shoulder against the door. It creaked when he pushed it.

The girls gasped with fright. Wess lowly called, "Who's there?"

Iain ignored Wess to push the door until there was enough room to pass through.

"Uncle!" cheered Wess.

"Hush." Iain swiftly crossed to the cells that stood side-by-side. "Easy, girls. Getting here was too easy. I don't want to alert them."

"Too late!" Latham arrived with four soldiers. "I knew it was bait you could not resist."

Sword ready, Iain placed himself between the children and danger. "Now that I'm here, let the children go."

Latham's eyes narrowed. "You presume to command me? *Cummhachd!*" The talisman glowed when he spoke. By a wave of his hand, he struck Iain's sword. To his surprise, Iain retained his grip. "Impressive. Still, you are no match for me."

"If you fought like a man, I'd kill you in one stroke."

Latham smiled, cold and lethal. "Let's see what you do against four. Kill him!"

The soldiers hesitated. This made Iain cock a cynical smile.

"You're sending them against their general. They know better."

Latham clenched a fist. One soldier grabbed his chest. He moaned in great pain. When Latham jerked his hand, the soldier fell dead. "Kill him!" he ordered the others.

This time they didn't hesitate. Ignoring the cries of the children, Iain met the attack. Even for the renowned general, three against one proved difficult odds. Iain sustained a slight wound to the arm.

One soldier held back, while two launched themselves again at the wounded Iain. Using a stunning move, Iain parried both and seriously wounded one. When the soldier who held back went to join the attack, the unscathed soldier stepped in front of him to lunge at Iain. The general stepped aside. The momentum carried the man face first into the wall. Rendered unconscious at impact, he collapsed.

With his back to the third soldier, Iain was in no position to parry the attack. A hard shove sent him tumbling to the floor. Iain landed partially on the unconscious soldier. The third soldier went after Iain. The blade harmlessly passed Iain into the body of the unconscious soldier beneath him. Iain stared at the bronze haired man with a goatee whose face hovered inches from his face.

"Play dead," he whispered to Iain. His frame blocked Latham's view.

Iain's momentary surprise turned to calmness, as he looked into a pair of eyes that became clear silver. The soldier withdrew his weapon. Iain feigned a groan. He fell to one side into a heap.

"Uncle!" Wess shouted in horror, only to be ignored.

The soldier stood. "He's dead."

"I need to be certain." Latham stepped toward them.

The soldier grew in stature to well past seven feet wearing a tan uniform. A flash from the soldier's hand sent Latham across the room into the far wall. Latham struck his head and sank to the ground, unconscious.

"By the heavens!" Iain bolted upright.

He ignored Iain to break the cell locks with his bare hands. "We must leave before he wakes. Quickly. Through the ditch." He nudged the children to the tunnel door.

Once they were inside the tunnel, he struck the wall with his sword. A rockslide blocked the interior door. He ushered them through the tunnel. At the exterior entrance, he made certain the way was clear.

"Go as far as you can into the forest. I'll be right behind you," he told Iain.

They ran until the girls became painfully out of breath. He gathered them in a protective hollow for recovery.

Iain curiously looked up at the towering being. "Who are you?"

"I am Avatar, a Guardian warrior."

"I thought Guardians didn't exist, Uncle?" asked Wess in confusion.

"They must." Iain still regarded Avatar in wonder. "How did you come to Ravendale?"

"Jor'el sent me in response to your prayer. *'For the children's sake.'*"

Iain smiled in awed relief.

Cassie, one of twins, embraced Avatar about the hips. "Thank you."

Avatar kindly smiled and knelt to reply. "Don't thank me, small one. Thank Jor'el, and your uncle. Without them, I would not be here."

"Where would you be? In heaven?"

Avatar chuckled. "That's a long story. Your uncle knows what is happening. Perhaps he'll explain it to you."

Iain sheepishly shrugged. "My knowledge is not what it should be."

Avatar stood. "Then make it so. You now have that chance. I will take you to safety. The rest is up to you. Be assured, Jor'el heard you at Ravendale, so he will hear you anywhere."

<hr>

Back in the nether dimension, Latham's image hovered over the basin in Dagar's chamber. Witter stood behind Latham.

"A Guardian warrior?" Dagar questioned Latham then demanded of Witter, "How did you not sense him?"

"I wasn't here. I just returned from my assignment," Witter replied. "Form what the Grand Master told me, I suspect it was a *certain* Guardian," he spoke with an inflexion that piqued Dagar's interest.

Dagar's mahogany eyes narrowed on Latham. "Describe him."

"Tall, with bronze colored hair, goatee and silver eyes. Very powerful. With a wave of his hand, he sent me into the wall where I was rendered unconscious."

"Avatar!" Dagar spat the name, and sent a glare to Witter. The Shadow Warrior nodded.

Unaware of the meaning behind the visual exchange, Latham said, "The book of Legends says Avatar is Captain Kell's aid and protégé."

Witter seized Latham's shoulder upon mentioning *Captain Kell*.

Dagar gave a throaty growl. "Ay. Avatar is a meddlesome wretch I should have destroyed long ago. It would have dealt *him* a serious personal blow." He then demanded of Witter, "Did you sense anything? Which way he went?"

"No, only the presence of the enemy, which is why I returned. By then, he was gone and the trail cold."

Dagar's sneer turned to a small, pleased smile. "I too sense something wrong. Our full restoration is close at hand. Yet, there is more than one presence." His eyes darted back to Latham. "Was he alone?"

Latham shrugged ignorance. "I don't know. He acted so fast." He touched the talisman. "My lord, if you and Witter sensed him then how come I could not since I have your power?"

"At full strength Guardians can sense each other immediately. It is also the way we communicate over long distances, by focusing on the essence of the individual we want to contact. This," Dagar lifted his talisman, "is a simple conduit. It does not heighten your innate senses rather gives you access to power beyond your mortal ability."

Though he accepted the explanation, Latham cautiously continued. "My lord, speaking of the Guardians, Avatar's clandestine arrival brings up a rather delicate matter. *He* may be deploying his forces to take tactical measure of our strength."

Dagar's mood instantly soured. "Don't you think I know that?"

"My lord, I merely seek to remind you not to underestimate *him*. The Enforcers have reported trouble."

"More Enforcers have met with success, than failure," said Witter.

Dagar nodded to Witter's assessment. "Despite minor interference, I am aware of *his* forces. *He*, on the other hand, cannot get a full assessment of mine. That is where I have the advantage," he spoke to Latham. "Any further reports from Tyree about the Son of Tristan?" he asked Witter.

"No, although I am investigating multiple sightings leaving Midessex."

To this, Dagar showed a new interest. "They may have split up? Time to reactivate our spy."

Latham slyly smile. "I have already taken the liberty of dispatching Musetta again."

"Excellent." Dagar stretched his limbs with a smile. "The time grows near to leave this cursed place! Contact me when she has been successful." He waved his hands and the image instantly vanished.

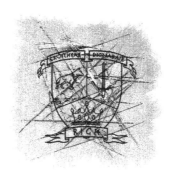

Chapter 19

IN THE FADING AFTERNOON SUNLIGHT, SHANNAN PLAYED WITH Torin on the beach of in front of the cave hollow. Each afternoon, rain or shine, she insisted on taking Torin for a romp by the water. She claimed both needed exercise and fresh air. Wren secured the cliffs while Priscilla made the wind blow so ships stayed away from the cove. This insured that no innocent, or not-so-innocent eyes spied Shannan.

From a respectful distance, Vidar kept watch. His crossbow slung across his back in such a way as to be instantly in hand. Occasionally Shannan convinced him to participate in a game of tag with Torin or engaged him in conversation. More often than not, he kept silent vigil over his charge.

When they first met, Vidar sensed Shannan was special. After months of guarding her, he had no doubt about her special connection to the Guardians. Centuries of imprisonment had worn down his spirit. When Priscilla found him weak and disoriented, he felt content to remain in the cave hollow for eternity if need be. He never wanted to see a spurean whip or stygian cage again.

His response to Jor'el's prompting to help Shannan and Wren began a healing process he didn't think possible. Since then, he grew more confident. Wren commented on noticeable differences in his character prior to the Great Battle. He used to be more outgoing, given to quick-witted amusement. Perhaps he could still banter with wry quips, but more content to listen and observe. Protecting Shannan gave him a new purpose and hope for the future.

As he watched Shannan played with Torin, Vidar wondered if she realized how significant she was to him and the others. With a small knowing smile, he answered himself. "She knows. One look in her eyes, and she knows."

"If you were mortal, I'd say you're in love with her."

Startled by a female voice, Vidar hopped off the rock with crossbow in hand. He rolled his eyes at Priscilla. "Kell's right. Your sudden comings and goings are annoying."

She took a casual seat on the rock. "I admit it. What about you? The way you keenly watch every move she makes with a fawning frown. Or is it a smitten smirk?"

His copper eyes flashed with irritation. "I do my duty, nothing more, nothing less."

She laughed with light mockery. "Nothing less, definitely. Nothing more? I'm not so sure."

"You can tease all you want, but you have no idea what Dagar is capable of! That girl is our hope. If you stop playing the flighty windbag you'd see reality."

"Better a flighty windbag than a lovesick Guardian."

"I'm not lovesick," Vidar began, only to end up grumbling under his breath when Priscilla vanished.

Wren arrived. "Who were to talking to?"

"Our favorite come-and-go-as-you-please-to-tease windbag."

She knowingly chuckled. "Don't let her get to you like she does Kell." She saw him scowl. "Oh, she did get to you."

"No," he said with bravado. "I'm going to fetch firewood. We need some for supper."

"Maybe Kell isn't the only one with a mortal ego."

Vidar bit back a reply as he headed up the cliff in large strides. He muttered complaints of Priscilla's nature while he gathered firewood. A nearby sound made him stop to listen. He heard it again. When he turned around to determine the noise he froze, a cry of surprise caught in his throat. Before him stood a large female Guardian dressed in black. Her dark hair was starkly pulled back while the violet eyes haughty in their regard. She placed her hands on her hips.

"Shaka!" he barely uttered the name.

A cold tight smile crossed her lips. "Vidar. I'm glad you haven't forgotten me."

He cautiously looked her up and down. She was unarmed. "What do you want?"

She took note of his inspection. "To talk."

"Right. Then say what you want and leave."

"Oooh. Found courage, have you?"

"Vidar?" His eyes darted sideways at hearing Shannan's call.

Shaka's eyes followed his nervous glance. "Who's that?"

"No one you know."

"Really? Let's see."

Shaka took a step toward the sound of Shannan's second call. Vidar struck her hard with the load of firewood he carried. The unexpected blow sent her stumbling forward. She recovered with lightning quickness before Vidar finished loading his crossbow. She knocked his weapon aside. A brief wrestling match ensued in which Vidar did his best against the larger, more powerful Shaka. Unfortunately, it ended with him on all fours and she in a dominant position. She had one arm locked about his throat in a chokehold, while the other grabbed his hair to pull back his head. Whereas he was a master archer, she was a master at lethal hand-to-hand combat. No need for a weapon. She knew the right amount of pressure to hold him in suspended agony.

"Not very smart, Vidar. You were never a match for me. I could end it here and now!"

"Then do it!" he painful grunted under her crushing grasp.

"Who was that?" she demanded. At his hesitation, she exerted more pressure, which made him cry out.

Brilliant light filled the area. It blinded them. A fast stunning blow to the head sent Shaka backward. The same time, hands ripped Vidar from her grasp. With a shout of outrage, Shaka struck out in her blindness. Her offensive was short lived. She gasped in surprise when a blade passed through her chest. She collapsed to the ground. Grey light surged in brightness around her then faded. When the light disappeared, so did Shaka.

Vidar recognized his rescuers. One held him in support; the other had his sword drawn. "Mahon. Cyril."

"Good to see you too." Mahon lowered a shaky Vidar to sit on the ground.

"It felt good to deal with Shaka." Cyril sheathed his sword.

"Vidar!" called Shannan. She, Wren and Torin rushed over. She knelt beside him. "Are you hurt?"

"No. Thanks to Mahon and Cyril." Vidar patted Torin when the wolf nuzzled him.

"I saw someone trying to kill you," Shannan insisted.

"Shaka won't be trying that with anyone again," Cyril said stoutly.

Shannan surveyed the two new Guardians. Cyril appeared older with thick shoulder length grey hair. His light brown eyes told of suffering. Mahon was blond with a youthful face. She noticed a hint of liveliness to his almost translucent blue eyes. Both wore warrior uniforms similar to Kell and Armus, only patched in places where the fabric was torn or tattered.

"You are the warriors who escaped with Vidar," she said.

"Ay, my lady. I am Mahon and this is Cyril."

"How did you find me?"

"After our escape, we headed toward the West Coast. On route, Zinna confirmed rumors of the Son of Tristan and Daughter of Allon," replied Mahon.

"Zinna is the Guardian of Midessex," Wren explained to Shannan.

Mahon continued. "Zinna took us to Kell. He armed us with instructions to aid in your protection."

"Which we are more than happy to do," added Cyril.

Shannan's gaze lingered on Cyril. "You suffered under Dagar."

Mahon smiled with compassion. His hand clasped Cyril's shoulder. "Being the eldest, Cyril was made an example to the warriors. He endured horrendous torture. I know he bears scars I should have received."

Cyril grew uncomfortable at the declaration. "If I had a chance, I—" he passionately began, yet unable to finish.

Shannan gently touched Cyril's arm. He stiffened. Her reassuring smile made him relax. She reached up to brush the hair from the left side of his head. Doing so revealed the reason he wore his hair long; his ear was missing.

"You have nothing to be ashamed of. This is no different than if you have been wounded in battle. Even as a prisoner, you fought bravely for your comrades, and bear the scars to prove it."

Cyril responded low and humble. "Thank you, my lady."

"Vidar!" came a desperate shout. A badly injured Guardian staggered from the shrubbery. He fell hard to the ground.

"Elgin?" Concerned, Vidar hastened to Elgin. The latter's face was swollen from bruises. His left hand broken and bloody. The torn clothes revealed more cuts and bruises. "What happened to you?" When Elgin reached for Vidar with his right hand to sit up, Vidar obliged.

"Shaka! I came to warn you," Elgin said between labored breaths.

Vidar tightened his supporting grip when Elgin became wracked with pain. "It's all right. Cyril and Mahon have taken care of Shaka."

Shannan knelt beside Elgin. He balked with confusion at sight of her. Her smile placed him at ease. "Let's get him to the cave," she told Vidar.

Elgin fainted upon movement.

Inside, Vidar placed Elgin on the bed. Shannan gave instructions for treatment. She then asked Vidar: "Who was Shaka?"

He didn't answer, rather went to the cupboard to retrieve a sheet. His copper eyes narrowed as he tore the sheet into strips of cloth for bandages.

At Vidar's piqued reaction, Mahon answered: "Shaka was an Enforcer with a knack for preying upon weaker Guardians. Vidar and Elgin have felt her might before. She was the one you saw trying to kill him when we intervened."

Unsettled by what was said, Wren queried Vidar. "I thought you said you weren't tortured?"

"Not officially. Griswold is Dagar's primary torturer. Shaka was his apprentice. My abuse was mild compared to Elgin. Being a vassal, he became her particular favorite. Easy sport for any new technique." Vidar looked at Elgin with compassion.

"You were a Trio Leader," Shannan said.

Vidar tore more cloth, his voice strained in reply. "Shaka became an Enforcer. I'm an archer. Only warriors of great strength and ability can match an Enforcer's might."

"Under our present limited circumstances, it took both of us to bring her down, and we're warriors," Cyril said of him and Mahon.

"Shannan!" Kell rushed in. A ripple of relief crossed his face at seeing her unscathed. His expression turned to curious at the scene before him. "What's going on?"

"Elgin came to warn Vidar about Shaka," Mahon replied.

Kell moved toward the bed. His jowls tightened, as he gripped the hilt of his sword upon sight of Elgin's injures. Golden eyes of fire flashed to Mahon. "Where is Shaka?"

"She is no more, Captain. Cyril and I just rescued Vidar from her when Elgin stumbled upon us. Apparently, she found Elgin first. Dagar probably sent her to track down and finish those of us who escaped."

Kell's passion was slow to ebb when he spoke to Shannan. "Now it begins, and will escalate until the final climax."

Shannan stood to ask Kell, "What will we do?"

"I don't know, yet. By sending Enforcers, Dagar seeks to thwart the return of the Guardians. Using gullet worms and kelpies against the mortals, he hopes to prevent their uniting with us against him."

"That means mortals of the Dark Way will begin to emerge also," Vidar said in warning.

"Perhaps we should counter him by moving against those mortals," suggested Mahon.

"No," refuted Kell. "Such actions mean Dagar is in control, and we simply respond to his choices."

"Then take the offensive," Shannan said, simple and direct.

Kell flashed a thin smile. "We are too few to launch any offensive."

"I meant an offensive to increase our numbers. We have four Guardians who escaped Dagar's prison. Between them we should be able to locate it and rescue others."

"No! Out of the question."

"Why?"

"Because we would be walking into his domain."

"A move he wouldn't expect," Mahon said to Shannan's pleasure and Kell's chagrin.

Shannan pressed her advantage. "Kell, you said that by countering Dagar we would be responding to his choices. We must to take those choices from him."

"I said, no!" Kell drew her away from the others. "I won't risk your life," he said in a low thick voice. His black brows level with golden eyes steady on her.

At that moment, Shannan fully understood why her grandfather spoke so fondly of Kell. He took everything to heart. He had taken her to his heart. He would protect her at all cost, just like Vidar. "Dear Kell, you can aid me, give me advice, even protect me, but you cannot stop me from doing what I must. What is my destiny," she gently countered. Yet no amount of gentleness could ease the hurt that crept into his eyes. Eyes, which more often, showed with unshakeable confidence.

"There could be other ways."

She shook her head. "If we allow Dagar to do as you have said, how many more Guardians and mortals will suffer? We must make a bold strike against him."

Mahon acted circumspect in his approach of them. "She's right, Captain. Just one word would spread like a wild fire in the nether dimension. All they need is their hope restored. Hope that years of imprisonment and torture have smothered." He glanced shifted to Shannan. "*She* is our hope."

"Kell, we know what it's like to be driven to the point of hopelessness," said Vidar. He titled his head toward Elgin.

"And to have it restored," added Cyril, who softly smiled at Shannan.

Kell's gaze swept over each Guardian. Elgin the abused vassal, Cyril and Mahon brave warriors, Wren loyal in her duty, while Vidar a former Trio leader. He turned back to Shannan "It will require a great amount of planning. Anything could go wrong."

"I don't fear that. You will be with me."

A bright light appeared. Swords and bows were instantly ready to make defense. Kell shielded Shannan. Cyril and Mahon at his shoulders. Wren and Vidar flanked them.

"Did I miss anything?" asked Priscilla.

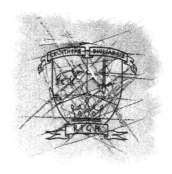

Chapter 20

DESPITE ALLARD'S ORDERS, WORD SPREAD OF ELLIS' PRESENCE AT Milton. Tyree paid Allard a third visit. Using his shrewd mind, Allard convinced Tyree that Ellis and his group secretly left. Unknown to Allard was Ellis' charge to Armus and the night twins to help fool Tyree. This gave the others more time to recover before they really left. Being the second longest duration they stayed in a single place, Ellis took the opportunity to consider the inevitable confrontation in light of everything they encounter.

Tyree's visit made Ellis renew his vow not to allow such evil to go unpunished. To fulfill that pledge, he spent time at sunrise and before retiring in meditation with Jor'el. During those quiet moments, he reflected upon his strengths and weaknesses, as he recalled each event of the Contest. So much already happened, with so much still left to do. At times he wondered if it would be worth the hardship and sacrifice.

Since leaving Dorgirith, what he read about his family from history books and Prophecy became starkly real. True, Niles recounted his time as King's Champion to King Rogan then King Berk I. However, the journey drove the knowledge from Ellis' head to his heart. Words written long ago became the flesh and blood of the present. Those closest to

Ellis became part of his consideration. Although, he accepted the fact that Angus and Agatha were not his real parents, in his heart that would never change. They loved him unconditionally, and encouraged him with unwavering conviction.

Shannan displayed similar confidence. Ellis smiled. Even apart he drew strength from her steadfast commitment. Despite a temporary interruption with Erin, Shannan was never far from his thoughts or heart. Memories of her filled his mind's eye, as he wondered what she was doing or how she felt about the situation. He could almost hear her verbal response. The two most difficult questions he could not answer: has she begun her part of their enterprise; and when would they be reunited? Upon those questions he dared not dwell lest he become gripped with concern for her welfare. Others and past situations, he did dwell for those impacted his current situation, along with any decisions.

Darius, Edmund and Jasper remained stoutly loyal. The deaths of Nando and Brody grieved him. They were barely older than Darius. It was so like Nando to give himself in the protection of another. Such a kind gentle soul of a man who was wonderfully patient with animals and children. Not a selfish bone in his body. As for Brody, he always tried to prove himself. Why? Ellis never knew, yet Brody was the first to volunteer and the last to question an order.

Kemp and Erin disturbed Ellis the most. Even as children, Kemp acted contrary, always ready with a snappy retort or snide comment. He usually did so with a wry smile or deadpan expression, but an evil heart? Since being reunited, Ellis noticed a sharp edge to Kemp's manner not present when they were younger. The chilly sense he felt connected to Kemp still puzzled him. Then Erin. Their encounter proved what Niles and Armus told him. Perhaps someday, he would thank her for helping him to realize just how much he loved Shannan. About how united purpose was vital to the survival of the kingdom.

Ellis' mind drifted to Niles. No words could express his gratitude for what the old Knight taught him. What reward could possibly begin to repay Niles? Being the King's Champion was enough for Niles.

"Oh, no," chuckled Ellis under his breath. "To see me crowned and married to Shannan will complete his joy." He opened his eyes to look heavenward. "May it be so." He clapped his hands together three times then bowed to conclude his prayers. He just returned inside from the balcony when there came a knock. "Enter."

Niles arrived fully dressed. "Did I wake you?" he asked.

Ellis still wore a dressing gown. He didn't immediately answer. Instead, he took a moment to regard Niles. In his generosity, Allard specifically ordered his tailored to make a new suit for the King's Champion. What a stark contrast to the old faded suit with its indistinguishable crest and numerous patches. Niles tried to keep the old suit clean. Alas, time took its toll. It often needed to be mended. The new rich azure blue suit brought a sparkle to the old blue eyes. Ellis noticed a swagger he had not seen before. Considering his advanced age, Niles remained fit. With a full head of dark hair, strong features with no sign of age, Ellis could only imagine what a sight Niles must have been in his younger days.

"Ellis?"

He smiled. "I was meditating. Have you seen the others?"

"Lord Darius is on his way to breakfast. The mild exercises I prescribed are doing wonders for his appetite, and increasing his strength. Edmund is also better. They will be ready to leave when you say the word."

"What of you? How have your old bones being doing?" Ellis teased. To his surprise, Niles answered in a more somber tone than expected.

"I'm managing."

"Is something wrong? Some physical malady you're not telling me?"

Niles arched a scolding brow. His words were laced with biting sarcasm. "Old age always brings on physical maladies which the young cannot comprehend."

"Cynicism for one," said Ellis, which drew a caustic snort from Niles. "Come, tell me what is wrong."

"I am concerned for Shannan. She must be about to start her part, if she hasn't already."

Ellis' smiled, warm and tender. "I was just thinking about her. As she is confident in my destiny, I must show her that same confidence." He placed an arm about Niles' shoulders. "Jor'el appointed you to instruct us, which you have faithfully done." Another knock came at the door. "Enter." His arm dropped from Niles.

Allard cordially greeted them. "Forgive this intrusion along with my neglect of you as host, my lord."

"Not at all. In fact, I appreciate your discretion while allowing me to secretly witness your dealings with people's troubles. It is obvious my enemies wish to stop me."

"Not all enemies are mortal," said Allard, who continued at seeing their keen regard. "I have diligently searched Verse and Prophecy. In doing so, I've come to believe the calamities are a preemptive strike to prevent you from gathering your Companions. The more difficult they make it, the more you are pressed. So, I have taken the liberty of accepting a proposal."

Interest piqued, Ellis folded his arms across his chest. "Go on."

"Arrangements have been made for a clandestine meeting of the Council of Twelve at a location suggested by Vicar Archimedes . . ."

"You've been in contact with Archimedes?" Niles interrupted.

"The other way around. The Vicar contacted me."

"Where is this place?" inquired Ellis.

"Arundine. To reach our destination we must leave within the hour." Ellis's laughter perplexed Allard. "My lord, I realize this sounds strange since it is rumored to be the legendary Council Hall of the Guardians—"

Ellis stopped Allard with a hand on the man's shoulder. "On my journey, Jor'el has directed my path. My next destination is Arundine." He saw Allard gape in wonder.

"That takes us back into Midessex," Niles warned Ellis.

"So be it. I don't think Owain will be eager to challenge me. While I dress, tell the others to make ready to leave," he instructed them.

Despite the hazardous of crossing back into Midessex, the group proceeded. This time the mortals rode horses, in case a quick escape became necessary. Daren and Darcy led the way. Two packhorses carried materials for a small tent along with provisions. The tent accommodated Erin while the men slept on bedrolls.

Being a Council member obliged Kemp to attend. Erin wore a feminine riding habit rather than men's clothes. Her attitude remained aloof, even a bit hostile toward Ellis.

Armus kept a discreet rear guard. Kell joined Armus in the clandestine effort. Their presence after so long an absence would alert the enemy. They didn't need to tip their hand to let Dagar just yet. That would happen soon enough.

Using short bursts of transverse contact, Kell and Armus maintained communication with Daren and Darcy. Along the route, Kell and Armus quietly secured locations to camp. Once the group crossed the border from the Meadowlands into Midessex, Gresham covertly joined Armus and Kell in watching over the mortals.

Half a day's travel into Midessex, Daren and Darcy led the group off the main road. The less visible they were to the general populous, the better chance for arriving safely at Arundine.

Four days later, they wound their way deeper into the forest to arrive at Arundine. According to legend, the Council Hall of Guardians stood in the most central part of Allon. Since the Great Battle, no mortal had been able to find it, though many tried. To their amazement, there it stood, a six-sided domed shrine of white marble, similar to that used to build the Temple of Providence. Vines grew around the pillars. A grayish-brown moss hung from the dome.

"It used to be splendid," said Daren to Ellis, a hint of pain in the Guardian's voice. "Now, the overgrowth serves as camouflage."

Niles noticed other horses along with a carriage. "It appears we're not the first to arrive."

"Jasper, Edmund, keep watch," instructed Darius.

"That is not necessary. We shall be your eyes and ears," said Darcy of himself and Daren.

Allard walked beside Ellis to enter Arundine. Niles flanked Ellis with Darius on the other side. Kemp and Erin followed with Jasper and Edmund in the rear.

The interior appeared larger than anticipated by the exterior. Six pillars held up the dome. Twelve marble chairs were arranged in a semi-circle. Under the dome on the marble floor, was a map of Allon. The name of each province etched in gold before its respective chair.

In the Highlands chair sat a virile looking man of fifty whose hair was completely white. The piercing dark blue eyes shone with a strength and fortitude Ellis always imagined Lord Ranulf possessed. With a smiling nod, he acknowledged the Highland lord. He did not expect to see Owain while Darius, Kemp and Allard took their places. Erin moved behind Kemp. Jasper and Edmund remained at the door. Niles stepped to one side, just inside the shadows to observe.

Archimedes sat in the high chair. He spied Ellis. "My lord." When he rose to pay respect to Ellis, so did the others.

"Malcolm. You shouldn't be here." Ellis gently eased Malcolm into his seat. "Gentlemen, be seated."

Malcolm tried to stifle a grunt of pain as he sat. "I would be remiss in my duty if I were not, my lord."

"You were remiss in your duty by losing the North Plains," complained another.

Ellis turned a critical eye to the speaker, a gruff-looking man of forty-five with a salt and pepper beard and dull brown eyes. "I don't believe we've met."

"Lord Zebulon, of the Lowlands."

"Ah," said Ellis with recognition at the name. "You struck a bargain with Tyree similar to Owain. How can you speak so basely of one who did not yield, rather had his province taken by force?"

Zebulon became rigid at the question. "My bargain was not the same. Owain yielded in cowardice. What of Allard? He too bargained with Tyree."

"You are quick to point the finger of blame, yet when you fall under the same charge you avoid responsibility. Tell me, Lord Zebulon, why did you come if you are already disposed to being contrary?"

Ellis' rebuke momentarily stymied Zebulon, who quietly replied, "I don't know, my lord."

"Then I suggest you remain silent until you can answer." Ellis heard soft laughter coming from the man beside Zebulon, who sat in the South Plains chair. He appeared ten years younger, stout, with whisker stubble, but no serious growth. "You laugh at your brother's thwarting, Sir Gareth, but you offered no resistance."

Gareth's swallowed back his mirth to answer. "My lord, my lack of resistance was not an act of cowardice, or self-preservation, rather strategy. Prophecy predicted Tyree's march. It also spoke about the scourges that now plague Allon. The time to fight is when you are ready, not before."

"Well said." Ellis slowly changed focus from Gareth to a man seated in the East Coast chair. He reckoned the occupant to be an older teenager. "You can't be Sir Fergus. Who are you?"

"I am his eldest son, Hollis. We received word prior to the summons that my father died in prison."

"My condolences."

Hollis made a quick nod of acknowledgement. He maintained his composure to speak. "It was my father's wish, and mine also, that you count us among your loyal supporters, my lord."

Ellis grinned, as he spoke to Zebulon. "From the mouth of babes."

"You're not much older," said a man from behind Ellis. A dashing dark-haired, mustached man of thirty-five sat in the West Coast chair. "Baron Mathias, at your service," he introduced himself with a swaggering smile. A gleam of confidence radiated from his hazel eyes.

Ellis chuckled. "You gave Tyree quite a smarting, Baron."

"And will do so again when you say the word, my lord."

Archimedes stepped forward. "Now that you have met everyone, we must test you. To see if you are who you claim before we pledge allegiance and fealty." He held Ellis' shoulder. "We all know you as the son of the late Sir Angus of Garwood, and brother of Lord Darius. Angus could have given sworn testimony of your birth. Alas, he died during his attempt to bring you to the Temple."

"I can give such testimony," said Darius.

Archimedes shook his head. "Verse requires eyewitnesses. Only Sir Angus and Master Ebenezer could provide such testimony. Alas, both are dead."

"He is not your brother?" Zebulon asked Darius.

"No, the story was a ruse to shield Ellis until the appropriate time. The Vicar knows this. Why can't you testify to the truth?" Darius asked Archimedes.

"I only know of what I was told by Angus and Ebenezer. I have seen nothing to confirm their story."

"I have this." Ellis produced the royal amulet from around his neck.

A small smile of pleasure appeared, as Archimedes examined the back to find the initials. "The Royal Seal. This is a start."

"My Lord Vicar." Jasper stepped forward. "I was with Sir Angus when he found Master Ellis as a babe. His dying mother told us of his heritage before she gave him to Angus for protection. That amulet was wrapped in his blanket."

"When was this?" asked Mathias.

"Three days after the Slaughter of the Innocents began."

The significance of the events was not lost upon the Council.

"Jasper, how long have you known Ellis?" asked Ranulf with a wink at Ellis.

"All his life. I taught him how to hold a sword, to ride a horse. Edmund has also known him since a babe."

"Were you an eyewitness to his finding?" Gareth asked Edmund.

"No, sir. I was at Garwood when Jasper and Sir Angus returned. They told me what happened and showed me the amulet."

"That's only one eyewitness," complained Zebulon. "You said Verse calls for three."

"My Lord Vicar, I have a document written by Master Ebenezer," said Jasper.

"How could you have such a document?" snapped Zebulon.

"He gave it to me the day the Fortress of Garwood was attacked by Latham's men. That's how I got this," Jasper chided about his eye patch. "At the time I didn't know what it was, only that he instructed me to give it to Sir Angus. Alas, I never saw him again. I showed it to Lord Darius."

"That he did. It bears Ebenezer's seal," confirmed Darius.

"Where is this document?" asked Archimedes.

Jasper pulled it from the breast pocket of his doublet. Though worn, creased with slightly forayed edges, the seal remained intact. He gave it to Archimedes. The Vicar broke the seal to examine the contents.

"Well?" asked Zebulon with impatience.

"It is Ebenezer's writing, and bears his seal. Give heed, my lords." Archimedes read aloud:

"I, Master Ebenezer, Priest of the Fortress of Garwood, take pen in hand to write this historical account in hopes of explaining the actions taken by Sir Angus of Garwood, Lord of the Southern Forest, member of the Council of Twelve, and myself.

"Almost ninety years have passed since the demise of the House of Tristan. The worship of Jor'el has faded to almost nonexistence, though the Temple Fortress remains unscathed, a force not permitting Dagar and those of the Dark Way from marring a single stone. The present ruling family uses their connection to the Dark Master of the Heavenlies to ruthlessly put down anyone who remind the people of Jor'el or Allon's glory days. Under such harshness, most chapels are empty, or only attended by the most faithful believers.

217

"The Fortress of Garwood has seen a drastic decline in attendance while the locals shun us. Threat of uprising from the Fortresses is considered minimal due to our dwindling influence over the populace. That was until rumors of Prophecy began concerning the promised Son of Tristan with the birth of a prince, heir to the throne.

"Praise to Jor'el, it is no rumor! How anyone of the royal line survived is a mystery. Sir Angus found the babe wrapped in his dying mother's arm during the Slaughter of the Innocents. With my own eyes I have seen the evidence to confirm his identity when Sir Angus brought the babe to me for advice on what to do. We agreed that Ellis would be raised as Angus' own son until the appointed time.

"Alas, betrayal has forced us to abandon our original course of action. Thus I write this testament, for a deep foreboding in my spirit tells me I may not live to see the Son of Tristan crowned. I fear Allon will experience evil the likes of which has not been seen since Magelen. Many questions remain unanswered about Prophecy. If the Daughter of Allon exists, we have yet to learn of her. Howbeit, we have not wavered in our duty to protect him, rear him, and instruct Prince Ellis, the Son of Tristan, rightful born king of Allon.

May Jor'el have mercy on us at this time! And may the Son of Tristan be restored to the Throne. Long live, Prince Ellis.

"Signed,
Master Ebenezer
Twelfth Priest of the Fortress of Garwood
15 Dàmhar 1584."

A profound silence followed Archimedes' conclusion of the letter. At length, Mathias broke the silence.

"Ebenezer's testimony confirms Jasper's story."

"That makes two eyewitnesses. We need a third," said Malcolm.

Niles stepped from the shadows into the light. "There are three alive and present, who can testify to his identity. Fulfilling the need for both young and old eyewitnesses."

Archimedes snorted with sarcasm. "Niles of Pollux. I should have known you'd survived all these years to come back to haunt me."

Hollis' grew wide-eyed. "The same Sir Niles of legend?"

Niles grinned at Hollis. "I can hardly be a legend if I'm still alive." He turned to Archimedes. "My haunting is by way of presenting the Son of Tristan to the Council."

"Then you were with Jasper and Angus?" asked Ranulf.

"No. I was honored with a direct word from Jor'el for my part in saving Prince Akilles from Zared's coup. I have been doubly honored to be the grandsire of the *Daughter of Allon*, who at this moment is fulfilling her part of this venture."

"Can you prove this? Or are you some daft old man with delusions of grandeur?" challenged Zebulon.

"Vicar Archimedes just confirmed my identity." Niles removed his amulet to hand to Zebulon. "If you want proof, this is the amulet of the King's Champion."

Archimedes gave Zebulon the Royal seal. "Compare it with this."

"Anyone can make an amulet from what is described in the Book of Prophecy. Either one of these could be fake." Zebulon continued in his dispute.

"True," began Archimedes. "However, if one were to make a copy of the Royal seal from the King's Champion, it would include an eagle clenching a crown and sword, not the royal eagle by itself. If the reverse, then only an eagle would appear, ignoring the symbols of the Jor'ellian Knights of the Temple. Also, you should find initials on the back of the royal amulet. All royal symbols are carved with initials. One would have to be well versed in Prophecy, royal customs, and an accomplished metal smith, to make perfect copies."

"APR?" asked Zebulon with a shrug of confusion.

"Akilles, Prince Royale. My great-grandfather," said Ellis.

"There is something the book of Prophecy does not mention. There is a nick on my amulet at the top. Do you see it?" Niles asked Zebulon.

"Ay. Was that on purpose during the forging? As an identifying mark perhaps?"

Niles chuckled. "No, purely accidental. Or should I say, providential," he spoke the sentence while looking at Ellis and Archimedes. "It happened when I instructed Prince Akilles in armed combat, shortly before the coup. Archimedes witnessed the accident. In recompense for my enthusiasm, I was ordered to replace the broken chain, yet since the nick did not mar the amulet too severely, no need to forge a new one."

"I would recognize a duplicate," confirmed Archimedes.

"So you *can* bear witness to Ellis' identity," Darius said emphatically to Archimedes.

"I can bear witness to authenticity of the royal amulet. Whereas others make its connection to the Prince himself."

"Then the requirements of Verse are fulfilled?" asked Malcolm hopeful.

"Ay," declared Archimedes. "Gentlemen, behold Jor'el's chosen, the Son of Tristan, true King of Allon!" He placed a hand on Ellis' shoulder.

Niles clasped his sword and knelt. "My liege."

Darius knelt beside Niles. Erasmus, Ranulf, Hollis, Allard and Mathias followed. Gareth did so when Ellis' gaze passed to him. Malcolm moved painfully slow to kneel beside his chair.

Ellis took note of Zebulon's confusion. "Do you have your answer now, my lord?"

"Ay, my Liege." Zebulon respectfully bent a knee.

Ellis focused on Kemp, the sole man remaining in his seat. Ellis' expression was not of compulsion or judgment; rather hopeful. He knew no matter Kemp's personal feeling, the facts of his parentage were undeniable. For Kemp not to acknowledge that among his peers was an unspeakable effrontery to him and the Council. With clenched jaw and stiff back, Kemp forced himself to one knee.

Erin gave Ellis a quick half-hearted curtsey. For a brief moment their eyes met. True, he wounded her affection, however, at that moment, he realized the great gulf between them. Like Kemp, her affection became easily bruised. Such fragile emotion doesn't make a stalwart heart. He felt a twinge of regret.

Ellis caught Erasmus' studious gaze of he and Erin. When he acknowledged Erasmus with a small nod, the normally affable Erasmus barely responded.

Ellis addressed the Council. "Vicar, and noble lords, I accept your homage. I solemnly pledge before the Council to do all Jor'el has ordained to take back the throne. The question is, will you help me?"

"Ay!" said Darius, Erasmus, Gareth and Hollis individually.

"Ay," said Allard, Mathias, Ranulf, and Malcolm in chorus.

Zebulon curtly nodded. "Ay."

"Ay," droned Kemp in contrast to the other's enthusiasm.

"Your Highness, time is short. Even as we speak, the Dark Way is creeping across Allon. We must begin preparations," said Archimedes.

Ellis nodded to the Vicar's statement. He addressed the Council. "My lords, return to your provinces to begin secret preparations of gathering supplies, enlisting men and forging weapons. When the hour is near, I shall send word of where to meet me."

The more enthusiastic quickly followed Ellis' instructions. Gareth and Zebulon left together. Erasmus approached Kemp and Erin. He paid special attention to Erin. Ellis noticed Erasmus gallantly kissed Erin's hand. Her return smile was polite, yet she replied to his words with a nod of agreement. Kemp also appeared to agree.

Archimedes' address interrupted Ellis observation. "Your Highness? Is something wrong?"

"A moment, Vicar." Ellis approached them. "Erasmus, I didn't get a chance to greet you earlier."

"It's good to see you too, Ellis, my Liege," he corrected himself. "Although the last time we met, you were a wiry lad of fifteen."

"At Erin's wedding."

"Ay. Since her birthday is next week, I invited she and Kemp to Deltoria for celebration."

"I told Erasmus my intent is to go home, only he informs me the Northern Forest is under Lord Byrne's rule," said Kemp in bitter complaint.

"I'm sorry," said Ellis sincerely. His eyes lingered a moment on Erin.

She turned to Erasmus. "In our position, it is a generous offer we cannot refuse." Not standing on ceremony of leaving royalty, they departed Arundine.

Niles appeared at Ellis' shoulder. "It's for the best."

"I know. Perhaps Erasmus can give her what I could not."

"What now, Highness? Will you return with me to Milton?" asked Allard.

"I'm not certain."

"Could I persuade you to join me and the Jor'ellians?" asked Archimedes.

"Ask me later. Both of you." Ellis went outside to walk among the ruins of what was a garden that surrounded Arundine.

Armus appeared beside him. "There's no need to wait too long."

Ellis heaved a casual shrug as he kept walking. "I thought it would give either you or Kell time to speak with me in private."

"With the Guardians returning, we hardly need to speak in private." Armus stopped Ellis. "As the time approaches, Dagar grows stronger. Kell summoned all Guardians to meet here this evening. Why, I don't know exactly. However he left instructions for you to go straightway to the ancient ruins of Magelen's manor in Dorgirith. Take only Niles for the final phase of the Contest."

"What of Shannan?"

"I'll find out this evening. You must concentrate on your task."

A look of melancholy furrowed Ellis' brow. "I miss her terribly."

Armus kindly smiled. "I'll be sure she knows that. Now, you must leave." His hearty grip on Ellis' arms made the moral look up at him. "I won't see you again until the hour has come. Jor'el is with you, Son of Tristan."

"And with you, Guardian of Allon."

Ellis returned to the front of Arundine. Archimedes and Niles conversed on the steps. He passed them to where Erasmus and the others were by their horses.

"Erasmus! Will you extend hospitality to Darius, Jasper and Edmund?"

"Of course."

Darius was within earshot. "What about you?"

"I have business I must be about. Niles will accompany me."

The answer did not set well with Darius. "Just the two of you?"

Ellis drew Darius aside to ask; "Are you jealous of Niles?" Darius' sheepish scowl answered his question. "You know Jor'el appointed him as my teacher before we were born. Rest assured, no man is as dear to me as you, brother."

"Then tell me where you are going, so I can at least have some knowledge and not be fretful of the unknown like before."

Ellis cocked a smile. "To where it began. I must come full circle to complete the Contest. That is why I can only take Niles."

"Dorgirith," snorted Darius. "Goes along with Arundine." He embraced Ellis, though he didn't want to let go. "Don't take too long."

"I won't. When I have completed my test, *you* will be the first I call. I won't go into this venture without you."

"Darius, we must leave if we are to reach shelter before sunrise," called Erasmus.

Ellis escorted Darius to his horse. There he bade good-bye to Jasper and Edmund. He also wished Kemp and Erin well though the brother and sister barely acknowledged him.

Archimedes approached. "When you have completed your task, return to Allard. He knows how to contact me. Until then, Jor'el be with you, Highness."

"Vicar. Allard," said Ellis in farewell. He motioned Niles to the horses.

"Where to?" asked Niles.

"Dorgirith and the Final Contest."

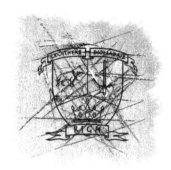

Chapter 21

WHEN ALL GREW STILL FROM THE MORTALS' DEPARTURE, small white flashes signaled the arrival of other Guardians. Armus had the night twins usher them inside Arundine.

A large flash caught Armus' attention. Wren, Vidar and Priscilla arrived with a hooded Shannan. Three other Guardians with Torin also appeared. One Guardian in the russet and tan uniform of a vassal showed signs of abuse. Armus smiled at Mahon and Cyril.

"By the heavenlies! Warriors." As Armus watched them go inside, he felt a tap on his shoulder.

"You can count on my sword." Avatar gregariously smiled.

"Avatar! It's been too long." Armus greeted Avatar with a bear hug.

"Indeed, old friend." Kell heartily embraced Avatar. "Only tell me you are here to help, not just bring a message."

Avatar chuckled at Kell's reference to the last time they spoke before the House of Tristan fell. Avatar slapped the hilt of his sword. "I'm here to unite the High Trio to face what is to come."

"That makes five warriors," said Armus to Kell.

"Let's see how many others there are."

Kell entered. He stopped beside Shannan, who remained concealed under the hood. He counted a total of twenty-two Guardians with six warriors among them. Including the High Trio made for a total of twenty-five and nine warriors.

"Mahon!" Avatar happily shouted.

Kell smiled, as he watched the reunion between Avatar and Mahon. They served together for centuries before Mahon's capture just prior to the Great Battle. After a brief moment of basking in some satisfaction, Kell ushered Shannan to the high chair. She kept her hood up. Standing in a room full of Guardians, her diminutive size along with a large wolf beside her drew attention.

Kell's voice rose above the chatter. "I'm sure all of you are wondering why I called this war council. In times past, such a gathering was restricted to Trio leaders." He fought a smile to say, "The time *has come* for all Guardians to unite!" His gaze swept over the room to gauge the guardedly curious reaction. "At present, the Son of Tristan is heading for his final Contest, which I must administer." With pleasure, he announced, "Guardians! I present the Daughter of Allon." He removed Shannan's hood.

Armus clasped his sword, as he bent one knee in homage. "My lady."

Avatar, Cyril, Mahon, Valmar, Jedrek and Barnum followed suit. Wren, Vidar, Eldric, Gresham, Chase, Zinna, Mona, Priscilla, Elgin, Darcy and Daren bowed.

"How can we be sure this is not some trick of Dagar?" asked a gruff looking Guardian warrior. He had a weather-beaten face framed by golden hair with amber eyes. His expression grew apprehensive as he watched Shannan's approach. Her gentle gaze held a reassuring confidence that began to place him at ease.

"Your question is one of concern, not rebellion, though you harbor great anger for what you have suffered." Her focus went to his left arm, which he protectively shielded with his right hand. "It is useless as a result of torture. You escaped with Vidar."

"I recognize him. Though I don't know his name," said Vidar.

"I am Morrell. You are correct about my arm," he said with a hint of awe. He bowed to Shannan. "My lady."

"I think that answers all doubts," said Kell.

"What now, Captain?" asked Valmar.

"Her ladyship has proposed a bold strike against the enemy's stronghold. Ay, against the Cave." Kell affirmed at the wary reaction from those unaware of the proposal.

Unnerved, Elgin shook his head. Several females muttered under their breath. Avatar braced himself by gripping the hilt of his sword. Most of the others warriors also covered the initial surprise by following Avatar's lead of stalwart silence. Morrell paled with worry.

Surprise briefly rippled Armus' brow. As second-in-command, it was unusual for him not to know what was happening. After two millennia together, looks between he and Kell often conveyed thoughts that made words unnecessary. Thus, Armus asked the obvious question, "Why?"

"To free more Guardians, and interfere with Dagar's efforts to cause premature conflict. Hopefully, this will give Ellis time to finish his preparation," answered Shannan.

"As long as Dagar keeps sending plagues on the mortals and Enforcers against us, our energies are split, lessening our strength for when he emerges," Kell added to the explanation.

"So this is a preemptive strike," said Armus to which Kell agreed.

Elgin remained fretful "I don't know! Returning to the Cave is not something I planned."

"None of us who escaped did. Yet, if it will delay Dagar and serve the Daughter of Allon, I will return," said Cyril stoutly.

Kell placed a supportive hand on Elgin's shoulder. "Penetrating the inner sanctum is a warrior's task. Each will have an assignment according to ability. However, the execution must be swift and precise for maximum effectiveness, and to allow for ample exit time."

"How? We don't even know exactly where the Cave is," said Valmar.

"We entered it from Midessex," said Mohan of he and Avatar.

227

"That was before the Great Battle. Those of us captured during the fighting were transported from the Region of Sanctuary," said Vidar.

"Which could mean multiple entrances," said Barnum with discouragement.

"Doesn't change the location of the Cave, merely different access points," said Armus.

Shannan interrupted the conversation. "From the description of those who escaped, along with the recent plagues, everything seems to originate from near Ravendale, which *is* in Midessex.

"Her ladyship is correct," began Avatar stoutly. "Ravendale is near the location where Mahon and me entered. Also, I encountered Latham when on assignment at Ravendale." He proceeded to describe his activity to an attentive audience. "It is likely the Cave is either underneath or very near the castle."

Kell nodded to Avatar's concluding statement. "We know Dagar uses a talisman as a link to a mortal *Grand Master*. The closer their proximity to each other, the better the access. So we will go on the assumption of the Cave being in Midessex." He turned to Avatar. "Take Morrell, Elgin, Priscilla, Mona, Jedrek, Gresham and Daren for reconnaissance, and establish a perimeter."

"Watch for Enforcers and Shadow Warriors. We don't want them showing up unannounced," Armus warned Avatar. He received an acknowledgement before Avatar's group disappeared in a bright flash of white light.

"Captain, we're not as strong when separated," said Darcy.

"We must go tonight, and will need your abilities on two fronts. Once I have given out the other assignments, we go," said Kell.

"That quickly?" asked Morrell still a bit uncertain.

"Ay, time is of the essence. Valmar, take Nixie, Luann, Chase, Barnum, Darcy and Zinna. Post watches at all roads leading to Ravendale." Kell turned to the two other warriors, Ewert and Bailey. "North of the castle is a hollow. That will be our place of rendezvous, and escape route, should it be necessary. Secure it. Eldric, go with them in case your skills are needed."

"Take Torin. He makes a good sentry," said Shannan. With a few words in the Ancient, she sent Torin to Ewert and Bailey.

The wolf disappeared with the warriors. Valmar's group also vanished in dimension travel.

Once the light from departure faded, Kell spoke to those remaining. "The rest of us are the main strike force. We will give the first three groups ten minutes to complete their assignments. Cyril, you and Vidar take the point. Shannan will stay with Armus and me. Wren and Mahon will be rear guard. We must move swiftly."

"Won't we risk being sensed upon arrival?" asked Wren.

"No," Mahon answered instead of Kell. "One of the things we discovered last time is a lack of sensory perception. Part of the punishment for those sent to the Cave."

"You were captured on reconnaissance, not sent there as punishment," said Wren with some confusion.

"Jor'el originally created the Cave as a prison for turncoats," Kell said with distaste. He waved Wren silent. "No time to argue—" A flash of light interrupted him. Avatar returned, which made Kell ask, "Trouble?"

"No, we have an opportunity," began Avatar with enthusiasm. "Immediately upon arrival, I felt that the resistance is gone. So using my senses, I confirmed the location of the Cave *is* under Ravendale. We can also bridge the dimension gap."

"Are you certain?" asked Kell with some skepticism.

"I tested it myself. Easier access with no physical side effects—"

"You gave away our element of surprise!" Armus chided.

"No!" insisted Avatar.

"Lack of sensory perception," Mahon added as a reminder. He statement satisfied Armus' objection.

Kell drew his sword. He held it straight out. "May Jor'el's strengthen us for this venture!"

The warriors drew their sword to overlap Kell's blade. They repeated in one voice: "May Jor'el strengthen us!"

"Return," Kell instructed Avatar. "It's time. Cyril. Vidar." He waited for the light to fade from dimension departure. "We leave when all is secure," he told the rest.

Deep within the cavernous domain of Dagar's nether Cave, two dim flashes appeared in a small passageway. Vidar and Cyril softened their arrival so as not to draw attention. Vidar crept to the edge of the wall. He carefully peeked around the corner. Seeing no one, he motioned to Cyril. The warrior closed his eyes.

A moment later, Kell and the others appeared. Shannan clung to Kell in an effort to keep from fainting.

"Take several deep breaths. You'll be fine in a moment. Dimension travel is difficult on mortals," Kell instructed Shannan.

"I sensed a disturbance when I summoned you, Captain," said Cyril.

"Ay, but we'll tend to it later. Which way?"

"To the right leads to Dagar's personal hall. To the left is the Reconditioning Chamber. Beyond that is the garrison."

"Secure the point," Kell told Cyril and Vidar. After they left, he spoke to Shannan, who now stood on her own. "Stay close to Armus or me. Wren, Mahon, bring up the rear.

Carefully they moved down the intersecting corridor to where Cyril watched. The warrior crouched at the corner to another corridor. Vidar continued around the corner. Kell, Armus, and Shannan knelt beside Cyril. Mahon and Wren kept the proper rear guard, both stopping a short distance behind the others.

"The Reconditioning Chamber is several corridors beyond where Vidar went," said Cyril. He didn't hide his contempt when speaking of the chamber.

Suddenly they heard the whiz of a shaft followed by a dull thud. They rushed forward to Vidar's position. He fitted a new bolt in his crossbow.

"What happened?" demanded Kell.

"A Shadow Warrior crossed my path. When I hit him, he fell off the crosswalk. I don't think anyone heard," replied Vidar.

"Where does the crosswalk lead?"

"It goes to the garrison quarters. Another discovery we made last time," said Mahon. "Not too far from it is an area where some creatures of infrinn are held."

"We don't want the garrison coming down on us," said Armus.

"Is there a way to deny access to the reconditioning chamber?" Kell asked Mahon.

"Sure, *if* we can block the garrison entrance."

"We can do that," Vidar said of him and Wren. He patted his bow.

Kell spoke to Mahon, Wren and Vidar. "We'll give you a few moments before heading for the reconditioning chamber."

Mahon took the lead with Vidar and Wren close to his heels. Fifty yards from the others, the tunnel turned. Around the corner, they heard voices. They ducked into two crevices: Vidar and Mahon into one and Wren in the other. Two Shadow Warriors proceeded past them without any notice. Vidar sent a puzzled glance to Mahon, who simply flashed a confident smile. With the passage clear, Mahon again led the way.

Mahon stopped in a clearing. Another tunnel veered off from the clearing while a short passage stood opposite them. Mahon waved to take cover behind a very large stalagmite capable of shielding all three of them. Muffled voices came from the tunnel across the clearing.

"That tunnel leads to a area holding some creatures. The voices are from the garrison chamber through a short entrance," Mahon whispered.

"The impact will make noise that can't be helped," said Vidar.

"The garrison first then the creatures," said Mahon.

Vidar nodded to Wren. She moved to the other side of Mahon at the edge of the stalagmite. The archers fitted a bolt into their crossbow then placed another bolt between their teeth for quick shooting.

Vidar carefully stood. He nodded to Wren. They fired at the rocks above the garrison entrance. The sound of impact echoed, followed by falling rocks. Immediately, they reloaded to fire at the same place above the tunnel to the creature's holding area.

Angry shouts came from the garrison while loud snarls, screeches and howls emanated from the startled creatures. Unfortunately, the rock slides at the entrances caused instability in the surrounding walls. Rocks and dirt fell on them from above. Wren covered her head. Vidar dodged falling rocks. The debris threatened to block their escape route.

Mahon sheathed his sword. He shouted in the Ancient; "The speed of flight!"

Mahon seized Wren with his right hand, and Vidar with his left. He raced toward the crumbling exit. His speed made the archers stumble. He half-dragged, half-carried them through the gathering rubble. They made it to other side just before a rockslide blocked the entire passage.

Vidar staggered a few step to regain his balance. He brushed the soot from his hair.

Wren fell to her knees coughing from the settling dust. "Thanks for that. I think," she said between coughs.

Mahon helped her to stand. He brushed some dust from her face. "You're welcome. Now let's rejoin the others."

At the main group, Kell waited with impatience. "That should be enough time—" They became alert at hearing nearby movement.

"It's us," Vidar harshly whispered.

"Done," Mahon said with a nod to Kell.

"Vidar, Cyril, take the point," Kell said.

They followed Vidar and Cyril down the steps to take up positions on either side of an opening. Shannan, Kell and Armus came up behind Vidar while Mahon and Wren went opposite with Cyril.

"The Reconditioning Chamber," Vidar grimly whispered.

Kell observed the infamous chamber. It rose one hundred feet tall and just as wide. Thousands of cells and cages filled the chamber. Each contained at least one Guardian. Instruments of torture were scattered about the cavern. Kell's jowls tightened with dismayed fury.

"We'll free as many as we can," said Shannan at Kell's reaction.

Armus fiercely sneered during his scan of the chamber. "How?"

Griswold appear from behind several cages. They slightly pulled back to avoid being seen.

Griswold jeered at a poor wretched female in the cage close to their concealment. "You're next, Jakki. Perhaps this time, you'll reconsider."

Cyril visibly tensed when Griswold jerked Jakki out of the cage.

Mahon tried to soothe Cyril. "Easy. She's still alive."

Griswold struck Jakki. Cyril bolted forward, Mahon not quick enough to grab him. Cyril's attack caught Griswold off guard. He tossed Jakki aside. She hit her head on the cage, which rendered her unconscious. The sounds of disturbance brought three Shadow Warriors from an adjacent corridor.

Kell snarled at the miscue. "Targets!" he told Vidar and Wren.

The archers immediately emerged from their concealment to fire. Two Shadow Warriors disappeared in the gray light of demise.

"Keep sight on the openings," Kell ordered Vidar and Wren

The archers moved to take up better positions for better viewing of the various corridors. So many levels each with multiple entrances, it would take all their energies to focus on covering them.

"Kell!" Shannan pointed to corridor from which came two more Shadow Warriors.

"Stay with Shannan," he told Armus and Mahon. Kell raced for the Warriors.

Two Shadow Warriors quickly fell under the mighty captain's sword. Each vanished in a flash of grey light. *Twang! Whiz!* Kell loudly hissed in pain when a crossbow dart slashed across his upper left arm. It lodged into the cavern wall. Fortunately, it cut flesh and not muscle. At the sound of another bolt being launched, Kell jerked to one side. The dart just missed his face. He glared up to where it came from. Two Shadow Archers stood one level above and across from him. Enraged, Kell bounded up the stone steps in two strides to deal with the archers.

Try as they might, Vidar and Wren couldn't prevent total incursion by Shadow Warriors. At the arrival of two more Warriors, Mahon said to Armus, "I'll take care of them."

For all of his skills, Cyril proved no match for Griswold's size and strength. The crafty Griswold used a spurean whip to keep Cyril at bay. At a misstep, Cyril found himself entangled in the whip unable to move. Like a coiled snake, it tightened. Cyril gritted his teeth against the strangling pressure that threatened to squeeze the air from his lungs.

"He'll kill Cyril!" Shannan readied her bow.

"Your weapon is no match for him." Armus drew his sword.

At Armus' charge, Griswold left Cyril to snatch up a nearby sword to parry the attack. "Puny warriors coming out from under rocks, how quaint."

Shannan went to aid Cyril. He lay gasping for air beneath, being smothered by the whip. She hurried to try to find a way to free him.

He grimly shook his head. "Useless—I'm powerless—you're mortal." He began to choke. She worked feverishly to try to free him, yet struggled against the whip.

Although more powerful than Cyril, Armus too was hard pressed against the larger Griswold. A backhanded blow sent him staggering sideways. He touched his face to discover blood from a split lip. He caught a glimpse of Kell engaged with two Shadow Warriors. Mahon also engaged several Warriors. Vidar and Wren continued to provide cover.

Griswold advanced. Armus used all his strength to turn away another hard blow, but with mild success. He felt the tip of Griswold's blade cut into his left breast.

Griswold reached for a stygian chain. "You know you can't last."

Armus set his jaw. He gripped his sword with both hands. His eyes uneasily shifted between Griswold and the chain. Griswold's fake thrust made Armus flinch, but not fully fall for the deception. Griswold became more aggressive. He stepped forward to lunge at Armus' body. This made Armus parry in such a way that exposed the back of his shoulders.

A savage blow from the chain sent him down on all fours. A glancing blow to the forehead made him collapse into semi-consciousness.

Kell finished with the Warriors in time to see Armus struck down. Several levels separated them. Griswold moved in. The only way to reach Armus in time was a frantic, death-defying leap from the walkway. With a rising war cry, Kell took the necessary strides and launched himself.

At the same time, the twang of a bow sounded. When the shaft lodged in Griswold's throat, a sudden blinding light erupted in the cavern. The intensity of the force altered Kell's trajectory. He crashed into the wall behind Armus. Nearby cages were shaken.

Wren, Vidar and Mahon shielded their eyes against the intense light. When the light faded, Griswold was gone, and an armed Shannan stood protectively in front of Armus.

"Armus?" she spoke over her shoulder.

"I'll recover," he grunted. He wiped the blood of his head wound from his eyes. His vision clear, he saw Kell lying in a heap not moving. Too groggy to stand, Armus crawled to Kell. He seized him by the shoulder. "Kell?"

Shannan saw Armus try to rouse Kell, but told Mahon, "Help Cyril."

Stricken, Mahon motioned to the empty coil of whip. "He's gone."

She stared at the whip that once ensnared Cyril.

"Kell!" Armus desperately shook Kell, who still did not respond.

Shannan joined Armus. Kell's face was unusually pale. He didn't appear to be breathing. She touched his face. "Kell! It is not your time. I need you. Ellis needs you."

"Kell, listen to the Daughter of Allon," urged Armus.

"Daughter of Allon?" murmurs began among the Guardian prisoners. The questions were ignored since their focused on Kell.

Shannan seized him by the shoulders. *"Kell! Duisg, do dleasdanas."*

Kell's eyes snapped open. He quickly sat up; his breathing labored and expression confused. He stared at Shannan. "You called me back. I was almost free. But it didn't feel right." He swayed, still weak and dazed.

Armus caught Kell against his chest, which made him flinch at the pain of his own wound. Kell quizzically regarded Armus. Sight of the wound made Kell sit up.

"If the racket from Griswold's demise didn't attract notice, I think we'll be safe for awhile," said Wren, tentative and respectful.

"We lost Cyril." Mahon spoke with choked words.

Vidar clapped Mahon's shoulder in an attempt to comfort. Wren too lent her support. Mahon didn't look at either of them, rather stared at the coiled stygian whip.

"So you dispatched Griswold on his behalf," Kell said to Mahon.

"I did," said Shannan.

The reply surprised them.

"Kell!"

"Who calls me?" Kell needed Vidar's help to stand.

"It's Gulliver," said Vidar.

"That old seafarer still around?" Armus chuckled. He gingerly stood, yet doubled over in pain. He held his head. Wren aided him to sit on a boulder. "I'll be all right in a few minutes."

"You don't have a few minutes. It's only a matter of time before Dagar arrives," warned Gulliver.

Crossing to Gulliver, Kell didn't see a cringing being in the back of the cage. Once at Gulliver's cage, Kell used his sword in an attempt to hack open the lock.

"That won't work, lad," said Gulliver.

"I won't leave you. Any of you!" Kell repeatedly tried to break the lock with his sword.

When Shannan moved to join Kell, the cringing mass sprang forward, and thrust a hand threw the bars to seize her. She cried out at seeing a pitiful male Guardian with one eye badly bandaged, a hand missing and one leg gone below the knee gone.

Kell turned at her cry, sword first. The wretched being in the cage made unintelligible wheezing noises. Rather than strike, Kell balked at the sight. "Rune?" he asked in a thick discord.

A pitiful nasal wheeze and nod came in response.

"Dagar ripped out his vocal chords so he couldn't cry out when watching others being tortured with his remaining eye," Gulliver said with remorse.

Rune's imploring eye looked at Shannan. He again tried to communicate.

"I am," she said.

Rune wept. He took her hand between the bars to kiss it.

"You understand him?" Kell asked.

"Ay. He wanted to know if I am the Daughter of Allon. I told him I was." Rune again communicated with her, so she interpreted for Kell. "He wants to come with us."

Kell seized the lock on Rune's cage. "I can't open the cages!"

Shannan grabbed Kell's hand to stop his gesture. "I know this." She withdrew her necklace. What hung on the chain matched the lock.

Kell's eyes grew wide with surprise at seeing the necklace. "Where did you get that?"

"Grandfather gave it to me the day they left Dorgirith. He said Vicar Wilbur entrusted it to him before he died. Grandfather didn't know why. Now I do."

"I gave it to Wilbur," said Kell in a hushed tone of awe.

Armus came to Kell's shoulder when Shannan used the necklace to unlock the cage. The click echoed in the chamber. "By the heavenlies!" he exclaimed.

"Quick, open the cages." Shannan gave Vidar the necklace. "Wren, Mahon, help Rune."

"Better hurry," said Gulliver. He was the next one to be set free.

"Halt!" shouted a voice from the direction of the main entrance. In the archway appeared Tor. Behind him, and at other passages were Shadow Warriors.

Vidar stopped his tracks. He paled in fright. "Tor."

Kell waved at Vidar to continue. "Ignore him."

Tor's sword flashed at Vidar. "Another step, Vidar, and I'll slice you in two!"

Vidar froze with indecision.

Shannan stepped in front of an irate Kell to confront Tor. "Vidar will do what we came to do. You will not stop him."

Tor haughtily laughed. "Puny mortal, what business have you here?"

"She is the Daughter of Allon!" declared Kell.

Tor's laughter caught in his throat. His eyes grew level on her. "You?"

"*Mise.* I am," Shannan replied with serene confidence in the Ancient. "We are leaving, Tor. You will not stop us. The time for the Guardians has come."

Tor stared at her. She didn't flinch under his intense inspection. Most mortals cringed when a Guardian invoked heavenly power. Instead, the truth reflected in her eyes. His jowls tightened with realization, and he lowered his sword.

Kell spoke for everyone to hear. "All of you who joined Dagar thought this day would never come. That he was able to prevent it. He deceived you! Here is proof." He snatched the necklace from Vidar. "No Guardian could unlock Spurean Chains and Stygian Bars. Only by the hand of Daughter of Allon could the Guardians be renewed." He gave it back to Vidar along with a wave to proceed. "Those of you strong enough to dimension travel, come with us," he continued above the clicking locks. "The rest," he said to Tor, "you will hide until they are strong enough to leve."

A ripple of concern crossed Tor's brow. When he replied, it was with a submissive tone. "Ay, Captain."

"Dagar will kill us for letting them go," protested one at Tor's back. "We're already dead!"

⁂

Torin's bark alerted Ewert, Bailey and Eldric just seconds before multiple flashes filled the hollow. Torin eagerly greeted Shannan. Some

Guardians fainted; others sank to their knees. What little strength they possessed became exhausted by one travel between dimensions.

Rune collapsed. He took Wren with him to the ground. Kell and Shannan knelt beside him. Upon seeing her, Rune tried to communicate.

Shannan signaled him quiet. She spoke to Wren. "Help the others." Wren obeyed, leaving Shannan and Kell with Rune.

"Slowly," Shannan warned when Rune became excited. "You don't have to apologize." He became insistent. "Very well. I forgive you."

Rune seized Kell. He began to gesture and wheeze. Befuddled, Kell looked to Shannan for clarification. For a moment she remained silent, the weight of what was said evident on her face. She spoke after Rune motioned her to Kell.

"He says it was Jor'el's wish for him to forge the cages and chains. It was planned before Dagar captured him. It's why he was created." She gazed steadily at Kell.

Rune tugged on Kell to get the Captain's attention. Confused by the confession, Kell looked from Shannan to Rune when he whizzed.

Shannan gasped in horror. "No, Rune!" He vigorously nodded. Woeful tears filled her eyes, in telling Kell, "He wants you to kill him so he can be free."

Pricked, Kell tried to turn away. Desperate, Rune pulled himself up on Kell's neck with pleading nasal whimpers. Rune's sudden gasp startled Shannan.

"Thank you," Rune spoke in full voice to Kell. He collapsed. Before his body touched the ground, he vanished in grey light.

Kell clenched a dagger, his face pale while the golden eyes void of expression. Shannan never saw him reach for the dagger. When she compassionately touched him, he snatched her hand to stand and moved to join the others.

Vidar noticed them return along with her stricken pallor. "Shannan?"

"Rune is free," said Kell flatly. "How long before we can leave?"

"It would be best if we found shelter for the night."

"No! Dagar will have his forces out soon. We must leave now."

239

"Kell, that's not possible. Dagar's hold extends at least a day's journey on foot from Ravendale. After that, they will begin to recover," Vidar argued.

"Some may take longer than a day to regain their strength," Mahon added to Vidar's assessment.

Shannan tried to soothe Kell. "At least they are alive and free."

"Kell!" Avatar came running. "Witter's at Ravendale."

"That's it!" snapped Kell. His glance swept over the Guardians, his voice rose for all to hear. "Witter is here! I don't think any of you want to return to the Cave." He was met with determined negatives. "Then on your feet! Those who can, help the weaker. We'll find shelter as soon as possible."

⁂

Dagar stiffened with alarm a second before Tor came running into the main chamber.

"Kel—" Tor began then corrected himself. "*He* was here! Thousands are freed!"

Dagar pushed past Tor so hard that the Warrior flew across the room. Arriving at the reconditioning chamber, Dagar pulled to a skidding halt. Hundreds of cages and cells stood empty. Furious beyond measure, he let out a thunderous shout that echoed in the chamber for several moments.

Tor staggered into the chamber to hear Dagar bellow, "Find them! Destroy them all! I will not be thwarted!"

A Shadow Warrior rushed in to give a report. "Access to the garrison and creatures of infrinn has been blocked!"

Dagar turned red-faced. "Unblock it!"

"We're in the process of doing that, my lord. Only uncertain of how long it will take."

"What about the winged section?"

"No word yet, just the land creatures."

Dagar issued new orders to Tor. "Send out scouts to find them. Use Enforcers, if you must. I'll tend to the creatures for dispatch when available."

With great effort, the Guardians reached the safety of the deep wood just after nightfall. Vidar and Wren combined their special strength to call upon the night animals to act as sentries and create a defensive shield. It was a risk to their own lifeforce, but a necessary one. Avatar posted extra security using warriors. For the present, they could rest.

With this bold strike into his domain, all knew Dagar would vehemently come after them. They determined to rest long enough for some of the weaker one to take some nourishment. Food wasn't essential to Guardians, but when injured, it helped in the healing process. Armus organized providing food.

Kell separated himself from the group. His body still sore from slamming into the wall while his spirit heavy over Rune. Weary, he sat on a log at the fringe of camp. He reflected on events that led to this day.

It was a dark time when Jor'el removed Dagar from his position as Trio Leader. Naturally, Kell had the authority to carry out Jor'el instructions, though inwardly he always felt Dagar more clever than he. Not more powerful or skilled in arms, but superior in intellectual shrewdness. Perhaps, if he had more cunning, he could have prevented Dagar from rebelling thus avoiding all that had come since. Regrets could not erase the past. When the time comes for them to finally meet, he hoped he would be at full strength. Until then he had Shannan and the others to protect. To do that, he needed to dismiss such distracting thoughts.

A hand on his shoulder briefly startled him. Shannan sat on the log.

"You should be asleep," he said.

"I wanted to speak to you about Rune, but you've been avoiding me. Why?"

Kell stared at some unseen stop on the ground. "Not since the Great Battle have I killed my own kind. I hated it then. I hate it now."

"Dear Kell, you didn't kill Rune out of hate. It was out of compassion. You're a caring and noble being. I've come to understand why Grandfather calls you his good old friend. I also consider you a friend. Don't blame yourself for something that wasn't your fault. I suggested we free the Guardians, so the fault is mine." She spoke with a dejected sigh.

"You're not to blame."

"Neither one of us is to blame." She steadily regarded him.

Kell frowned at her ploy to shift blame. "You sound like Niles."

She sighed for real. "I miss him terribly. And Ellis."

"You'll be reunited when all this is over. I promise. Now, come," He helped her to stand, "you need sleep. I too will rest," he added to forestall her protest.

Vidar met them upon return to the main group. Without any exchange of words, he took charge of Shannan to escort her to a prepare pallet for sleeping.

For a moment, Kell observed Vidar and Shannan. Since the writing of Prophecy he knew about the Daughter of Allon. Over the centuries he encouraged others with the hope of her appearing. Yet, now, in reality, her depth of understanding surprised him.

Avatar and Armus joined Kell. Armus' wounds had been cleansed. The gash on his forehead was surrounded by abrasions with some bruising. Armus carried a bowl of stew with a spoon. He held them out to Kell.

"Don't refuse. You need nourishment just like the rest of us."

"We already ate," Avatar added.

Kell accepted the bowl. "How are you feeling?"

Armus smiled. "Better. Eldric mixed ingredients for strengthening tonics into the stew for everyone rather than individual doses."

Avatar flashed a wry smile. "I made sure he took a double dose," he told Kell in reference to Armus.

Kell sniffed the contents of the bowl. "Boar? How did you manage that?" he asked Armus.

"Wren, of course."

"She hasn't lost her touch," chuckled Avatar.

"Nor has your dry wit been tempered by time off in heavenlies," snickered Armus

Kell shook his head with a grin at the banter. He ate.

Avatar's smile faded in regard of Shannan. She appeared to be sleeping. Vidar sat on a log beside her with a loaded crossbow on his lap. "Humor aside, there are times I wondered if we'd ever see this day."

"Think what it's been like for those of us here. The difficulties we faced," said Armus.

Avatar stirred with slight offense. "Don't make the mistake of thinking that my being in the heavenlies freed me from angst or dismay. Quite the opposite. Prior to the House of Tristan's fall, Jor'el sent me to Kell with a message that all Guardians, regardless of whereabouts, are affected by events."

Kell swallowed the latest bite to say, "That he did."

"Sorry. I do remember the message," Armus recanted.

Avatar accepted the apology with a smile and nod. He then continued his early thoughts. "Where do we take them, Kell? Arundine or Melwynn?"

"Melwynn is safer from Dagar's forces. Once there, we formulate our battle plan."

"Will we be at full strength by then?"

"According to Prophecy, ay. Until then, we manage as best we can."

"Any way to arm the warriors before then?"

Kell pursed his lips to consider Avatar's question. "Perhaps if we had raided the Cave's armory. However, trying to create weapons will take time away from escape."

"At least Mahon, Vidar and Wren sealed the area containing creatures of infrinn," said Armus, as some encouragement.

"Let's hope what they did last long enough to reach safety. Dagar knows the secrets of the Cave, and even enhanced it," groused Kell. He finished eating.

"Jor'el lifted the barrier so we could bridge the gap to come with no ill effects," Avatar reminded Kell.

Kell grinned, as he patted Avatar's shoulder. "Hold that thought, because if at any time Armus and I need to leave, you will be responsible to get them to the safety of the Temple. From there, all should have the strength to dimension travel to Melwyn. Now, show me the perimeter." He handed Armus an empty bowl before he left with Avatar.

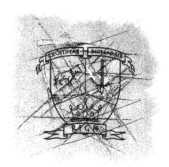

Chapter 22

THE YEAR-ROUND MILD CLIMATE OF THE DELTA MADE THE Castle of Deltoria open, spacious and luxurious. The splendor of the grounds held numerous gardens with fountains and pools containing the famed healing waters. Even the style of dress was lighter than other parts of the kingdom.

Upon arrival, Erasmus showered his guests with all manner of finery. He particularly doted on Erin. Kemp's gruff attitude grew more agreeable. Darius, Jasper and Edmund bore it with some wariness. When Erasmus ordered an elaborate feast, they became cautious. Hardly a time for celebration, however, Erasmus assured them of added security.

Not wanting to insult their host, Darius, Jasper and Edmund agreed to attend. Darius wore a suit of burgundy and gold; Edmund in cobalt blue while Jasper chose to remain in brown and gold, akin to his uniform. They met Kemp and Erin on their way to the banquet hall.

"This is a change from tramping about the countryside like vagabonds. More suited to our station," said Kemp of his mahogany brocade suit with apricot accents.

"Your taste, perhaps, not mine," groused Darius.

"And me, cousin? Do you dismiss my taste?" Erin wore a gown of peacock blue with silver and peach accents.

"No, you look stunning. I'm just concerned."

"Concern won't change the situation. Enjoy yourself. Ellis did at Milton." Kemp steered Erin into the grand hall without waiting for a reply from Darius.

"Leave it be," Edmund warned a putout Darius.

Garlands and flowers, along with all manner of decorations adored the Great Hall. The tables were filled with food. Darius, Edmund and Jasper joined Erasmus at high table. Kemp and Erin were already seated.

"For a bachelor, you live well," said Erin in observance of the feast.

"I hope not to be a bachelor for long." Erasmus eyed her over the goblet when he offered her a salute.

Erin smiled, her eyes playful on Erasmus. "Which of these lovely ladies will have the honor of becoming your wife?"

Erasmus set down the goblet to take hold of her hand. His regard earnest and direct, while his voice passionate. "I hope it will be you. I have always held you in the highest regard. I found it difficult to drink to your happiness with another." His eyes showed the ardent truth of his words.

"Erasmus, I'm overwhelmed. I don't know what to say."

He gallantly smiled. "You don't have to say anything … yet. Simply allow me the privilege of showing you the depth of my affection." He kissed her hand.

"Indeed, sister. This is the life you were born too." Kemp enjoyed his gayest mood in years. He felt hands caress his shoulders followed by a whisper in his ear. He smiled with pleasure at a thirty-year-old fair beauty. "Musetta. I wondered where you had gone." He pulled her to sit on his lap. In height she reached his shoulder yet light upon his lap.

She made a pout while she played with the lace on his shirt collar. "After hearing of Lord Phineas and Sir Lavi's deaths, I feared the worst. When the soldiers overran Denley, I fled. I found safety here in the Delta with an old uncle of mine," she said with a somber sigh.

Kemp caressed her cheek. One look in her deep green eyes and he was captivated. "You did right to flee." They kissed.

"Kemp's found a friendly face," said Erasmus to Erin.

"Musetta was one of mother's maids. Her relationship with Kemp has been on and off for years." She spoke with disapproval.

Her scorn made him curious. "What of Nancie?"

"We believe any liaison ended when she and Kemp married." Erin leaned closer to Erasmus. "Personally, I never trusted her. Except with Kemp, she has always been secretive and mysterious."

Musetta caught Erin's sideways glance. She flashed a cool smile. "Can we find a place more private?" she asked Kemp.

Kemp wickedly smiled. "Of course." He turned to Erin. "Enjoy."

With inviting lips and teasing kisses, Musetta led Kemp to the garden. "That's far enough, my little vixen." He pulled her to him for a passionate kiss.

She mewed under his advance. "If I yield, what will you give me?"

"Anything you want," he muttered.

She took his head in her hands to look deep in his eyes. She spoke in the Ancient with determined purpose. "What the Dark Master Commands, no one denies."

The merriment instantly fell from Kemp's face. His eyes became transfixed upon her. "What does the Dark Master Command?"

She switched back to Allonian. "Are you listening closely?" she asked, watching his face.

His features remained riveted on her. "I am," he flatly replied.

"Where is the Son of Tristan?"

"I don't know."

"You mean he's not at Deltoria?"

"No."

"When did you last see him?"

"Five days ago."

"Did you see which way he went?"

"No."

"Do you know anything?" she lashed out in frustration.

"He spoke with Darius before we separated."

For a moment, Musetta considered her next move. Kemp remained focused on her. "Learn what he told Darius. Employ whatever means needed. Then tell me."

"As you wish." Kemp began to leave with his expression still stoic.

"Not like that. Remember, this is a party." She smiled to show him.

His face brightened into a grin. He entered the grand hall. Erin danced with Erasmus. Jasper and Edmund laughed as played a game of chance with several noblemen. Darius remained at high table in better spirits than earlier. A sly smile appeared as Kemp returned to high table. With a hearty laugh, he slapped Darius' back.

"Enjoying yourself, cousin?"

"Actually, I am. I wasn't sure at first, not with Ellis leaving."

"Don't fret over Ellis. Niles will see to him." Kemp refilled Darius' goblet with wine. "Drink up. How long has it been since we made merry? We were too injured at Milton. Come! Even Uncle Angus knew when to enjoy life."

Darius smiled with remembrance. "Only he could hold his wine better than me."

Kemp raised the goblet. "To Angus." He drained the goblet in one long drink.

"To father." Darius didn't drink all the content.

Kemp noticed Darius' goblet still contained wine. "Uncle would have drained that goblet and filled it again." He refilled both goblets. "To Angus," he said again and drank.

"To father." Darius drank the full goblet.

With raised brow of surprise, Kemp laughed. "You can drink."

"I didn't say I couldn't. I just don't do it often."

Kemp laughed as he refilled the goblets a third time. "To my father." He drank, yet watched Darius.

"Uncle Phineas." Darius emptied the goblet again.

Kemp stabbed a knife onto a tray of fowl a servant offered. He put it on Darius' plate then fetched another for himself. "Eat."

Darius followed Kemp's lead of eating. "Suppose Ellis—"

"A bit dry," Kemp interrupted. "Needs to be washed down." He took a drink from his goblet. "Tastes better too."

Darius drank. "Decent wine," he began to slur. "As I was saying - what was I saying?"

"Something about Ellis," Kemp said nonchalantly as he ate.

"Ay, Ellis. What if he sends for me tomorrow?"

"Is that likely? Would you know where to go if he did?"

"Ay," said Darius, more into his goblet then to Kemp. He frowned at seeing his goblet empty. In pouring the wine, some overflowed the rim.

Kemp observed Darius' inebriated demeanor. "Then I shall accompany you since I know too."

Darius paused in mid-drink. "You do?"

"Of course. Why wouldn't he tell me? He claims me as kin." He moved closer to speak confidentially. "He said in case you forget, I can remind you."

Darius frowned at the brotherly insult. "He said I'd forget?"

Kemp feigned the wine affected him also. "Shhh! I wasn't supposed to say that. Ellis didn't want you to feel bad. Something about being forgetful in your old age."

"Old age? As if I'd forget such a name as Dog, Dog-it." Darius paused in mild confusion. "Not Dog. Dor. Ay, Dorgirith," he said with a triumphant smile.

"That's exactly what Ellis told me. Now we won't let the other forget." Kemp clapped Darius' shoulder.

"No," groaned Darius with a deep, sour frown.

"What's wrong?"

Darius turned pale. "I suddenly don't feel well."

"Must be the fowl. I saw," Kemp leaned closer, "worms."

Darius clapped a hand over his mouth to contain his stomach from erupting. He rushed from the table.

Kemp let the fowl fall back on his plate. He left the hall.

In the garden, Musetta pulled Kemp into the shadows. "Well?"

"He's on his way to Dorgirith with Niles."

"Excellent." She then switched to the Ancient. "Now into sleep straight away, and remember nothing, but what I say." While she spoke Kemp became sleepy. By the end, he collapsed into a heap. Musetta acted quickly. She made their clothes appear wrinkled with leaves and twigs. "My lord!" she exclaimed and roughly shook him.

Kemp was slow to respond so she persisted in her efforts. He raised himself to his elbow. She appeared frightened. "Is something wrong?"

"How can you ask that after what you've done?"

"What are you talking about?"

Musetta fearfully bit her lip. "You don't remember? Oh, that excuse won't serve when your cousin or Baron Erasmus learn that you betrayed the Prince."

"Betray Ellis?" he repeated with surprise. "No. I wouldn't."

"You did!" she insisted with high anxiety. "You told me while we made love. You said he deserved it because of Erin."

Kemp gaped, thunderstruck. "I admit anger – betrayal - no!"

She wept. "You deny it, yet threatened me if I did not agree to be your alibi. To say you never left me. I agreed because you said you loved me. Now I'm in danger."

Confused, he asked, "When did I leave?"

She sniffled back the tears. "Perhaps twenty minutes ago. You went to speak with Lord Darius only came back drunk."

Kemp looked completely befuddled. "Truly, Musetta, I can barely remember what happened. Although, I did speak with Darius, my head is fuzzy with details." He blinked his eyes against some pain.

"We must flee before we are discovered! I have an uncle in the village who will help us when he learns what you did for Allon."

"For Allon?" he echoed, still trying to comprehend.

"Ay, you avenged your sister's honor, and saved the kingdom. The same as when you rode out with Lord Phineas and Sir Lavi. They were going to betray *us* when you stopped them." She ignored his new bewilderment to draw him to his feet. "You are a brave man. Now we must act quickly if are to escape alive!"

Musetta moved swiftly at night. Several times she stilled his questions though never paused in her course to lead Kemp from Deltoria. They arrived at a small house on the edge of the local village. A man of sixty answered her call. While she explained the situation to the man, he closely scrutinized Kemp, who still appeared uncertain yet very groggy.

"The King will be pleased by your service, my lord. However, judging by your condition, you won't get far. Best sleep it off. You'll need a sober mind and body to face what lies ahead. Niece," he said.

"I'll come to bed after we've worked out an escape route." Musetta escorted Kemp to a bedchamber where she said in the Ancient, "Now fall asleep, dreamless and deep, but remember all when you wake."

Kemp made no comment or fuss, as he fell into a deep slumber.

"Well?" asked the man when she returned alone to the living room.

Musetta's smile filled with disdainful pleasure. "He'll sleep for hours. A weak mind is the easiest prey."

"Our special escort is waiting." He handed her a cloak.

<hr />

By sunrise, a Shadow Warrior helped Musetta and her companion to reach Ravendale. Normally it would take ten days to travel from Deltoria but with the need for haste, Latham dispatched the Warrior to aid Musetta. She received immediate admittance to Latham's study.

"I have done what you asked," she said with triumph.

"I never doubted your abilities, my dear."

"Abilities in the bedroom. Yet, I hope by this, I have proven myself skilled in other ways to become your official apprentice."

Latham kissed her hand. "When this is over, we shall begin your formal instruction."

She placed his hand on her abdomen. "*Our* instruction. I'm certain it will be a son."

His smile beamed "Ay. A son." He drew her to sit on his lap and deeply kissed her. "Now what did you learn from Kemp?"

"The Pretender is heading for Dorgirith in the company of a man called Niles."

"He came from Dorgirith. Are you certain?" he asked, a bit dubious.

"The information came straight from Lord Darius."

Surprised, Latham asked, "You swayed Darius into betraying him?"

"Not exactly," she was forced to admit. "Once I had Kemp under my influence, he tricked Darius into revealing the destination."

Latham grinned in admiration. "Does Kemp know he betrayed his cousin like he did Phineas and Lavi?"

"I made certain he knew *that*, along with references to them. When he wakes, he'll be a hunted fugitive." She smiled with warped pleasure.

Latham regarded her with admiration. "Truly, you deserve to be my apprentice as well as the mother of my son." He again kissed her.

Hearty laughter came from across the room. Dagar's image hovered over the basin, his eyes merrily on her. "So this is the lovely Musetta."

She paled with fear at seeing Dagar and stood to bow. "My lord!"

Dagar lewdly smiled. "I can see why she pleases you, Latham. For now, be gone, wench."

With a smile and nod from Latham, she hastened from the room.

Dagar laughed. "Dorgirith! Do you know what this means? Freedom! He sets foot in Magelen's ruins and he is mine! Now, what of Witter?"

"He is in pursuit of them, but no word yet."

Dagar slyly grinned. "In truth, it doesn't matter. Once I am free, I'll deal with them. Even *he* won't be able to stop me." His mocking laughter lingered after he vanished.

At Deltroia, Darius furiously paced his chamber. He passed in and out of the morning light filtering through the window. He wore bedclothes and slippers. He paused to ask Erasmus, "Are you sure?"

"I wouldn't have told you if there were any doubt." Erasmus was dressed.

Darius groaned with angry regret. "What have I done?"

"Kemp tricked you into drinking—"

"I fell for his deception and told him Ellis went to Dorgirith!" Shouting made Darius grab his head, which still rang from drinking. "Where is Kemp now?" he spoke in a more controlled voice.

"He could be anywhere. I dispatched men to find him, only Jasper insisted on saddling horses. He said you'd want to search for Kemp."

"Ay! It'll take me only a moment to dress."

"Longer for your head to clear," Erasmus lowly groused.

Erin burst into the chamber. Pale with anxiety, she balked at Darius' grim expression. "So it's true about Kemp."

"Ay!"

Erasmus shot a warning glare to Darius for the harsh response. Erasmus comforted Erin when she wept. "The shame is his alone."

Jasper arrived with Edmund; both dressed for travel. Darius' hand them from speaking. He approached of Erin to speak in a softer tone. "Stay with Erasmus while go to warn Ellis."

"What of Kemp?"

Darius tried to keep an even tone in reply. "I'll deal with him in time.

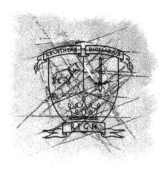

253

Chapter 23

WHILE THE REST OF THE SOUTHERN FOREST RECEIVED A good amount of snowfall, only a few inches ever fell in Dorgirith. An early spring snow was rare, though it did not hamper Ellis and Niles' journey through familiar territory. They dismounted outside the ruins of Magelen.

"I wonder what Kell has in mind for the final test?" snickered Ellis.

"Knowing Kell, it will be a challenge." Niles surveyed the area. "I'm surprised he's not here yet."

Ellis drew his sword, which made Niles arch his eyebrows. "He said I needed to defeat a Guardian in armed combat. I assume this is the test to see if I can."

"Kell is a powerful and skilled warrior. You won't match him blow for blow. It will require cunning quickness."

Ellis cocked a grin. "I learned that from Valmar."

Niles' hollow chuckle ended in melancholy. "Even if you defeat Kell and successfully complete the Contest, you still have a long road to travel before becoming king. A road upon which, someday soon, our journey together will end."

"Not before I'm crowned," Ellis said with bravado.

"Whenever it is, I thank Jor'el I have been a part of your destiny." Niles heartily embraced Ellis. He sniffled when they parted. "Come. I would have you take a few practice swings." He drew his sword.

They no soon stopped into the center of the ruins than the earth violently shook. The tremor brought Ellis to all fours. An unseen blow sent Niles hurling through the air. He landed hard against a cornerstone where he lay unconscious.

The shaking ground prevented Ellis from rising to aid Niles. Bright light engulfed the ruins. When it faded, the tremor stopped. Ellis blinked to regain his sight from the temporary blinding. Two booted feet stood before him. A large being with a taunting smile, and narrow mahogany eyes towered above him. Fear gripped him.

"Dagar?"

"Ay, Son of Tristan. Though I guess you were expecting someone else?"

Ellis gripped his sword to stem his fear. True, this was not the Guardian he expected. Nor the time or place he thought to meet Dagar. Then again—Ellis snatched a handful of dirt. He threw it in Dagar's face then rolled to one side. He quickly rose to his feet.

Dagar wiped his face. "That may have saved you for the moment but you won't escape!"

With a confident smile, Ellis placed himself on guard. "I have no intention of escaping."

"Then prepare to die!" Dagar attacked.

Ellis met the first blow with a partial parry. He ducked to roll under the blade. He came up in a crouched *en garde* position for retaliation. "Nice try," he began with a growing smile, "*Kell*. Good disguise too."

Dagar roared with anger. With a wave of his hand, he sent Ellis flying across the ruins. "Never say that name in my presence!"

Ellis shook his head clear. He winced with sudden realization that it was not Kell in disguise. He truly faced the Dark Lord! He scrambled to his feet. He gripped his sword in an attempt to calm his racing heart. His mouth went dry.

Dagar attacked. Ellis did his best to parry the blow. He stumbled forward. He quickly regained his balance to whirl about in anticipation of another attack. Instead, he was sent flying backward again by an unseen blow. He landed on some stones. He grimaced in pain, slow to move.

Dagar snorted a mocking laugh. "I see you believe me now, boy. I can crush you with one hand. But," he waved his sword. "This is fun, and I need the exercise after so long."

Ellis rose to make defense. Dagar's speed proved so stunning that Ellis make no sound when Dagar's blade plunged into his abdomen. His surprised look went from the sword to Dagar. A rough hand shoved him backward. Ellis cried out when the action made the sword withdraw from his body. His vision dimmed before he collapsed.

Niles just regained his senses to watch in horror. Ignoring personal pain, Niles launched himself at Dagar. For all his age and injuries, he would not be easily battered aside a second time. Dagar grew irate at the interference. He spoke the Ancient then heaved his shoulders in such a way as to knock Niles on his back. Niles lay unable to move. Dagar kept him pinned by sheer will, eyes locked on the old Knight.

"Still trying to play the champion? The death of one king wasn't enough? Well, Knight, you can witness my ultimate victory."

When Dagar turned to Ellis, Niles felt a release. He pulled the dagger from his belt and leapt upon Dagar's back. He plunged the blade into the Guardian's right shoulder. Howling in anger, Dagar seized Niles by the collar. He hurled Niles over his head. Niles' back slammed against the same boulder he hit earlier. This time his back cracked, causing his chest to cave in. He desperately gasped for air. The world became a swirling haze. A huge hand grabbed his tunic to hoist him to his knees. He could barely see. The sounds in his ears began to fade.

"I told you I would have the ultimate victory, Knight." Viciously Dagar turned Niles' head to look where Ellis lay unmoving. "See Allon's salvation now? I have destroyed it, just like I have destroyed you." With a violent jerk, he ripped the amulet from Niles neck. The motion sent

Niles hard to the ground. Dagar raised the amulet heavenward. "You have failed, Jor'el! I have crushed your pitiful mortal under my feet!"

Brilliant light consumed the area with such force that Dagar went crashing into a large oak. He lay in a semiconscious heap. From the fading brilliance emerged Kell and Armus, their swords swung to one side ready for retaliation. Armus raised his sword for another strike at Dagar. Kell stopped him.

"I can finish him!" Armus insisted.

"No. It took our combined strength to knock him aside. He already stirs. Quickly!" Kell shoved Armus toward Niles.

The seriousness of Niles' condition concerned Armus. "He's not breathing well." He sheathed his sword to lift Niles in his arms.

Kell fetched Ellis. Light from their departure filled the clearing

Dagar scrambled to his feet ready to confront whatever waylaid him. The clearing was empty. He crossed to where he left Ellis. He discovered light scorching of the ground. In a mighty bellow, he spoke; "Hear me, Kell! You can't win. I have defeated Jor'el's pathetic mortal. I will become more powerful than you can imagine. All the Guardians' combined strength will not stop me!"

The echo of mocking laughter lingered in the clearing after Dagar vanished.

Barely a moment later, three riders arrived. The tired, lathered horses staggered to a stop. Darius leapt from the saddle before the animal stopped. Jasper and Edmund were quick to follow.

"The snow is melted away and the earth gouged - blood!" Darius examined the spot where Ellis laid. "What are these strange marks? I've never seen anything like them."

"A battle?" asked Edmund.

Darius became worried. "Whatever they fought, it was not mortal. Ellis!" he shouted and began to search the area.

After about ten minutes, Darius said, "It's no use. No tracks, no more blood, nothing! It's as if they vanished."

"If what Niles said about this Dagar comes to pass, Allon won't last much longer," said Jasper with dread.

Darius snarled with vengeful anger. "Jor'el help Kemp if that happens, for I'll kill him with my bare hands." He vaulted into the saddle. "We must find Archimedes."

Melwynn, Castle of the Guardians, was a large splendid palace that dominated a vista in the Highlands. It offered a magnificent commanding view of the countryside. One could almost see the Temple in the Region of Sanctuary.

Like Arundine, Melwynn had been shielded from mortals for centuries. Jor'el sealed it from Dagar and his followers. However, that did not stop Kell from hearing Dagar, as he laid Ellis on a large cushioned bed in an opulent chamber.

"See to them," he ordered two Guardian physicians concerning Ellis and Niles. Kell stepped out onto the balcony. Painful fear clouded his brow, as golden eyes stared southeasterly.

Armus joined him. "Is it true? Will he become more powerful?"

Kell soberly nodded. "Fortunately, he doesn't know Shannan's location. As long as she is safe and Ellis alive, there is hope."

"Ellis maybe dying. Niles—is dead."

Kell reeled at Armus' declaration. He raced back inside where he drew to an unsteady halt. Niles lay still upon a bed. His face ashen with eyes closed. The Guardians charged with care of the mortals looked awkwardly at each other, then to Kell.

"There was nothing we could do, Captain. He was even beyond our special power to heal."

"We believe the other will recover." The second Guardian motioned to Ellis in an attempt at encouragement.

Kell's jowls tightened, as his golden eyes grew misty. He swallowed back emotion to grip Niles' shoulder. "I'm sorry," he murmured.

Armus sent the physicians from the room. "What now?" he asked when alone.

Kell gave a hapless shrug, unable to reply, as he still stared at Niles.

Armus forced Kell to look at him. "Dagar has slain the King's Champion and laid low the Prince. You cannot falter now!"

Pricked by Armus' admonishment, Kell winced with angst. "You don't understand."

"Oh, but I do. Remember, we are counterparts," Armus spoke with confident reassurance. His chestnut eyes were unwavering in their steadfastness.

Kell took a deep breath to gather his composure. He bowed his head and closed his eyes. After a moment, the golden eyes regained their gleam of certainty. "We wait and pray. If Avatar can get those we rescued just to the Temple to regain their strength, then perhaps when Ellis recovers we'll have a chance."

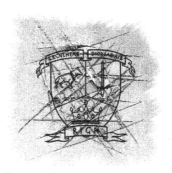

Chapter 24

AVATAR DID ALL HE COULD TO URGE HIS CHARGES IN THEIR FLIGHT from Witter and the Shadow Warriors. Since the group consisted of mostly vassals, he couldn't press them too hard or risk losing some to capture or worse. The warriors among them were unarmed, and not returned to full strength to face the enemy. They had to continue the on foot, and use whatever means necessary to keep the enemy at bay.

Avatar paused to assess the progress. He managed to lead the group to the hill country of Midessex near the Region of Sanctuary border. So far they had not suffered a single loss. The Pass of Peace leading into the Region lay just over the next ridge. Vidar and Shannan joined Avatar in his observation.

"Once we cross the border, most should be strong enough to dimension travel. At least to the Temple, going to Melwynn will take more strength," said Vidar.

Avatar's gaze swept over the group to consider what Vidar said. He became braced when Mahon raced from the rear of the group. The younger warrior didn't look pleased.

"Shadow Warriors. About four miles behind us," Mahon reported.

"Go back and urge everyone to hurry over the ridge. From the high ground we may be able to shield those who can dimension travel to the Temple," ordered Avatar. As Mahon left, Avatar shouted his order to those closest, "The enemy is sighted! Over the hill to the Pass of Peace!"

Avatar raced to the top with Vidar and Shannan at his heels. "Take the Daughter of Allon to safety. I'll help the rest," he told Vidar. From the crest, Avatar called to the lagging Guardians. "Hurry up! Move! You can make it."

Sight of the enemy prompted urgent flight. Several stronger Guardians raced back to help their weaker companions. Mahon brought up the rear. He urged the stragglers in the climb.

Avatar aided the last climber to the ridgeline. "I knew you could do it," he said with an encouraging smile to a winded male vassal.

"Now can I make it down is the question," he said between deep breaths of recovery.

"Avatar!" Wren came running along the ridge. "Hunter hawks!" She pointed to the sky's horizon. Three ugly, large vulture creatures with rotten flesh and feathers flew towards them. "Three miles at most."

"I think you'll want to climb down rather than face those," Avatar said to the vassal.

Without argument, the vassal began the descent to the other side.

"Mahon, organize defense." Avatar nudged Mahon on his way to the group at the bottom of the hill. "Think you have a shot at them from here?" he asked Wren.

With wary consideration, she studied the horizon. "I maybe good, but at half-strength, if I can't kill it with one shot, a wound will only make it worse."

"We don't have much a choice!" At her continued worry, he added, "I'd rather take my chances with you at half-strength than not at all."

At Avatar's voiced confidence, Wren again studied the approaching hunter hawks. "If there was way to distract the others while I site a target, I believe I can do it."

"I'll give you that distraction." Avatar drew his sword to place the pommel in front of his face.

Wren seized him. "No! Using your power will deplete your strength. We need you whole right now."

The hunter hawks appeared closer. Avatar looked to the fleeing group. He spied his quarry. "Priscilla! Get up here, now!"

"Vidar also," shouted Wren. She armed her crossbow.

Within a moment both summoned Guardians arrived.

"Hunter hawks." Avatar pointed the horizon. "Priscilla, we need your winds to separate them for destruction. Wren. Vidar."

Priscilla raised her arms. She recited the Ancient to call upon her power. Winds rose to cause updrafts that altered the course of the hunter hawks. While two fought the currents, one continued towards them.

Wren loosed a shaft at the advancing hunter hawk. The creature slipped right. The arrow missed its chest to strike its body near the left wing. She prepared a second shot.

Priscilla's attempt to keep the others occupied didn't last long. One righted its course to resume a flight towards them. Vidar took aim at the second creature. His shot flew faster. The hunter hawk could not avoid the arrow. Struck in the throat under the head, ensured an instant kill. It plummeted from the sky.

Wren recalculated her aim in anticipation. She guessed correctly. When it dodged to the left, her shaft hit it between the eyes.

Priscilla grew weak from the effort. She swayed so Avatar steadied her. The moment her created winds died, Vidar took down the third hunter hawk.

"That saved us from them. Now to deal with the enemy," groused Avatar. "Are you well enough to rejoin the others?" he asked Priscilla.

"I think so."

"I'll take her. I need to return to Shannan," said Vidar.

Valmar arrived. On the horizon, the Shadow Warriors grew closer. On the other side of the crest, the fleeing Guardians made little progress toward the Pass of Peace.

"Where is Kell? We can't keep this up!" complained Valmar.

"What could he do that I haven't?" chided Avatar. He spoke more forcefully when Valmar appeared unconvinced. "I may have been gone a while but I'm still a member of the High Trio."

Valmar yielded with a nod. "That you are, lad." His gaze shifted from the fleeing group to the advancing enemy. "We risk losing all if we don't act to at least save some."

Avatar grimaced. It pained him to think of losing even one fellow Guardian. He tried everything he could to keep them all together. Alas, he was running out of options.

"Have those of the strike teams form a defensive perimeter. We'll hold off the Shadow Warriors for the rest. Tell any who can dimension travel to go to Melwynn. Those weaker will have to hide until they can reach the Temple," ordered Avatar.

"What about the Daughter of Allon? Vidar, Wren, Priscilla and Mahon are part of our armed force."

"Tell Vidar to take sole charge. Go! I'll keep watch."

Avatar lingered a moment to observe the approaching enemy. When he lost sight of the Shadow Warriors behind a ridge, he ran down to the group. He heard Shannan argue with a frustrated Valmar. Vidar tried to add his voice to bolster Valmar.

"Why hasn't she left yet?" Avatar demanded of Valmar.

"She refuses to go."

"Avatar, you can't hold them off with just a few, and you know that. It's me Witter wants. Let me lure him away, while all of you return to Melwynn," said Shannan.

"Oh, no! If you got into trouble, Kell would have my hide." Avatar impatiently waved to Vidar. "Get her out of here!"

Arrows from the crest cut down several Guardians. Avatar drew his sword. "Dimension travel to Melwynn if you can or make defense!" he shouted to the group.

The warriors responded by ushering the weaker ones to safety then grabbed anything they could find to face the enemy.

Shannan broke from Vidar to run parallel to the attacking Shadow Warriors on a lower plateau. At the whizzing of an arrow, Vidar tackled her in time for it to miss. He rose to one knee to fire. His shaft hit the offending Shadow Archer in the chest. Shannan scrambled away in an attempt trying to draw attention. Vidar pursued. He snatched her arm to pull her behind some large boulders. Torin joined them.

"Do you want to get killed?" Vidar chided.

"No. Nor do I want to lose any more Guardians."

Vidar looked back at seeing white flashes of light. "Some are leaving. Avatar is organizing resistance to protect their departure."

"That's not good enough. Do you want any of them to go back to the Cave?"

Vidar spoke with frustration. "I don't know which is worse, your stubbornness or Priscilla's goading." Her sly smile infuriated him. "I'm supposed to protect you! If Avatar believes Kell will have his hide, what will he do to me?"

"Kell won't do anything I don't want him to. Nor will you, my gallant Vidar. Once we're certain they're following, you can take me to Melwynn." She didn't wait for his answer. She bolted from concealment. Torin followed.

Vidar grabbed Shannan in mid-stride. A short distance away, was a patch of wood. He could cover the distance quickly, but with Shannan, he could not move as fast as normal. Sounds of pursuit drew closer. At the edge of the clearing she fell, exhausted.

"Can you run anymore?"

"I don't think so," she spoke with difficulty.

Vidar slung the crossbow on his back to lift her in his arms. "Hold on tight."

Vidar moved at dizzying speed, dodging trees. Shannan buried her face in his shoulder. Even at full speed, Torin could not keep pace. When they broke into another clearing, Vidar slowed and dared a glance over his shoulder. He saw nothing.

"I think it worked," he said, pleased.

"Vidar!" Shannan screamed in warning.

He turned just in time to see the cliff. In a wild move to steer away, he stumbled. Both fell hard to the ground. He rose to his knees. "Shannan?"

She pushed herself onto her elbows. "I'm in one piece."

Witter's mount burst through the brush into the clearing. He and four Shadow Warriors surrounded them. "You disappointment me, Vidar. Why lead me on this futile chase? All you had to do was hand her over. Do so now, and I may convince Dagar to forgive your mistake."

Vidar's face grew taut as he stood his ground. "You'll not take her."

Witter caustically chuckled. "You defy me? Defy Dagar? Since when have you had courage?"

Vidar braced himself in front of Shannan.

"Take her. And kill him," Witter commanded.

"Run!" Vidar managed to take down a single Warrior before being disarmed. He dodged away. He snatched a dead branch to use as a club.

Shannan raced back toward the trees. Witter used his stallion to block her. *"Na h-eich, leig mi a'dol!"* she ordered the horse.

"A spirit horse will not listen, even to the Daughter of Allon."

"Then take this!" She hurled stones at them.

The stallion became angry. It reared, which forced her to retreat to avoid the flying hooves. She fell flat on her back, completely knocking the wind from her lungs. The stallion's hooves barely missed her head when it touched the ground. She couldn't move, desperately trying to recover her breath.

A long loud screech came from overhead. Kato dove at Witter's head. This momentarily distracted him from Shannan. Witter swatted at the bird. Instead of sending Kato sideways, his hand became entangled with something. When he ripped his hand away, he found he held a brooch attached to a strip of cloth.

Kato screeched in anger as it circled for another attack. *Twang!* Kato screamed. A crossbow dart from a Shadow Archer pieced its left wing near the body. Horrified, Shannan watched Kato drop from the sky.

Witter shoved the brooch in his pocket. He leapt from the saddle, and jerked Shannan to her feet. She offered only minimal resistance.

A Shadow Warrior drove Vidar dangerously close to the edge. Vidar's foot slipped. He instinctively looked back, thus never saw the blow that sent him over the edge.

"Vidar!" Shannan cried in panic.

The Warrior peered over the ledge. "I don't see him."

"Good. You've saved Dagar the trouble." Witter lifted a stunned Shannan off the ground to place her on the stallion. He mounted behind her.

Tyree's platoon reached the cliff. "I see you captured her. Well done. I'll take her from here."

Witter stiffened with disdain. "She is my prisoner."

"Are you forgetting the King's command? Hand her over."

Although outnumbered five to one, the Shadow Warriors took up position around Witter's stallion.

Tyree signaled his men to ready their bows. "Refuse again, and they shoot to kill."

Unseen, a bloody hand reached the top of the cliff, followed by a second hand. Gingerly, Vidar pulled himself up to his chin. His face battered with a large scrape over his half swollen right eye. Trails of blood ran down his face. He painfully stopped at seeing more soldiers. Witter lowered Shannan from his stallion.

"Wisely done." Tyree had a soldier bring Shannan to him. Once she was mounted behind him, he addressed Witter. "I'll put in a good word for you with the King." He wheeled his horse about to leave the clearing.

"What about Dagar?" a Warrior asked Witter.

"It's not our time yet." Angry, Witter spurred the stallion. The Warriors followed.

Vidar finished his climb. He dragged his broken right leg over the ledge where he collapsed in agony. The large gash in his right side bled heavily. He had numerous cuts and bruises of various severities all over his body. Something wet touched his face. Torin whimpered, nudged and licked him. Picking up his ears, Torin yipped before he bolted to the wood. The wolf returned with Mahon and Wren.

"By the heavenlies!" Mahon exclaimed at sight of Vidar's wounds.

"Where's Shannan?" asked Wren with anxious concern.

"Witter. Tyree. Shadow Warriors. I did what I could," Vidar groaned. He fought to stay awake. "I'm sorry," he murmured to Wren before he lost consciousness.

Mahon felt Vidar's forehead. "He's cool. We must get him to Melwynn quickly."

Torin tugged hard on Wren's sleeve. Torin led her to where Kato lay on the ground wounded and breathing heavy.

"*Furasda, Kato, furasda.*" She gently lifted the eagle in her arms then returned to Mahon. "Looks like we have two patients. You take Vidar." Torin nudged her leg. "I'll see Kato gets well. You must find Shannan."

Torin whimpered at Kato. The eagle replied with a low squawk. After that, Torin ran in the direction Tyree left with Shannan.

❧

The moment Kell entered the infirmary; Ellis knew by his expression that something was desperately wrong. Only yesterday, Kell told him of Niles' death. He stirred on the bed in an attempt to rise. Eldric, the Prime physician, came to help. Ellis waved him aside to focus on Kell.

"What is it?"

Kell pursed his lips in an effort to form the words. "Shannan has been captured."

In utter disbelief, Ellis ignored the pain of his wounds to sit up. "What? You said she was safe with Vidar and Wren!"

"Vidar and Kato were nearly killed in a battle with Witter and Shadow Warriors trying to protect her! Wren and Mahon brought them here for treatment."

For a moment, Ellis could not speak. The tide of events changed so fast it was difficult to comprehend. "Why is Jor'el permitting this?" Kell didn't answer, so Ellis pressed him. "You rescued Guardians from the nether dimension, can't you rescue Shannan from Ravendale?"

Angst filled Kell's reply. "Don't you think I want to? She saved me. I would gladly give my life to see her here with you. But they'll be expecting us to make such an attempt. I'd risk more than my life. The fate of Allon hangs in the balance."

Ellis couldn't stop the tears. "I can't lose her, Kell!"

"None of us can," Kell replied in low husky voice.

"I told you not to upset him anymore, Captain!" scolded Eldric. His pale violet eyes flashed with warning. He shooed Kell from the bed. "Please, Highness, you can't recover if you don't rest."

"I can't rest," Ellis tearfully refuted.

"Listen to Eldric, Highness. Until you are recovered we can do nothing," urged Kell.

"Drink some more remedy." Eldric took a cup off a small table beside the bed.

Too weak to resist, Ellis drank when Eldric help the cup to his lips. Eldric helped him to lie down. Within a moment, he was asleep.

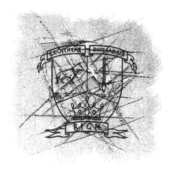

Chapter 25

IN HIS APARTMENT AT RAVENDALE, HUGH'S ATTEMPT TO RELAX MET with little success. He recently buried his wife, dealt with the disappearance of his children then learned of his sister Vera's death. Not news he wanted to tell Iain. Of course, he heard nothing from Iain regarding the children's safety. For all he knew, Latham may still have them hidden somewhere. Day and night the situation gnawed at him, and prevented him from sleeping. Still, he had to find a way to remain calm so he could reason with Marcellus. However getting a moment alone with his brother became increasingly difficult since Latham occupied nearly all of Marcellus' time.

Hugh couldn't venture far from his apartment before being confronted by guards. He even took his meals in his chamber. It pained him to think that Latham succeeded in thwarting him on all fronts. Yet, with each passing day, the stark reality of that fact took hold.

Hugh picked at his dinner. The entrance of two guards created a knot in his stomach. The sensation proved short-lived when he spied a disheveled man with them.

The lieutenant whispered in Hugh's ear. Surprised by what he heard, Hugh dismissed the guards. When alone, he addressed the man.

"You come with an interesting claim. You also look familiar."

"I am Baron Kemp of the Northern Forest."

Hugh's initial surprised turned to incredulity. "Phineas' son? You betray your kinsman?"

"No, Your Grace, I bear no relation to the House of Tristan. The story was a ruse to cover the truth."

Hugh regarded Kemp with skepticism. "Why come to me?"

"I was unable to gain audience with His Majesty."

"Why do you want to see the King? To gain reward for your alleged service?"

"In a manner of speaking, Your Grace," said Kemp, a bit uneasy.

Hugh snorted with incredulity. "You're as bold as your father. Can a traitor be trusted?"

"I saved Allon from civil war."

Hugh raised a sharp scolding brow. "You have a sharper tongue than Phineas. Why should I believe you? You could be a spy for this Pretender."

A hint of pain crept into Kemp's face. "In the eyes of many, I have forfeited their trust and allegiance. I am completely without means or friends. Even my sister, has denounced me." His voice slightly cracked upon mention of his sister.

For a long silent moment, Hugh studied Kemp. What was he to do with such a person? If he didn't take Kemp to Marcellus, he could go to Latham. That would not go well for Hugh personally.

During Hugh's consideration, a servant entered. "Your Grace. His Majesty requests your presence in the council chamber."

"I'll be there shortly." Hugh waved the servant away. For a moment, he studied Kemp. Abruptly, Hugh stood and said; "Come with me."

Kemp knew he took a risk coming to Ravendale. What other alternative did he have? Returning to Denley was out of the question with the Northern Forest under the rule of Lord Byrne. Musetta's words of *betraying Ellis* caused many hours of racking his brain to recall what happened at Deltoria. Nothing. He had no memory past speaking with Darius. Her mention of a connection between Ellis, his father and Lavi only added to his puzzlement. In short, he needed answers. The best way to obtain those answers was at the source. With nothing left to lose, he arrived at Ravendale. Now he accompanied the duke to the royal council chamber. He hoped whatever he learned would provide clarification.

In the chamber, Marcellus sat at the head of the Council table. Latham stood to his right. Tyree, Witter, two Shadow Warriors and a teenage girl stood opposite Marcellus.

"Who?" Marcellus asked Hugh in regards to Kemp.

"Baron Kemp of the Northern Forest, Phineas' son. He claims to be the one who betrayed the Pretender," said Hugh.

Although Hugh introduced him to the King, Kemp couldn't take his eyes off the girl. Her gaze turned sharp on Kemp when Hugh mentioned the word *betrayed*. Kemp forced himself to look from her to Latham when the Grand Master spoke.

"It's true, Sire. The baron has been most helpful," said Latham.

"You knew of this?"

"Naturally. The baron had been of great help in the past concerning his father and brother-in-law." Latham deliberately turned to Kemp.

Kemp shivered though not due to coldness of the Grand Master's icy blue stare. Rather, hearing Latham confirm what Musetta said in regards to his family. How could that be? He recalled nothing. Confusion stabbed at his heart.

Latham continued speaking, "The baron has secretly gathered information among the Pretender's associates. However, his latest action caused him to flee."

"Why didn't you tell me this before?" Hugh asked Kemp.

Befuddled, Kemp didn't know how to answer, so Latham replied.

"A matter of security."

"You're lying," said Shannan.

271

Kemp studied the girl. She spoke the words his mind desperately wanted to say but could not voice. Despite her age, there was something different about her. Something he couldn't quite place his finger on.

Latham sharply rebuked her. "You shouldn't be so quick to speak." He waved a man forward. He carried a small satchel. Latham took the satchel and opened it to let the contents spill out onto the table. "Recognize these?"

If she didn't, Kemp did: Ellis' brooch and Niles' amulet. Neither would surrender personal items to Latham. *That must mean* ... He heard the breath catch in her throat. She too recognized them. Though she swallowed back fear, tears rose in her glare at Latham. For being young, she bravely stood her ground against the Grand Master.

"What are those things?" inquired Hugh.

"Proof of the baron's story. This is the Pretender's brooch, and this is Sir Niles' amulet," said Latham.

"Why should they matter to her?"

Marcellus smirked. "This girl is his intended queen. Tyree was fortunate to capture her."

"The Daughter of Allon," Kemp muttered with sudden recognition.

"So Prophecy claims," said Marcellus, having heard Kemp. "Though she is hardly noble. What say you of this supposed queen, brother?"

The suppressed tears intensified the green of her eyes. Hugh shied, yet covered his discomposure by asking Marcellus, "What do you plan to do with her?"

"Marry her, of course," he said to Shannan's surprise, Hugh's trepidation and Kemp's concern.

"No!" she exclaimed.

"You are hardly in a position to protest."

"You just said she wasn't noble, so why marry her?" Hugh asked with confusion.

"What better way to triumph over my enemy than take what was his? Besides, it would be a terrific blow to those who supported his quest."

"Your Majesty speaks as if he is dead," said Kemp with care.

"A very good assumption, Baron."

Overcome with emotion, Shannan cried, "No! You're lying."

"Take her to Lady Blay for preparation," Latham ordered.

"No! I won't marry him. Ellis!" she sobbed, while forcibly taken from the room.

Unable to watch her departure, Kemp lowered his eyes. Hugh couldn't take his eyes off Shannan.

Latham keenly observed their reactions. "Perhaps the baron would assist His Grace in delivering the invitations."

Kemp swallowed back his surprise. Hugh became more vocal. "What?"

"As Duke of Allon and brother of the king, it is your privileged duty to ensure the invitations are properly sent," said Marcellus. "The wedding will be in three weeks. That should allow enough time to notify the Council."

"With the help of Shadow Warriors, of course," added Latham.

Hugh's sobriety kept him mute, so he simply nodded.

Kemp knew what was expected, though the words difficult to speak. "I would be honored to help, Sire."

Marcellus grinned then waved them out.

In the morning, Kemp left Ravendale to deliver the formal invitations. He was provided a new suit of clothes along with a horse. Hardly a task Kemp ever thought to undertake. It would have been so easy to create a ruse that he had been waylaid by robbers or ambushed by his former comrades. However, Latham made certain to prevent such action with the inclusion of Shadow Warriors. To aid him in his speedy travels, so said the Grand Master.

What manner of fate dealt him such a harsh hand that he lost his home, his family, and now compelled to act on behalf of a King he personally disliked? Surely there had to be an answer. Unfortunately, he was powerless to do anything other than to complete his task.

With less than three weeks, Kemp dared not linger in any one place. Not that he desired to, for the task would bring him into contact with each member of the Council. Some would consider him a traitor.

Latham chose the route that bypassed the Southern and Northern Forest, which made the Highlands Kemp's first stop. He longed to see his sons again, only not under such twisted circumstances. He hoped the boys were not present when he delivered the invitation to Ranulf. Alas, Ned and Fagan were with Lady Tilda in the family salon when Kemp was admitted. At first the boys were pleased to see him, however, their eagerness became cut short at the sight of Shadow Warriors.

Ned lashed out, "So, it is true! You betrayed Ellis and joined them!"

"It's not that simple," argued Kemp.

"Then why are they with you?" Fagan shouted in anger at the Shadow Warriors.

Lady Tilda tried to calm the boys. "Perhaps there is a good reason. Let your father explain." She flashed pleading eyes to Kemp.

"By order of the King, I come with an invitation to a royal wedding. All members of the Council are commanded to attend," said Kemp.

The declaration shocked Tilda. "Is that all you have to say?"

Kemp fought to keep his wits and temper. "What more can I say? I am commanded to undertake this task."

"Commanded?" she said disconcerted. His firm stance told her reality. "You have aligned with Marcellus."

"Traitor!" Ned spat, which caused the Shadow Warriors to reach for their swords.

"No!" Kemp placed himself between his sons and the Warriors. "He's a child. Wait in the hall." The Warriors didn't move. "I'll only be a moment. You can leave the door open," he said more forcefully. Once the Warriors left Kemp approached his sons. Ned and Fagan retreated from him. Pricked, he said, "You don't understand what has happened."

"We understand enough," said a deep male voice from behind Kemp's left ear.

Kemp came face-to-face with Ranulf. By the look of the open door behind Ranulf, he entered by a way unseen by the Warriors.

"You dare show your face here after what you've done?" chided Ranulf in a low throaty voice so as not to be overheard.

"I am their father."

"Our father is dead! He died when he betrayed his honor, his kin and Allon," rebuffed Ned.

Stunned to the core, Kemp stared at Ned. "You can't mean that?"

Ranulf stepped into Kemp's line of sight. He continued to keep his voice low. "You are dead to them. They are *my* sons now."

Rage moved Kemp to confront Ranulf. He halted when a dagger pressed against his mid-section. His eyes flashed from the dagger to Ranulf. The cold glare, told him Ranulf would not hesitate to kill him. With a last look at his sons, Kemp left.

Riding from Clifton Castle, a steely resolve grew. He just endured the ultimate injustice and indignity, being renounced by his sons. His own flesh turned against him. The incident provided one more reason to justify his personal malice against Ellis.

In the North Plains, Kemp's dealing with Lord Harkan proceeded in a more pleasant manner. He learned that Malcolm went into hiding shortly after the calamities began.

During the rest of the journey, Kemp encountered various reactions from members of the Council. To those favorable, or rather didn't press him, Owain, Gareth and Zebulon, he acted courteously. To those vocal against him such as Mathias and Allard, he relied upon the strength and fear of the Shadow Warriors to silence their complaints.

With only a few days left, Kemp reached Deltoria. He was in a foul mood having left a combative Allard at Milton. He set his jaw to address the Shadow Warriors.

"At our last meeting, Baron Erasmus made known his intentions toward my sister. He may be our greatest challenge. Stay sharp."

They followed Kemp into the grand foyer to wait while a servant fetched the baron.

Erasmus showed unusual visible anger when arriving, yet checked up at seeing Shadow Warriors. "What do you want?" in asked in a voice strained with emotion.

"I have come charged to deliver a royal invitation. The King is to marry Lady Shannan at the Temple in five days."

Erasmus stared with disbelief at Kemp. "You're joking?"

"This is no joke." Kemp shoved the envelope into Erasmus' hand. "All members of the Council of Twelve are commanded to attend."

"If I refuse?"

Kemp glanced at the Warriors. "That would be unwise."

The invitation became crushed in Erasmus' grip. "At first I didn't want to believe you capable of betrayal. Alas, your own actions have proven it. Have you no shame for how you've hurt and humiliated Erin?"

The Warriors drew their swords when Erasmus' passion compelled him closer to Kemp than they approved.

"No!" Erin rushed to stop Erasmus. With misty, woeful eyes she stared at her brother "Kemp?"

Kemp's façade began to crumble. Abruptly, he whirled on his heels and marched from Deltoria.

Erasmus restrained Erin from following her brother. "He's changed. He came to deliver a wedding invitation. Marcellus is marrying Ellis' lady in five days at the Temple. All Council Members are commanded to attend."

"Then Ellis is—" fear prevented her from finishing.

"I don't know," Erasmus quickly said. "There's been no word from Darius. I thank Jor'el he wasn't here or blood would have been spilled."

She wrapped her arms about herself as if warding off a chill. "Will you go?"

He heaved a hapless shrug. "To refuse would incur Marcellus' wrath. The Delta, no, Allon, cannot withstand another onslaught of Shadow Warriors."

"I'll go with you."

Her statement concerned him. "I'd rather you remain here in safety."

"This is the only safe place in Allon." She snuggled under his arms.

"Very well. We leave in two days." He kissed her forehead.

***

At their hiding place deep in the forest near Arundine, Jor'ellian sentries alerted Archimedes to incoming riders. Allard accompanied Darius, Jasper and Edmund. All were dirty, winded and weary from a hard pressed ride.

"Lord Darius. Were you successful in finding the Prince?" asked Archimedes.

"No. I fear the worst. Coupled with what news Allard brings, the end may be near."

"What news?" asked Archimedes. Knights gathered around to listen.

"Marcellus is marrying Shannan at the Temple in three days," Allard spoke loud enough for all to hear.

"No! Not the Daughter of Allon!" A chorus of objections rose vehemently from the Knights, forcing Archimedes to call for order.

"The Duke of Allon sent invitations by way of Baron Kemp to all members of the Council," said Allard.

A man pushed his way the crowd. "Did I hear right? The duke is party to this?" Iain came to stand beside Archimedes

"General Iain?" Darius' stirred in the saddle to draw his sword.

Archimedes seized Darius' arm. "All is well. He came to us by way of a Guardian in search of sanctuary. He has seen the error of his ways. We have tested him, and he has accepted Jor'el's path."

Satisfied at seeing Darius subdued, Allard answered Iain's question. "I received the invitation from Kemp, who confirmed the Duke's involvement."

"Latham must be threatening him with his children. If Hugh knew they are safe, he would not act so," Iain argued to Archimedes.

"I believe you. However, the Jor'ellians cannot allow this marriage to take place," the Vicar firmly stated.

"What do you plan to do? Storm the wedding?" asked Darius.

"If we must."

"They will have Shadows Warriors for security," warned Allard.

"Naturally. However, they will not be expecting me to be among the enemy's force," said Iain, flashing a sly smile.

Darius slapped the saddlebow in frustration. "If only there was some way to get word to those on the Council favorable to Ellis. We would rise in support of the Jor'ellians!"

"Leave that to me," said Archimedes. "Will you attend the ceremony?"

"It would be too dangerous for Darius. They would kill him on sight," began Iain in refute. "He should stay here to help with our plans," he suggested, to which Darius reluctantly agreed.

"Return home to make secret preparations, then attend the ceremony as commanded," Archimedes told Allard.

"How will I know when to act?"

"You will know. Now go with Jor'el's blessings and protection."

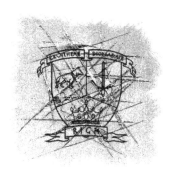

Chapter 26

ELLIS STIRRED UPON HIS BED IN A FITFUL, NIGHTMARISH SLEEP. The Temple of Providence was decorated for celebration. Royal banners along with those of Latham's house replaced the usual tapestries. Evergreen garlands hung from pillar to pillar. A kaleidoscope of bright colors streamed through the windows adding to the festival atmosphere. A crimson carpet ran down the center aisle from the door to the Altar steps. Grim faces of the nobles starkly contrasted the colorful display. Add to the contrast, the Shadow Warriors who flanked the nobles. In front of the High Altar, Vicar Archimedes stood rigid with Tyree and Witter standing ominously beside him. At the base step, Marcellus and Latham waited. Both wore ceremonial attire fitting the occasion.

A trumpet sounded the call for attention. From the rear of the Temple, came a veiled and gowned woman accompanied by the Duke of Allon. When the nobles lowered their heads or turned aside, Warriors forced them to watch.

When the woman stopped beside Marcellus, Latham preempted Archimedes to say; "Dispense with the formalities. Make the pronouncement."

"It will not be sanctified if I do not," Archimedes argued.

"Sanctification does not matter," Latham huffed.

The Vicar stiffened yet continued, "By the power vested in me by Jor—, I mean royal decree," he corrected at a harsh look from Latham. "I pronounce this man and this maid, man and wife."

Marcellus no sooner pulled back the veil to reveal Shannan then a thunderous roar sounded. An explosion of light filled the Temple. Dagar appeared in all his glory wearing a knee length cloak that matched his black and crimson suit. A large jewel encrusted chain held the cloak in place. From a golden belt round his waist hung a magnificent scabbard with a bejeweled hilt at his left hip. A golden coronet encircled his brow. A chill of evil seized those in the Temple. Women screamed while the men reached for their weapons only to be reminded that they were unarmed. Tyree quickly placed himself on guard at Marcellus' side.

"What do you want, Creature of Darkness?" demanded Archimedes.

Dagar smiled with wicked pleasure. "You know who I am. That is good, Lord Vicar."

"You have no place here."

Dagar's loud mocking laughter echoed in the Temple. "Not according to Prophecy!" He snatched a terrified Shannan to mount the steps of the Altar. With a clenched fist raised to ceiling he shouted; "Witness what I think of your chosen one, Jor'el!" He drew Shannan close. She struggled to resist him.

"No! Ellis," she cried—

"Shannan!" Ellis bolted upright from his nightmare. His heart raced, body trembled, and drenched in sweat. He anxiously looked about the dark room. Shafts of moonlight cascaded through the window's shutter. It took a moment to realize he was still in his sick bed at Melwynn.

Kell rushed in. "What's wrong?"

In a panic, Ellis replied. "Dagar has taken Shannan! He did so at a wedding. I saw her with Marcellus and Latham at the Temple, and then Dagar appeared."

Kell tried to keep Ellis from rising out of bed. "What you saw is in the future. Earlier I sent Elgin to Archimedes to tell him about Shannan's capture. The Vicar sent back word that she is to marry Marcellus at the Temple in a few days."

What little color remained on Ellis' face, drained away. "No! You can't let it happen."

Kell ignored the outburst to ask, "Do you know of Latham's parentage? Of Dagar?"

"What does that have to do with it?"

"Everything! Do you know?" insisted Kell.

Ellis shrugged with befuddlement. "I know that he is from the lineage of Ram, Dagar's son by a mortal female. She helped in his rebellion against Jor'el."

Kell shook his head. "That is what most believe. If it were true, each succeeding generation from Ram would become more mortal and less heavenly, losing their power. A half mortal, half Guardian would command much power."

"How can Latham be half Guardian? It's been over five hundred years since Ram and Razi were born," Ellis refuted with confusion.

Kell was deliberate in his answer. "Just as Jor'el has preserved Razi's descendants, your lineage; so has Dagar, only in a more self-serving manner. A pact was made with Ram that when the king married, the bride was turned over to Dagar to conceive the first-born, who would eventually become *Grand Master*. Being half Guardian is how Latham and his predecessors command the Dark Way. If Shannan bear Dagar's child—"

"No! I won't let it happen." The outburst sent pain through Ellis.

"You're in no condition to do anything. Archimedes said the Jor'ellians would mount an offensive to stop the wedding. He urged me to dispatch Guardian messengers to the Council for their support. I have done so."

"What about the rest of the Guardians?" Ellis asked between teeth clenched in pain.

Kell couldn't look at Ellis when he replied. "We can't help. It's up to the mortals."

"Why? Your fate is linked to Shannan," Ellis stammered in disbelief.

"So I argued with Jor'el, but to no avail. However, if the mortals fail there is only one alternative to prevent calamity."

The tone in Kell's voice joined with a glint of distress in the golden eyes alerted Ellis to something undesirable, something he wondered if he wanted to hear. All the same, he asked, "What?"

Kell was unable to keep the pain from his face. "If Shannan dies before—" Ellis sat upright, blue eyes hard and lips taunt. The reaction caused a momentary pause in Kell's speech. "It's the only way!"

"Do you truly believe Jor'el would permit us to come this far only to allow Dagar the victory? What of Prophecy concerning the subduing of the Great Enemy?"

"Perhaps this is the way to that subduing."

"No! We were meant to be together," Ellis' voice cracked despite his bravado.

Kell spoke with halting sobriety. "We cannot wait long to make the decision, Highness." With nothing else to say, he withdrew.

Ellis let out a yowl of great heartache and bitterly wept. The agony too great at such an unthinkable sacrifice! So many already suffered or died for him, he could not lose the most precious person, his heart and soul. How could he come this far only to fail? What was left now? Niles was dead, Shannan in grave danger, Darius—somewhere unknown. What would become of Allon if Jor'el were usurped? Was it all for nothing? He cried out in angry frustration.

"How could you let this happen? What more do you want from me? Answer me, Jor'el! I deserve that much."

"Your complete trust and obedience," came a calm voice that filled the room.

Ellis saw no one. "Kell?" he tentatively asked, though the voice didn't sound like Kell.

"No. It is I, Son of Tristan, the one who chose you."

A misty veiled figure appeared beside the bed. Only the opalescent eyes were clearly visible. The gaze radiated with soothing reassurance.

"Jor'el," Ellis said with reverence. "What do you want from me?"

"Do you trust me, Son of Tristan?" Jor'el spoke, but no lips moved.

"I want to. But—"

"No, doubts. Remember the pouch."

Ellis took a deep breath. He closed his eyes to focus on the Jor'ellian Knight's meditation. Jor'el's presence felt stronger than ever. Images of the wedding invaded his mind's eye. "What of Shannan?" he asked, eyes still closed.

"Do you believe my word and trust my judgment?"

"You haven't answered my question."

"You asked me what I wanted from you, and I told you. Now answer me," Jor'el spoke with serene authority.

"It hurts so!" Ellis' sobbed. His head fell into his hands

"Pain is an emotion that passes with time. Trust and obedience are actions that surpass all emotions."

Ellis wiped the tears from his face to again begin his meditation. After a few deep breaths, he slowly exhaled. A hand caressed his head. A wave of calm swept over him. He no longer felt troubled in spirit, or experienced pain from his wound.

Jor'el's eyes smiled upon Ellis. "I ask you again, Son of Tristan, do you believe my word and trust my judgment?"

"Ay," replied Ellis in strong voice of confidence.

"Then be at peace and sleep."

From the terrace, Kell watched the first light of morning break over the horizon. He had been there since leaving Ellis. Everything stood on the brink of catastrophe. It took every ounce of self-restraint not to rush out to rescue Shannan. The last time he acted rashly, Dagar nearly killed him during the Great Battle. If not for Armus' quick thinking then, he would not be watching this sunrise.

The burden of total failure gave way to a low lament; "How many more sunrises will I see? How many more will any of us see? Or have I doomed us all?"

"Kell."

Kell started in recognition of the voice. A figure bathed in haze appeared beside him. He fell to his knees, his head bowed to the ground. "Jor'el! Forgive me. I have failed." His choked voice filled with remorse.

Compassionately, Jor'el gazed down upon Kell. "Have you as little faith as the mortals, Captain?"

Head still bowed, Kell forced a reply. "Your silence swayed me to actions that resulted in tragedy leading to our present situation."

"You thought Archimedes' revelation of the Knights too early would be a hindrance. It was not. Why should this be different?"

Unable to look up to give an answer, Kell's words faltered in painful admission. "Because I allowed Dagar to escape prematurely."

"You take too much upon yourself, Kell. By doing so, you minimize me." Jor'el spoke the rebuke with gentle firmness.

Stunned, Kell dared a glance up. "I didn't mean that, Holy One!"

"I know." Jor'el kindly smiled. "Despite your many diligent efforts and inquiries, I purposely kept you ignorant.

> "*When the Great Enemy has gathered together his minions,*
> *Uneasy shall lie his crown.*
> *For when peace has come to his camp,*
> *They shall behold him who is to come,*
> *To lay at the feet of Jor'el,*
> *The subduing of the Great Enemy.*'"

"Arise, my Captain. The Son of Tristan wakes. Go to him." With that, Jor'el vanished.

Ellis stretched with a great yawn. The room appeared lighter than before. For a moment, he wondered if everything was a dream. He sat up to allow his mind to collect his thoughts so he could focus his attention on the present. During his reflection, Ellis absentmindedly tossed aside the covers to stand. Not until his bare feet stepped off the rug beside the bed onto cold stone did he realize he was standing. He felt no pain. He looked and felt for his wound. Instead of bandages he discovered bare skin—healed, and no scars! He quickly crossed to the balcony doors where he threw them open to step outside. He raised his hands skyward.

"Praise your mercy, Great Jor'el! Add your strength to my arms this day so I may do that which you have appointed for me."

"Highness?" Ellis heard a concerned Kell. He turned to see the captain approach the empty bed. He went back inside. "I'm here, Kell."

Kell's eyes grew wide in surprise at Ellis' naked and healed torso. He fell to his knees. He seized Ellis' hand to place it reverently against his forehead. "Forgive me, my Prince!" he said in urgent pleading.

"For what?"

"When I told you it was no longer safe at Dorgirith it was because Jor'el lifted his seal. The seal kept Dagar bound, unable to return by way of Magelen's ruins until the appointed time. It wasn't Jor'el who sent you back to Dorgirith. He had been silent since the beginning of the Contest." Kell swallowed back his emotions, then hastily said; "I took it upon myself to prevent the calamity that now threatens to engulf Allon. I intended to be there when you arrived, to allow you to defeat me, slay me if necessary. All to prevent Dagar's release. Everything that has happened since is *my* fault! Niles' death, Shannan's capture, your wounding."

Ellis regarded the contrite Kell, who did not look at him. Ellis' initial confusion turned to sympathy. "What has Jor'el said to this?"

"That he purposely kept me ignorant and quoted Prophecy."

Ellis quoted the same verse;

> *"When the Great Enemy has gathered together his minions,*
> *Uneasy shall lie his crown.*
> *For when peace has come to his camp,*
> *They shall behold him who is to come,*
> *To lay at the feet of Jor'el,*
> *The subduing of the Great Enemy."*

"Kell, if Dagar did not believe me dead by his own hand, could he believe he won as the Prophecy says?"

Kell glanced up. He replied in a calmer voice. "That peace will come by way of Marcellus' marriage to Shannan, and she conceives his son."

"So he thinks." Ellis slyly smiled. He tugged on Kell to stand. "Assemble the Guardians, Captain. We go to stop a wedding."

"Ay, my Prince." Kell saluted. He left to fulfill the order. In the hall, he shouted, "Armus!" Shortly Armus appeared with Avatar, which surprised Kell. "Avatar. What of the others?"

Avatar grinned. "Thank Jor'el, not a single loss. All are here safely, and being tended by the physicians."

"Captain!" Wren and Mahon arrived in a rush. "Vidar is gone!" she said.

"He's left Melwynn. We think he went to find Shannan," said Mahon.

"That was foolhardy," chided Kell.

"So was going into Dagar's nether dimension. But what's that to a love-struck Guardian?" said Priscilla, who appeared from behind Kell.

"You think Vidar is in love with Shannan?" asked Avatar.

"So is Kell."

"Priscilla, you go too far!" Kell scolded.

"Love of duty then."

Kell ignored Priscilla to issue orders. "To your posts! Our time has come to face the enemy. I'll deal with Vidar later."

"But the Prince—?" Armus stopped when Kell smiled.

"It is by *his* command we go to stop a wedding," Kell announced.

"At once, Captain," said Armus with a hearty salute.

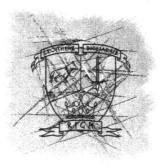

Chapter 27

ONSIDERING THE VAST NUMBER OF GUESTS AND SHADOW Warriors required for security, the area surrounding the Temple became crowded with tents of various sizes. The compound adjacent to the Temple was only capable of housing a hundred guests, those of Marcellus' choosing. This left the rest to arrange their own lodgings.

Amidst a flurry of regal display, those on the Council in support of Marcellus arrived a few days before the ceremony to establish their quarters. Those who objected to the wedding, waited until the last possible moment to arrive. They even kept company apart from the others.

Tilda and Ranulf entered Allard's tent. Inside they found Malcolm and his mother in conversation with Allard and Mathias.

"Malcolm, you look better," said Ranulf.

"I'm not as strong as I would like."

"That is coming with each day," Matrill said with encouragement.

Mathias tossed a surly glance at Ranulf. "Did you notice Owain, Zebulon and Gareth keeping company with Marcellus' new jack-in-napes Kemp?"

"It is best to keep your tongue in your head if you want to keep your head on your shoulders," countered the Highland lord.

Mathias scoffed a laugh. "Since when have you kept your tongue?"

Ranulf flashed a cunning smile. "Only for a few hours then."

"Is all well, my lord?" Allard asked Ranulf the coded phrase.

Ranulf spoke the reply, "All *is* well."

"What about Erasmus and Hollis?" inquired Mathias.

"Erasmus arrived an hour ago. I haven't seen Hollis," said Ranulf.

"If only Darius were here," murmured Malcolm.

"It is best he is not. His family has suffered the worse of any," said Tilda with concerned compassion.

"Come tomorrow, the rest of us will suffer. The only question is how, with success or failure?" said Allard with dread.

Tilda covered her mouth to stifle a gasp. Matrill also displayed distress. Malcolm comforted his mother while Ranulf scolded Allard.

"No need to upset our women."

"I'm sorry," Allard apologized to the ladies. "I know your presence is a comfort to your husband, and your son," he said to Tilda and Matrill respectively. "Still, I am glad Natalie's delicate condition kept her home."

"Shall we partake of food to strengthen our resolve?" Mathias spoke while motioning to a table prepared for dinner.

"Indeed. I don't mean to a gloomy host," said Allard with a gracious smile.

As Erin and Erasmus left the registration area inside the Temple compound, she faltered in her gait at sight of Kemp. She tightened her grip on Erasmus' arm in an attempt to ignore her brother. Erasmus took her cue and kept walking.

The arrival of the royal carriages in front of the Temple forced them to stop. The King emerged from the first carriage followed by Latham. From the second carriage, came Hugh. He extended his hand to help a hooded woman in regal dress from the carriage.

Erin had never seen Shannan before. Due to recent events the woman with Hugh had to be her. Before going inside, Shannan paused. She looked directly at Erin! In that brief meeting of the eyes, Erin shuddered with distress. Her face instantly turned pale. Shannan and Hugh entered the Temple.

Erasmus noticed Erin's stricken pallor and felt her quake. "Erin?"

Her disturbed voice barely rose above a whisper. "This shouldn't be happening. She should be marrying Ellis."

With a warning hand on her shoulder, Erasmus indicated another group. Shadow Warriors escorted Lord Archimedes into the Temple. "Heaven help us now," he said.

Hugh escorted a somber Shannan to a room off the nave inside the Temple. An inexplicable anxiety gripped him, as he watched her sit on a small cot. He tried to determine the cause of his anxiety. Perhaps it was Latham's last words to him before leaving Ravendale when given charge of her. The warning laced with reminders of his children's fate, sent a shiver through him. Or perhaps it was being at the Temple? Allon's most holy place would become the stage for a marriage he felt uneasy about.

She must have sensed his regard, for she glanced up at him from under shrouded brows. At that moment Hugh knew the source of his discomfort. Since the first time he saw her, memories of Lida and Vera's fate haunted him. Shannan had not spoken a word to him. In fact, he had not heard her speak since that day in the Council chamber, but heard stories of the difficult time she gave Lady Blay.

Now, dressed in an ivory gown with her hair pampered she no longer appeared the forest urchin. She may not have been noble of birth, yet there was nobility about her, especially when she stiffened to his overly long gaze. Again, the gesture reminded him of Lida.

"I'm sorry," he said, which made her brow furrow. "I, too, lost someone I deeply loved to—"

"To what?" she asked when he hesitated.

He tried to wave it off. "It doesn't matter."

"Did you lose that loved one to your brother?"

"No. Someone close to him."

"Latham," she said with certainty.

Hugh painful grimaced. "I've said too much. What happened is in the past. Tomorrow you will marry Marcellus."

"Because of Latham's evil." Her poignant gaze direct on him.

"*That* is why I apologized."

"You are nothing like your brother. Compassion stirs your heart, though you feel powerless to act on that compassion."

Hugh regarded her with admiration. "You speak with such maturity. You can't be more than twenty years old."

"Seventeen."

Hugh lowered his head to gnaw on his lower lip. This was too much! So similar in strength of character to Lida and Vera it was unnerving. They too were sacrificed to Latham because they posed a threat for not bending to his will. *What will my children think of their father's cowardice if I let another brave woman be sacrificed?*

With a look of determination he spoke to her. "Can I trust you to remain here? Not that you would get past the guards."

"I will stay."

Hugh went in search of Marcellus. He found him near the altar with Latham. This time the Grand Master's presence would not deter him from his course. Too much was at stake to back down now.

"I would speak with you privately," he said. He tossed a harsh side-glance at Latham.

Marcellus followed Hugh's glance. Latham carefully shook his head. "I'm afraid there is no time."

Hugh also saw Latham's action thus spoke directly to him. "I, the Duke of Allon, brother of the king, command you to leave."

Marcellus laid heavy hold of Hugh's arm. "There is nothing you can say to me that Grand Master Latham cannot hear."

"That's not good enough."

"It will have to be, if you wish to speak with me."

Hugh noticed a cold harshness to his brother he had never seen before. He reckoned the change due to Latham's dark influence. With such a stalwart front, he wondered if he could reach Marcellus. He had to try! For the sake of his children, Shannan's fate, and Lida's memory.

"Very well. I will say what needs be said, whatever the outcome." His eyes flashed to Latham then back to Marcellus. "This marriage should not take place!"

Marcellus laughed. "Is that what you came to say? Well, you could have saved your breath. Despite what you think, I've been assured this marriage is for the best, both for our family and Allon."

"Assured by him? Since when does he care what is best for anyone but himself?"

"Tread lightly, Hugh," warned Marcellus.

"Or what? You'll have him silence me like Vera or Lida?"

"Grand Master Latham never silenced anyone."

Hugh was beside himself with rage at Marcellus' refusal to listen. "By the heavenlies, he has my children!" he lashed out. The outburst did not have the reaction he hoped.

"You mean he is keeping them safe until the wedding is over."

The answer stunned Hugh to the core! Marcellus knew Latham had his children. Latham coolly watched them. "This creature has changed you, Marcellus. Have you no concern for my children? Your flesh and blood also?"

"They will not be harmed."

Hugh's shoulders sagged. His last attempt to reach his brother failed. A hand upon his arm made him look up. Marcellus casually smiled.

"Once the wedding is over, you'll see the children. I promise. In fact, you can toast me as a father. Latham says my bride shall conceive a son, who will be the most powerful king Allon has ever known. My throne shall be secure."

Until now Latham remained silent. When he spoke, it came with a heavy warning. "Your Grace can share in the good fortune, unless you proclaim public opposition to this marriage."

Hugh could not tolerate the cold regard. "I have no choice," he said low and hapless.

"A wise decision, brother."

Shannan didn't feel as certain as she sounded when dealing with Hugh, but anything was worth a try. She suspected he went to speak to the King. She tried to curb a spark of hope. Thus far other hopes of avoiding the marriage were dashed. Vidar fell off the cliff and Kato shot from the sky. If Vidar were not dead, he would have come for her by now. Her thoughts turned to Kell. He went to help Ellis when they sensed Dagar's release. However, if what Latham said was true about Ellis and her grandfather then more than likely Kell was dead also. He would protect Ellis to the end.

In company of the Guardians, her intuition grew keen and precise, surprising in clarity of perception. She didn't possess the Guardian ability to stretch out her senses, rather a general awareness of attitudes and feelings. What her grandfather spoke in the abstract regarding her destiny became reality during those months with Wren, Vidar and Priscilla. Through interaction with them, she learned to hone her abilities. Since capture, she felt as if all her innate senses were being blocked. Similar to what Vidar did with Witter to hide their escape from Dorgirith. She knew Shadow Warriors were once Guardians yet unable to discern their heart or minds.

In her heart of hearts she could not discern if Ellis was truly dead. More frightening was the absence of Jor'el's presence. It had to be Latham, or worse, Dagar! She knew he was free when a terrifying dark coldness seized her on their flight from Ravendale. Her voicing of fear sent Kell and Armus to aid Ellis.

Hugh was the last remaining hope to avoid the marriage. Alas, he had been gone a long time. With each passing moment, she wondered if something dreadful happened to him. Finally he returned. His downcast features told her that he was not the same determined man who left. He restlessly paced and tossed woeful glances at her. After a few moments, he mumbled '*good-night*' and left. She lowered her head to silently weep.

Hour after hour passed in the deep stillness of the night, as she sat on the cot looking up through the small high window. The solitary candle long since burned itself to nothing. Moonlight softly played across her face. Her eyes puffy yet dry from weeping. Lips silently moved in forming unspoken words.

From outside the window, she heard a soft whimper. At a second whimper, she careful crossed to the window. Another whimper. An animal!

"Torin?" she carefully called.

An affirming low bark became louder. She bit her lip to stifle a sob of relief. Her loyal wolf found her. What help could he be? She had to think fast before Torin's presence was discovered.

A dim flash of light came from behind. She backed into the corner, fearful of the fading light. "Vidar!" she breathed in wondrous relief. Overjoyed, she embraced him. "I thought you were dead."

"*Shh*," he silenced her then listened for sounds of alarm.

"You're hurt badly," she whispered in reference to her wounds.

"I'm fit enough to get you out of here. That's all that matters." He took several deep breaths. "Hold on. This could be rough."

Under the cover of darkness, Erin emerged from the quarters she shared with Erasmus. She wore a dark cloak over dark clothes. She pulled the hood up. She headed for the Temple. Since her brief encounter with Shannan, she had not been able to shake the deep sense of doom concerning the marriage. The most intense feeling was that she could do something to help. Not for her own sake, somewhat for Shannan and Ellis, but more for the man she just left, for Erasmus.

Ellis hurt her terribly, or so she believed for a time. Her bruised heart felt bitterness towards him and jealousy for Shannan, the rival she never met. At Deltoria, she found a surprising source of comfort along with a renewal of heart and spirit. All because of Erasmus. He declared his love for her without reservation or resentment toward Ellis. His liveliness of character was markedly different from Ellis' dark determination. The more time she spent with Erasmus, the more her heart mended. She grew to appreciate his strength of character, gentleness and genuine passion for her. She only fooled herself in thinking she could ever be what Ellis needed to fulfill his destiny. That is what he tried to tell her at Milton.

As her heart changed toward Ellis, so did her feelings about Shannan. When their eyes met, she saw what Ellis tried to tell her. Shannan was the Daughter of Allon, Jor'el's chosen. A mere glance told of a strength and singleness of heart that she could never share with Ellis, but had come to know with Erasmus. That kind of love should not be forsaken. Those feelings, coupled with the shame of Kemp's betrayal, compelled her to take a course of action.

Erin crept behind the tents to circumvent the Shadow Warriors at the Temple entrance. She was uncertain of how to enter the grounds or even reach Shannan. Perhaps the postern gate would be easier. At the back of the compound, a dim flash of light eye caught her attention. Hearing a soft female voice, Erin moved to investigate. Near a crop of bushes, Shannan knelt beside a man on the ground. Erin let out a surprise, short cry when something brushed by her. A wolf! Shannan became alerted to her presence.

"Be easy! I mean no harm. I came to help," Erin quickly said, and lowered her hood.

Shannan studied Erin. "I saw you earlier."

Erin shied from Shannan's probing glance. She noticed Vidar's wounds. "He's hurt."

"I'll live, but we must leave," he spoke the last part to Shannan.

"Alarm will be raised when they find she is gone," said Erin.

Vidar stood with a grunt of pain. "That can't be helped."

"Take my clothes!" Erin impulsively offered Shannan. "If we switch clothes, I can go back and pretend to be you, giving you time to escape."

"Why would you take such a risk?"

Erin boldly met Shannan's gaze. "You know why. Allon needs you."

Vidar watched the visual exchange with marked interest. "Can she be trusted?" he asked Shannan.

She didn't immediately answer, still studying Erin. "Who are you?"

"Erin, daughter of Phineas the brother of Sir Angus of Garwood."

Shannan grinned. "Ay, she can be trusted. Yet she has no way of getting inside."

"Say no more. I'll keep watch while you switch clothes." Vidar turned his back. He leaned against a small tree for support.

Shannan notice a glint of silver attached to Erin's petticoat. "What is that?"

"A dagger. Just in case." Erin readjusted the weapon in its hiding place.

"Are you strong enough?" Shannan asked Vidar when they finished.

He reached for Erin. "That remains to be seen."

Once inside, Erin fainted. Vidar had difficulty carrying her to the cot due to his wounds. A scraping at the door alerted him to someone coming. He flattened himself against the wall beside the door, hoping not to be noticed. The peephole opened. A brief light shone through to land on Erin. He tensed. Fortunately, he laid Erin with her face away from the door. At the closing of the peephole, he slightly relaxed.

When Vidar reappeared outside, he collapsed from exhaustion. Shannan helped him walk the short distance to the wood surrounding the Temple. Once in the shelter of the trees, he gingerly sat against an oak.

"We were fortunate not to be seen. Were you able to block us from being sensed?" she asked.

"No. With my wounds, I had to conserve my strength to get here and free you. I'm not certain how I managed to dimension travel without alerting Shadow Warriors to my presence." He glanced back to the Temple with a disconcerted brow. "There is a deep sense of darkness overshadowing this holy place."

She followed his gaze. "Ay. But there must be some grace in the midst it for all this to happened."

He groaned when he shifted to get comfortable.

"How bad are your wounds?"

"I'll be all right in a little while. Who was she?"

"Someone in love with Ellis," she said while examining his wounds.

He snatched her hand to stop her. "What?"

"You remember when I sent my pouch because of my dream? I did so because I saw her and Ellis together."

"So how could you trust her?"

"It's all right. Nothing happened. Ellis wouldn't—" She became choked by tears.

He gently wiped away her tears. "Don't cry. You'll be together soon."

She shook her head. "They said Ellis is—dead."

"He's not dead. He's wounded, and recovering at Melwynn."

With joyful relief, she hugged his neck. "Grandfather? They had his amulet along with Ellis' brooch—" she stopped at seeing his dismay. "He is dead."

Vidar slowly nodded. "I'm sorry."

Torin lay beside Shannan to place his head on her lap. She stroked the wolf's head. "At least you're here."

Vidar bit his lower lip with discomposure. "Shannan—my lady. There is something I must to tell you. About what Witter said."

She noted his change in speech, his expression remorseful. "You mean handing me over to him?"

He sluggishly nodded. "I knew what Shaka wanted the moment she arrived. Although Rune's escape plan surprised me, I was to be set free to find you—" he couldn't finish for shame. With eyes screwed shut, he lowered his head.

She gently lifted his face. "If you didn't turn me over to Tor in the nether dimension, you weren't going to give me to Witter at the cliff."

He went from contrition to confusion. "You knew?"

"From your encounter with Shaka, Tor's attempt to bully you, and Witter's cruel abuse, I knew you overcame much more than a lack of confidence. I first noticed your reticence at the cliff cave when I told you to be more confident in yourself."

"Confidence is one thing, but this is something else," he droned.

She wouldn't let him turn away again. "Tell me, when did you determine not to give into Dagar's desire for you?"

"Practically from the moment I saw you. Most definitely during Kell's interrogating when you seemed so confident in me."

She smiled, soft and gentle. "Then, my dear Vidar, Dagar never really had a hold over you since your determination was from the beginning. That is why I trust you completely. I never sensed duplicity or falsehood in you, then or now."

His gratitude for her understanding became cut short by a nearby rustling. He hushed Torin's low growl of warning. When the danger passed, he said, "At the present, I don't have the strength to dimension travel us anywhere to safety."

"You will after some rest," she said with confidence.

"We can't rest long. The early grey light of dawn is breaking over the horizon. We need to find more secure shelter."

They began to move when Torin growled a second time. A twig snapped. Vidar snatched Shannan to head deeper into the forest. Vidar's speed and agility didn't last long under the limitations of his wounds.

At hearing louder sounds from nearby, Vidar nudged Shannan into a sinkhole under a log. He struck his right leg on the log when taking cover. His bit his lip to stifle a cry. Footsteps and low voices came closer. Numerous feet passed by the log. They waited several moments before the area fell silent again.

"Shadow Warriors?" she whispered.

"I didn't sense any evil. Besides, what would they be doing in the woods? Except looking for you."

"Maybe he means to slay the Council."

Vidar peeked out. He scanned the area with deep concentration. He caught a glimpse of figures. He ducked back. "I believe they are mortals yet unable to determine their identities. Whatever is going to happen, we can't stay here."

More nearby muffled voices.

"Can you hear what they're saying?"

Vidar closed his eyes, his brows furrowed in concentration. His face relaxed into a smile, his eyes opened. "Come. It is time to fulfill your destiny, Daughter of Allon."

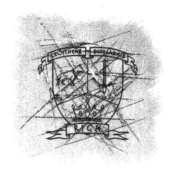

Chapter 28

A T DAWN, THE TENT FLAP FLEW OPEN. ERASMUS EMERGED. HE made a quick search of the nearby area. Anxiety rose at seeing Shadow Warriors. Kemp spoke with Owain. Maybe Kemp knew where Erin was or—"Allard."

Erasmus spied his friend with another a man wearing a grey cloak. He rushed to intercept him. Startled by Erasmus abrupt arrival the man moved to withdraw. Allard stopped him by taking hold of his arm. Erasmus ignored the man to inquire of Allard.

"Have you seen Erin? I can't find her."

"She's missing?" asked the man in a low, husky voice of disguise.

Curious at his question, Erasmus tried to see under the hood. Allard leaned close to Erasmus to whisper a name in his ear. Erasmus quickly recovered from his surprise to answer.

"I think she may be with Kemp." Erasmus discreetly nodded in the direction of Kemp.

They carefully followed the indication. Kemp noticed the interest. He sneered at them before storming away.

"He could have invoked his authority over her," Allard suggested to Erasmus.

"I don't believe she would yield. She accepted my marriage proposal en route here."

"*That* would incite Kemp," chided the man. His hooded head turned in the direction Kemp left.

"Steady," warned Allard in a confidential voice. "Remember your task."

"I do! The question is will you and the others be ready?" He continued to maintain a disguised voice.

"Of course. You can reassure our mutual *friend* that all is well."

"What of Erin?" Erasmus interjected.

"How long has she been gone?" asked the man.

"I'm not certain. We partitioned the tent for privacy. When she didn't respond to me, I looked in only to discover she wasn't there. I summoned the maid, but she didn't know where she went."

Allard pursed his lips. "No way to mount a search with the wedding in two hours."

"I must find her!"

"Later. Too much is at stake," rebuffed the man.

"You know I won't jeopardize anything," Erasmus refuted.

The man gripped Erasmus' arm in acknowledgement. "Afterwards, we will search for her," he said with reassurance.

"Jor'el protect her until then," Erasmus murmured.

"Go make ready." Allard nudged Erasmus on his way. He then escorted the man to the rear of his tent. "Don't let this distract you."

"No, but it does add an uncomfortable complication."

"Jor'el be with you." Allard held out his hand.

"And with you, my friend."

Assured of no prying eyes, the cloaked man raced to the forest. Once under cover, he made his way to where a group of men waited.

Iain, Jasper, Edmund and two Jor'ellian Knights lay on the dew-covered ground watching the Temple. All wore splotched olive, brown and gray cloaks to blend with the forest. Upon joining them, he removed his hood for a better view. Darius.

"Are they in place?" Iain asked Darius.

"Ay. Only there may be a problem. Personal, not detrimental to the plan." Darius told Jasper and Edmund, "Erin is missing."

"How?" Edmund asked.

"Erasmus doesn't know exactly. He discovered her missing this morning. Thankfully, he agreed to wait until after to take up a search. When the action starts, keep a sharp eye out for her."

"Who is Erin?" asked Iain.

"My cousin, sister of Kemp," Darius spat out Kemp's name.

"You trust her?"

Darius stirred with insult. "You assume wrongly to ask such a question. She bears Kemp's shame most of all, and is betrothed to Erasmus. If she is missing because of Kemp, is it by compulsion, not voluntary."

Iain spoke with contrition. "My lord, I ask out of an abundance of caution, nothing more."

A Jor'ellian arrived. "General, the archers are in position."

"Very well. Let's return to the main force." They crawled backwards into the shadows before moving deeper into the forest.

In the room off the nave, Erin lay awake listening to the noises outside. Her face remained turned toward the wall. She carefully moved the dagger to her hand. *What am I doing?* Then she answered herself. The only thing she could to help Shannan and Ellis; to protect Erasmus and Allon from the doom she felt. She froze with fear when the door opened then closed.

A female spoke; "It's time, my lady."

"Are you alone?" Erin asked over her shoulder.

"Ay. Come. I must dress you."

At a touch on her shoulder, Erin sprang into action. One hand covered the woman's mouth; the other hand pressed a dagger to her side. Erin whispered a warning in the terrified woman's ear.

"One sound and I'll kill you. Answer my questions with a nod or shake of your head, no sound. Understood?"

The woman nodded.

"Is there a veil to conceal my identity?"

She nodded.

"After you dress me are you to leave?"

She shook her head.

"You are to remain until the ceremony?"

She nodded.

"Good. Now, I will release you to help me dress, but remember, I *will* kill you if you utter a sound of alarm." Erin carefully removed her hand.

"I could betray you after we leave the chamber."

"I would implicate you as an accomplice."

The woman saw Erin's determination. "Once the veil is removed you are undone."

Erin spoke sharply with rebuff. "So why risk your life when you will have time to escape while I'm walking the aisle?"

The woman curiously studied her. "Who are you? And why do this?"

"That doesn't matter. Now dress me."

The Temple interior was decorated for celebration. Royal banners of Marcellus and Latham's houses replaced the usual tapestries. Garlands hung from pillar to pillar. The kaleidoscope of bright colors streaming through the window added to the festive atmosphere. However, grim faces of the nobles standing on either side of the crimson carpet starkly contrasted to the colorful display. Shadow Warriors flanked the nobles. By the High Altar, Lord Archimedes stiffly stood with Tyree and Witter ominously beside him. At the foot of the Altar, Marcellus and Latham waited, both in ceremonial dress.

Erasmus fidgeted in standing beside Allard. He especially grew agitated at the sight of Kemp near the altar. He averted his gaze when Allard whispered to him.

"Courage."

Malcolm appeared pale as he and his mother waited on the other side of Allard. Tilda held Ranulf's arm. Mathias and Hollis stood behind the Highland couple.

"I feel naked without my sword," grumbled Mathias.

"Did you think they would allow us to keep our weapons?" Ranulf carefully said over his shoulder.

"We'll be armed when our men arrive," said Hollis out of the side of his mouth.

The sound of a trumpet drew attention to the rear of the Temple. A veiled and gowned woman walked down the asile escorted by the Duke of Allon. Some nobles somberly lowered their heads or turned aside. Warriors roughly forced them to watch.

Archimedes' jowls tightened when Hugh stopped beside Marcellus to present the bride.

Latham sneered at Archimedes. "Dispense with the formalities. Just make the pronouncement."

"It would not be sanctified if I do not," Archimedes argued.

"Sanctification does not matter.

The Vicar stiffened with piety but obeyed. "By the power vested in me by Jor'el—I mean—royal decree," he corrected himself after a harsh look from Latham. "I pronounce this man and this maid, man and wife."

With a thunderous roar, brilliant light filled the Temple. From the fading light appeared Dagar in all his glory. A knee-length cloak that matched his black and crimson suit was draped over his shoulder, held in place by a thick jewel-encrusted chain. From a golden belt hung a magnificent scabbard with a bejeweled hilt. A golden coronet encircled his brow. As the cloak settled about him from his abrupt entrance, a chill of evil seized those in the Temple.

Some women screamed; others fainted. Men instinctively reached for their weapons, only to be reminded they were unarmed.

Shadow Warriors kept the royal soldiers from interfering. Marcellus drew back a few steps. Tyree appeared at his shoulder ready to make defense. Hugh gaped in fear at Dagar and Latham standing side-by-side.

"What do you want, Creature of Darkness?" demanded Archimedes.

Dagar smiled with wicked pleasure. "You know who I am. That is good, Lord Vicar."

"You have no place here!"

Dagar's loud mocking laughter echoed in the Temple. "Not according to Prophecy."

"Who are you?" demanded Marcellus.

"The Dark Master whom your father acknowledged, and to whom you shall soon pay homage!"

The intensity of Dagar's glare surpassed anything Marcellus experienced from Latham. At that moment, he stared in the face of pure evil. Terrified, he paled to the point of near fainting.

With a haughty laugh, Dagar snatched the frightened bride from Marcellus. He mounted the step to the altar. "The Daughter of Allon is no more!" He ripped off the veil.

"Erin!" Kemp gasped in horror.

When Erasmus stepped forward, Allard seized him. "No! Wait," he hissed in warning.

"She is not the Daughter of Allon," Latham declared.

"What trickery is this?" demanded Dagar.

"I don't know, my lord." Latham vehemently turned to Hugh. "You did this!"

"No! I did," Erin bravely said before a stunned Hugh could reply.

Dagar's eyes narrowed upon her. She struggled to breathe. She fell to her knees, desperate for air. Allard fought to contain Erasmus from going to Erin's aid. Mathias added him when Erasmus struggled hard. They stopped when Kemp launched forward to protect Erin. He became Dagar's focus. Erin gulped for air at being released. Alas, air would not be what Kemp needed.

Kemp grabbed his chest. All the color immediately drained from his face. He collapsed beside Erin, ashen with death. She gathered him in her arms and wept.

Panic seized those in the Temple. People scrambled to escape. Erasmus broke free with the intent of going to Erin only a Shadow Warrior struck him aside. Mathias helped Erasmus to his feet. Blood oozed from a cut where the Warrior struck him.

"Marcellus! You brought this evil upon us," Hugh shouted.

Dagar shouted, "*D'uin!*" in the Ancient while he waved his hands. The huge Temple doors slammed shut. "Silence!" he commanded. A deep hush of terror fell over the crowd.

"Dagar!" a booming voice echoed in the chamber. All eyes searched for the source.

Dagar half scowled, half smiled. "You may serve me yet." He jerked Erin to her feet. He replaced the veil on her head. "Come!" he ordered Marcellus and the Shadow Warriors.

"No, Marcellus, don't!" Hugh spoke in desperation

Unable to tolerate Hugh's pleading eyes, Marcellus ran after Dagar.

"You shall remain with the traitors!" Latham told Hugh. "No one else is to leave," he ordered the royal soldiers.

Once outside, Witter and Tyree led the way by ordering the crowd to part. Dagar ignored the apprehensive mortals to move from the Temple to the main gatehouse. There they mounted the steps to the rampart. Dagar's pulling grip made Erin stumble in her effort to keep up with the powerful Guardian. Marcellus followed Dagar. Latham arrived in a rush. He pushed past Tyree to flank Marcellus.

The entire Temple plain could be seen from the rampart. Dagar's fierce gaze stared at the hilltop beyond the tents. No sign of his foe.

"You're too late, Kell! I have your precious Daughter of Allon!" Dagar jerked Erin around to stand in front of him. "She will bear my child and I shall be supreme ruler of Allon!"

Erin screamed, "No—" Dagar clapped his hand over her mouth to press the stifling cloth against her face.

Tremendous thunder roared and lightning spread along the hillcrest to engulf the entire area. The sound grew deafening with the light so intense it blinded everyone. Even Dagar shielded his eyes. He balked at feeling Erin ripped from his grasp. The thunder stopped and the light faded. Erin was gone. Dagar's head snapped back to the vista.

Upon the hillcrest, appeared Shannan wearing a white mid-calf tunic with breeches. The light brown leather boots were fastened by gold bindings. A golden girdle with a small dagger encircled her waist. She held a gold-tipped bow of rosewood, a handsome matching quiver across her back. Her gold coronet sparkled in the sun. Flowing dark hair stirred in the breeze.

Beside her stood Kell, Armus and Avatar, all renewed in might, and dressed for battle. Armus' chestnut eyes gleamed with confidence. His warrior clothes transformed to white with gold trim, leather gilded belt, scabbard, gauntlet and boots. He wore a plain golden breastplate. Avatar mirrored Armus in uniform. His silver eyes flashed like a shiny sword.

Kell's appearance commanded attention. He wore a gold cuirass emblazoned with the ancient symbol of Jor'el. Instead of a belt, a purple sash held his scabbard. His face glowed warm, golden eyes sparkled with full heavenly power and authority.

"You're wrong, Dagar! *I am* the Daughter of Allon, and the Guardians have returned!" she shouted in declaration.

Upon Shannan's announcement, Guardians materialized behind her all along the ridge. Thousands arranged in ranks, some on foot, others mounted on white spirit stallions. They consisted of archers, rangers, element Guardians and warriors.

Vidar joined them. He wore a white uniform. He steadied Erin, as she recovered from the dimension travel.

Shannan compassionately spoke to Erin. "I owe you my life, but this is no place for you. Nixie," she summoned a female warrior. "Take her to safety and stay with her."

Erin touched Shannan's arm. "Jor'el is with you, Daughter of Allon."

"There goes a brave woman." Armus watched Erin leave with Nixie.

With pride and determination, Shannan spoke to Kell. "Captain. The field is yours."

"My lady." Kell saluted. He cocked a grin at Vidar. "I should scold you for your foolishness. Instead, guard her well this day." In response, Vidar readied his crossbow. "Avatar!"

Avatar vaulted into the saddle. He rode a white spirit stallion to the right flank to take up the forward position of his command.

Kell drew his sword. He held it in front of his face. His voice heard across the Temple plain. "For Jor'el and Allon!"

Armus, Avatar and all Guardians echoed the battle cry.

"There must be thousands!" Marcellus marveled.

"Ten thousand, at rough count," chided Dagar with a huff. "Half of our force." He looked to the Temple courtyard to shout, "Witter!"

Now mounted on black spirit stallions, Witter signaled the Shadow Warriors from the Temple compound onto the plain. In a hard gallop, they rode past the tents to meet the Guardians on white spirit stallion. The tremendous clash of forces resounded on the field like a long rumble of thunder slow to fade.

Several eruptions of gray light signaled the vanquishing of an opponent, both Warrior and Guardian. Most were equally matched in strength. They exchanged vicious blows. When one became unhorsed, the battle continued on foot. Lesser Guardians and Shadow Warriors met in hand-to-hand combat using short swords or quarterstaffs.

The Shadow Archers sent a barrage of arrows onto the field. Wren hurried to assemble the Guardian Archers under her command. Unfortunately, they weren't quick enough. The rain of arrows took down mostly Guardians, although a few Shadow Warriors fell. A hasty order to launch counter-strike forced the Shadow Archers to regroup.

To avoid a direct attack, Wren kept her archers darting from cover to cover. They eluded the enemy to inflict what damage they could.

On the right flank, Avatar rallied his forces. He rode along the line speaking orders along with words of encouragement. His forces consisted of Guardians from lesser ranks with only a handful of mounted warriors against an entire company of mounted Shadow Warriors.

Guardians fell in a barrage of arrows from Shadow Archers. A dozen vanished, while those badly wounded were forced to withdraw.

Avatar tried to dodge the flying projectiles. He managed to avoid being impaled yet suffered a deep graze to his left leg from a passing arrow. He no sooner recovered from that wound then the sounds of hooves alerted him to a charge. A Shadow Warrior bore down on him. He moved in time to parry the first attack. His spirit stallion received a large gouge in the flank as the Warrior passed. In response, the stallion reared and threw Avatar.

Unhorsed, Avatar scrambled to his feet to repel a new attack. His parry deflected the sword aimed at his head. The blade clipped him in the right shoulder. Avatar backed away to assess the injury. Not bad, the shoulder guard took most of the force with only flesh nicked.

Outraged at two wounds within a short period of time, he growled, "Enough!" He summoned his power, "*An dealanach siuthad!*"

A shaft of lighting flew from the tip of his sword to strike the Shadow Warrior. The enemy vanished in grey light of demise.

Avatar shouted to his troop. "Give no quarter, spare no power! Remember the Great Battle!"

The sound of rushing footsteps followed by the swooshing of a sword made Avatar duck. The blade passed over his head. Blindly, Avatar placed his sword over his shoulder to parry an expected attack. At clanging of a blade, Avatar twisted himself under his sword to disengaged and face his opponent.

"Roane!" Avatar scoffed. "Didn't you learn anything last time."

"That a coward runs when being chased!"

They exchanged several blows before two more Shadow Warriors joined Roane. Avatar managed to put some space between he and them.

"Remember us?" demanded Bern of himself and Cletus.

"Ay, you needed swimming lessons." Avatar engaged all three with a war cry that made them recoil a few steps.

Cletus slipped, which gave Avatar an opening to land a crippling wound to Cletus' left hip. Avatar pulled back to avoid Bern's wipe at his face. Avatar tripped when making a sudden dodge to evade Roane's counter-attack. A sword blocked Roane's second attempt to get at Avatar. Mahon. While Mahon engaged Roane, Avatar dealt with Bern.

Bern drew for his dagger. This made Avatar jump back. Bern knocked Avatar's sword aside to lunge at his body with the dagger. Avatar caught Bern's wrist to hold the dagger at bay from reaching his throat. A swift knee in the groin sent Bern backward in pain. Avatar clouted Bern in head with the hilt of his sword.

Mahon disarmed Roane with a slash across the chest.

"*Astar de leus!*" came a shout.

A powerful force of speed ran passed them, knocking Avatar and Mahon to the ground. When they recovered, they noticed two other Shadow Warriors helping Bern, Cletus and Roane in a hasty withdrawal.

"Nari!" Avatar shouted. He bolted to his feet.

"Let them go," said Mahon with a hint of pain. He reached for a hand up. Avatar obliged.

"Are you hurt?"

Mahon rubbed his chest. "Something struck me as they passed. Just sore, no wound. Old friends of yours?"

Avatar huffed a sarcastic laugh. "Shadow Weaklings I bested when serving as a decoy to help Tristan." He viewed the faltering troops. "Regroup!" he called.

Valmar experienced great difficulty in maintaining the left flank. At the initial clash, an unexpected blow sent him off the spirit stallion. The head wound bled heavily into his eyes, impairing his vision. He wiped the blood clear to view the battle. Shadow Warriors gained the upper hand.

Daren and Darcy responded to Valmar's downing. They employed night blindness to shield his recovery. He acknowledged the twins with a short nod before he snatched his sword to rejoin the fight.

Darcy cried out when an arrow struck deep in his side. He collapsed to the ground. Daren knelt beside his fallen twin. A shout made Daren look up. A Shadow Warrior ran towards them with sword raised. Before he could strike him blind, Torin launched at the Warrior. Briefly brought to his knees by the wolf's attack, the Shadow Warrior battered Torin aside. Upon rising, a shaft exploded in his chest. He vanished.

Vidar lowered his crossbow. "How is he?"

"Bad," said Daren with grave concern.

"Take him to the field hospital, by the river. Torin, go with them."

Shannan came alongside Vidar. Anxious, she watched Daren carry Darcy from the field. The fierceness of battle sounded all around. Two shafts landed beside them. Two Shadow Archers and three Shadow Warriors headed towards them.

"Run!" Vidar shoved Shannan toward their line of defense. He raised his crossbow to quickly fire. One Shadow Archer vanished in grey light. Vidar swiftly readied a second shot. An arrow flew past him from behind. It struck another Shadow Warrior. He went down, seriously wounded though not vanquished. Shannan fired the arrow.

"I said run—!" Vidar began. A blow from a Warrior caught Vidar in the upper right arm. The forced knocked him sideways to the ground. The crossbow fell from his hands, as he cradled his wounded arm. The cut went deep, perhaps to muscle.

A shriek from above followed Kato's attack of the Warrior that saved Vidar from being killed. Jedrek and Gulliver joined Shannan. They engaged the Warriors. She vanquished the Archer with force from her golden bow most mortals did not possess.

A Shadow Warrior appeared from a flash of white light behind Shannan. Vidar grabbed his crossbow.

"Down!" Vidar shouted.

He used his crossbow to block the blow meant to strike her. The Warrior's blade buried itself in the wood until it struck the metal shaft running the length of the weapon. The blow would have shattered any normal bow. Vidar grimaced at the pain shooting through his wound

310

caused by the impact. His wounded arm could not withstand much more. A swift kick to the Warrior's leg, and Vidar gained the momentum. He shoved the Warrior to the ground with his crossbow. The action dislodged the blade. The Warrior barely got to his knees when a sword took him down. Jedrek.

"Get her back behind the lines, and see to your wound," Jedrek instructed Vidar.

"No, I must be seen for encouragement," she refuted.

"It'll go worse if you are killed!" Jedrek waved Vidar to Shannan.

"He's right. I need my wound tended so I to continue protecting you," Vidar spoke of his wound.

In the initial clash, Kell and Armus fought side-by-side. They did not need spirit stallions. They easily defeated any foes without calling upon their special powers. Only a handful of Guardians or Shadow Warriors could match their full strength. During the course of battle, they became separated. Each took command of a group in need of strengthening.

Armus paused to catch his breath. In surveying the field, he counted more Shadow Warriors than Guardians. However, they were initially outnumbered by two to one, so he could not fully assess the situation as dangerous. Tents of the mortals, wagons and possessions were strewn on the field, trampled beneath the force of conflict. He heard the shout a moment before a dark Guardian leapt in front of him.

"Griswold," chided Armus in recognition.

"You didn't think the mortal's arrow finished me, did you?" Griswold's voice sounded raspy. A scar on his throat showed where Shannan's arrow struck.

"I was hoping for that pleasure." Armus attacked.

At full strength, Armus equaled Griswold blow for blow. Griswold's added size gave him an advantage in reach. This proved a nuisance by forcing Armus to keep his distance. He dodged swipes or lunges each time he tried to close the gap.

Griswold appeared to stumble. Armus stepped forward into an attack. Griswold spun around. At the crack of a whip, Armus tried to halt his momentum. Unfortunately he couldn't, and stepped into the path of the stygian whip. The whip ensnared him. It pinned his arms to his side. His sword fell to the ground. Searing pain spread through his body at the initial contact.

Sneering against the pain, Armus bent his arms at the elbows. Movement caused more shooting pain in his body. He ignored it to continue his effort of reaching for the whip. Griswold jerked the whip to stop Armus. Despite an outcry of pain, Armus managed to grab it. More burning radiated from his hands up his arms. Despite his fingers beginning to feel numb, Armus pulled with all his might. The whip snapped between himself and Griswold. The force sent Griswold backward to the ground.

With a deep intake of breath, Armus shouted the Ancient, *"Bho neart gu Jor'el!"* to call upon his special power. He heaved his arms to break the whip holding him.

Armus staggered in pain from the stinging, numbing effects of the whip. He couldn't take much time to recover, not with Griswold down. Awkwardly, Armus grabbed his sword in both hands. Griswold tried to brace for the attack. He didn't make it. Armus' mighty swing caught him in the chest with a deep lethal wound. The impact sent Griswold flying. He landed in a huddled mass. His whole body jerked twice before he vanished in grey light.

Weakened from the pain, Armus took a knee. He drew in several large gulps of air in an effort to recover.

Concerned, Priscilla raced over. "Armus?"

After a long exhale, Armus used his sword to stand. "I'm better." His eyes widened in alarm. "Hunter hawks!"

Three of the grotesque birds flew over the Temple.

"I can handle them better this time," said Priscilla with confidence. "Wyndy! Zinna!" she called for another wind Guardian and archer.

Kell just defeated a large Shadow Warrior when a blast from behind sent him crashing into a large tent. He took half of it with him to the ground. He angrily batted the tent off him to see who waylaid him. He barely recognized Witter before another attack. Not by sword, rather Witter used a wave of his hand to hurl a crate at him.

"*Bi rach a dol!*" Kell spoke. With a flick of his wrist, the crate broke into pieces then disappeared in midair.

"We're both at full strength. In fact, the Dark Way has made me your equal. This should be interesting." Witter swung at Kell.

Kell leapt up and did a somersault in the air. He landed behind Witter where he promptly sent a blast of his own against Witter's back. The same tent became Witter's landing zone, which took down the rest of it around him. Kell charged. A slice from his sword ripped through the tent to land a blow. Witter growled in anger at the wound in his side. His blind thrust through the tent forced Kell to retreat.

Freed from the tent, Witter roared as he whirled about to add momentum to his swing. The swords met with a loud clang. Witter's eyes grew wide with surprise that his added strength did not budge Kell from his stance. The brief moment the swords hung together was all the advantage Kell needed. With a circular motion, he disarmed Witter and lunged. His blade passed completely through Witter.

"You were never my equal," Kell sneered to Witter before removing his sword. Witter vanished into gray nothingness.

A seriously wounded Valmar stumbled toward him. Kell caught Valmar when the Highland Guardian collapsed. He suffered a serious chest wound while blood ran down his pale face from the head injury. His left eye was bruised, bloodshot and swollen shut.

"We're outnumbered. I lost half my command!" Valmar gasped.

Kell viewed the field being overrun by Shadow Warriors. Some Guardians valiantly fought. Alas, many wounded and exhausted began to retreat. Mortals caught in the midst of the chaos fell under the Shadow Warrior's advance. This was not the outcome he expected.

Jedrek arrived. He pointed to the Temple where Marcellus' army gathered. "Captain! Reinforcements!"

Although mortals could not kill Guardians, their numbers could inflict enough damage to give Dagar and the Shadow Warriors a great advantage. "Take him to Eldric," Kell instructed Jedrek about Valmar.

"Captain!" Valmar painfully protested.

"It's all right. I know you did your best."

Jedrek was gentle in dealing with Valmar.

Dagar's voice over the battlefield made Kell turn. "You are defeated, Daughter of Allon! Now, I will have complete victory!"

Kell helplessly watched a blast from Dagar's hand race across the field to where Shannan tended Vidar's wound. "Shannan!" he shouted.

She began to move out of harm's way when the blast hit. She tumbled down hill while Vidar was knocked backwards off his feet. She crashed into a wagon wheel at the bottom of the hill. Kell reached her just before Vidar did. He anxiously felt for a pulse.

"Shannan," urged Kell. He held her face in his hands.

She groaned. Her eyes blinked then opened.

"Thank Jor'el, you're alive." He helped her sit against the wagon.

"How badly are you hurt?" asked Vidar.

"I don't think anything's broken. Although I'm very sore." Her eyes filled with tears, as she asked Kell, "How can we lose? Where is Ellis?"

Kell couldn't answer. Nothing had gone according to plan.

Chapter 29

THE SOUND OF MULTIPLE TRUMPETS RESOUNDED OVER THE battlefield. Men in olive cloaks materialized from the forest that surrounded the Temple. Dagar, Latham and Marcellus had descended from the rampart. Marcellus sat mounted upon his stead in front of his personal cavalry at the main gate. They, along with the Shadow Warriors turned to view the extent of the new enemy.

Marcellus rose in the stirrups. "We're surrounded!"

"They're not Guardians—" while Latham spoke, another trumpet sounded. The men shed their cloaks. "Jor'ellian Knights! Archimedes."

"He's trapped in the Temple," disputed Marcellus.

"That means—" Latham did not finish for Dagar's hateful stare.

Marcellus pointed to the crest of the hill. "Look!"

Wearing the gleaming gold armor, Ellis rode a white spirit stallion through a gap in the line to take his place at the head of his troops. He appeared every inch a king, stronger and more determined than Marcellus ever anticipated. Kell, Armus and Avatar joined Ellis.

"It's him. The Pretender," murmured Marcellus.

"Do not falter now, mortal," sneered Dagar.

"That's easy for you to say, Guardian, or whatever you are!"

315

At Dagar's fury, Latham intervened to scold Marcellus. "You would do well to mind your tongue, if you want to keep your throne."

"And your life!" Dagar's added. Narrow mahogany eyes focused upon Marcellus.

Marcellus swallowed back the bile burning his throat. He stared at a distant Ellis. At least he was a mortal foe.

Only a moment passed between Ellis' appearance and his voice calling across the battlefield.

"Marcellus! I am Ellis, Son of Tristan. By birth and Jor'el's divine appointment, rightful King of Allon. I have come to claim what is mine!"

"How do I know you are who you claim and not some vile usurper?" Marcellus shouted in reply.

"You know I am. Why else steal my bride and ready yourself for battle? Stand down and I may have mercy. Take up arms with the Dark Master, and you will die!"

Marcellus' steadied his horse when Dagar hurled a blast toward Ellis. Ellis simply raised his shield to bat it aside. Marcellus marveled at the easy thwarting.

"He is the Promised One."

"Another word will get your brother killed," growled Dagar.

Marcellus snarled disgust. He had no alternative. He drew his sword. "Long live the House of Patrin! Charge!"

The Sword of Allon hummed and glowed when Ellis drew it. "For Allon! For Jor'el."

Inside the Temple, they heard three quick burst of a trumpet followed by a long blast. Archimedes snatched a sword concealed behind the altar.

"For Jor'el and Allon!" shouted the Vicar.

At Archimedes' rally cry, those wearing cloaks cast them off to reveal their identities as Jor'ellian Knights. They attacked the soldiers. Malcolm ushered the women to a corner for safety. Council Members joined the foray using fists or anything available until able to secure a weapon.

Owain bolted for the door. Armed with the sword of a fallen soldier, Allard stopped him. Owain raised his hands in surrender. "I'm unarmed!"

"Back up." Allard prodded Owain with the sword until he ran into the wall beside a large wall sconce. "Give me your belt." Owain did so. "Hands out!" When Owain hesitated, Allard poked him with the sword. He lashed the belt around Owain's wrists then attached it to the sconce so that Owain's arms were raised above his head. Allard flashed a caustic smile. "That should hold you for now."

By sheer number, the Knights and noblemen defeated the soldiers.

"Malcolm, take the women out the rear! Jor'ellians and nobles to me!" shouted Archimedes.

Hugh picked up a fallen sword.

"You would turn against your brother?" Archimedes questioned.

"My brother turned against the people."

After a nod of understanding, Archimedes waved his sword at the front door. "Forward!"

Once outside the Temple compound, Council members eagerly went to their prearranged assignments. Archimedes and the Knights moved to secure the field to contain the battle to the Temple plain.

Keen in guerrilla warfare, Ranulf's Highlanders aided Iain and Darius in the forest. They formed the second line of defense should some of the enemy seek to escape.

Upon sight of Ellis, Darius' spirit soared. He did not want to believe Ellis dead, nor Allon's fate doomed. This was the day his father believed would come, but never saw. "Oh, Father, you would be proud of him." A hearty clap on his shoulder made Darius turn.

"Angus would be proud of you as well," said Jasper.

Darius flashed a modest smile. "Where is Edmund?"

"I sent him with a squad to help Lord Malcolm guard the women and elderly. War is not his strength," Jasper said with a teasing smile.

"Look sharp!" called Iain. "The battle is fully engaged. Contain them! Cut down any enemy who flees."

Darius and Jasper joined the battle. The eye patch did not hamper Jasper's ability. At one point, Darius was knocked to the ground by mounted solider. Stunned, he had difficulty rising. Jasper intervened to keep Darius from being trampled.

Both turned at the sound of snarling animals. Five rabid wolves surrounded them. Salvia dripped from the wolves' mouths while the eyes unusually red and large. One leapt at them only to be batted aside by a staff. A redheaded, bearded Guardian ranger arrived. Darius and Jasper barely had time to notice him when the wolves launched a group attack.

Darius dodged one wolf but couldn't avoid the second. It landed on top of him. He clouted its head with the hilt of his sword. The wolf caught Darius' arm in its jaws. The thick metal armguards prevented the fangs from ripping into his flesh. It yowled when Jasper's dagger lodged in its shoulder.

Darius rolled away, which allowed Jasper to finish the wolf with a sword hack to its neck.

The Guardian ranger dispatched three wolves before howls alerted them to the arrival of more. "Get behind me!" he told Darius and Jasper. *"Talamh cobrach!"* he called in the Ancient. He lifted his staff then struck the ground with the end of the staff.

A minor tremor started. The earth opened from his staff to underneath the wolves. Darius and Jasper watched in amazement as the ground swallowed the wolves before closing on top of them.

"My lord, are hurt badly?" asked the ranger.

"Eh, no, I don't think so, sir—" Darius replied, searching for a name.

The Guardian smiled. "My name is Ridge." He examined Darius' arm where the wolf caught him. "The armor seems to have saved you from suffering nothing more than some bruising and minor cuts."

"Can you help us keep other creatures from entering the battle?" Jasper asked Ridge.

"Captain Kell sent me to do just that."

318

Being skilled warriors, Allard and Mathias commanded experienced troops. They aided Ellis' main attack force. Each displayed leadership that gained the advantage against Marcellus' mortal cavalry.

When a group of Shadow Warriors reinforced Marcellus' troops, it became a desperate struggle. Neither Allard nor Mathias would yield, even against such overwhelming adversaries. Both suffered wounds, as the situation grew desperate.

Seeing the mortals in trouble, Chase and Barnum used their Guardian troops to reinforce the front. Their added strength drove a wedge in Marcellus' cavalry by diverting the lethal attention of the Shadow Warriors. Now the battle was equal.

On the left flank, Ewert and Bailey lead Valmar's group in support of Hollis and Erasmus. The mortals found mounts from which to lead their troops. Loud multiple caws alerted them to the arrival of one hundred ravens. The birds dove at them.

"By the heavenlies!" Erasmus tried to avoid the ravens.

The force of the attacking birds unhorsed Hollis. On foot, he fought against the birds. Erasmus helped Hollis by killing a couple of ravens with his sword.

Hollis wiped some blood from where talons cut his left cheek. "We can't fight both birds and the enemy!"

Erasmus rose in the stirrups to shout, "Bailey!"

The Guardian warrior no sooner arrived then they heard screeching. From high above, Kato led fifty large eagles in a dive. The ravens broke off the attack to engage the eagles. Being nearly twice the size, the eagles made short work of the ravens. Only a few ravens managed to retreat.

Ellis rode in the thick of battle. Mortal foot soldiers closed in. He used his spirit horse to scatter the enemy. When the stallion's front legs touched down, two-mounted Shadow Warriors charged. One of them was Altari. Ellis recalled being told how his shield and sword could turn a Guardian's weapon. Now came the test.

Ellis met Altari's attack. His sword broke Altari's blade near the tip. With barely a few seconds pause, Ellis parried the second Warrior's attack with his shield. The force unhorsed the Warrior. Dazed, the Warrior was slow to rise. A slice from the Sword of Allon nearly bisected him. He disappeared in a flash of grey light.

Altari whirled his horse about for another attack. He noticed his broken blade, which made him realize, "Son of Tristan," he muttered.

"Do you yield?" demanded Ellis.

"He does not!" Tyree whipped his horse to charge. Ellis made quick defense, but Tyree held. "See, Altari! He can be engaged." He fought to turn his horse for another pass. The animal acted contrary to the command.

Altari lowered his broken blade at Ellis. With a war cry, he charged. This time, it wasn't his sword that gave way. In a rapid move, Ellis batted the sword aside with his shield and swung at Altari in passing. The blade caught Altari in back, slicing deep. Altari vanished in a grey flash.

Through the fading light, came a charging Tyree. The clash made Ellis rock in the saddle. He grabbed the horse's neck to keep from falling. After regaining his balance, he glanced back. Tyree lay in a crumpled unconscious heap on the ground. The horse galloped off. Tyree had not vanished like the others, so he wasn't a Guardian. All the same, the encounter was over.

Ellis noticed Chase and Barnum rally the Guardians. The flank would soon be secure. He allowed himself a moment to catch his breath before rejoining the foray on the opposite flank.

Gareth and Zebulon's men attacked Marcellus' right flank, which consisted of infantry. Suddenly, unseen arrows flew into the melee, but from where? No archers were visible. If a mortal was struck, but not killed, a Shadow Archer materialized to finish him then disappeared as quickly. The mortals could not defend against the tactic.

320

Armus raced over while shouting a command, "Wren! Assemble your archers to intercept the enemy."

"How will that help? We don't where the arrows are coming from," argued Gareth.

"What is invisible to the mortals we can detect. Now, rally your men and leave the rest to us." Armus nudged Gareth on his way.

"Not so fast!" shouted a voice from behind.

Armus came face-to-face with an bow pointed at him by …"Carvel!"

The Shadow Archer Commander balked. "Ar—Armus?"

Although a brief pause, Armus' flashed back to a time before the Great Battle when his friend Carvel served as his Archer Commander. He steeled himself against the memories to use his sword to knock away the bow. He held his sword level at Carvel.

"Tell your archers to cease," ordered Armus.

"I can't. Not even for you," said Carvel with regret.

Armus could not back down. "I said, cease! Or you will leave me with no choice."

Carvel spoke with anxiety, "I must do as Dagar commands!"

Armus lowered his sword in an effort to convince Carvel. "Not if you yield to me."

Carvel shook his head, his voice hopeless. "It's too late." He turned aside, which shielded his movement. With a shout, he drew his dagger to slash at Armus.

"Don't be a fool, Carvel!"

"Leave me at least the dignity to choose my own demise!" Carvel came at Armus with wild abandon. He landed a lucky blow that ripped Armus' tunic to inflict a flesh wound. His next attack would be his final one. He fell beneath Armus' sword, and vanished in grey light.

Armus fought back a flood of rage against Dagar, as he stared at the spot where Carvel stood. He disliked killing another Guardian but until Carvel, he had not encountered a familiar face. He sprang to defense at a flash of white light. It took a moment to recognize Wren and keep from striking her.

"Armus? Are you all right?" she asked to his angry sneer.

"Who can be all right with the work we must do today?"

"Ay," she agreed soberly. "The Shadow Archers are all dispatched. The flank is secure."

"Keep it that way while I report to Kell." Armus vanished in dimension travel.

Kell engaged eight mortal soldiers when a determined Armus reappeared. Four quickly fell beneath Armus' wrath.

"How much longer?" Armus chided, his expression of anger laced with pain.

"I wish I knew. Yet with less Warriors, mortal resistance—Dagar!" Kell indicated Dagar, who stood by the Temple with sword in hand. Dagar stared at them.

With a deep throaty growl, Armus moved toward Dagar. Kell tried to stop him, but Armus wasn't about to be deterred, and jerked away. Kell stepped in front of Armus to seize him. Armus' whole body grew rigid while his narrow eyes focused on Dagar. It was the deadliest look Kell had seen from Armus in centuries.

"Armus!"

Through clenched teeth Armus said, "I had to kill Carvel."

Kell winced at the statement. "I'm sorry."

"I'm waiting, Kell!" Dagar called.

Kell's hold on Armus tightened when Armus again tried to move toward Dagar. "You can't take my place! This is between Dagar and me. In that, Carvel, Rune, Cyril and others can be avenged."

"He nearly killed you before. I won't lose two friends in one day."

Kell cocked a smile. "You won't."

Armus held up his sword. "I'll be close by."

Kell gave Armus a parting clap on the shoulder.

Armus watched Kell with such intensity that he didn't see the blow from behind. He cried out in surprise when the sword passed through his body from the back to under his sternum.

Kell whirled about in time to see the sword withdrawn. Armus collapsed, but did not vanish. Despite a now vacant eye and scarred face, Kell recognized Tor as the one who waylaid Armus. Kell's golden eyes flashed with fire.

"No!" he exclaimed.

"Ay!" Dagar launched himself at Kell.

Kell barely managed to parry the deadly chest high blow. He felt Dagar's blade cut through the shoulder guard into his left shoulder. He staggered to one side to assess his wound. He maintained a guard against another attack.

"Poor Armus. Now, you're all alone. Finish him, Tor!" Dagar said over his shoulder.

Blind fury erupted into a great howl, as Kell went to intercept Tor. Kell wasn't thinking, only reacting. Dagar let him know it with a mighty blast that sent him hurling backwards twenty feet.

Armus sluggishly stirred at hearing Kell's war cry. Tor's foot crashed down on his back, driving him to the ground. The impact rendered him unconscious. Tor raised his sword to finished Armus. To his surprise, his attack was blocked. A voice said:

An dealanach siuthad

Tor barely recognized Avatar before being blinded by a flash of lightning. Avatar finished Tor. When the grey light of Tor's demise faded, Shannan knelt beside Armus. Vidar kept his loaded bow ready for defense.

Shannan bit her lip at seeing Armus' ashen features. "Avatar!"

Avatar sheathed his sword. "I'll take him to Eldric. Get her back to safety," he told Vidar.

Dagar focused on Kell, thus ignorant of what happened with Armus. "Don't make this easy. I've waited too long to kill you. I don't want it over so soon."

323

Kell witnessed Armus' rescue. He could now concentrate on Dagar. Kell leapt into the air to avoid the attack. Another blast from Dagar altered Kell's course. He managed to correct himself to land on his feet.

"Keeping to your old tricks because you don't have the courage to face me sword to sword?" Kell challenged.

Dagar squared his shoulders. "I almost killed you before. Now, I will."

Their swords met. It became sheer strength against strength. Kell shoved Dagar backwards fifteen feet. He charged to engage Dagar again. Their heated battle took them from the plain into the Temple compound.

Marcellus just finished an engagement with one of Allard's cavalry officers when—"Marcellus!" He turned his horse to see Ellis charge.

On the first pass, Ellis' sword chopped off a corner of Marcellus' shield. The blade narrowly missed the left side of Marcellus' face. His riposte clipped Ellis' left shoulder guard. No damage to Ellis, but the impact caused a nick in his sword. Marcellus did not have time to comprehend the differences in armor or weapons when Ellis turned for another pass.

This time they exchanged several blows. He saw Ellis' determination and felt his superior strength. At the end of the exchange, Marcellus suffered wounds; one to his right side the other to in the left leg. Ellis remained unharmed. Marcellus pulled away to check his wounds. Nothing appeared life threatening.

Arrows whizzed about them. Ellis raised his shield. He deflected one arrow. A second passed under the shield's edge. Marcellus stared in awe when the arrow harmlessly bounced off Ellis' left leg armor. Ellis charged again. Marcellus wanted none of it. He turned his horse to retreat.

Ellis' horse overtook Marcellus' mount. Using the flat of his sword, Ellis sent a sharp slap to the horse's rump. It bucked to throw Marcellus. Ellis vaulted from the saddle, his sword ready.

Marcellus slowly rose to his knees. His painful wounds kept him from standing. Ellis' sword leveled at him. Marcellus carefully felt for the dagger in his belt by pretending to cover his wound.

"Kill me quick," he said in despair.

Ellis' brows leveled in angry surprise. "You send mercenaries to wreak havoc on the innocent, but refuse to fight your equal?"

"My better." Marcellus offered his sword to Ellis. "I yield."

Ellis slightly lowered his guard to accept the surrender. Marcellus bolted up, seized Ellis and thrust the dagger upward. Instead of inflicting a terrible wound, the dagger broke. Marcellus' stunned expression suddenly became a gasp of horror. He fell against Ellis. His weight began to drag Ellis down. Ellis stepped back to shove Marcellus away.

Behind Marcellus, stood Hugh. His agonizing gaze focused on Marcellus, a dagger buried in Marcellus' back where the neck connected to the shoulders. Hugh's face was pale as he fell to his knees before Ellis.

"Do with me what you will," he said with fatal resignation.

"I owe you my life. For that, I restore a father to his children."

"What?" Hugh asked, slow to understand.

"General Iain!" shouted Ellis.

"Iain?" Hugh questioned.

Iain arrived dressed in a Jor'ellian Knight's uniform. "Hugh." Iain's quizzical glance shifted from Hugh to the dead Marcellus then Ellis. "Highness?"

Ellis kindly smiled. "Take him to his children."

Iain grinned in relief. "Ay, Highness."

"They are alive?" asked Hugh, still baffled.

"Ay. There's much to explain. Come." Iain left with Hugh.

A clapping from behind Ellis followed by Latham speaking, "Bravo, Son of Tristan. You saved me the trouble of disposing of him." He motioned to Marcellus

Ellis raised the Sword of Allon. "Surrender, or face your own destruction."

"It is you who will die," Latham calmly said before he unleashed an attack. "*Cummhachd!*"

Ellis' chest tightened as if being squeezed. He gritted his teeth against the pain to attack. He made a feeble swing at Latham. The momentum brought him to all fours. He tried taking deep breaths to stem the pain.

"Your Guardian armor is no match for the power of the Dark Way."

Through the pain, Ellis glared up at Latham. The talisman glowed.

"Time to end this." Latham eyes narrowed. He clenched his fist.

In excruciating pain, Ellis collapsed. "Jor'el! Help!" he pleaded.

"You'll have to speak louder for him to hear you."

At that moment, Ellis ceased struggling. His features became fixed. He stared at Latham, unmoving.

"I know you're not dead. I haven't killed you, yet."

No response, only blankness in the unblinking eyes. A look so unnatural that Latham cautiously stooped to examine Ellis. In doing so, the talisman dangled from his neck. Suddenly, Ellis launched himself at Latham. He seized the talisman and ripped it from Latham's neck. Ellis cried out in pain as intense heat from the talisman penetrated his gauntlet. He dropped it. The talisman still glowed when it came to rest on the ground, where it scorched the grass. The glow faded. Frantic, Latham lunged for the talisman. Ellis intercepted him. The Sword of Allon plunged into Latham's chest.

"No magic can save you now." Ellis swiftly removed the sword.

The horror of death on his face, Latham turned toward the Temple. "Dagar—Father!" he called before dying.

Dagar clenched his talisman, as he doubled over in agony. The action surprised Kell. He hadn't landed a blow, yet a serious wound appeared on Dagar's chest. Kell took advantage of the distraction to attack. Dagar parried enough to deflect Kell's thrust for the heart, only the captain's sword passed completely through his lower abdomen. At the second attack, Dagar frantically waved both arms to create a shield of light to temporarily blind Kell.

Kell assumed a defensive stance as he listened closely for movement. When his vision cleared, he saw Dagar stagger into the Temple. He rushed to pursue.

Inside, Kell pulled up short. No time for Dagar to reach the rear exit in his injured condition, so where was he? Did he dimension travel to safety? No. Dagar was bent on revenge. No wound would stop him. With careful steps, Kell crossed the floor. His eyes darted from side-to-side. He held his sword ready.

"I know you're here, Dagar! You've proven you can only fight the coward's way."

Kell no sooner finished speaking then Dagar leapt from behind a pillar onto Kell's back. The action sent Kell to his knees. He snatched Dagar's hand to keep the dagger from his throat. Dagar strained to press the blade closer.

"Fitting I should kill you here," Dagar jeered with effort of the struggle.

Kell heard pain in Dagar's voice. Kell winced when the blade pricked his throat to draw blood. He mumbled the Ancient. He forced the dagger away, but still held onto Dagar. Kell threw a hard elbow into Dagar's wound. He spun out from under Dagar's arm. He used Dagar's own hand to thrust the dagger hilt deep into Dagar's chest. Bitter anger filled the mahogany eyes, as Dagar sank to the floor.

Ellis raced inside. Wren, Avatar, Gulliver, Mahon, and Priscilla were with him. All showed various signs of battle. "Kell?" asked Ellis with uncertainty.

"I'm fine." Kell moved towards them, which exposed his back to Dagar.

"Kell!" Priscilla rushed past him.

Dagar viscously struck Priscilla aside. The force sent her sliding across the floor into the opposite wall.

"*Bi falbh!*" Kell shouted the Ancient, as he used a tremendous backhand to propel Dagar into the air.

Dagar struck a pillar with such force pillar that his spine broke. The crack echoed in the chamber. When Dagar hit the floor, the earth trembled. Thunder accompanied an eruption of gray light that engulfed the Temple. When the light faded, the thunder stopped. Dagar was gone.

Kell quickly knelt beside Priscilla. She groaned in distress while she reached for his help to sit up. In pain, she leaned against him. "You were right. I appeared once too often for my own good."

"No, no, I didn't mean it!" Kell clamored in apology.

"Really?"

"Ay. I'm sorry."

"I accept your apology." Priscilla suddenly stood up. "You're so cute when you're flustered. Bye." She waved at him and vanished in dimension travel.

Kell heard laughter. Avatar straightened, and bit his lip to stifle his amusement. Mahon coughed to one side to halt his mirth. Wren could barely contain herself, while Gulliver made no pretense. He doubled over laughing. Ellis smiled. He shrugged when Kell looked at him.

"At least Vidar wasn't here to see it," groused Kell.

"Who said I wasn't?" Vidar quipped. He escorted Shannan.

Shannan and Ellis embraced. Kell waved everyone out to allow them privacy. He paused by the pillar where Dagar vanished to make a quick search of the surrounding floor. He scowled at seeing nothing, so he left the Temple.

Ellis tried to imagine what their reunion would be like, how good it would feel to have her in his arms again. He never expected to feel all their time apart melt away in that embrace. "My armor's cold," he said.

"I don't care. You're alive! I never felt so hopeless as when they told me you were dead." She sniffled.

He lifted her chin to brush away the tears. "I know. The vision of you marrying Marcellus—" He passionately kissed her then once more held her close. "You realize what this means?"

"Ay. I'm sorry Grandfather didn't live to see it."

"Who told you?"

"Vidar. He also told me you were alive."

"Your Highness." Archimedes approached. His clothes soiled from battle, but his companion caught Ellis' attention.

"Darius!" Ellis grabbed Darius in hearty embrace.

Darius surveyed Ellis with misty eyes of pride. "You look like a king."

"You look horrible," laughed Ellis. He again embraced Darius.

"Father would be proud of you. I am," said Darius in Ellis' ear.

"My Prince, the day is yours. What would you have done with the prisoners?" asked Archimedes.

Ellis thought for a moment. "Have them held until the coronation. At that time, they shall have one last chance to pledge fealty or face the consequences."

"Do you think that wise?"

"Vicar, this is a new beginning for Allon. I would rather it start peaceful than with executions."

Archimedes nodded his reluctant agreement before he departed.

"My lady, how did you manage on be in two places at one time? The rampart and hill?" asked Darius.

"What?" Ellis asked, confused by Darius' question of Shannan.

"It wasn't me with Dagar." Shannan answered Darius then to Ellis, "Erin took my place when Vidar rescued me last night. She is safe now."

"What made her do it?" inquired Ellis with eyes intent on Shannan.

"You know why." She motioned to her pouch on his belt.

Darius curiously regarded them. "I must be missing something."

Ellis chuckled. "Nothing that matters anymore." He hugged Shannan.

Outside, Barnum approached Kell. "Captain, some Shadow Warriors surrendered in secret. They fear retaliation if discovered. Jedrek and I have isolated them, but don't know what else to do."

For a brief moment, Kell stared in the direction Barnum indicated. "Keep them secure until I can deal with them."

Kell headed toward the area designated for the Guardian hospital. A cloaked figure wearing the hood ran across the field ten yards in front of him. It stopped, snatched something off the ground then darted into the wood. A curious sight, but he had more pressing matters to be concerned him about then an urchin stealing a war souvenir.

Kell arrived at the hospital to find Valmar unconscious. Fresh blood soaked through the head bandage. Small streams of blood ran from under the bandage down Valmar's haggard face. The left eye was completely swollen shut with dried blood caked on the lid. The chest bandage proved a feeble attempt to stop the bleeding.

Distressed by the sight, Kell knelt. He compassionately touched the Highland Guardian's shoulder. "Valmar?"

The response came slowly. The right eye was half shrouded. The normal spark now dull. "Captain? We were outnumbered! I tried—"

"It's all right. We won."

"We won," Valmar repeated. "I can return to my Highlands now?"

"Ay," said Kell with a catch in his voice. He swallowed back grief when a small smile crossed Valmar's lips. The Highland Guardian closed his eye. Grey light surrounded him. Kell choked back a whimper of sorrow at the loss.

Eldric arrived, sympathetic in demeanor. "Captain."

Kell's voice was thick. "How many?"

"Five hundred. I anticipate twenty more come morning."

Kell bit his lip to stifle more grief. He turned further away from Eldric. He knew the cost of battle would be high, but not since the Great Battle had so many Guardians fallen. The few who survived became dear to him, Valmar among them.

"I realize that is unusually high. However, considering the battle, and what causalities the mortals inflicted on each other, we did well."

Kell swallowed back his upset to ask, "Where is Armus?"

"By the willow." Eldric delayed Kell's departure. "I don't know *if* or when he'll wake. The wound would have killed a lesser Guardian."

Kell briskly made his way to the willow. His jowls tight as he recalled Armus' declaration of not losing two friends in one day. Heaven forbid that he would lose his most cherished friend on top of what he suffered as captain.

Armus lay the grass with his eyes closed, his face ashen. A large bandage wrapped around his entire bare torso. Blood stained the bandage. Kell knew the wound came through from behind. Indeed, such a wound would have been lethal to many a Guardian.

Kell knelt. He reached to touch Armus' face then hesitated. He wanted to sense the extent of Armus' life force upon touch, but did he dare? He took a deep breath before he placed his hand on Armus' forehead. Cool. Not a good sign.

"Armus. It's Kell. You didn't lose me."

No response nor did Armus stir. His chest barely rose with breath.

Kell pressed his hand firmly against Armus forehead. "Armus, hear me, old friend," he said in pleading command.

Armus' eyes flickered then slowly open. It took a moment to focus his gaze. "About time you showed up," he said a raspy whisper.

Kell made an impulsive short laugh of relief. "Dagar wasn't very accommodating." He held Armus' left shoulder. "Tor's attack was meant to incite me. I'm just glad it didn't kill you."

"Close."

"Too close. I lost five hundred. I feared you among them."

Armus attempted a smile then asked, "Ellis?"

"We won. Dagar is defeated, and our restoration complete. Recover quickly. I want you by my side at the coronation."

"Nothing will stop that," Armus said in his strongest voice yet.

Kell shied. "Perhaps, if you knew the truth about Dorgirith you'd think differently."

"You mean about it being your idea for Ellis to go, and not an order from Jor'el?"

Disconcertion filled Kell's voice. "You knew?"

Armus took a painful breath before speaking. "When you gave me the message for Ellis, you couldn't look me in the eye. Despite your feeble attempt at dishonesty, your heart would never allow you to jeopardize our mission. I only wish you had confided in me."

Kell squeezed Armus' shoulder. "The risk was too great. If it failed, I didn't want you to bear any blame."

Armus wearily he rolled his eyes.

"I've made you talk too much. Rest and recover, old friend."

Avatar arrived. His wounds bandaged. "How is Armus?"

Kell stood. "I believe he'll live."

Avatar titled his head to the contrary. "You don't look so certain."

"The cost of battle weighs on me. All the same, stay with him while I tend to what is necessary."

❦

The hooded individual Kell noticed ran deep into the wood surrounding the Temple. The steps grew staggered while the breathing labored. Finally, the individual fell to the ground and doubled over while gasping for air. Grunts of discomfort sounded like a female. The hand opened to reveal Latham's talisman. A few sobs came.

"What have we here? An escaped mortal?" said a husky male voice.

When her head snapped up, the hood fell off to reveal Musetta. Five Shadow Warriors surrounded her. "You would do best to help me," she said with bravado.

Roane, Nari, Cletus, Bern and Indigo laughed.

Their amusement angered her. She placed the talisman around her neck. "As the Dark Master commands!" she spoke in the Ancient.

The laughter immediately ceased, and Nari spoke in rebuff. "Latham is dead. Who are you to command us?"

She rose. "His mistress. I carry his son!" She opened the cloak to show her abdomen. Her narrow gaze shifted to each Warrior. "Do not press me. I know his secrets, those entrusted to him by Dagar." At their hesitation, she spoke the Ancient command of obedience. *"Sleuchd gu an Dorcha Slighe!"*

Her words forced the Shadow Warriors to their knees. "We hear and obey, mistress," they said in unison.

The effort needed for flight made Musetta sway.

"You are unwell, mistress?" asked Roane.

"I am burdened with grief while the child makes me fatigued. Though I am not incapable of action if needed," she added in warning.

"The talisman binds us to the Dark Way. We are at your command." Nari stood to make a salute. The rest mimicked her. "Let us take you to safety where you can rest."

"And plan my revenge."

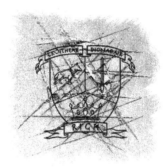

Chapter 30

K ELL SAT ON THE STEPS OF THE TEMPLE WITH HIS BACK RESTING
against a pillar. The first shafts of dawn broke over the horizon.
He sat there all night. The burden of Guardian losses prevented
him from resting. Although unrealistic to go into battle without any
losses, he felt each death, even of the Shadow Warriors. They were once
Guardians despite what Dagar had done to them. If Armus had died, the
personal loss would have been overwhelming. For more than two
millennia they served together as captain and lieutenant. He couldn't
imagine another by his side.

Kell became roused from his pondering when Ellis and Shannan sat
on either side of him. He balked in awkward surprise when Shannan
kissed his cheek.

"That's the least I owe you," she said.

"You owe me nothing. Though I have something that belongs to
you." Kell reached into his tunic to pull out Niles' medallion. "It was
found among Latham's belongings."

Though she fondly smiled, she refused to take it. "You keep it."

"Oh, no." He tried again to give it to her only this time Ellis stopped
him.

334

"Keep it, Kell," insisted Ellis. "My first royal act is to name you as the King's Champion."

"Me? I'm a Guardian not a Jor'ellian Knight."

"This is a time of transition. Until I can establish my reign, I need someone I can trust implicitly to help keep order."

"Jor'el has given permission," Shannan encouraged Kell.

Ellis took the medallion to put around Kell's neck. "I don't think you'll refuse me and the Almighty."

"Of course not." Kell regarded the medallion. "This will be a first for me."

"You've not served as a protector or advisor to the king?" asked Ellis.

"Before the Great Battle, Allon had no mortal king. Jor'el reigned supreme while we administered the provinces in his name. When banished for Dagar's rebellion, we rarely interacted with mortals, reduced to obscure legends. Even when Tristan became king, we kept to clandestine roles. Oh, we maintained close watch on him and his descendants to ensure survival." He again regarded the medallion. "Since we've been restored to a new age in Allon's history, it appears our roles will change."

"It's nothing to fear," soothed Shannan.

Kell chuckled. "No fear. Adjustment, perhaps."

"Come. There is much to do before the coronation," said Ellis.

The Temple once more played host to a royal event. This time, the wedding and coronation of the long awaited promised king. Banners from the House of Tristan hung from the rafters. The golden eagle with wings spread overhead, a jewel crown clutched in its talons stitched on purple velvet. Tristan's coronation crown and scepter had been secretly stored in a lower vault.

Ellis and Shannan walked to the High Altar. Both wore regal clothes of white with diamonds embroidered by gold thread, and purple trim. He kept glancing at her. The gown shimmered with sparkling jewels as she moved. Her hair pampered into luxurious curls. She grew curious at his repeated glances.

"What? Is something out of place?" she whispered.

"No," he replied with an amorous smile. "I just realized I've never seen you in anything but breeches and a tunic. You're beautiful."

She blushed brightly when they stopped at the foot of the altar.

Archimedes waited near the Altar. Upon the Altar were two crowns and a scepter. Archimedes held the original Book of Verse. This time he wore a proud smile. His attendants stood a step below the platform. Two of the best chairs in the Temple were arranged behind Archimedes. These would serve for the coronation portion of the ceremony. Armus and Kell flanked the chairs. Both wore the gleaming white Guardian dress uniforms. Armus appeared a bit pale, but on his way to a complete recovery.

Archimedes motioned for Ellis and Shannan to mount the steps. They knelt before him. He opened the book to read:

> *"'And the King shall return to Allon, and the house*
> *Which was once laid desolate shall be rebuilt.*
> *Unto himself shall his bride be restored*
> *And all the people shall gather to rejoice*
> *That the time of peace has come,'"*

He closed the book and gave it to one of the attendants. The man in turn gave him two bracelets. Archimedes continued, "What Jor'el has ordained let no man object." He addressed Ellis and Shannan. "As Jor'el joined you in spirit, so now are you joined in marriage." Upon the left wrist of each, he clamped a bracelet with the intertwined etchings of Tristan's eagle with the ancient symbol of Allon, a wolf.

When Archimedes finished, an eagle was heard. Through the open doors of the Temple flew Kato to land beside Ellis. Torin moved from beside Vidar to sit next to Shannan.

"A sign of Jor'el's blessing," said Archimedes happily. As the people cheered, he bade Ellis and Shannan to the chairs. Once they were seated, another attendant gave Archimedes the Book of Verse. "These words were spoken when Tristan was first crowned, and has served for each king from his royal house using their name. Give heed to the charge given your ancestor, Son of Tristan:

> *'O blessed Ellis, chosen of Jor'el, from this day forth serve the Great Maker with all your heart and might. Rule with wisdom from the heavenlies. If you are true to your vow, you and your heirs shall be blessed. If you stray, beware the wrath of Jor'el. Having heard the charge, Tristan answered; For him only will I accept this crown. Be it done to me as you have said if I fail in my duty. The charge being accepted, the crown was placed upon his brow.'"*

Archimedes closed the book and handed it to Kell. The Captain placed it on the Altar. Kell picked up the larger of the two crowns. Armus took up the scepter. They moved to flank the Archimedes.

The Vicar continued. "Each descendant has been reminded of the sacred duty to which Tristan swore. What say you, Ellis, Son of Tristan?"

"Blessed be Jor'el for his mercy in restoring peace to Allon. As my forefather said in reply; *may it be done to me as the Almighty warned if I should fail in my duty.*"

Archimedes accepted the scepter from Armus. He gave it to Ellis. "To your oath be true." Kell handed the crown to the Vicar. "With Jor'el's blessing, I crown you, King Ellis."

Ellis bent his head to receive the crown. Cheers rose from the crowd.

"Daughter of Allon," began Archimedes. "You are the bride of Jor'el's chosen, raised from the people to be queen. You are blessed with the insight and wisdom of the Guardians to unite the two races. Having heard the King's charge, what say you?"

"Blessed be Jor'el, who makes wise the simple and rich the poor. Be it done unto me as the Almighty said if I fail in my duty to Jor'el, my King, and all of subjects of Allon, mortals and Guardians," she said.

Archimedes stepped back. The honor of this crowning fell to Kell. Shannan dutifully bent her head for him to place the crown. When she looked up, Kell widely smiled. His golden eyes filled with pride and hope. Kell moved aside.

After a moment of cheering, Ellis raised the scepter to quiet the crowd. "Allon has suffered terribly for many years under the Dark Way. From this day, there shall be no traces of it found! Those who have practiced its evil shall be brought here to the Temple for Jor'el's judgment. To aid in this task, my first royal act is to appoint Captain Kell as the King's Champion. Along with his lieutenant, Armus, the Guardians will be the keepers of the peace, responsible for eliminating the Dark Way from Allon."

Ellis held up a stiff hand when some murmuring began. "Fear not! The Shadow Warriors are no more. Many of you are familiar with Captain Kell. He is a being of high integrity. He will carry out his commission without malice. Remember, the Guardians are our allies. They have served our Queen with honor and distinction. Treat them with respect, as befits their station." He handed the scepter to Archimedes. "There is a particular Guardian the Queen wishes to thank."

Shannan happily said, "Come forth, Vidar."

The archer moved to the platform where he bowed. "Your Majesty."

"How can I ever thank you?"

"Majesty, it is I who should thank you. You restored my faith along with belief in others, and *myself*. That is sufficient," he modestly replied.

"No, it is not, Vidar. Kneel," said Ellis. He stood to draw his sword. He placed the flat of the blade on Vidar's right shoulder. "From this day you shall be the Queen's Protector. Arise, and to your duty be true."

"Sire. Majesty," Vidar said, overwhelmed.

Ellis motioned for Vidar to join them on the platform. Armus gladly moved aside for Vidar to take his place by Shannan's chair.

Ellis sat. "Now, for the justice of mortals." He signaled to the back of the Temple where General Iain waited. Under guard came a group of twenty men. Among them were Lord Harkan, Lord Owain, and a wounded Tyree. The crowd hissed and tossed barbs at Tyree. Once at the altar, Iain presented the prisoners.

The crowd quieted when Ellis raised his hand. He harshly regarded the prisoners. "I have interviewed you individually. However, since your crimes were against the people, I shall judge you publicly. Lord Harkan, Sir Kerwin, Lieutenant Reece, Lord Skylar and Captain Tyree, you are condemned to death for treason and heinous crimes against the people. May Jor'el have mercy on your souls. General."

Iain ordered them escorted them out of the Temple.

"The remainder of you have offered fealty by surrendering lands and swearing upon your word. This is done with the understanding that justice will be swift if you fail to keep your pledge. I have accepted most pledges—save one." Ellis viewed Owain with a critical eye. "Duplicity marks your character."

"My lord—" began Owain in protest.

"Silence!" Iain cuffed Owain on the neck. "If you are permitted to speak the proper address is *Your Majesty*."

Ellis continued. "To accept your pledge, more proof is required. Considering the length of time you made a pact with the late king, along with the time you caused me to lose in my pursuit, it is only fitting the length of sentence match. Thus four years. For two years you shall be a servant of the Temple under the strict rule of Vicar Archimedes. During such time, the Crown will hold your lands and possessions in trust. *If*, at the end of the first two years, the Vicar approves of your conduct, your possessions shall be restored, and once more allowed to sit on Council. This will begin the second probationary period of two years, where *I* shall judge your mettle. If you fail during any portion of your sentence, you shall be condemned to the gallows."

"As you command, Majesty," stammered Owain.

Ellis waved for Iain to remove the prisoners. "Now," he began in a agreeable tone, "For the more pleasant side. Lord Darius."

"My Liege," said Darius from his spot on the front row with Jasper and Edmund.

"To you, I grant the title Duke of Allon, second to me in authority."

"Sire," said Darius with humility.

Ellis grinned. His gaze passed to Jasper and Edmund. "If I could convince you both to leave Darius to join me, I would, but I know better than to try. Still, accept tokens of my friendship and gratitude." He signaled Avatar from his place at the end of the platform. The Guardian held a sword and royal medallion. "Use the sword well, *Captain* Jasper."

Jasper smiled upon receiving the sword from Avatar. He bowed. "Thank you, Sire."

"Edmund, you are now *royal* steward of Garwood, along with any future holdings the duke acquires," Ellis continued.

Avatar placed the royal medallion around Edmund's neck.

"Sire." Edmund bowed to Ellis.

Ellis waited for Avatar to resume his place before he continued. "Lady Erin," his voice slightly choked. "Words cannot express our gratitude for your actions. By taking the Queen's place you saved Allon from eternal destruction, and me, from bitter heartache."

"I need no thanks, Sire. I am content with having learned what is most treasured in life," Erin said. She held Erasmus' arm.

Ellis widely smiled. "We expect an invitation to the wedding, Baron."

"Ay, Sire!" said Erasmus.

"Until Waldron Castle is rebuilt, we shall hold court at Clifton Castle in summer and Deltoria in winter," Ellis announced, smiling at Lady Tilda and Lord Ranulf. "For now, let us enjoy the fruits of victory. Praise Jor'el for his mercy!"

Kell drew his sword. Armus and Avatar joined him in proclaiming, "Long live the King!"

Explore the Kingdom of Allon

www.allonbooks.com

Featuring:

- Read excerpts of Allon books
- News and Events
- Photos and Videos
- Links to:
    - o Facebook - The Kingdom of Allon Page
    - o Newsletter
    - o Contact Shawn Lamb

Made in the USA
Middletown, DE
12 April 2022